JOSLIN DAY is the pseudonym of Val Tagg
with her husband over twenty years ago. She
many years and this is her first novel.

A lover of wild, unspoilt places, she ha
stories she writes in the seascapes and barren moorland that surround her.

She has three grown-up children and four grandsons.

The SEW|NG *Place*

JOSLIN DAY

SilverWood

Published in 2020 by SilverWood Books

SilverWood Books Ltd
14 Small Street, Bristol, BS1 1DE, United Kingdom
www.silverwoodbooks.co.uk

ISBN 978-1-78132-913-9 (paperback)
ISBN 978-1-78132-914-6 (ebook)

British Library Cataloguing in Publication Data
A CIP catalogue record for this book is available from the British Library

Page design and typesetting by SilverWood Books
Printed on responsibly sourced paper

To Bill, partner ad infinitum, without whom this novel would have remained unread.

Exeter

1763

1

Roving like a zephyr along The Bear Lane, the late February wind caught the back of Latimer's neck, fanning his dark lank hair to his head, insinuating itself between stock and collar. The gallows crowds were out in force. Detached from the hum of the city, he had misplaced days and had he paid even scant attention to the calendar he would not have come, would have delayed and spent yet another day in confines of his sick room waiting for Vetch to bring his posset and take away his slops, searching the elaborate mouldings of his ceiling in the vain hope of finding unhindered sleep.

Viewing the lane with pale judgmental eyes, he assessed the density of the crowds. The offering of a public holiday seemed to have given them impetus. Mob-like revellers moved in a nebulous mass, slowly bleeding out of the city towards the Heavy Tree to watch the last struggling dance of the luckless – the gin-soaked and the ragged rubbing shoulders with the mercantile affluent and gentlemen in dun breeches and dull coats; a consequence of changing views he supposed, a rejection of the peacock fashion of the French Court during the long wars.

The sky over Rougemont Castle was the colour of indigo serge; the city had recently been deluged with icy rain and he weighed his chances of another drenching, letting his eyes scan the moor-scape and forested slopes to the west and the meandering hampered river working its way to the sea. Always more prevalent here during this raw month, the north-west wind ran unhindered across the plateau of the moor. Suddenly prey to its unpredictability, he felt the wind lift his coat, encouraging the skirts to flap about his knees like an untethered sail.

A clutch of pamphlets discarded by the gallows crowds moved in the vortex, dancing in the cold air amongst the detritus of the street. Supported by his stick he caught a pamphlet with his boot, bent and retrieved it, the pain that stalked him reminding him of his decrepitude. He huffed to himself; a list of those to hang, coarsely printed, ink smudged, impersonal. He read: there were embellished descriptions of the felons' crimes, the obligatory pleading of their innocence and the conclusion of certain guilt. Two men condemned for highway robbery, an elderly servant for the theft of his employer's pocket watch, and a tanner for the rape of a vintner's daughter. A sudden gust of wind caught the paper and bent it in half – he shook it, irritated, and squinted again at the print.

The bottom of the page had been obscured by a boot print and the name was impossible to read. The description of the crime, however, was not: a young woman in her seventeenth year to hang for the murder of her male bastard child – a crime too common, a life forfeited before it had begun. Closing long fingers, he screwed the used paper into a tight ball and dropped it to the foetid cobbles.

More by determination than his easy knowledge of the city, he found the coffee house he sought. Less frequented than its more popular cousin in St Catherine's it sat almost unnoticed in a dingy lane behind Goldsmiths, but the place suited him well enough and the opinion there often ran in parallel with his own. Pausing, leaning heavily on his stick, Latimer studied the elongated building, the square-paned sashes of yellowing glass which sat in reasonable symmetry across its front, the decaying mullions supported by incongruous pagan carvings. It was a place he had visited regularly for some years; although this regularity had been curtailed these last weeks.

Two men were leaving as he entered. The mutterings were all about him; he understood it, he was stooped and deathly – the city had given him up for dead. Hanging on the leather strap, he closed the door behind him, moved crab-like between the tables. The familiar face he sought was sat on the far side of the room close to a struggling fire, and he pushed awkwardly forward until he was adjacent to a small circular table. A broadsheet was spread amongst the coffee cups, the three men who huddled about it too deep in conversation to notice his arrival. A decade ago he had put a fraternal arm about this young man's shoulder; he had come to him as a slight fifteen-year-old, literate, willing and determined to support his widowed mother – they had been firm friends since.

"A momentous and meritorious time," Latimer said, looking down.

The familiar face lifted his head. "Henri." The younger man stood, surprise spread across his compact features. He offered his hand, allowing the merchant to take it in his own now insubstantial grip. "It has been too long, far too long, sir – too long away." He spoke enthusiastically sitting again, eying the darkly clad man with poorly hidden concern.

"Misadventure has brought me down to a place I cannot yet climb out of, Edmund, but I am here at least and glad to be so. Besides I am done with sickroom food and feigned sympathy." Latimer lifted his skirts and sat, aware of the constant pain in his leg.

A boy was moving about the rooms filling tiny china cups from a silver coffee pot. Edmund Elcott waited for them to be served.

"We discuss the Treaty, sir."

"I see that you do," Latimer said bringing his slim lips together and nodding. "Do not wait upon me. Go forward with your discussion and forgive me if I am dull-witted, there has been little to make me anything other these last weeks."

Latimer's pale eyes flashed up momentarily to meet the younger man's. His friend and confidante of some years, the slightness of his build matching the sharp compact features of his face, would be running a concerned eye over the spectre that he had become.

The conversation resumed.

"What think you, sir, of this news? The Treaty finally signed despite the not inconsiderable disagreement amongst our politicians over the terms." An elderly man in a cheap horsehair wig was speaking. "Surely we must be pleased with that?"

Latimer waved a hand. "I know only the barest bones of the thing. I have had little chance to study any broadsheet and news does not filter easily beneath the door of a sick-room – and most especially when a man's servant is determined that it shall not." He leant forward, rubbing his thigh with a weathered long-fingered hand.

The other man continued. "They argue only to be contrary, sir – I am sure of it. There is no worthy reason why any should complain given such an offering. This country has done well, has she not? Who would not agree to such a treaty? Canada secured and all of French America?" There was a mumble of agreement. "Surely we must be satisfied with what we have been offered?"

Elcott raised his eyes to look about the group. Distracted and perhaps a little disturbed by the arrival of Henri Latimer, he spoke deliberately and without theatre in his quiet unhurried way. "Indeed so, dear sirs – the West Indies, Florida, the Island of Minorca – I believe we should all be satisfied with what has been won and indeed with the Treaty in total."

Latimer rested his head back against the settle and felt his chin. The ending of this long, protracted war was the reason he had come – crossed the city in the mayhem of a hanging day, dragged his decrepit body forth when it would have been easier to have stayed in his rooms. But he was glad he had come, simple conversation was balm to his soul and given his general look and the rumours of his misfortune that had undoubtedly been circling the city, he expected to be allowed to take a back seat. Listening, but not part of the conversation, he let his thoughts trace a more personal route: his daughters, the cessation of his business, the need to resurrect it and the consequences if he could not.

The elderly man with the bulbous nose and coarse wig was addressing him again, bringing him up from the mesh of deeper thought. "My understanding is that we have been offered a free hand in India. None should argue over the benefits of this."

Easing himself into a more upright position, Latimer rubbed the part of his leg which gave him most pain. He waited for the heads to stop nodding. "Putting acquisition aside," he said levelly, folding his arms about his spare coat, "this Treaty brings an end to hostility and this country has warred long enough over its colonies. Some will say that war brings a kind of prosperity and I would say, yes, to a few; but the soul and the heart of the land must surely be better fed by this offered peace. With the need to consider allegiances gone, trade may now continue unhindered."

Tired from his journey across the city, Latimer let the conversation run.

"I read London silk weavers have already rioted over French imports," the elderly gentleman said tentatively.

The subject was closer to the business Latimer knew and he answered casually. "London weavers are London weavers. I do not believe we need concern ourselves over what happens in Spitalfields. I doubt this discontent will filter down as far as Exeter and this is about silk we talk – wool is altogether a more solid proposition, ancient, enduring and familiar and cannot be so easily upset."

Elcott answered him. "I would agree, Henri, it is the Rotterdam trade that we must continue to look to, and although my business is only indirectly connected it is most certainly dependent upon the prosperity of this city and thus the lucrative trading of serge. Let us hope that the end of these long wars will see our vessels sail freely along our coastal waters again, not only to Rotterdam but upon other trading routes – even my mother has begun to complain of the lack of choice in our cellar."

There was a mumble of agreement. Latimer considered his own circum-stance. Unable to trade, visit his weavers or do much else for weeks, he knew there were more pressing things to concern himself over than the emptiness of his cellar. He considered the beginning he had had in life and where he sat now. Refusing to follow either his grandfather's trudging reverence to business or his own father's genteel disaffection, he had over time become a rather non-conformist maverick mix of merchant, clothier and fuller. He knew his trade well and had done acceptably well by it.

Another emaciated boy was coming towards them, pressing through the debaters with determination and a very large pile of split logs. Henri watched the child settle the fire, see to the ash and restore its warmth. The trouble with beginning life in debt was that the debt needed to be cleared away before any indebted money could be made. Without reserves a man and his family were vulnerable. He was so now.

The child had finished. Resting his head again on the hard back of the settle, Henri closed his eyes and allowed the conversation to continue around him. The young King, the Earl of Bute, and the power and influence that the elder had over the younger, the state of the highways, the changing markets. Conversation had distorted time, and before midmorning the older men had risen to face the wild weather, and Latimer was left alone with the young notary.

Glad to be able to enjoy the easy companionship of a long-held friendship he stretched his leg in the heat of the open fire, regretting that even this simple action gave him pain. For weeks his life had been blighted by this injury – a moment of indecision, a sad lack of judgement on his part, had caused him to be beneath a crate containing several bales of serge being offloaded from his ketch in Rotterdam. Ropes had been poorly secured, and it had not been the falling of the cargo but the unforgiving edge of a buttress that had caused his injury. Meeting the full force of a south-westerly gale on their return, they had laboured up the channel, damaging the bowsprit and a yardage of sail. After several days they had limped into Topsham. Confined to a tiny cabin, his leg tied to a board, he remembered little of the journey home.

"How is your health, sir? I did not like to ask when in company." Elcott broke into his thoughts.

"The wound seems knit, although it causes me some pain." Latimer ran a hand through his hair.

"And the surgeon?"

"Still comes, and takes his coin. The leg may be heeled but the body becomes ever more decrepit with time and he cannot give me reason. Insists that a bloodletting would help me forward but he has already sharpened his knife above my wound long enough. I have my leg and I shall keep it – and the blood that remains."

"Although I understand the reasoning I am always at odds with such things, Henri." Elcott paused, considering his reply. "I have heard many a case where some comfort is given, but I cannot always see the logic in letting the blood as many seem to die away through lack of the stuff."

Latimer rasped his unshaven chin subconsciously. "What do they say about me, Edmund, what gossip runs about this walled city?" He raised his eyebrows and then answered his own question. "That I am down on my luck, never seen, the question being not when will I recover but when I am likely to die?"

"Your observation is far too brutal, Henri. I cannot deny there is talk but not quite as you describe it."

"Supposition verified by the sight of me, eh?"

"Indeed not, sir; proof of your recovery confirmed by your presence."

"Perhaps?"

"Your nephew, sir, is he settled now, and a help to you in these difficult times?"

"My nephew, Edmund, encourages Peruvian Bark, swears by its efficacy, visits the apothecary in St Paul's Street and has a draft made for me each day. I have felt little benefit but I intend to reward his concern with perseverance. And whether he is settled, I believe him so – at the least his mother is appeased. And I cannot yet say if he is a help to me or no." Latimer replaced the fragile cup on its saucer. "How goes the law writing, Edmund, and business in general – perhaps some changes now; keeping legalities and advising your gentlemen now that peace has come?"

"You need not ask of my prosperity, Henri. I have been settled throughout these hostile times and little troubled by them – but I must ask of yours?"

"Ha, mine – I have enough to buy a little more time but I shall be better pleased when I have moved *The Lady Rosamunde* to a place where she can be repaired, and I am able to source an agent to collect cloth from my weavers – I think it will be a long while before I am able to sit a horse for any length of time."

"Can your nephew not act as agent, sir? It seems an obvious solution."

"At nineteen perhaps he ought, but being raised as he has the boy has never had need to see for himself or take responsibility beyond his own constantly refilled purse. I would not have him go out alone yet awhile, he must learn the trade from the floor up and then we shall see." Latimer searched the fire, considered the unexpected arrival of his dead brother's son and the implications that his presence in the Latimer household presented. "The boy must find his own way up, as I have and my grandfather before me. My grandfather found no help in learning the idiosyncrasies of trade, but he survived his humble beginnings in the tanner's yard because he had the ability to view the world in a broader sense, the determination to succeed, and unlike my father, keep a frugal eye upon his purse."

Elcott nodded his agreement, the merchant's history was well known throughout the counting houses and gossiping places of Exeter.

Latimer continued, "My father, in contrast, spent his life as the gentleman money allowed him to be – carousing, womanizing and gaming and proving quite outstandingly good at spending the gains of his forefather. During my life I have preferred to follow the example of my grandparent, although sometimes I question my rational, for who lived the better life?"

"Perhaps there is a balance between the two, Henri. And a fortune must be made before it can be lost. Are your daughters well, sir?"

"They are, thank you, Edmund – a little boisterous at times, the younger more headstrong than the elder, but their nurse attempts to set them to their samplers and I to their letters, and then they must look to themselves for I am poor company."

Finding the thread of their conversation finished, Elcott stabbed at the fire with the poker. The street door, which had been opened and closed throughout the morning, now seemed to be permanently open, allowing a blast of cold air to penetrate the rooms. The fire, disturbed, exuded a cloud of wood smoke into the room. Latimer glanced up; a young woman was standing on the threshold, indecision keeping her from entering and shutting the door, further indecision preventing her from leaving. Affront ran around the rooms, floating on the top of mumbled comments – this was no gin shop and the girl, whoever she was, had no place entering an establishment where wives and virtuous women chose not to go.

Distracted, Latimer manoeuvred his injured leg so that he had clear view of the entrance. He was, although it had to be said quite loosely so, acquainted with this girl and took some interest in her unexpected appearance. She was his neighbour. The elegant merchant's house – won and paid for by his grandfather, and in its prime existing betwixt other like-residences – was now flanked by a bawdy house on the one side and the home and studio of an itinerant artist on the other. The girl, it seemed, had connection with both these establishments.

Unpainted, dressed in plain skirts and a woollen coat, her dark hair tied with a ribbon and with no tell-tale signs of rank or position, her indecisiveness had the effect of keeping the mumble active and fuelling the interest in the room – including Latimer's. Amused, he viewed the door from the safety of the fireside settle. The young woman was struggling to find the coin she had been given to complete her errand and rummaged again in a pocket of her skirts. Successful she caught the attention of a boy, offered him the coin, waited whilst he collected a scarlet-headed harlot from an adjoining room and left the house to the audible relief of the room.

Latimer turned back to the fire. The presence of the girl had brought to mind the pamphlet. The ending of lives, so simplistically put; no substance, no history, nothing about what had gone before. He folded his arms across his waistcoat, ill-fitting now from weeks of sedentary living and sick-room food.

"What say you to today's hangings, Edmund?" He lifted his leg and rested it in the heat of the fire again. "Every man, Jack, and Jenny his wife, out and heading to the Drop."

Edmund began to fold his broadsheet. "I have followed the trials, Henri, a mixed bunch and guilt not in doubt, I propose."

"I feel I must agree, although I believe there are times when society should offer clemency."

"Perhaps, but to what end? They will be dealt with swiftly and there will be more to follow. Our gaols are poorly placed to hold every law breaker without end."

"I do not doubt the logic, Edmund, only the morality. And the young woman – what level of desperation pushes a mother to murder her newborn child?"

"I have no answer to it, Henri." Elcott looked away and picked up the poker again.

"Take no heed of me, friend, I have become maudlin these last weeks. Lighten my mood and tell me what has been happening in the markets and the mills. I will have all the gossip that has come to your ear – spare me none."

2

Just after midday Latimer picked up his stick and faced the fickle and unpredictable west wind. The skies had changed a dozen times between his entry into the coffee house and his exit and now they were dark again, fast moving, rolling at pace across the moor-scape, beginning to shed rain on the already drenched city. He made haste, choosing to cut down Smithern Street towards his home – he had made better choices.

At the head of Butchers Row the rains had come on without mercy, flooding the narrow street and washing the detritus of butchery into the central gutter – blood and entrails rushing downwards towards the receptive Exe in obnoxious rivulets of red. To add to this gruesome picture, at intervals from either an open shop front or the dark recesses of a squat doorway, a butcher's boy would discard a bucket of slop with the hope that the contents would find its way to the river via the facilitating open sewer.

Fortunately the crowds had now moved on to Gallows Lane and the Inns of Heavitree; it made for easier movement and before the next deluge he had reached the end of Billiter Lane and the cobbles of Exebere Street. He had been born here, his wife was buried a street away in St Mary's burial ground – he expected to die here. The thought suddenly shocked him, and made him pause and indulge his memory a little, unbalancing his thoughts. A piss cart came level on its way to Trews Mill, the pungent smell of ammonia following in its wake bringing him back to the reality of the wet day and the need to find his own door.

Time had brought only subtle changes to this street. The houses along Exebere sat shoulder to shoulder in this southern quarter; some three and some four stories high, one level incongruously balanced on the next, some teetering on granite piers and squat basements and others decorated with pargeting or Flemish tiles. Latimer's family house sat squarely in the centre of the street, its timber frame supporting a mixture of tiny paned leaded casements as well as more functional sashes replaced in the time of the first George. These buildings had been Merchants' houses since mediaeval times, some still so, but now with an air of neglect and a feeling that perhaps tastes had changed.

Latimer stood in the central hall of his house, clutching his stick, leaning on it until the swoon and lightness of head had passed; with his hair dripping on his collar and his face pallid and colourless, his servants might have been forgiven for thinking him a cadaver recently pulled from the Exe.

He called, almost a bark, the pain in his leg making him irascible. "Vetch, if you are within earshot I would have you attend."

Despite having been divided from a much larger space some one hundred years before, the hall was still cavernous. Now, this floor, level with the street, was enclosed by oak screens and wattle walls, creating two large square rooms dominated by huge fireplaces and thick beams. An ancient pole-staircase – the central post upon which the triangular treads were built, reputed to have come from a Spanish Man of War – connected the floors above. The sound of heavy shoes on slate flags made him look up. A male servant, a retainer in his father's time, came from the kitchens and looked him over with some distaste. The man had a spare neck and greying unwashed hair tied at the nape – without direction he began to relieve his master of his wet soiled coat.

"Is my nephew about, Thomas?" Latimer was perched awkwardly on the hall settle attempting to remove a soaked and muddied boot.

"No, sir. Not these last two hours." Vetch helped him with his second boot.

"Did he say what might be his errand?"

"He did not, sir, but I believe he may have gone to Blackaller."

Latimer sat a while. The man was irritating, and rarely fluid with his information, especially where his nephew, Geoffrey, was concerned, purposely articulating less than he knew.

Vetch followed him at a respectful distance as Latimer worked his way to the top of the spiralling oak staircase. Both men were silent until they reached Latimer's bedchamber on the first floor.

"And my daughters, Thomas?" He pulled impatiently at his stock freeing the wet cloth from his neck. "Not out in this, I hope."

"No, sir." Vetch hung the stock over his arm and waited for his master's shirt to follow. "I heard talk of an outing, sir, but not since the rain has come on."

"Above then, and all is well, I did not see them before I left." Vetch passed him clean linen.

"As far as I am aware, sir, Mr Geoffrey was present at breakfast, although Mrs Sarah did not come down." Latimer considered Sarah's sloth-like progress around the house, likening it to his own.

"No? I well see her reasoning."

A change of clothes and a tot of brandy improved his appearance but not his general mood. Vetch had gone, taking with him a bundle of soiled and wet clothing. Reaching for his stick Latimer crossed the room, sitting heavily in a stuffed chair beside the meagre fire and stretching out his leg. He thought of his daughters a floor above, unobtrusively doing whatever it was they did at this time of day. He felt they were somewhat isolated up there, kept away from him at his request – but happy and well, he hoped, and surprisingly robust, in fact. Today he would have liked their company but since his accident and his near imprisonment in his room, he had avoided such. Now it was a habit he seemed unable to break.

Since his marriage he had desired separateness – a poor husband, he knew it, and his marriage as with so many others had been one of convenience; it had filled a need, sealed a business transaction, in fact. Sailing with *The Lady Rosamunde* had never been a necessity but he had chosen it in preference to remaining at home; he had absented himself for weeks, sometimes staying in Rotterdam. He rubbed his leg and stabbed at the fire with the poker, looking about the room. Nothing much had changed here over his lifetime – the drapes and the darkly polished furniture, not his wife's choice, not even his own: the leftovers of other's lives, lives that had been lived long ago. He ran a critical eye over what he saw, almost as though he had never seen any of it before. Absurdly, there seemed nothing left of Mary now.

When his wife had died of puerperal fever following the birth of Sophia, he had been away. The relationship had never been comfortable when she lived but since her death it felt frayed and without closure; he could hardly make amends with a corpse. Some would say he should make his peace with God – he did not take this view.

At first his daughters' needs had been basic. Old Sarah had been employed to assist the wet nurse – he had not intervened. As they grew he had found more reason to visit them, and had begun to teach them their letters. But since his accident and subsequent sickness he had kept them at arm's length. His illness could not be explained by his injury alone and although rationality told him that the prospect of contagion was remote, he had continued to stay away.

He refilled his glass and drank, waited for the spirit to settle and then pushed himself wearily from the chair. His stick was leaning against the bed end and he took it and moved slowly towards the open door, tapping his way to the head of the stairs. Vetch had likely taken himself back to the kitchen fire. He looked over the rail into the void and bellowed.

"Vetch! Vetch!" God damn the man. Well used to his servant's inconsistencies he had hardly expected a response. He wanted to have his daughters brought to him but if this could not be achieved then he would visit them above instead. He took the narrower staircase to their rooms, tapping his stick laboriously up the worn treads. The door to their rooms was ajar and he could see Old Sarah nodding in her chair; the fire was bright and her feet were in the hearth. Mary, his eldest child, sat with a picture book on her lap; Sophia lay on the rug playing a game of her own devising. He pushed the door with his stick, the alertness of youth turning their heads in an instant – their nurse did not stir and he put a finger to his lips and entered.

"Papa." They came to him and with only a moment's hesitation he embraced them, holding their soft heads to his coat and stroking the pale hair and the dark with an affection that was instant – a salve to his own disaffection. "Where have you been, Papa?" Mary at just eight knew well to speak quietly for she had no wish to experience Old Sarah's befuddled, woeful nagging, which was often the consequence of her being woken.

"I have been below, but also about in the city." Latimer sat and presented his good leg to Sophia who perched there contentedly, whispering to him in a voice louder than if she had been talking from the other side of the room. He asked of their schoolwork, of the unfinished samplers that awaited further attention; they told him of games they had played with their blocks and beads and complained that they had missed him, until Mary – who had all along been considering where her father might have been without her – asked:

"Have you been to Fore Street, papa?" Occasionally Latimer had taken her there, before his accident, to purchase ribbons and embroidery thread.

"No, Mary, not this day – it is not a good day for shopping. I have been to meet with Mr Elcott, he asks of you both and I have told him that you are a constant trouble to me and give me no peace." Mary's pout was followed swiftly by a smile, but Sophia, more confident in her father's presence, responded in an instant with laughter. He remembered what Vetch had told him. "So, you have seen your cousin today, Daughters." He watched them. "Thomas tells me you broke your fast together."

Sophia swung her short plump white-stockinged legs back and forth as she perched on her father's knee. At six her reasoning and thoughts were never deeper than the surface. Secrets burned within her like excited sprites waiting to be free. After a pause, during which time her long eyelashes fluttered repeatedly across her blue eyes, she responded. "Mary has no need to go to Fore Street to buy ribbons, Papa, for Cousin Geoffrey has given her new ones this very day." She was suddenly prevented from continuing by the thought that she may have been disloyal.

"You were not to tell, Sister. It was a secret and besides you have new ribbons also, blue ones, and you were not to tell Papa."

Sophia put a small hand over her mouth and buried her head in her father's coat. Intrigued more than angered and more than a little surprised, Latimer removed his daughter's face from his coat and speaking directly to his eldest daughter he asked:

"But why would your papa be angry at such? Would I deny you presents? Presents I am happy with, secrets I am not, for you must see that a secret and a lie are often akin to one another." He considered his perpetual absence from their lives and its consequences. "I think I would wish to know all from this morning's breakfast table, Mary."

Mary remained silent, coyly rubbing a leather slipper along the edges of the rug. Sophia seeing an empty stage stepped on to it. "We turned cards, Papa, and Cousin Geoffrey had a helping of oysters with all the shells piled up and the insides shining like pearls."

"Cards, my daughter?" Her father was surprised by this revelation, the previous run of the conversation had amused him but not so this. "Amongst your breakfast china, Mary, how was this so?"

"It was quite after breakfast, Papa. Cousin Geoffrey asked us to turn a card and remember it and he could see what was in our heads for he knew what card we chose and we played a game where all numbers must add up to less than a guinea."

Latimer made a disapproving 'humph' sound and brought his brows together. He did not think he would like his daughters to become proficient at cards before they had learned their letters, especially in the light of family history. Letting Sophia gently slide back to the floor he stood her beside her sister, rubbing the thigh of his injured leg until the ache was lessened. If there were things to say, reprimands to be made, then he would make representations to his nephew, not his small and malleable daughters.

"Then I have missed a merry time," he said lightly. "I would that I had joined you, but no matter, perhaps I shall do so tomorrow. But before then we must keep one another good company at supper time. I will have Mrs Sarah told that you are to come down." He stroked his younger daughter's peach-like cheek and his elder's soft head with a cool hand. "And now, Mary, you must show me your picture book and you, Sophia, this game. Then I must go down and you, my daughters, will be as good as you are."

Coming slowly to consciousness from her gin-induced slumber, Old Sarah had begun to mumble disconnected words from whiskery lips, intermittently reprimanding and then immediately exonerating. Latimer rose, placed the tip of a finger across his lips again, and picked up his stick leaving them to the guidance of their nurse.

In his absence, a small glass of cloudy liquid had been placed on his writing table. Latimer moved to the table, rested his weight on his palms, idly looking out through his window at the changing day; whatever else Vetch may choose to misremember, this daily ritual he did not. Behind the house, below him, a small courtyard remained. Owners of the properties on either side had long since built over, and then above this space, leaving just a small square of a yard where all manner of work was carried out. Legally this was his property but it was accessed and often used by other residencies for the less pleasant tasks that any household might need to perform and prefer to perform outside – whether or no these tasks related to the Latimer household. The activities in the courtyard were a distraction. Over the last weeks, watching what happened here had eased the monotony of his days – although there had been times when he had felt voyeuristic. He looked down on the heads of two young women. A painted harlot with a crude wig and open bodice was talking to a younger girl. Between their intermittent conversations the harlot drew tobacco smoke from a long clay pipe, the other woman was splitting kindling with all the concentration that this task required – the tap, tap, tap of the axe head reached him through the closed casement and he drew back, standing as erect as he could but still watching.

On the table behind him the glass of physic awaited; he considered it and the benefits this foul liquid might be offering in his progress to recovery – he was not convinced that there were any, and he could not help to question the efficacy of drinking a mix so foul it made him retch. Drinking this draught had become habitual over the last month, this last week he had begun to avoid it. Leaving the glass untouched and the women to their work, he pushed open the door and called loudly for Vetch. He would be heard, and to make certain that he was, he left his room and standing at the head of the stairs lifted his stick and pounded on the oak boards. Vetch could shave him and then he would pass instruction to the kitchen for caraway cake, jellies and syllabub to be served at supper time.

3

Entering The Phoenix towards the mid-afternoon of that day, unavoidably sober, Geoffrey Latimer had a look of singularity about him. Newly shaven angular chin, clean lace, neatly tied dark hair all defining him as the gentleman he felt he was and separating him from the riff-raff that had wandered there straight from the gallows tree. He made his way through the busy inn to a snug at the rear. The rooms were full and the din in the hostelry was rising by the moment, the noise swimming about in a sea of familiar odours – the smell of mutton stew running above the rest. The good breakfast he had eaten mid-morning with the Latimer cousins was beginning to slide away to be replaced with something he supposed to be hunger – although he had never been hungry in his life. Hearing from Vetch that his uncle was up and intending to walk across the city, Geoffrey had postponed his own breakfast by an hour, visited his cousins a floor above and, ignoring the gin-soaked old woman who acted as their nurse, had suggested they come down. Small girls were prone to honesty and he liked to know what was being talked of on all levels of the house.

He settled himself in a corner, ordered the cold mutton and a bottle of claret. The snug was only half-heartedly divided from the rest of the inn by a panelled screen, allowing him a good view of the comings and goings of those in the low rooms. Looking idly through the drinkers towards the window, Geoffrey could see a broad, coarse shaven man hanging over his tankard. The thick neck and grizzled hair were familiar. A luckless gambler, Geoffrey Latimer had so far escaped the consequences of earlier debt, but like all gamblers the habit must be fed and he had borrowed unwisely from moneylenders; a confrontation with this man would not be welcome.

At the insistence of his uncle he had visited Blackaller earlier, walking briskly to the tucking mill avoiding the worst of the rain. Josiah Mudge, owner, Alderman and Quaker, had been absent, but his son William, distinctly unlike his father, was there in his stead. They were peers and gambling partners, drank together in most of the better inns and often shared the same whore; although the young man's father would have been scandalised if he had known it. There was nothing much in the way of business to discuss, just a loose overseeing of some of his uncle's cloth between pack-pony and tenterhooks, and they had spent an idle hour in the counting house agreeing to meet later.

A girl brought a plate of mutton and boiled potatoes and a near full bottle of claret wine. He filled his mug and looked about the room before beginning to eat, reassuring himself that the grizzle-headed man had not left his seat in the window. He considered his time here and the reasons for it. It was surprising just how far gossip and tittle-tattle spread about this rural county even when begun in the city. His uncle's accident and the consequences that this was likely to bring had reached his mother some weeks ago. And where some might have seen misfortune his mother had seen only opportunity. The money that had been left to run and repair her small Dorset estate was dwindling fast – gone on the trappings of a genteel life – and it was at her behest that he had come, to pay his respects, to sit beside the dying man's bedside.

John Latimer, his father, had died within three months of his wedding day, leaving a young widow and a living father. Geoffrey had been born posthumously, and the Latimer estate – although much depleted by this dissolute grandparent, a man whom Geoffrey secretly admired – had passed sideways to a much younger half-brother: to Uncle Henri. These circumstances had been known to him since boyhood, the wrongness of the situation being fed him constantly by his embittered widowed mother.

He lay down his knife and looked at his empty plate. He did not believe the suggestion that his uncle was poor; the man may live as a shabby recluse but he had done well in business, had he not? Thrift would have filled his purse, a purse where the strings were ever drawn in tightly – fate must surely turn in Geoffrey's favour eventually.

The girl returned with a tallow candle and lit the sconce; he found the pack of cards he always kept in a pocket, cut them ran the corners together and placed them prominently on the table. It had never been his intention to remain long in this place, but it seemed Uncle Latimer had not been as close to death as the city had reported; fate was taking its long slow course to any acceptable end. The meagre allowance his uncle had offered him did not pay for boot polish – the obstinate man's newfound energy and improving health was a disappointment and a complication.

A shadow obscured the light from the sconce and he looked up to see William Mudge standing above him – his wet felt hat tilted towards the table, excess water dripping from the brim.

"Saints and martyrs William, do not stand above me and dispense city water into good claret. You are like a dog drowned in a sluice. Take the thing off and have it settled somewhere."

Mudge removed his hat and cloak and hung them over the back of a chair.

"I am quite done with this weather, Geoffrey, and glad to be out of it. A man may not plan his journey with any certainty in this watery county, it was only at last thought that I sent for my cloak and I am still soaked through to my neck."

A few months beyond his twentieth birthday, as Geoffrey was before his, they were like in build and height but not in temperament. William's observations of the world were more sanguine, less complex; his Quaker father had yet to force his views upon him and since his mother's death he had kept his only son in comfort and coin with the expectation that he would eventually find his way. Removing the wet ends of straw-coloured hair from his damp collar he sat down.

"You have a quiet corner here, Geoffrey, and a seat and two to spare. The crush in The Swan is worse than a corn riot."

"Then you should have avoided the place and come here at the start – I am lose-ended, William, and in need of entertainment."

"You are rarely loose-ended, Geoffrey, but I believe I can save you from it. I have met with a couple of clodhoppers in The Swan; they have a countryman's purse and a lively desire to be rid of it – I have bid them find us." The Quaker's son settled himself closer to the fire, adjusting the damp lapels of his woollen coat. "I see your plate is promisingly clean, Geoffrey, I am tempted to join you but my papa will have me dine at eight and I must offer a healthy appetite else he will query my whereabouts."

"How long before you were let lose, William; did that compliant little clerk keep you busy with mill sums and signings?"

"He may make a show of keeping me there but I believe he is better pleased when I am gone; he has fidgety little fingers and cannot wait for me to leave so that he may look again upon my numbers and rearrange them – he do so like counting and I am quite an ass at the occupation."

Geoffrey raised an arm to get the attentions of the pot boy. "That infernal noise at Blackaller, I do not know how you go along with it. Your papa must be quite deaf from the racket."

"Not a bit of it, sir, I know for sure his ears and indeed his eyes are as good as yours and mine, we must remember this when we are out and about, Geoffrey. Not only does he have the eyes and ears of a youth, but he is a man with many associates and many watchers."

"I will be mindful of this, William, now that my uncle is up and walking these streets."

"Is up, sir – surely this is quite unlikely?"

"Indeed it is, William, unlikely – I would have said impossible a week ago."

"What takes him from his bed, Geoffrey? Not the hangings; the gallows tree is hardly an agreeable destination, not for a man who has so recently been pounding on death's door himself?"

"Some rash, hair-shirt determination to reach that derelict coffee house in Goldsmiths, I believe. I have been out since breakfast and do not yet know if he has returned." A barefoot girl of about twelve was standing behind Mudge waiting for instruction. "I have taken the claret, William, whether or nay it began life in a French vineyard or the brew-house at the back of The Phoenix I cannot confirm, but the pallet is satisfied – especially upon the third jar."

"I have no real taste for it, Geoffrey; the Sidwell house is as dry as a saw-pit by necessity – one wine is as good as any, but I will need a headful of it before I return to that dull house. I am sure my father asks for the fire to be kept low so that he may call himself frugal. His God requires it in all things but I cannot say I go along with it; the Mill does not stop its pounding day and night and all with good profit."

The girl returned with a bottle and stood waiting for payment – Mudge felt for his purse and paid what was due. "Are you minded to return to your mama, now that your uncle seems to have left crisis behind him?"

"I am not William. I believe I will bide my time here a little longer, the health of a man is ever unpredictable."

Darkness had descended on the streets bringing with it changing custom: the whores were out – not to Geoffrey's liking; an irritant he felt, more than opportunity to satisfy his needs. Brash, outspoken and filthy. When he wanted a whore he would chose his own. He looked through the bodies to the table in the window; the heavy-shouldered man had gone. Life perhaps would be a little more comfortable if he were to settle his debt, but he would rather keep the coin in his pocket as long as he could. Empty pockets often meant missed opportunity. Besides, avoiding such men had been a necessity since he was able to turn a card – he was familiar with the practice and felt himself to be rather proficient at it.

"If your clodhoppers do not appear shortly, William, the tether upon which your papa holds you will be drawn in and any chance at a profitable outcome curtailed. I'll wager 'tis beyond the seventh hour already." He took out his watch, agreed that it was and stood unsteadily, brushing a hand down the front of his new coat. "I must piss, William; whatever the origins of that bottle, pissing is a consequence of drinking the stuff same as any."

The yard at the rear of The Phoenix was poorly lit, heavy with the smell of urine. Pissing barrels were set in each corner, easily accessible to the carts that would collect them in the early hours of the morning. He guided himself through the open door; cold and dank, the odorous air quickly reached him, making him take a step back, upsetting his balance. Crossing the yard unsteadily to the nearest pot, he adjusted his stance, unbuttoned his flap and settled to the pleasure of relieving himself indirectly into the pot.

Too muddled in drink to take heed of his surroundings, and oblivious that he had been observed leaving the taproom, Geoffrey did not note he had company until company was beside him. The shadowy bulk of a large man loomed from the darkness. He turned automatically without pausing what he had begun, saying nothing in greeting, hoping to remain unobserved in the shadows; his earlier sense of infallibility was disturbed by the gradual and then recognizable sensation of warm piss running in a steady stream down his leg and over his foot.

"Master Latimer. Well, fortune do find me. I have had a mind to communicate with 'ee since I were first aware of your presence in these lively rooms."

"Saints, sir!" Geoffrey moved his foot and shook it. "You have pissed upon my foot and I believe your aim to be quite direct."

The stream of urine eventually ceased, the bulky man moving about beside him in the darkness, shaking himself and adjusting his breeches.

The art of money borrowing was a familiar practice to Geoffrey Latimer, but avoiding settlement was often confounded by the accurate unearthing of a name – it was what came of being related to a man with a finger in every pie and a nose poking through every door. Premonition told him that things were not likely to play out well.

Moneylenders and their collectors had a certain odour to them and this he caught strongly now. "You know I am ever obliged and happy to have the lending of coin to those in need, even if they be fool enough to play Ruff and Honours with cheap-jacks and tricksters, but when 'tis lent it must be paid back and the interest upon 'n added." Geoffrey felt his stock go tight. He looked into the blackness of the yard and felt the man's hand on his collar. "Since I have had sight of you sitting so comfortably in these hospitable rooms, I have spun my head around the rights and wrongs o' things; do the young man have manners? Will he come to me and offer what is owed, or will he no?"

"Speculation is quite unnecessary, sir, if you wished to speak with me then you should have sought me out and asked your questions direct." Geoffrey inserted his fingers between his hampered windpipe and the chocking linen of his stock. "We might have settled this like gentlemen."

"Gentlemen, now there be a questioning thought. Born of gentlemen you may be, rigged out fine in gentleman's clothing you are, but gentleman you are not." Geoffrey watched the moneylender conjure up a mouthful of spittle and direct it towards his boots.

"You must unhand me now, sir, for how else am I to find my purse and settle this dispute?"

"Now there, sir, is a question I am able to answer directly."

The obligatory frisking, the fumbling in the dark, Geoffrey had experienced it all before. Fortunately his purse was nearly deplete – let the ox take what was left. He waited passively for the rough handling to be over.

"Now what have we here, Latimer, in this gentlemanly coat? A purse all tied up and put away, and close to it a nice snugly stored pocket watch. A man ought not to leave his friends in want and requirement when he has such a rounded little purse hidden in his breeches and such a delicacy hiding in his fob pocket."

"Your rough handling is quite unnecessary, sir, I had every intent to seek you out before the evening was done." Geoffrey felt his half-strangled neck and straightened his lapels.

"Impatience do sometimes take a hold o' me, Master Latimer; since I was as tall as my father's shoulder, impatience has taken me and will not be laid down until 'tis fed."

The dark night seemed suddenly darker than it ought, the stinking yard more foul and the lighted interior of The Phoenix less hospitable. Shaking his foot and straightening his back he walked briskly through the busy inn, ignoring the hunched form of William Mudge hung over his claret, and stepped gratefully into the unlit street.

4

The merchant's house – its foundations begun in the time of the seventh Henry and displaying a variety of architectural influences upon its modest footprint, was loosely known as Latimer House. Squeezed against its flanks were similarly tall buildings, not so grand now and suffering from the indifference of their owners. Apart from Latimer House, these had ground-floor shops fronting the street. On the one side was a much-visited milliner's shop and whorehouse. On the other a bootmaker shared his shop with his son – with no interest in his father's craft the boy was much more likely to be found bobbing up and down on the Exe in search of salmon than repairing boots; the consequence of this unlikely arrangement was that the bootmaker also sold fish. Rising stately beside the fish-sellers' trestles and immediately next to Latimer house was a grand fortified door. Behind this rose the three-storey home and studio of a successful, although itinerate, artist.

A man of loose morals and liberal sexual tastes, Alexander Trelawney was a proficient painter, patronised by the top end of Exeter society. When in residence – and he was often away for large parts of each year – the artist made good use of his studio's close proximity to the whorehouse; the young women there offered infinite possibilities, and whether for personal pleasure or a penny pose the whores satisfied his needs. Rich men's wives rarely made good models: their sense of class and poorly hidden arrogance gave them airs that did not paint well. Having the young harlots sit for him, entertaining them in the easy relaxed nonconformity of his private rooms, allowed for a certain intimacy – and their virtues were well known to him.

In portraiture a flat aged bosom might be substituted for a rounded upstanding one, and swan-like shoulders put to use in any number of portraits. Perhaps there was some morality in the inclusion of whore and lady in the same pose, and this fed his black sense of humour – he found great pleasure in noting, quite to himself, that the wife of the mayor or the daughter of a rich landowner displayed her head and grandest gown on the bosom and neck of a slattern.

Although the milliner's shop ran as a milliner's should, with two sickly young girls working away at their craft towards the back, gaudily dressed and brightly painted young women often busied themselves towards the front where they could be easily seen by any passing customer, or they loitered in the darker corners of Exebere Street soliciting their trade. When his wife was alive Henri Latimer had bothered much about the proximity of the bawdy house on her behalf, but now that she was dead, he did not. Apart from the steady trade that ran above the milliner's shop there was not much else to note. Besides, until these last weeks when he had been almost permanently confined to his bed chamber, he had been away, returning briefly, mollifying his wife and seeing to land-based business; more latterly, concerning himself with the care of his daughters, appeasement for a conscience grown guilty through his lack of earlier connection.

Clinging to the backhouses of the artist's dwelling and set at right angles to Latimer's ran a strange affair of balustrade, slate roof and balcony, forming a kind of derelict gallery. All was in a poor state of repair: the floors missing boards and the small jutting roof missing slates. The balustrade itself endured intact. From here the view was westwards across the river out towards the wooded hills that preceded the great open empty moor; the light was good for working or reading and it was a regular sitting place.

On the Tuesday of that week Henri Latimer was standing at his open window looking out at the late afternoon sky. The young woman he had watched at the coffee house was perched on a stool, a bundle of lace and a cambric petticoat resting in her lap. She wore bawdy house cast-offs: an undyed dress which was pulled in tight to fit her young shape with the help of a short woollen jacket of faded scarlet, the former being too large for her, the latter too small. Her cap was in her lap along with the lace.

"Book or needle, Rae?" He began as he often did, easy talk often the promised ending to a long day of isolation and discomfort.

"I have needle, Henri. It is needle today."

"Needle." He paused. "Godly seam or whorehouse frippery?"

"'Tis neither, Mr Latimer, you must guess again, although I believe you can see quite clearly what I do." The girl was about seventeen, although even she was not sure. When asked, the artist in whose house she lived would offer very little about her background or beginnings. If his mood was one of indifference he would often say that he had been robbed of a shilling when he had bought her seven years ago; if she had pleased him, sat well for him, mixed pigments, cleaned oily pallets, delivered food and beverage as she should, he might say that he had purchased her for a guinea and that she was worth five.

"Guessing has become customary, Rae, and I prefer to keep to the practice – I am in favour of custom."

"You know well and good, Henri, that I am not free to choose my pass-times, and must do as I am bid before I can do as I choose, so your guessing is made much the easier. 'Tis more like that I should have necessity resting in my lap rather than any book or fancy work."

"Then I propose, by your lack of your immersion in the task, that it is necessity that has you seated on this rickety outshoot in the half-light."

Rae was thinking now. "Necessity, yes, I believe it is necessity. I sew because I am mending." There was a pause and then she continued almost in a conspiratorial whisper. "I am returning the lace to the bawdy mother's delicates."

Henri adjusted his weight, perching awkwardly on the sill, he imagined her smile – she would be smiling to herself. "This perhaps involves some skill?" he said.

"'Tis not much of a skill, Henri – I believe you do tease me. Once you have learnt to put thread through needle and needle through cloth there be no skill at all, just a determination to get the thing done. I was taught the need for sewing long ago before I came here, and such a thing can never be un-learned."

"And was there a time before you came here, Rae?"

Latimer knew that the time before she came here was hardly known to her any more than it was to Trelawney. He wondered why Trelawney had picked her out, the black-eyed child that she must have been: gaunt and hungry faced. Perhaps he had seen beyond the hollow eyes and unsmiling mouth or had seen her as a possession, as a man might a beautiful but empty-headed wife or a pretty black serving child – a talking point at gatherings, an investment perhaps. The haunted half-starved waif had disappeared long before these meetings began, but he doubted maturity had changed her overmuch.

"You do know for sure that there was, Henri, I have told you before and many a time."

Their thoughts were private for a while. Henri adjusted his position and remembered his first painful visit to this window; the injury that had near seen him out, the expectation of death and then the slow repairing of his health. He assessed the changes in the sky and the progressing dusk. Thin cloud was spreading from the west, obscuring the dying sun.

"I think you must work quickly, Rae, the light will soon leave us."

From the encompassing gloom the companionable silence was abruptly broken. "Hell's Gate, this spiky little needle has stuck my forefinger and I shall bleed out all over this good cambric."

He muffled merriment and responded. "Then put the thing away and talk to me in its stead, else you will bleed upon the whore-mother's delicates and I cannot help you with the consequences." He drew to surface the thought that had been in his mind since he had seen her sitting on the gallery and opened his window. "I saw you," he said.

The dark head bobbed up, sloe-black eyes searching the dusk. "You saw me? Where did you see me? How is it that you have left the house, Henri?"

"Goldsmiths, the coffee house in Waterbere Lane – I cannot mistake you. You held the door ajar for some while, and I may say put the fear of God into many who take their coffee and gossip there. They were fearful you may have the audacity to enter."

Ignoring his comment, she said, "You have been out, to Goldsmiths?"

"Yes, I have," he said deliberately. "It might not have been the best of times to go for I received a drenching there and a drenching back, with the wind finding me on every corner."

"This testy weather do ever catch a person out, Henri." He waited for her to continue, he knew she would be assessing what he had said. "Was the hill not hard to climb?"

"Hard enough, but I had no reason to make haste – time is something I have too much of. I had no agreed appointment – there were no demands for my return."

"Then you are well again, Henri?" Hope danced undisguised in her voice.

"No," he said absently. "No, I do not think that I am, but there is improvement – I believe there is improvement." There was a pause whilst he considered his own unpredictable and seemingly fragile health. "Besides, I refuse to rot away here whilst the whole city anticipates my death. I will not stay locked away in these rooms, Rae, despite fate dictating that I must."

"Nor could I, Henri, I mean to stay locked in any room – not in this guarded coup and it is only coming here that keeps me from the fidgets."

"There seemed some urgency to your visit to the coffee house. Why so?"

"I was sent upon an errand. There was a title in the house and he would have no other but Jane, and the mother says that Jane must come and must be found."

"A title?" Lust, he supposed, needed to be obliged – aristocrat or pauper, it was the same. "In a back street brothel in Devonshire, Rae – who was your title?"

Dusk had come to the courtyard, having the effect of further obscuring her features. Although conversation had passed between them not infrequently over the last few weeks –whether daylight permitted it or not, each did not have a clear view of the other.

"You know I cannot say, Henri, so you must not ask me." He did not ask her. "Will you go out tomorrow?" she said.

"Perhaps I shall, and if I do will you not find your way to Goldsmith's again and lighten the mood?"

"Fool's talk, Henri."

"Why so? You could amuse me, Rae, and my friend, Elcott."

"Those dark-suited old men would have me gone as soon as set eyes upon me, Henri, and you do know it."

"Perhaps they would? Perhaps we must have some place to hide from the distractions of your sex. But do not think yourself unworthy of these houses, Rae; you have your letters and I know for sure that many of those who take their coffee and chocolate in these places, the most eminent of orators, do not."

"Letters have uses, Henri. 'Tis not so hard to learn such when you are driven by a need, and I must read Mr Trelawney's letters, and who else is there to do it when you do know that Elijah Flood, despite his bible searching, cannot read beyond his name?"

He sensed she was gathering up her needles and thread. "What work calls you in now, Rae?"

"Supper, Henri – the fire, the pot and an old man determined to keep me from ungodly talking."

"Is this talk ungodly, Rae?"

"I am sure that it is, Mr Latimer. Elijah would think it so and I must be gone, Henri, for I cannot have him know that his door-locking do not keep me in."

She was leaving; opening the window behind her, pushing the bundle of cambric and threads inside her coat, and gathering up her skirts, she was returning the way she had come. He waited until she had gone, looked one last time at the grey, silhouetted buildings and the snaking river before reluctantly dropping the sash.

There were tasks that needed to be got through other than just the mundane tasks of domesticity. Elijah Flood would return from his meeting house soon, watch her as she ladled food upon earthenware, watch her until she settled to the evening, waiting for her to sit before the bible and read to him, losing the hours in the dimly lit room beside the spluttering candle.

5

The strong winds of the previous week had returned, blowing up the Exe valley and bringing with them a salty tang. Watching Elijah Flood walk purposefully away from the house along Exebere Street, collar pulled up to his ears, Rae had turned back from the upstairs window and gone down to the kitchens, stood for a moment considering the heavy bolt pulled shut across the top of the door. Collecting the stool from the hearth she lifted her skirts, stepped up and pulled back the bolt. Rain-washed crates and pools of muddy water lay about the partly-cobbled chaotic court yard – she drew her coat about her, tucking the needlework she had completed inside its fronts, taking large irregular steps to avoid the worst of the water. Henri Latimer's window she noticed was closed to the elements – she would not have expected it other.

She let herself into the bawdy-house kitchen, shaking out her hair and stamping her wet feet on the flags. The young whores who were sat about the permanently lit cooking fire looked up, accepted her as one of their number and continued with conversation. Rae put down her bundle, kicked off her wet slippers and nimbly sat herself on the edge of the large scrubbed table which dominated the room.

At the other end of the table a girl of about thirteen was working away with a heavy knife slashing at a scrag-end of mutton, cutting collops, then laboriously throwing them one piece at a time into a pot dangling from a chimney crook. The girl raised her face without smiling and then continued with her work. In a society where labour was cheap, servants were easily come-by; if there were enough shillings to pay for one then no matter what class or level of household a servant could be got. But the mother may just as well have saved her shillings, for the young woman who worked at the table was surly and very seldom willing, a clumsy girl with large red hands and unwashed matted hair who viewed the world about her with an eye of resentment.

Pushing back the clutter of millinery – a bundle of bright ribbons, a flat straw hat and a brace of long feathers – Rae found herself a more comfortable position. Her feet were damp and she stretched her toes towards the fire.

"You are late today, Rae. Did that fool dissenter lose his pocket watch or have a change of heart and forgo his meeting-house visit?"

"He was busy with the fire and waiting on the rain – you know he would never miss his Methody meeting." She shook out her bundle and placed the contents neatly on the table. "Will you see your gentleman again, Jane, your Lordship – the one I was sent for to bring you back?"

"A lord here, Rae?"

The voluptuous whore they called Jane was sitting in a low chair close to the fire, skirts drawn up, examining her legs with a contrary expression of satisfaction and distaste. Five years in the bawdy house had not eroded Jane's bloom and she was a favourite in the house.

"Oh, Jane, you know which she do mean. Do not lead us along a slow path when you know that you must answer what is asked at the end of it."

Fragile-faced, pale-headed Mag did not like game playing. She raised her face to look at Rae, her long fair hair hanging lose over her shoulders, a small scar showing prominently below her left eye. Rumour had followed her when first she came here, when first the bawdy mother decided to take her beneath her roof: she had once been married; she had fought her husband and had killed him to escape his brutality, fragile like a bee's wing, this seemed unlikely but the rumour would never leave her.

"I have sworn upon my life to keep a secret." Jane spoke with mock reverence, twisting a finger in her tangle of coloured hair, a hand spread across her exposed ample breasts.

"You must enjoy the dance around, Jane, but you will out the story in the end and be more 'n glad to tell it." Mag narrowed her blue eyes and picked at a broken nail.

Swinging her legs idly before the heat of the fire Rae listened to the talk as she had since she had first come here in the early years of her adolescence. Listening and watching and forming her own, and perhaps irregular, opinions, her education during her informative years was an eclectic mix of bawdy-house gossip, Trelawney's ambiguous rantings and the regular almost incomprehensible teachings of the bible. Although she had never considered joining them, the bond between her and the harlots endured, the connection their mutual practicality and undiminishing desire for survival.

"I will not talk freely upon the man – the mother will not here of it. Besides one man is the same as any other when he is buck to a doe and I cannot say as I've seen any more coin from this one's pocket than I have from any other jack in the pack."

Slumped in a wooden chair, high brown wig obscuring her pinched features, white paint and rouge obscuring her thoughts, a third whore drew on a clay pipe she held between filthy fingers.

"As long as they've got coin to pay I don't see as there's any difference between those who've slunk sideways from their marriage bed to seek their pleasure and those who do take it with their liquor like it were due to them." She drew again, allowing the smoke to drift up above the cooking pots to the low beams above. "A youngish gentleman's coin be easy come and easy go, but if he is older the man will sit upon it even if he do have plenty; but as long as the Lordship do drop his money in the mother's box when he drops his breeches, we should not care what name he goes by."

She stood, placed a foot on a firedog warming the uncovered flesh beneath her skirts, angular almost masculine shoulders showing white above her bodice. "If I were set down any place but this then I should be turning these fool drunks and collecting up the coin that falls from their unbuttoned breeches and forgotten purses; this house is becoming more like a gospel meeting hall than a bawdy house."

"Then you would have the magistrates down upon us, Lisa, and 'twould be a poor thing for us all." Mag was speaking, almost fierce in her opposition.

Rae listened to the talk, similar talk she had heard before. It was in common knowledge that the bawdy-mother had viewed gaol from the wrong side, had watched many a young girl kick their last at the end of a rope; now her business was prostitution and to a lesser degree the trade of millinery and nothing more. Rae had heard of the rookeries of London and of those growing northern cities where mantua-making and millinery was just a front for deeper criminality; in this undisturbed western city it was not so.

Hardly listening, lost in a private daydream, Mag gathered up her hair and began to divide it into three even strands. "I should like to have a lordship for my very own one day."

"And why would you wish for a lordship – for to keep you, I'm supposing?"

"And why should I not – a room of my own and one man visiting instead of many, a press full of silk – why should I not?"

"You misremember, Mag. You misremember from whence you came and what you came away from; your lord would soon turn keeper. Keep you in finery one week and drop you heavy into the gutter the next."

"Hush, Lisa, and leave me to my own thinking." Mag drew in her laces, pulling in her bodice about a waist that was already as small as a child's.

"Do Flood still make you read him all those long words from that great book o' his, Rae?"

"And he does, Jane, he says I must read and read again and he says I must stay away from whorehouse kitchens and whore-mothers."

"I suppose he thinks we shall all end in the fires of Hell and you along with us." Jane paused, restless fingers touching the paper spot on her rouged cheek. She had been raised by devout parents who had turned her out onto the streets when she was carrying her first bastard – religion and bible teaching was not for her. "You must tell the dissenter that you shall never fall into that pit of his miss-imagining, not whilst you have Jane to watch over you. There is none better to save you, Rae, than those who are journeying there themselves." She smoothed her skirts over fleshy legs and pointed her feet to the fire.

"So, what says your last letter, Rae?" Mag raised a subject which held some interest for her. "Any news of Trelawney bringing his living back amongst us?" she said hiding her eagerness. "I have missed him and all his mischief-making."

Hetty had finally completed the task of cutting and transferring mutton from table to pot, a task which had taken her some long while. Many a sharp tongue-lashing had discouraged her from joining in the conversation, not that she wished it, and to remind them that she was still present in the room, she begun to throw large muddied tiddies onto the littered table allowing them to roll in a variety of unwanted directions. Rae slid from her perch and walked without comment to the opposite end of the table, picked up a root and began to peel it with the small knife that Hetty had put down.

"And what of the Merchant?" Mag asked, now plaiting her hair so that it hung in a sleek tail over her shoulder. "We all expected a burial, to see him put in the ground with his pious wife, and those two young girls to be left to the world as orphans."

Hearing Henri Latimer talked about so freely, when her intimacy with him – no matter how oddly detached – was known only to her left Rae with an odd feeling of confusion – somewhere between guilt and something she could not quantify.

"I have heard he goes along much the same," she said dropping a root into the pot.

The wet world did not penetrate this room but the chimes of St Mary's Church did. She put her head up, listened, counted the foreboding ring of the single bell. "Hell's Gate! I must go before Mr Flood do find me and bother me for repentance." She put down the knife, wiped her wet hands on her skirts and let herself out into the courtyard.

6

The unpredictability of the weather in these westward counties never failed to begin a conversation – never allowed a room to stay silent for long – and the following day all traces of the harsh weather were swept away by a brisk south-easterly. Latimer had eaten breakfast with his daughters and then bade them farewell as they started on their short walk towards the river marshes with their nurse. Geoffrey had not yet left his room. Ascending the stairs with more ease than he anticipated, Latimer returned to his room, removed his shirt and plunged his head into a bowl of tepid water. Washed and dressed in clean linen, he left the house, making his way across town to Blackaller Tucking Mill.

He was shown into a back room, the deafening noise barely deadened by the heavy door that was closed behind him. Josiah Mudge was sat behind a wide oak desk. The Quaker wore a short periwig, his bushy eyebrows almost connecting with the coarse horsehair. He was friendly faced with thick lips and broad ruddy hands.

"Latimer, a pleasure, sir, to find you abroad. God has seen fit to bring you back to us and I am grateful for it." Henri was not sure that his improvement was all God's work but he would not contradict.

"Josiah, how goes business?"

"Do sit, sir." Apart from his lack of perception with regard to his only son, Josiah Mudge was an astute man and although he could see an improvement in Latimer, he was still aware that all was not well. Henri sat, leaning forward over his long legs, elbows resting on knees. He took breath, ran a hand through his dark hair.

"I do not wish it to appear that I check upon the boy, Josiah, but I am keen to know how my nephew does. I have encouraged him to come along and see how the fulling process operates. I hope you have had chance to meet. His mother is ever concerned for his prosperity and wellbeing and is pleased with his situation here, but I would be glad to have your view of the boy."

"We have made acquaintance but I have not seen him this last week and more, these mawkish throats have a rare contagion and I was also confined to my bed for a while; but my son has spoken to him, reports him studious."

Feeling relieved at being able to speak on a subject that had long since troubled him but which he had not been able to air, Latimer continued, "The boy keeps himself within himself, we have little conversation. As you know I have hardly left my rooms and have found no heart for company. My nephew is scarce at home – I assume he moves about the city. I have advised him to get an overview of our industry and although there is no trade for him to deal with at the present time, I hope this situation will change."

Mudge placed his broad hands on the desk before him. "I also have concerns for William, so like his mother – such soft colourings and no head for figures. Perhaps we were too grave in our youth, Latimer. I am Quaker and expect it; it is in my nature and my nurturing to be sombre minded, but we need not all be so. They are young, Latimer, they will come right."

"Since I have been able to make sense of the world, found strength to drop my legs to the floor and leave my bed I have begun to considered this very sentiment, Josiah. I have dealt with life with unquestioned gravity since my father's death and my abrupt discovery of his failings – it seems habit disallows anything other." Henri sat up and gave the businessman a clear look. He did not wear his heart on his sleeve, deeper thoughts were rarely aired and most especially in a counting house in the stead of business. "How goes my cloth, Josiah?"

With just a ten per cent share left in the fulling mill, Latimer had never expected riches. The agreement that had been made when the mill was sold on in his father's time allowed for an approved amount of cloth to go through the fulling process in lieu of any dividends – and without charge. He supposed this had been small beer as part of an agreement that had seen the Latimer Mill sold on to the family Mudge – and with no more than the payment of debts coming to the Latimers.

The Quaker was an upstanding God-fearing man, honest to the bone, and Latimer had great respect for him.

"You have a dozen serges on tenterhooks, do you have a market abroad still or will you sell in the city?"

"Alas not, I have not set foot upon *The Lady Rosamunde* since my injury. The crew has long since dispersed. We are not trading."

Josiah Mudge contemplated his broad purple hands.

"Those we have, would it assist you if I sold them along with mine? I can allow them to run on through with our own, and whether or no we sell here in these markets or send them on to Rotterdam there will be some profit to come from it – I do not doubt that you will be glad to have it at these difficult times." The Quaker looked up and met Latimer's steel blue eyes. "Better still let me give you their estimated value and then the process will be made that much simpler."

It was a generous thought. He would not allow pride to display him as ungrateful.

"Your gesture, well meant, is well received, sir, I thank you."

Inconveniently and quite without warning a swoon now engulfed him, unexpected and unwelcome. Latimer allowed his head to rest in his hands, he hoped the Quaker would not take too much account of it; he had hoped to make this visit a starting point in his return to good health and then to trade.

"Are you quite well, sir? May I assist you? I have a good physician and can send for him in an instant."

Henri lifted a hand to show not. "This infirmity takes me without warning. It is damnable!" he said. "It will pass, it will pass. I have only been from my bed these last two weeks, so I must find patience."

"Just so, sir, just so. Well sit awhile before you leave. I can find someone to walk along with you if you choose."

"No, am better already."

The Quaker waited for a moment and then looked across his desk, his profuse brows meeting. "And what of other business, Henri, do you still use the Rack Lane carriers to collect your cloth, and the agent who oversees on their behalf; or has this link been broken also?" He rarely used first names; it was a sign of empathy and kindly meant.

"Not at present. I have had no heart for business even if I could put my mind to it. Indeed it has seemed altogether futile under the circumstances."

Josiah Mudge coughed into his hand to cover a slight awkwardness on his part. So the merchant had anticipated his own death.

"I must talk to my nephew on this very subject," Latimer continued, 'I am eager for him to ride up to the heart of the county and make contact with the farms and weaving families I have previously done business with – and the markets at Moretonhampstead and Crediton – observe our trade from deck to topsail. Beyond that…?'He did not finish his sentence. There was something altogether wrong about his nephew, something intangible that he could not explain. He considered how life might progress with his nephew trading his cloth. Latimer was well aware that his failure to delegate any part of his business to any other had brought about the near ending of it and he did not expect to sit a horse for a while yet.

"I must see *The Lady Rosamunde* made seaworthy and begin to move serge to Rotterdam again. The return trade is ever lucrative." Latimer had risen. He rested on his stick. "This stout stick," he said smiling, "I expected to use it whilst my leg healed, but now it has become an integral part of my existence."

Josiah Mudge rose behind his desk, a desk that had belonged to Latimer's grandfather. "Good day to you, sir. I hope we may see you here again soon."

Latimer turned and prayed to Josiah's god that this would be so.

7

Geoffrey Latimer had broken his fast with his uncle once already this week and did not wish to repeat the experience. Uncle Henri had left the Exebere Street house already, stepping out with that black stick of his tapping his way across the city on some business matter. He looked in the glass, tilted it and examined his appearance: the waistcoat was new, it had been made in best brocade by a tailor in High Street and had yet to be paid for. There was little he liked about this mercantile city of business; people seemed altogether obsessed with making money, so obsessed that they had not the time to spend it, but the Latimer house had a grandness about it that his own manor lacked. For a merchant's house in such an unpromising street, the rooms were lofty and genteel – it made dressing here a pleasure. He pulled on his coat, settled his lace and smoothed his dark hair. His wig must stay on its post; he had business on Exe Island in the oldest part of the city – a jumble of back streets, it was the breeding ground for opportune criminals, beggars and destitute slatterns and he did not wish to make a show of himself.

Vetch was waiting for him in the hall when he went down; the obliging servant, resident in the house since his father's time, effected to brush off his coat, duty and habit overtaking need.

"Travelling far, Master Geoffrey? I believe we have seen the last of the rain."

"Not far, Thomas, a stroll to take a little of this freshened air; it has been a long time since I have been able to breathe a lungful without the need to apply linen to my nostrils. The air about seems permanently laced with the stinks of the fulling industry."

A drying and cleansing wind may have been blowing across the city but in the dismal lower streets it did little to improve the state of the cobbles. The area was familiar and he found the hovel easily – a dank alley just off Frog Lane, it smelt of the river; he remembered the smell clearly. The squat door was chewed by worm along its base, allowing any passer-by to view the feet and ankles of those who worked within. He pushed it open and called into the dark cave-like room. "Blox!" When last he had visited this place the experience had left him feeling soiled and he felt no differently now. "Blox? Saints and martyrs, sir, how can you see in this gloom?"

The tiny low-ceilinged room was divided across its centre by a filthy piece of rag and behind it standing before a cluttered table, almost engulfed by the needs of his trade, was an ancient man. The bunches of drying herbs and tangled coils of brown-leaved shrubs and grasses hanging from the central beam of the low-roofed hovel brushed against the old man's head and shoulders as he worked.

"Impatient calling will not have my attention any more readily than none." The herbalist, known as Blox in the lower circles of the city, did not turn. Born high and come low he resented any interruption to his work, even though that interruption often meant the difference between penury and starvation. "Come in and state your business or leave me to work." Reluctantly the old man turned, running small bloodshot eyes over his visitor, taking in the fine coat and polished boots, returning his eyes to his work with a shrug of distaste.

"Can it be that you have yet another superfluous relative you wish to assist gently to his grave?" He bowed his head over the table, his tonsure giving him a monkish look.

"Your insinuation, Blox, is unsupported. You would be wise to keep such ideas within your insolent head and not allow them to seep out where they might find the light of day." Blox shrugged, his oversized coat, made stiff with the splashings of nameless substances and more than a year's dirt, moving as an entity with him. "I am surprised that you remember me after so many weeks? The light in this seething hovel is so poor I cannot imagine how you can tell one man from his brother."

"My eyes are as good as any and I misremember nothing. I have had dealings with many a coxcomb in my time and you, sir, sit well in my memory."

Dried seeds and burrs from the twine-hung herbage had found their way into Geoffrey's hair, even between his stock and his neck. He picked at them impatiently, considering the flimsy overloaded shelves that lined a wall at the back of the room. Ignoring him Blox begun to push pestle into mortar, grinding leaves into a pulp. The reputation of this revolting man preceded him: it was said that he had been born genteel, necessity having sent him to study and then practise the craft of apothecary amongst the rich. A misunderstanding had him spend time in the town's gaol – beyond that all was rumour and supposition.

"Do not loiter behind me and disturb my time. Speak plainly, state your business or take your foppery and expensive clothes to the houses of this city where they will find welcome."

The herbalist moved stiffly to another part of his work table and stooped, his dull coat accentuating his monk-like appearance.

"I will speak plainly if my only reward is to be gone from this pit. Your potion, sir, the decoction you supplied me at some cost to my pocket, has not worked. Indeed, on the contrary. So very nearly upon his deathbed the decaying man is up, Blox, and has left his home and will likely soon be poking into my affairs uninvited."

Blox put down the phial of liquid he was holding and frowned at the tiny lead window which was the only light in the hovel. His thoughts formed quickly.

"Then he has not been taking the draught,'" he said. He picked up the phial again and began adding white powder to the dark liquid.

"This cannot be so, Blox. His servant places the tonic beside his bed each afternoon and takes away an empty glass each eve."

"Then perhaps your determined relative has more intuition than you surmise. If he were taking what I have prescribed he would not be from his bed. Bittersweet Nightshade, even in its most weakened form, as we have offered, will lead to extreme fatigue, dizziness, even convulsions and paralysis in concentrate – the mix is rarely fatal but certainly debilitating." Returning to his mixing he added, "Debilitating in a man in full health, more likely fatal in a sickly one – but I believe you understood the risk."

Geoffrey kicked at the debris on the earth floor. The man had him over a barrel; he knew too much and now he must listen to his babble and attempt to hold his temper.

The herbalist reiterated his observation. "I'll wager he no longer takes the draught. I know not his reason but you may have been unearthed, sir."

"So, I am left between a rock and a hard place," Geoffrey mumbled.

"I supplied what you requested and you paid according to the sensitivity of your needs. Only you can know how to progress from here." Blox turned and ran an indifferent eye over his customer. "Money may offer many solutions. Only you can decide what it is that you require and I will tell you how much this will cost you."

Letting the plank door fall back against the stop, Geoffrey took a breath of air; even the dank smell of the river was preferential to the noxious evils of the hovel. Brushing his coat with his hand he began to climb the hill towards

Fore Street. How did a man become so base? Much must have happened to Blox between genteel birth and his hermit-like existence in the filthy hut. He felt his empty fob pocket; the incident with the moneylender was regrettable, he would make certain it was never repeated.

How much easier it had seemed to avoid the necessity of repaying his debts in his rural Dorset. If ever he were visited by any man he had done business with, and he much preferred not to be found, then there were always retainers who might fabricate a story, spin a yarn for small payment. Here, in this city with no servant to call his own, where judging a character was filled with pits and holes, life and moneylending had an added level of complication.

He had arranged to meet with William Mudge in The Swan before the midday – disappointingly The Swan and not The Phoenix. The Phoenix, always his choice previously, had lost a little of its bounce. William was sat before his tankard, waistcoat buttoned tightly to his stock, chin in hand – he had not yet mellowed into the day. He looked up.

"Sir, business done I see, and quickly so."

Geoffrey muttered a greeting and sat himself beside him. "And not quickly enough, William, I have had need to visit a hovel on Exe Island and the place is seething with drunken old women and half-clothed brats. I am supposing your good papa is back behind that grand old desk, William?"

William sat back, twisted the half-empty tankard in his idle hands. "He is Geoffrey, although I do not mind it; I would rather have him call me out for a fool than that little clerk – the man has no right to be as clever as he is with nothing much in the way of schooling and a pauper's beginnings."

"'Tis an oddity, William, a man should have the intelligence he was born to and nothing beyond it." A pot boy placed a full tankard on the table before him; he took it in hand but did not drink, sitting back and contemplating the irregularities of life.

"Think upon it, William: if the world had dealt with us differently it might have been my papa pushing numbers around a chalkboard above the workings of Blackaller, and that safe-box tucked so nicely within the wall-cupboard would have Latimer writ on its front in the stead of Mudge." Geoffrey picked up his tankard and drank the half, oblivious of how his comment had affected the Quaker's only son.

"And so it might, sir, and so it might – but all the same it do not, Geoffrey. How fairs your uncle, Geoffrey? My papa has reported him up and well enough to make his way to Blackaller – is his recovery complete or will he turn again as he has before?"

As it was Blox's physic that had caused his uncle's relapse, Geoffrey ought to have been able to answer this directly. Instead he said, the lie easily spoken,

"I have no answer to it, William. We rarely meet in that well-proportioned house and he is reclusive in his habits. Although I judge him sickly, still I cannot predict how his health will go, but I suspect he will continue to rise and stomp behind me in his dark coat and mended boots for a while longer."

Frustrated by the world about him, a world that seemed determined to trip him at every turn, Geoffrey rose, went to the fire and put his boot to a log, kicking it hard until sparks flew and a flame appeared. "Meantime I must run errands and live the life of an under-clerk." He leant his hands on the mantelshelf and watched the smouldering logs die back to nothing. "I cannot deny it, William, I have a need and a thirst for a full purse; my manor is hungry for it, my mama demands it and now I am sought by black-mouthed moneylenders."

"Life do indeed throw us up tricky evils, Geoffrey, I cannot see a way forward for you, and would offer it if I could."

The fire seemed to have given up altogether and he cursed it and began on a different tack – a seed of an idea forming as he spoke.

"That little safe-box – I am intrigued by its contents. As well as payments do it also hold scrolled documents and written papers? We have a similar affair in Marwood, it is under lock and key, although there is nothing of any worth beneath its lid."

"Full to the top, sir, and rolled parchments and sealed papers in every drawer and forgotten cupboard to add along with it. Why the query, Geoffrey? They are hardly looked upon and no interest to any."

"No interest to any, perhaps – save me. I suspect there is something amongst it all that I should like to borrow – if it can be found."

"My papa would likely set his clerk on the hunt if you ask it. What is it that you search for?"

"Saints, William, you must not ask your papa or his obsequious clerk for their help. I would not have them know a thing about it – this borrowing must be between us two and us two only."

William considered the proposition, although not quick-witted he had begun to learn that he ought not to trust Geoffrey Latimer fully.

"When the mill was sold to your family there would have been an agreement, a document allowing for the ten per cent share to remain with the Latimers."

"I propose that there was, but time has passed it by. A paper will be somewhere on those dust-filled shelves or in the box itself, and your Uncle Latimer will hold another similar agreement."

"And it has sat there for many a year, not note-worthy of even a second glance. If you could find it for me, William, I would quite like to second-glance it now; I have a purpose and a need to have it in my hand for a short while.

The thing surely will not be missed, you have said yourself that these papers are never looked upon."

"It seems a simple offering, Geoffrey, I cannot see the harm in it – if I can find the document. May I ask your need to have it?"

"I am done with these blood-hound moneylenders, William. Since my uncle no longer lies upon his deathbed, I must find solvency in another direction. I shall borrow, as any gentlemen engaged in business might, and for this I need to offer up a level of security – a ten per cent holding in the Blackaller Fulling Mill will surely appease even the most long-nosed lender."

8

A pleasing half an hour in his favourite coffee house had followed Latimer's visit to Blackaller and, returning in the later part of the afternoon, he had chosen not to climb the tapering oak treads to his chambers but in its stead settle himself in the large room at the front of the house – a thing he had not done for many weeks.

The sitting room, broader than it was high, was dominated by heavy oak cross-timbers and dark panelled screens; the fire was not lit and the huge bressummer-beam and stone fireplace seemed cavernous and lifeless. However his mood today was sanguine, even the neglected dusty hearth could not alter this.

He chose a wingback chair some distance into the depths of the room. The chair, like much of the furniture in this room, had been sourced by his grandfather and had been little disturbed in either position or upholstery since it had been placed there.

Although tired Latimer felt something that he had not felt for some time – optimism. It was a novel feeling and this feeling soothed all else that surrounded him, like the remaining pain in his thigh and his concerns over his nephew. He stretched his leg and looked at the day through the casement; the skies were unusually bright but the closeness of the surrounding buildings meant that the sun rarely penetrated this wide room.

He watched the mantle clock – cynicism so often crept in when he sat alone, and there had been enough of that over recent weeks. Today his mind-set was altogether lighter. Perhaps, in a week or so, if his health continued to improve, he might hire a nag and go north himself, visit some of the mid-county farms he had once done business with. Agents and pack boys could not always be relied upon; if he wished to resurrect his business he would need to go himself. He ran a hand through his hair and absently rubbed his injured leg – habitual now, it gave some relief. Although idleness had never suited him, sitting inactive in his own home gave him quiet pleasure – and he was waiting for Geoffrey.

In the time between, Latimer had slept – unknown for him – and when Geoffrey had entered the room towards the end of the afternoon, surprise was felt keenly by both uncle and nephew.

"Uncle Latimer, sir, I did not expect to find you here; I have become so accustomed to living with my own company and an empty room."

Stirred by what remained of his conscience – this enlarged by his recent duplicitous scheming – Geoffrey's fright at finding his uncle seated in this down-stairs sitting room had been genuine.

"I apologize, Nephew, if I have startled you, it was not in the least my intent." Henri roused himself after his unexpected doze. "I thought to stay down and now that you are here, I am glad that I have. We live under the same roof, Geoffrey, but we may just as well not for the little time we spend in companionship."

Henri adjusted his eyes to the new light that had crept in through a small casement on the west wall and looked at his nephew critically – not too critically he hoped. The boy was very well turned out – a new coat or waistcoat perhaps? Latimer chose not to ask himself how this was so when the young man had come to him but two months ago, pleading poverty.

"Uncle, you seem much improved – such a conflict of expectation." Geoffrey felt his stock; the thing had suddenly become tight. He came into the room and stood above his uncle – almost as tall but with less substance and none of the merchant's strength; there was an unmistakable family likeness.

"Come, sit along with me, Geoffrey, and let me have your company for a while."

Geoffrey took a chair some distance from his uncle's, lifting the skirts of his well-tailored coat before sitting.

"What has been your business today, Nephew, errand or pleasure? The air is softer than it has been for some days and I have taken a walk myself."

"I am happy to hear it, Uncle." Always prying – now he must run clear of the truth. "I have visited the Catherine Street coffee house, sir, as you suggested at the beginning of my time here; a lively place. Even if a man does not wish to do business there is a wealth of reason and knowledge to be sourced. We do not have the same in country districts, the inn supports all our gossip and at quite a different level."

"Forgive me, Nephew, you need not explain your day so fully, I have no wish to make checks and balances upon your doings. I have been poor company these last weeks and it serves me well to know of your advancement." Henri thought his nephew looked decidedly uncomfortable. He reprimanded himself; he must not put his boot where he did not intend it to be, but if conversation was to continue freely then their future here together, in this house and how they supported that, was more than pertinent. "I have been considering the future whilst I have been sat here in this quiet place. A future, I may say, that until quite recently I had not expected to have."

Geoffrey controlled the urge to run his fingers in that tight space between neck and stock again.

"When the time is right, what say you to a trip across this county? We must revive trade, make direct contact with those I have done business with in past years. There is something about shaking the hand of a weaver or farmer, man to man, that cannot be achieved by middlemen alone. The fulling is nearly done on our final serges, more must follow or business will die and not be so easily brought back to life."

Geoffrey pondered an answer. Nothing that had happened over the last few days had been as he had planned – and turn upon turn yet another surprise seemed determined to confront him.

"To ride out north and west across this vast county would bring me nothing but pleasure, sir. As you know I greatly miss having my own horse and would welcome a day or so in the saddle, but I concede I am not adept in business matters, and most especially in this woollen trade. I would not know a good fleece from a poor, nor a fine piece of woven cloth from a slovenly one." Geoffrey crossed one slim leg over the other and absently brushed an imaginary spot of mud from his new fustian breeches.

"It is a modest business we run, Geoffrey, not the level of trade our ancestors did, and we have not had ownership of Blackaller for decades. Wealth is unlikely to return to this family in this generation; but if bankruptcy and debt can be kept from our door, at least in my lifetime, then I am satisfied."

Affecting interest and deeper thought, Geoffrey looked at his uncle with unremarkable hazel eyes. Why was this man prepared to live in this penny-pinching way, deprived of comfort and the normal trappings of a gentleman's life? How unlike their aspirations; did this luckless man really expect that he would be content with a life of survival and no more? If ever the Latimer money came to him, the woollen trade could go to damnation.

"And there is the ketch, Geoffrey," Latimer began – another line of thought in his mind connected. "Prosperity will be better placed to find us if we can source our own fleece and see it through all its processes and this should include export. The Rotterdam trip has seen good coin return to this family's purse."

"Your ketch, sir, where is she berthed, Topsham dock did you not say?"

"Topsham has her, Nephew, you are correct – pulled up and sitting heavy in the mud and a-waiting repair."

Latimer's leg had become stiff. He rose, stretched, looked down at his own dress and compared the shabbiness with his nephew's new coat and breeches.

"Just as a business will not flourish without leadership, a ship cannot function without its master," he said, standing erect and adjusting his weight. "Despite my years of trading and sailing with *The Lady Rosamunde*, I am a poor sailor, have always been so, and never was I master – always sailed as owner and observer. A busy ship in past times she now sits with an empty hold and neither master nor crew to sail her."

There was only so much enthusiasm Geoffrey could offer upon subjects in which he had little interest – although perhaps the future of *The Lady Rosamunde* was easier to manage. He stood, eye to eye with his uncle.

"I would be glad to trot on down to Topsham with you, sir, if you will have me? We are a little more landlocked at Marwood and a distance from any trading port of substance."

"I would be glad of your company, Geoffrey; I will see it is a priority and now that my health improves we must make firm appointment to begin each day together. My daughters have little company, your entertainment of them both last week has been reported to me and I know they would be delighted if it were a regular occurrence."

Sensing the conversation near ended Geoffrey dropped his head and turned to leave the room. "Then indeed we must, sir."

Latimer watched him go, reflected upon what had been said during their brief interview and looked again at the mantle clock. He was tired, leaden in fact – he needed the solitude of his rooms. He found his stick and left the room, slowly climbing the stairs, feeling his way along the dark passage to his own door. His nephew was not easily read, his sincerity perhaps uncertain. Henri sat wearily on the bed and looked at the square-paned window. He would see his daughters later but not yet, not until he had done what he had a mind to do and then rested awhile.

Vetch had left the draught; perhaps the boy was well meaning – he had no faith in quacks and apothecaries. Rising stiffly, catching his breath and waiting for the pain to subside, he pushed the door closed with his stick. Holding the glass to the light he looked into the cloudy depths and then sniffed. His pot was quite visible from where he stood, moving slowly across the room he kicked at it until it was free of the bed, bent slightly and offered the liquid up. Time was running on, there was promise of a sunset tonight, be it dulled by thin drifting cloud, but a good night to look out at the wider world beyond the city.

Rae was not there yet. He waited for a short while, heard the familiar sound of the casement opening, sensing her there even though their view of the other was obscured.

"Needle, Rae?" He asked after a while, resting his head on the sash-box and waiting for a reply.

"Not so tonight, Mr Latimer. I am reading but it is not from a book."

"A picture pamphlet then, Rae – and the subject fallals and petticoats."

"You are quite mistaken, Mr Latimer. I believe you play foolish with me, Henri – you do know I have no interest in such. You must guess again and do not give me any mizmaized answer."

"Then it must be a letter, Rae. Is it so?"

"It is a letter, Henri." Her voice was clear and he saw her white cap just a space beyond his window.

"And now I reason you will ask that I guess who writes you?"

"You hardly need guess, Henri, for whom else would send words to me? The paper is thick, the seal well known and the message has travelled upon land and sea ending its journey this day upon the Teignmouth packet – and I have kept it away from Elijah since this morning so that I may read it alone and without his questioning."

"Alone, Rae?" Latimer folded his arms, settling to the routine of early-evening, companionable conversation, usually upon nothing of much importance – domesticity, the whores' progress and now a letter from her keeper. "Do you wish me gone?"

"No, Henri, I do not wish you gone. You know you are as eager as I to know what Trelawney says and cannot gainsay it."

"I will not, Rae, as I know you have been waiting this month gone to receive word from the man. Have we not both been waiting – although I more indirectly than you? Read and let us have his news."

Rae did not read as a story might be read from any book. Alexander Trelawney wrote with the same flourish that he painted: wild inconsistent strokes, numerous crossings out, and to make more confusion, a hurriedly drawn depiction of a new friend or visited place might be scrawled in the midst of the text – a third reading was usually necessary before his meaning was accurately understood.

She was quiet for a moment, Latimer waited.

"My dearest Rachael," she read.

"So, he is in good heart – and you in favour it seems."

"Yes, Henri, so it do seem, but wait until I have read further. He writes from Genoa – Florence has lost its appeal."

She read again to herself, there were parts of this letter that she would not read to any, not even Henri – though his confidence was sure.

"He is returning," she said.

"Is this the news you wished to hear, Rae?"

He had never quite understood what lay between Alexander Trelawney and Rae; their relationship seemed to fall through the gaps of convention – neither daughter nor servant, and he supposed not mistress either, although nothing Trelawney did surprised him.

"I believe so, although the man do have a way about him that is ever perplexing and wearisome." She was silent again. "A gentleman is to come along with him, he has made a friendship."

Henri thought about the man he knew in passing, his neighbour, and remembered his preferences – his company. Although he had only begun to make conversation with this girl since his accident, since he had been able to get to his window, he knew she had lived in Trelawney's house from childhood. She understood her master's ways – Alexander Trelawney would be returning with a new lover.

"When are you to expect him, Rae?"

Her head was down, he imagined her following the lines carefully with a finger.

"He is travelling from Portsmouth and not London. He expects to return to his home towards the end of this month." There was quiet again whilst she turned the page and reread the script to make certain she had not misunderstood. "Hell's Gate, then he has left and some time since."

"Ah, then I think he will soon be upon you, Rae." Her rising agitation amused him and he smiled to himself, allowing her to continue.

"And I am to send the linen out and Flood is to find a cook – and I have not begun to take the sheets from his furniture yet. He is keeping his rooms in Florence – we are to expect some crates," she said hurriedly.

Rae was returning her letter to its folds. Latimer looked at the late-afternoon sky. He saw her rise.

"How is your health, Mr Latimer?"

"It is well – it is improved, Rae."

"But I have seen you go out, Henri, and still you hang upon that old stick."

"I have some reliance upon it but I do not mind it, Rae, it is a concern you need not have; a letter from your artist is far more interesting than any reliance I may have upon this stout stick."

There was activity in the courtyard, Flood had returned and was moving kindling from the wood-pile to the kitchens. Time had run through, Latimer was satisfied. He waited for Rae to leave the gallery, rubbed his leg thoughtfully and let the sash down.

9

A few days from this time Latimer had made another foray to the Waterbere Lane coffee house. Elcott was seated at their usual table and this time Latimer was expected. The conversation in the house was centred around the growing unpopularity of The Earl of Bute.

Elcott had risen and gripped Latimer's hand. "Henri. It is so good to have your company again, sir. I had hoped it would be so. We discuss the Cider Tax, Henri, or more pertinently, the burden this has set upon our region's apple-growers."

Latimer nodded to the other gentlemen sat about the table. "I have heard the talk and read a little on their difficulties." He sat heavily, put his head back and listened.

"A cider tax may seem a simple solution to pay for our impoverishing wars, but when it is a staple of the working-man and the tax must be collected directly from the growers, such becomes an imposition. I do not believe it could have been thought through with clear sight." Elcott directed his comments to the table and then indirectly to Latimer.

"Are any of the decisions made by our politicians thought through with clear sight, Edmund? War is an expensive folly and must be paid for; ale already bears heavy excise so what is left but cider?" Latimer was served and the discussion continued.

"It is reported that small-holders have been taken to court; I cannot see this as popular in any county but most especially in these western regions where apple-growing and cider-making support many families." The conversation returned to Bute – they let it pass them, beginning their own.

"I had been hoping that we might take each other's company this week, Henri. I had a mind to call upon you and your good daughters tomorrow. I have an aged client out at Alphington and your home is but a street from my path."

"Was it a matter of some urgency, my friend?"

Latimer, the divided skirts of his coat hung over his knees, drew closer to Elcott, assessing that a measure of privacy might be required.

"Oh, no, not in the least, but I had need to tell you that I shall be away for a while. A will reading – but inconveniently in Bristol, not this comfortable city."

"How so?" Feeling a certain involvement in his friend's life – having been responsible, at least in part, for his education – Latimer had a genuine interest in the young notary's business.

"The beneficiaries are centred there; a Somerset family. The deceased had migrated to Exeter with a second wife – she died some short time before him. There is a daughter and some indirect kin in that large ocean city and in the villages round about who will inherit."

Latimer nodded, folded his arms across his waistcoat – an embroidered affair that he had got Vetch to pull from the back of his wardrobe that morning.

"I must attend," Elcott continued, "and besides, should we all not attempt to stir beyond the city walls on occasion? Is it not too easy to stay in the comfort of where we was put."

"Edmund, I do not think you will ever be accused of lacking breadth in your life – although there are some here who might be so regarded."

"How was your journey here, sir?"

"Tedious, but with far less distraction than my first."

"And health?"

"An improvement – was there something else you wished to talk of Edmund; is your mother in good health?"

"Yes, yes, she goes on well enough for a woman of near fifty."

Latimer viewed Elcott's slim clerkly hands as he toyed with his coffee cup. The young man's reasoning was sound and he was always glad to have his ear, but there was a suggestion of hesitancy in his speech this morning.

"Has your connection with your nephew improved, sir?"

"I believe it has in small measure, Edmund. My infirmity – confinement to my rooms – has created an unfortunate detachment and I admit we did not begin well. Now that a future seems possible I intend to change this. Today we took breakfast together." He allowed his dark brows to come together whilst he waited for Elcott to continue. "Is there reason why you ask?"

"Not especially, sir. I am glad to hear things push on well, but you know that the world and its news come easily to this house and indeed to my rooms at Northernhay."

"Come, Edmund, I am not a man of delicate sensitivities. And I know you not to be a man who runs around a subject in riddles. Speak of what you must and let us be wiser for it."

"Then I must, Henri. I hear, and it is on good authority, that there is a promissory note running unpaid about this city. The note raised by your nephew to settle a tailor's bill in Fore Street."

"Ah." Latimer felt his chin. "And in what direction does this promissory note travel? Up, down or are you suggesting that it now comes sideways?"

"This news does not seem to surprise you, Henri, are you already forewarned?"

"I am not; the boy has the needs and tastes of a gentlemen but not the purse to match it."

"I could see that it came to you – if you have a mind to discharge it? Perhaps your nephew is expecting that you will, that you will not allow his note to find its way to any court?"

Latimer hoped that this was not so. "I wish he had owned his predicament to me in the first instance, Edmund – if he could not settle the debt, surely it would have been prudent to ask for help rather than let the note run to other quarters where it might be picked up by any thick-necked moneylender smelling a young fool's blood? God in Heaven, I do not expect the boy to be grateful for his situation; I hold onto the thought that if his father had lived the boot might have been on the other foot – me seeking help from him. But he will need to draw in this propensity to spend money he does not have if he is to steer clear of our magistrates."

"I cannot imagine, sir, that the boot would ever be worn on the other foot. Will you buy the note, sir – do you wish me to enquire?"

"I believe that I must, Edmund, and I would be grateful for your help. The onus will now be on me to have the thing out with the boy – he will need to be confronted, warned of the consequences of not settling what is due. How much is the note for?"

"I believe it is less than five pounds – there will be a level of interest to be paid in order to secure it. A new suit and some additional linen were purchased at the beginning of his stay. These things do not come cheaply – their cost is disproportionate to other daily needs."

"When some men do not earn the price of a coat in a twelve month – can you arrange this, Edmund, and discretely so? I have spent a decade of my life keeping this family from the debtor's court – I will not allow this note to compromise my determination. Although my nephew may deserve to have the consequences of it, I will not have the note travel upwards to the courts, nor downwards for that matter; to owe any sum to the moneylenders of this city would be poor practice – such a place is hard to crawl up from."

The anticipation of death had mellowed Latimer, made him look in different directions. The expectation of survival returned some cynicism – he would buy the note and, as he had suggested to Elcott, have word with his nephew.

10

Rae had closed the heavy leather-bound bible with some relief. Breaking their fast meant that God must be thanked and repentance offered before food and then at length afterwards. Elijah Flood, a dissenter, a Wesleyan and a deeply religious man – who saw no complications in his faith, no contradiction in its doctrine and no areas between black and white where a young girl might fall down – pushed back his chair, satisfied.

"You read God's word well, Daughter; to have the meaning of letters easy come up from the written page it is a blessed gift."

Rae did not share his faith, but did not contradict this assumption and allowed him to consider her a daughter of that faith.

The dissenter rose and went to a high cupboard set in a corner of the low room and took down a small cash box. Seating himself again at the table, he searched an inner pocket for the key.

"You must go to the Bear Market, Rae, and make haste, the freshness of the day is already lost and we will be offered other's cast-asides if we idle back much longer."

She had made ash cakes in the early morning and she stood, took an iron from the hearth, pulling the trivet away from the fire and leaning over the heat, touching the warm mounds with a finger – assessing them done.

"You must stock the larder while our time is our own, Daughter." Flood unlocked the cash box, carefully lifted out a small leather pouch and began to count coin onto the table. Rae scrutinised him from beneath dark wayward curls.

"It is ever difficult to provision a larder in a household that do not yet have a master, Elijah. There is no prediction how long Alexander will stay or what his needs will be whilst he do stay along in this house." She crouched before the fire again and began lifting hot cakes from the trivet and dropping them into her apron.

"Indeed not, Daughter, nor what coxcomb of a young man he returns with, if 'tis only the one this time. We are no stranger to his ways and changes, so must think along with him and be grateful to have him home." He looked at the depleted coin on the table.

Rae listened, carefully laying the cakes on the table to cool. Elijah Flood's contradictory loyalties, to his own God and to a man whose life habits constantly confirmed his lack of affinity to any god, could not be explained. "There is still bacon in the settle chest, Elijah, and I will make cheeses this week and then we must wait and see what his needs be and meet them when they do come."

Flood pushed a small pile of coin towards her, she took off her apron, and finding her way amongst the folds of her petticoats dropped the coins into a pocket in her hoops.

"Will you go to the meeting house this day, Mr Flood?"

"I shall, Daughter, now make haste to the Bear Market and if you cannot manage the load you must give a farthing to a pauper and have him help you home." Flood stood pulling on his coat. He considered the young girl he had helped raise, had guided towards a sober and Godly life. "Unless ye should wish to come along with I?"

Rae had not accepted his offer and felt it unlikely that she would ever accept this offered path to salvation. Nimbly rising on her toes she took down the well-used flat straw hat from the nail behind the door and began tucking wayward tendrils of hair into her cap. She had already viewed the day through an open window – inviting; the promise of spring already dancing in the watery March sunlight.

Released from quite a different master Mag had met her in the street and they had stepped out together towards Bear Lane. Although there were markets and plenty in this still thriving city, often extending over three congested streets, this area of the market, this bustling square of open ground before The Bear Inn, sold predominantly field crops, meat and fish. The eighth hour had already rung from St Mary's tower and the lanes and back-allies were seething with industrious, single-minded shoppers – some already in drink, this encouraging hidden aggression and amorous tendencies.

The main serge market was being conducted a street away, where tuckers, clothiers and merchants, still with the comforting appearance of prosperity about them, would be moving between stalls and trestles to do business or mingling amongst the crowds with an interest in other goods beyond their serges – these precious long ells of loom-woven serge laid out under the comparative safety and protection of market house pillars in Fore Street.

Rae stepped over an accumulation of wilted leaves, fish heads and escaping tiddies, carefully placing her feet between discarded straw-filled crates and poorly clothed carefree babies, set down whilst their mothers did business. A long line of pack-ponies was being driven towards the South Gate, pushed on by a pair of bull-necked brothers; aggressive, determined, whips before and aft, their destination the Topsham Dock. The folly of the city's ancestors, who had freely dammed the Exe to enhance the capacity and prosperity of their fulling mills, had blighted the navigation of the river. But from this hindrance had come prosperity of another kind: carriers abounded in this city, their ponies and mules following in line, wooden pack-saddles laden with newly dyed serges, their movement accompanied by the sound of unshod hooves on cobbles and the distinct smell of horse and dung and indigo dyes.

"Rae, you must hold back." Mag had caught Rae's arm. "These brutes do think themselves above humanity with their whips and their calls and no thought for a girl's new slippers or laundered petticoats."

Rae allowed herself to be pulled back, waited whilst the train passed them, and watched them go on to the docks – there was a power and a force in the movement of so many beasts together, and the sight although fearsome was also exhilarating.

"So, Alexander is to lay his head on his own pillow again and drop his boots beside his own bed."

"He is, Mag, else I should not be walking these busy streets with this great basket upon my arm."

"Will you see him home with good heart or are you happy to continue running along beside that old man with nothing to do but whorehouse sewing and bible reading?"

"'Tis not for me to ask if I am happy, Mag. Mr Flood is well meaning and I do not mind his company, but I am more than ready to see Alexander return, I am glad to know he still wishes it and won't be choosing to make his living away from here for a twelve month instead of six. The coin-box is near empty and how can we continue to be servant if we have no master to serve?"

"He will always return, Rae, he would not do other; 'tis here that he makes his best mischief. I'm sure he do miss us as well as we miss him."

Did she miss him? In past times Rae had been glad of her keeper's return, putting her in mind of a newly shaken quilt laid down over a dull blanket, brightly coloured, busy and inviting. Perhaps she did, but this time his return was less welcome – her time would no longer be her own.

A small ragged child ran between them. Rae adjusted her hat, distracted by his hollow hungry eyes and reminded of her own history. The child had soon melted into the crowds and she pushed on through the mayhem of market day, holding close to the basket, catching sight again of Trelawney's favourite whore, straight-backed, slim waist laced into a gaudy bodice and skirts.

With no certainty of the day of the artist's return, there was little that could be purchased unless it could be stored. Rae gave coin for a sack of coarse flour and a crate of roots to be delivered to the Exebere house, as well as a cured pork hock. She bought a quart of vinegar, a rhizome of East India ginger and three pounds of Lisbon sugar, as well as a quantity of live yeast as the amount of bread required in the household would most surely increase.

Rae's pocket, and the carefully counted coin that Elijah had given her, did not allow for frivolous gewgaws and they had watched a hawker making a show of a box of intricate toys and persuasions, but did not buy any. A wooden monkey climbing unfathomably up a short stick, a clap-clap toy that folded and unfolded like an ever-moving ladder, some paste neck beads in blues as bright as any sapphires, and garish ribbons which Mag ran wistfully through her slim fingers. On another stall they tried a jelly-like substance finely dusted in white sugar that had come all the way from the Indian continent and tasted of lavender.

Turning for home Rae had seen Geoffrey Latimer pushing his way through the crowds from the direction of Fore Street. Knowing him by sight, and for Rae by reputation, they had bobbed to him – although class, status and occupation did not allow for more, he was Henri's kin and Rae could not help but find interest in his dandy's coat and buckled shoes, which seemed so much at odds with the Latimer she knew. Geoffrey had lifted his hat and moved on, the incident inconsequential. They had idled their time a little longer, enjoying the freedom. The days to follow would be busy enough, lost in flurries of activity – removing dust covers, polishing pewter and seeing to the linen store. Rae did not know when Trelawney would arrive home, only that he would and that his timing would be ever unpredictable.

11

Towards the end of the week, delivered up from Topsham Dock on a mule cart, a crate of worked canvases had arrived from Italy. The residents of the houses next to and close to Trelawney's were woken by a shrill whistle spilling from the lips of the insolent carrier's boy, followed by the loud banging of the carrier's fist upon the artist's door. The crate, expected but with no expectation of when, had arrived with the dawn. The barque had come into Topsham on the flood tide and the carriers were eager to begin off-loading.

Geoffrey, with his rooms set at the front of the house, had heard the disturbance, but with a head still heavy from a little private sampling of a very pleasurable French brandy – which he had been forced to take in his rooms now that his uncle Henri watched his every move – turned his face away from the intrusive daylight and tried to sleep. The promissory note had surfaced, and he had been summoned to the beamed sitting room to be ticked off and reminded of his vulnerability if such a note were to fall into the wrong hands and forewarned of the consequences of further extravagances. But the note had been paid – his uncle would not follow through if another came to light.

Remaining awake he lay on his back considering the place he now lived, the oddity of Exebere Street and the irregular mix of peoples who lived there. He had no interest or liking for the harlots who lodged in the bawdy house next to his uncle's unfortunately placed dwelling – whores and riffraff all. He freely used the services of other whorehouses in the city, these pleasures often paid for by William Mudge, but this house was altogether too close to his uncle's door to make his calling there anything less than uncomfortable. But knowing who they were and knowing what they did frustrated him, their continuous coming and going unsettled him.

He had been forced to show politeness to one of the girls earlier in the week, he had chanced upon her arm in arm with the artist's servant. The younger girl, robust as any gypsy, had recognised him and bobbed and he had tipped his hat. Alexander Trelawney was not known to him, had been absent from his home for the entirety of Geoffrey's stay, but he had heard rumours about this girl – she was the man's servant, she was his mistress, she was his private whore. In contrast, the other girl whom he had seen leaving and entering the bawdy house many a time, had small features and a rope of fair hair. He had always had a liking for slim-legged fragile women and this one had taken his eye some time ago, and if the house had been anywhere else, he would have paid his coin and had her. He had watched her moving through the market, noted the smallness of her hands and the neat buckled slippers that looked out from beneath her skirts, skirts that were held unnecessarily high he felt, perhaps for his benefit. There was a problem with fragility he had found – fragile things were so often broken in the handling.

Walking through the market on his way to The Swan he had lifted his hat and the pale whore had offered a rationed view of delicate blue eyes. If it had not been for the harsh rouge and forthright stance, her look might have been almost virginal.

Awake since dawn Henri was now standing in the small sitting room at the front of the house. Sensing some kind of disturbance in the street he had pulled on his long dressing-coat and limped his way past his nephew's room to settle his curiosity. A carrier's cart was drawn up under the window; Rae was there – the old man giving instructions. He rarely saw her like this. So many times over the last weeks, when health had allowed it, they had spoken freely to one another, but seeing her without the obscuring hindrance of the gallery roof was novel. He watched her for a while, pushing her hair unconsciously into her cap, moving around the crate with the vitality of a young cat. He wondered what changes the artist's return would bring – many he assumed. He knew Trelawney and he knew of Trelawney – there would be many demands on her time.

Having satisfied his curiosity he moved away from the window and returned to his room to wait for the day to fully begin.

Occupation pushed time on, the busy day was moving towards its end; she had already climbed the stairs and run the length of the house hourly it seemed with buckets and rags, bringing life back to mirrors, scrubbing floors, pulling back drapes, finding put-away china and settling it on sideboards. Left alone for a while she went into the large room at the top of the house that Alexander used as his work room, removed the last dust cover from a stuffed chair and looked about the room. The studio was just as it had been left almost six months before. Finished and partly worked canvases were stacked to one wall. A large table spilled over with pots and jars containing pigments, oils, spirits and crusty brushes. Dropped without thought amongst all this was a paint-covered stock, a cambric shirt that had been torn into rags, a fine feathered hat and one flat-toed buckled shoe. Furniture was spars: another smaller table, some high-backed chairs and dominating one wall, incongruously placed without reason, a roll-ended French bed. The Italian canvases had been brought up and placed randomly about the room.

The larger canvases were of barren landscapes with sparse pointed trees and yellowing shuttered buildings and did not interest her overmuch, but a small painting, a portrait of a straight-nosed dusky woman with dark hair and black shining eyes, did. She knelt before it and touched the worked canvas, following the fluid but textured brush marks with her finger. Did Trelawney have a life in Florence that ran parallel to the one that he lived here? Did he have similar servants, similar lovers? A city, so distant and so remote could not be imagined.

Unframed and wrapped in oilcloth was a bundle of sketches; she carefully took them out and laid them methodically on the floor boards. Flood was banging about in the next room – it would be a while before he called for her. A young man, three or four different young men, she could not say; they were loose sketches done in charcoal and chalk. Rae studied all the images together for a while; she knew of Alexander's preferences, and in a time when sexual pleasure had no limitations – provided it could be paid for – Trelawney's inclinations were not out of the ordinary and she did not expect her master to return without company.

She sat back on her heels. Alexander had never shown anything more than a benign indifference towards Rae – perhaps the occasional outburst of irritation – she had no particular place in his life, and yet he was her protector. Flood had finished laying shirts and undergarments in the old press, she heard the doors close. Thoughts done with for a time, she stood, gathered up the sketches and returned them to their protection. Beyond the window the day was still clear; now that the year was pulling away from its winter doldrums light would linger a little longer over the Exebere houses, and she would find reason to sit and work on under the decaying gallery roof.

Elijah Flood was calling for her; she must go to him, take her final instructions for the day and then she would slip away. Private time would be limited now and she would have no choice but to run along with the needs of the household and do as she was bid.

12

Not a man to shy away from responsibility, Henri had wasted no time before he had instigated a conversation with his nephew upon the folly of ordering a suit of clothes that could not be paid for. Deep within his being was the remembrance of his own father's extravagances and it would have been easy to lambast his nephew for a reckless fool. But he did not choose that path. Was not the boy here for guidance, to gain a rudimentary understanding of trade? Yes, Geoffrey had strayed from that course, overstretched himself, spent more than his allowance could sustain, but Latimer had already decided he would pay this debt, this time, and help the boy steer a surer course.

Despite what Henri saw as leniency – reporting frequently with description of daily activities and a proposed visit to the fleece markets of Moretonhampstead now becoming a certainty rather than a possibility – they had not parted well.

Looking thoughtfully about his room he pulled himself erect. The pain in his leg had returned. It tracked no pattern. His patience already thinly spread he had banged for Vetch, sending barked commands and a series of blasphemies through the silent house.

"Thomas," Latimer said evenly, attempting to show a kinder face now that he had his way. "I have a mind to shave before the evening."

There seemed no sign of urgency on his servant's face, just a blank, almost belligerent expression. Latimer observed the small tray and the decanted wine which was sat squarely at its centre. Vetch placed the tray carefully on a small table and moved across the room to collect Latimer's shaving box.

"Where has this come from?" Latimer said glancing at the decanter as he released his shirt from his breeches and began pulling off his stock. "Have you found another bottle of Peninsular? I thought we had long since drunk the last of that run."

Vetch poured water into the wash bowl and silently began laying out the cut-throat and soap on a clean square of muslin.

"The Peninsular has gone, sir, as you say."

"Then I suspect this wine's origin is closer to home."

"Quite close, sir."

Latimer kept an elderly cook who had been with the family for many years – other servants were purchased piece-meal when needed. The old cook had a way with fruits and could mimic almost any wine but it had been a long while since financial necessity had bade him drink the stuff. A little contraband would have been a welcome addition in these lean times.

"An English wine, then?" he said. The spurious description covered a variety of home-brewed imitations. And since the unpredictable climate would never support a good vine, the grape was not an option. "And what name are we to give this one, I suspicion the colour may come from the elderberry?"

"Yes, sir, coloured with the elderberry. A Cyprus, sir. 'Tis a rich wine and very much like it should be. Flavoured with ginger and cloves and tasting much as any Cyprus wine ought."

"I believe it, Thomas – at the least we may fill our shelves with something. I will take a glass before I go down."

Vetch began to scrape in long fluid strokes, bristle and soap coming away with the ease that only a sharp blade can achieve. Perhaps prompted by the lack of foreign wines in his cellar and the need to begin trading again, he said, "I have a mind to go down to Topsham as tomorrow's flood tide fills the estuary – run an eye over *The Lady Rosamunde*, see how she sits. I have an ancient keeper checking on her moorings – I am sure all is well." Henri watched his servant's face in the small triptych mirror that had been placed on the chest. "And what of my nephew this day? I suspicion you will have dressed him and understand a little of his activities."

"I did, sir. Although his activities are something I do not bother myself over."

"He must miss the attentions of a personal servant," Henri said ignoring Vetch's determination to tell him nothing, "now that he is no longer in his own home. He has been used to the attentions of many servants." More than his income allowed, Henri concluded, but he did not convey this to Vetch.

Vetch continued to remove Latimer's dark stubble in silence.

"Has he said whether or no he will dine here? We have had some disagreement and he chose not to join me yesterday," Latimer offered.

"Mr Geoffrey has not said that he will be leaving the house, sir. Would you like me to enquire for you? To save a tedious journey?"

"No, Thomas, I will make it my business to visit him. I am anxious that we will be two for dinner for I pray my solitary ways will not pass along to him."

Vetch finished, poured the soapy water into the slop bucket and then left his master to finish dressing alone. It was a choice Henri had always made. The day that he could not dress himself would be a sorry day.

There was welcome noise beyond his closed door. He limped towards it, drew it back to be greeted by his daughters – Old Sarah, as sloth-like as ever, was still descending the upper stairs.

"My daughters," he said. "You anticipate my visit to you."

"We could not wait for you, Papa," Mary said, standing correctly before him.

"You have been an age, Papa, and we are hungry." Sophia had already slipped her hand into her father's.

How distinctly different these girls were? he thought. Children seemed not to be a mix of both parents but rather to take on the likeness of just one.

"I will collect my stick and we will go down together," he said.

The shaving had taken a little longer than anticipated and his daughters were early. It was fast approaching late afternoon and his plans must be amended. He felt an unwelcome feeling of disappointment, which was swiftly replaced by a sensation of guilt. Latimer let his eyes casually scan the gallery through the window. No dark head bent forward over work and no cap or apron discarded over the balustrade.

"Then I am ready," he said turning away. "You must go first and slowly so, but do not begin until we are all met together."

They did not descend slowly, but he had no disagreement with that; there were enough sickly children in this prosperous city, too many. He could not condemn exuberance and he would not criticize good health.

13

On the evening of that day, Henri had not dined alone, Geoffrey had chosen to join him, intentionally avoiding any mention of the promissory note and successfully steering the conversation along a safer course – *The Lady Rosamunde*.

It was agreed that they visit Topsham at flood tide. Henri had arranged for horses from the livery in Holloway Street and they had followed the busy deep-rutted turnpike road as it ran parallel to the Exe. With progress hampered by mule-carts and laden pack-horse trains, farm wagons and straggling groups of pilgrims, conversation had been thankfully spasmodic.

"You seem at ease upon that nag, Uncle," Geoffrey offered as courteously as he was able, standing in his stirrups and then rearranging his rump in the cheaply made saddle. Riding along beside his uncle in this mayhem of a trading city, he suddenly felt an urgent desire to be rid of it all; he felt no cohesion with this place and would have his pampered, pleasurable but sadly indebted life in Dorset returned in an instant if he could.

"Not at ease, Nephew, but oddly free from pain; I would not have thought it would be so. Sitting a horse is not a thing I do with any proficiency or indeed pleasure."

As they reached the dock a hazy sun had begun to struggle through low cloud. "You must miss your own stable, Nephew," Henri said, searching the web of rigging and sail for signs of the *Rosamunde*. "A shared livery horse must seem a poor substitute?"

"And not a beast within it now, even my hunters gone to pay for repairs." It was a lie, but the statement he knew would have effect.

They had soon reached The Strand where the houses were built in the Dutch style from bricks brought back as ballast in the hulls of trading ships, the Exe showing intermittently through the paraphernalia of port life. A sharp westerly had stirred up the normally sheltered waters disturbing every halyard and buntline, every sail, furled and unfurled so that they sang together in tuneless chorus.

"I am sorry for it, Geoffrey, but you must be farsighted, Nephew; this busy turnpike is confirmation of the buoyancy of our trade here, there is good money to be made in the city and the ports about it – with a little hard work and perhaps an eye for a quality cloth. A few years hence you might return with a healthy bank balance and a heavy pocket; then you will be able to replenish your stables."

Geoffrey did not see his uncle as any kind of fool, but his determination to keep family together – and solvent – seemed to have clouded all reason. "I will hold to that thought, Uncle," he said turning his face away.

"Upon our return we will make plans for you to visit the moorland towns and villages."

"Indeed we must, Uncle." There was congestion ahead and Geoffrey came level with his soberly dressed uncle, concealing his irritation with a pleasant smile. How wrong could one man be about another? He had already resolved that he would not be sleeping on any bug-ridden mattress in any back-of-beyond hostelry on the moor and he would not be actively encouraging the return of connection between farmer and weaver. "I am surprised, Uncle, that you have never become a Guild member when you are so very much involved in that business."

"Such is not for me, Geoffrey," Latimer said releasing the stirrup and easing his stiff leg. "My grandfather, your great-grandfather, he of course belonged to the Fullers and Tuckers Guild – became wealthy on the back of it – but not so my father and I do not see myself in such a role. I am not for such close clubs. Besides, I have spent much time away from the city both riding the pack roads and running up and down the channel."

Before they could return to, what was for Geoffrey, uncomfortable territory, they had reached their destination. Latimer had dismounted, painfully easing his leg round, sliding to the ground, hopping in an attempt to keep the weight off it.

"I cannot see her," he said searching the shipping with sharp eyes.

They were standing before a large elongated building in the centre of the town; The Globe had an acceptable livery and they would have their mounts rested and fed before returning.

"It is not unthinkable that she has been moved to a different mooring place. She is quite distinctive and I have not had sight of any craft resembling her."

Geoffrey slid from his own mare, taking the halter of both and going through to the livery at the rear of the inn.

"I cannot help in the search, Uncle, I do not have an eye for boats nor can I tell one hull or sail formation from another. Might we not enquire?"

They left their horses with the livery boy and entered the inn. An hour or so before the midday, it was not so busy inside. There was still a while to high tide when the rising water would fill every quay and cover every stretch of mud and salt-marsh. The harbour side seemed to be waiting in anticipation. The landlord was tapping a new barrel as they entered – conversation with the man was not made easy.

"*The Lady Rosamunde?*" Geoffrey began tapping his fingers on the counter. "We understood her to be tied up in this port; no doubt you will know every ship and sailor who rests here?"

The man straightened up, slowly wiping his hands on a filthy rag wrapped about his portly middle, and looked Geoffrey over. Latimer folded his arms and waited for a response.

"No *Lady Rosamunde* tied up here, sir," he said moving away to another task.

"I am aware of that. We have already searched for her," Geoffrey continued. "That is not what I am asking." The victualler ignored him. Latimer moved towards the counter.

"Landlord, recommend you this ale?" he said. "The dust has kicked up badly this morning and a thirst is upon us both. Fill a tankard and two if you would be so good – and take one for yourself if you choose it?" A jug of dark ale was drawn from the barrel and two tankards carefully filled. "*The Lady Rosamunde* was berthed here some weeks ago and would not have gone to sea since. She is a small ketch, some sixty foot stern to bow-sprit. I make the assumption that she has been moved. Without cargo she would not need to be so positioned, and there has been requirement for neither crank-crane nor labourer these last three months."

"I have no time to be concerning myself over the comings and movings of any ketch, barque, row boat or frigate, sir." The man's reply, although terse, was more helpful than silence. "It is not my business to be making observations about what comes and goes from these banks. You must ask those as maybe do." He looked about the taproom. "A one or two sat around may know – aged men but sound." Latimer laid coin upon the counter, more than enough to cover the warm ale.

During the early days of his infirmity, Latimer had talked at length with the *Rosamunde*'s mate. The boy had come to Latimer's bedside, left reassurances – there were always old sailors who might keep a watchful eye on a vessel. He had arranged for this to be done, although Latimer had never met the man. By necessity the boy had left Latimer's employ and joined another crew – there was no requirement for crew on a boat that was going nowhere. Latimer left Geoffrey with his tankard and approached the group of men alone.

"Ill-fortune has kept me away from the dock for some months but I am looking for a certain craft." Latimer assessed his audience and ordered the empty tankards to be filled. A reply was quickly come by.

"I know'd her, sir. Come in mauled about. Moved, sir, moved along to Lympstone."

Latimer had sat and sipped his ale and listened to what the man had to say. The old mariner he had paid to watch over the ketch had died, what he had predicted was true, the *Rosamunde* had been moved.

They ordered victuals – paid well for a solidifying plate of mutton stew – and moved on as the waters of the Exe estuary began to ebb, picking up their livery mounts, returning to the main thoroughfare and continuing on to Lympstone. By the time they had reached the village the tide had left the mudflats and *The Lady Rosamunde* was lying over on her port side. It had not been the ending to the day that Latimer had expected. Through his weeks of inactivity he had held a picture in his mind of the *Rosamunde* – this was not the picture that greeted him now.

They had inspected the storm damage as best they could; mostly lost rigging and a broken spar. Latimer had paid the shipbuilder and secured the safe-keeping of the ketch for another month. There was nothing more to be done until money could be found to pay for repair.

14

Good winds had already brought the artist to the docksides of Portsmouth, and before the week was over, after having reacquainted himself with that bawdy town, Trelawney was back. He had arrived in the dead hours of the morning, in his cups and with a young dandy; they had literally fallen into the house and then slept for near on two days.

Flood had disliked the boy on first sight and referred to him the young princock – and under his breath as a sideways boy's whore. Trelawney's young lover was undoubtedly both these things, with his silk suit, overuse of lace and powdered wig; but beneath all that it was quite clear to Rae that he was very young, barely a year older than herself perhaps, and not as confident as was first evident. This was his redemption, for she did not dislike him and without doubt he was a very pretty young man.

On a day towards the middle of this changeable month, the painting rooms at the top of the old house were filled with thin orange light, penetrating deep into the cluttered space forming shapes of colour on the back walls. Rae was sat on a large oak carver and draped across her knees were the skirts of a rich velvet gown in the deepest of blues. These had been laid there to give the appearance that she was wearing them. In her lap, amongst the folds of the velvet, her slim fingered hands had been positioned in a sort of genteel clasp: demur, submissive, acquiescent perhaps, depicting the type of young woman that any new husband would be glad to receive. Trelawney was at his easel, a paintbrush in his hand, another behind his ear, throwing profanities in Rae's direction with no sign of remorse.

"Blast you for a whorehouse hussy, how can I replicate the hands of a lady when I am offered the hands of a farm boy in their stead?"

Rae did not move nor make comment and neither was she in the least disturbed or rankled by his disregard for her sensitivity; her black eyes merely flashed as he spoke but her thoughts could not be read. She had known this man since she was ten, he had been both her keeper and her saviour – words were nothing. Besides, she had always understood that his ability to reproduce a sitter with vitality and a personality, that in most cases they did not have, relied upon his ability to out his aggressive creativity. She was part of this process and did not mind it.

"Luca, what say you here? Do intercede on my behalf. This woman's nails are as black as any labourer's." Alexander Trelawney, an unexpectedly short man with a nose like a Caesar and a crop of copper hair cut tight to his head in the style of the day, addressed his comment to his companion and guest who lolled on a threadbare chaise placed just a little way from where Rae was sat. Gone was the wig and the suit of a dandy, in point of fact the boy had little upon his person baring a cambric shirt hanging loosely over his hastily laced breeches. His fair hair, with a hint of curl, was also free from restraint.

"Alexander, why show such petulance towards your ward when she has sat well and without movement for some long while." Having been born in the flatlands of East Anglia, there was not the slightest hint of the Italian in his dialect. His observations were spoken with a maturity that did not sit accurately with his boyish, effeminate looks.

"Ward? Ward?" Trelawney questioned, throwing the paintbrush in his hand away and exchanging it for the one behind his ear. "She is no ward of mine. What say you to that, my little Egyptian, this boy thinks you are better than you are?"

"Do not answer, Rachael." Luca indolently returned to a sitting position and viewed both sitter and artist without emotion. "He has a mood running and will disagree with whatever you reply."

Relying for most of his youth on dandy-like good looks and a well-proportioned and incontrovertibly effeminate body to make his way, Luca rarely worried about being anything more than he was. He had lived along with Trelawney's temper and mood changes for some months past and saw no need to appease him. Abandoned by his mother at puberty, discarded by his first lover, who at fourteen had taken him to Italy and introduced him to the usefulness of bi-sexuality, Luca had come far since those early insecure days – and he was confident of Alexander's continued patronage.

Rae, or Rachael as was her real name, the name she had been offered by

Trelawney when he had found her, did not reply nor move but neither was she displeased by the conversation.

"You shall be ward if you will assist me complete this painting before the unfortunate young woman I have been instructed to paint goes forth and joins her nabob of a husband in his white-pillared house on the Indian continent." Trelawney stabbed excitedly at a large globule of paint on his much-used mortar. "Assist, young woman, not hamper, not deter."

It was not in Rae's remit to speak. She understood that this portrait would be their bread and butter for a while. The unfortunate young woman spoken of – and only unfortunate in Trelawney's eyes because she was less than beautiful – was to leave for Bombay on an East Indiaman to join her husband in a week's time. The portrait had been commissioned by and for the grieving family that she was never likely to see again. As time elapsed and the true image of a daughter became blurred, it would not matter whose hands or breasts – for she was to assist in this as well – were displayed upon the manor house wall.

"I will speak for you, Rachael," Luca said. Bored, he had risen and had begun to wander the room. "If she is not your ward, Alexander, then she should be so. If she is servant then you ought not to expect her to be more." He paused, studying the extraordinarily sensitive sketches of himself done by Trelawney in Florence. "And if she appears to have the soil of the fields beneath her nails, then it is because she has scrubbed and worked for you as a lowly servant – the dirt beneath her nails is owned by you, Alexander."

The ruddiness of the artist's face was slowly subsiding; the hands he painted, quite beautiful hands as it turned out, were near perfect. The young upstanding breasts could be completed tomorrow perhaps.

"Why did I not ask the whores to sit for me? They are a slight more amusing and would offer a good romp at the end of proceedings." Said without malice, Trelawney refused to allow the adrenaline that unwarranted anger had brought him to run to nothing.

"You do not choose to entertain the harlots, Alexander, because you have noted upon your return that the child you keep in this house has become woman in your absence and sits very well indeed. You are pleased with these changes but will not accept them because they have caught you out. I wager I am right, am I not, Alexander?"

"Ha!" Trelawney threw down his brush and wiped his short-fingered hands on a cloth. "And so she has. My ward, my helper and so she has." He had finished and he was satisfied.

Rae had begun to fidget.

"Move now, my Rachael, you cannot do harm." Trelawney walked towards her and put an oily hand beneath her chin. "You are very quiet my child. Is it because my language abuses you so?"

Rae looked at the debris of paint, spilt spirits and hardening brushes that she would now spend her evening clearing away. "No, Alexander. You know that you do not offend me," she said.

"No, indeed I should not – not when you have been raised by a bully with a vitriolic tongue and a wayward fist; I am mere kitten to that man."

Such a man had existed in her life but she had not been raised by him; his ownership had been tenuous and easily severed. Trelawney liked to see himself as her saviour – she did not object.

"Is the work done? Am I to look or would you not have me do so?" The rich velvet was soft in her lap, she gathered it up and carefully laid it over a chair-back.

"I am indifferent, look or no, but the work is near finished and if payment is made directly I shall buy you a new gown and then perhaps we shall paint the whole of you. Would not that please you?"

Rachael thought that it probably would not – she had neither liking for forced inactivity nor an interest in dress-shop fittings and restricting finery. She stood before the portrait imagining the young woman saying her farewells to her family, imagining her being received by her new husband.

"'Tis a lively thing, Alexander, I am sure it will be well liked."

Luca had gone to stand by the window and was idly looking out across busy Exebere Street. He turned, listening to their interaction, understanding a side of his lover that he had not known of before. His own origins were as little known as Rachael's; taller than the painter, darker than a field hand – but then he had spent some months following Trelawney around the cities of Italy – he had a femininity about him that appealed to those with unorthodox sexual tastes.

"You may use your whores, Alexander, but they do not have the freshness and purity needed for such a work. Your Rachael has these things and you are well aware of the differences."

Trelawney's face was suddenly softer than it had been, the high colour almost gone. Rae watched him touch Luca's cheek, run a finger down the skin that was exposed between the fronts of his unbuttoned shirt.

"For a man with such an eye for things, 'tis wonder that you do not take up the brush yourself, Luca."

Rae put down the paints she had begun to order, moving away towards the door. Her knowledge of others' sexuality was greater than it perhaps should have been, but then when a thing has been commonplace it does not shock. She watched the young man, who, she admitted she had a liking for, reach out and reciprocate Alexander's advances. The light was fading, the dancing shapes had gone and the recesses of the room were beginning to grow shadows; she understood there would be no more work this day.

Rae closed the door and walked quietly away along the dark passage connecting the studio to the rest of the house. Wisps of hair had come loose from her cap; she felt them and began twisting them around her finger attempting to conceal them beneath the calico. The dim light in the hall was a reminder of time, a time when duty was often disregarded. Energy suddenly fuelled by brighter thoughts, she dropped down the narrow stairs, pulling off her cap and untying her apron strings as she went.

The larger rooms on the floor below were used by Trelawney. She passed them and opened the door to a smaller room – a jumbled mix of forgotten furniture, ripped and worked canvases and unwanted cloths were randomly stored here. Dropping her apron on a chair she opened the casement and slid over the window-board like a cat. The sound of the reluctant cords in the sash box made her look up expectantly, modesty making her drop her head again to the yard below. The roof of the gallery created a perpetual distortion and she waited for Henri to acknowledge her.

"You have been out, Henri." She spoke first.

"You watch me, Rae?"

"I have seen you walk out with your daughters."

"Indeed I did, and how do you see me, Rae, what spying place do you have that Trelawney does not know of?"

"I do not have a spying place, Henri. I was throwing out linen in the rooms above and saw you from the window there; 'tis such a vexing thing sheet changing and I had a need to look out at the world."

"Your master keeps you busy then? I am humbled that you have found the time to talk to me."

Looking out at the disorder of rooftops she considered how best to answer. "The man is such a contradiction, Henri. If I am turning butter then I must go to his rooms and clean his pallet. If I am to serve his supper I am at once set free and must not serve it 'till later. Alexander do not like to be predicted and he makes certain sure that he never is."

"Do not complain, Rae, I have a notion that the unpredictable sits well with you. It is the sameness of things that does not."

"'Tis deep talking, Mr Latimer, how can you know these things about me when I do not know them myself?"

"Observation and reflexion, Rae – it takes half a lifetime for most of us to know who we are, but sometimes others may see more clearly than we do ourselves."

"You are different tonight, Henri."

"How so – I do not see that I am?"

"You have a new waistcoat, I spy colour, Henri, hiding beneath the fronts of your solemn working coat."

"Do you? Does that make me different?"

"I believe it does. You do know how I mean."

"Does it please you that I am different?"

"It is unpredictable, Henri, so I believe that it does."

"Ah, then I am glad." She waited for him to continue. "I have made payment for a letter today. A sealed paper brought to the city on the Bristol coach."

"Who writes to you, Henri? Have you a life then beyond the one you have here?"

"Perhaps I do, Rae. It is Elcott who writes me. He has travelled to Bristol on notary business."

"'Tis such a journey, Henri, what makes him leave this place and travel so far from his home?"

"A will reading, Rae; he is charged with the reading of a will and stays with a family some miles inland from the port – by the mood of the letter I believe him to be quite happy with his time there."

"How do you know this, Henri?"

"Because, Rae, the meaning of a letter must always be looked for between the lines; there is a beneficiary, a young woman, he seems in no great hurry to return."

"I do not know your Mr Elcott, Henri, but I think that I would perhaps like him."

"You would indeed like him, Rae. I see Trelawney has not returned alone?"

"He has not, Henri, he has a companion."

"Do you like this companion, Rae?"

"I like him as much as I ought, but it is Alexander that must have his company. Mr Flood has taken against him."

"I can see that he might."

"The light has gone, Henri."

"And you must go in."

"I think I must and you also, you must return to whatever it is that you are so dandified up for to do."

15

In a slope-roofed room at the top of The Seven Stars Inn, Mag was returning white stockings to slender legs. The inn sat on the Alphington side of the Exe and although the windows were obscured by grime and the remnants of recent wild weather, there was still good view of the river and the city beyond. The young man she had recently serviced observed her from the crumpled bed, head haphazardly propped on a pillow, naked beneath the chaotic sheet. Without taking her eyes from the river she distractedly began to draw in the cords of her bodice. It was most unusual for her to service a man away from the protective and watchful eye of the bawdy-mother, but she had agreed to this regular and for her lucrative arrangement because of, in part, a secret desire to be more than she was, but also a worrying interest she had formed since he had acknowledged her in the street the previous week. Taking her eyes from the river for a moment she reached for her small full breast and began to examine the skin close to her armpit, stretching her neck round in order to see the mouth-sized red mark and swelling which was beginning to form on the otherwise white skin.

"Saints, Margaret, I have never had a whore with such a capacity for brutish thoughts." Reaching out for the pewter mug perched on a table close to the bed, Geoffrey finished what was left of the dubiously named fortified wine that had been served him by the landlord's doxy. Mag's eyes remained on the river.

"You do not know what my thoughts are, Master Latimer, and I do not believe 'tis I who holds brutish thoughts but you, sir, for biting me so."

"It is hardly a bite, madam, I should call it a pleasurable nuzzling and if

I have been harsh with you, Margaret, then it is nothing more than you deserve. Dishonest whores are two a penny but I did not expect such from you."

"Dishonest, sir?"

"Dishonest, madam."

Placing the mug back amongst the discarded and in his opinion quite unnecessary accessories of a harlot's life – a cheap periwig, a broken fan and a frayed neck-cloth – Geoffrey considered the small pouting features. A woman needed to be dandled and not allowed to plant her feet too securely upon any board-house floor, and he would dandle her as long as he felt it necessary. She was of course all that he had anticipated; the reality of her body had been as good as the fantasy, but this did not stop a perverse streak of malevolence from goading him into unpleasantness.

"I do not expect my bed-partners virginal, madam, but when a harlot is married she will have history beyond the whorehouse, and questions do jump about" – Geoffrey propped himself on one arm, watching her reaction – "and disappeared husbands have an uncanny knack of reappearing when a man is bedding their wife."

"But not this one, Master Latimer, for he is most certainly dead these last two years since and solidly buried beneath this red soil. You ought not to listen to street gossip, 'tis always twisted and turned to suit the teller."

"So am I to take a whore's word as truth?"

"I offer it so I think that you must, sir."

"Then I shall remain liberally undecided, but do not think you can play some cock-eyed double-sided scheme with any back-door husband; there are doxies aplenty in this city and my custom is well received in the best of houses."

Watching her form her long fair hair into strands he wondered how other men bedded her – dispassionately, brutally perhaps. The frown that had formed when she had inspected the mark of passion – which he had intentionally made – had not yet gone. She stood to reach for her skirts. A partially dressed woman always brought him forwards more than a naked one – he lay back and enjoyed what he had purchased, smugly pleased that he had prized one of the whore-mother's favourite harlots out from under her very nose and had her secretly service him in the attic room over the Alphington inn.

"I do not think I am yet spent, Margaret," he said watching her. "Come and lie with me and I promise to offer a gentler time." He could not be sure that he would.

He let her lay beside him, running his hand over the soft flesh of her inner thigh, finding the triangle of warmth, assessing her reciprocal desire. He covered the angry mark on her breast with his open mouth using only his lips this time and not his teeth. "You see, Maggie, am I not gentle now?"

16

Clarity had visited Latimer as Vetch had shaved him. Now that his health had returned to an acceptable level he would acknowledge and understand the workings of his own house again, take hold of the tiller – and he would know his nephew's doings even if his servant was hardly a helpmate in this determination.

Thomas Vetch had been his man-servant for several years but any friendship was lacking; shared confidences, unequivocal loyalty, he had learned to do without – although he felt he treated his servant fairly. Vetch had served Latimer's own father and he had lived in the household at the time of Geoffrey's father. Did this account for his reluctance to impart more than the minimum? Was this why he was more likely to be found in Geoffrey's rooms than his own? Henri could not say but it made life the more difficult for not knowing what was happening in his own house.

"I will break my fast with my nephew, Thomas." He viewed the man beside him through the small triptych mirror. "Be so good as to convey this to him and be sure to let me know when he is down."

"I believe Master Geoffrey is already down, sir." Vetch looked sideways at him through several strands of long unwashed grey hair.

His daughters' sing-song voices and innocent laughter met him as he entered the wide dining room. For most of their young lives they had lived and eaten in the rooms above. Running against the tide of opinion he had begun to have them join him at meal times. They were seated with their cousin, sharing some anecdote; the sight of their intimacy and the feeling of exclusion rankled.

"Good day to you, Nephew." Latimer observed the scene with cool blue eyes. "Mary, Sophia, my daughters, I see you are entertained." He had eased himself into a chair at the head of the table. "Laughter is a lively greeting, but what sees you in such merry heart?" His daughters had subdued a giggle and looked to their laps.

"Little of consequence, Uncle, an often told yarn, sir, regarding a bad tempered goat and a servant who was bade milk it; just a remembrance from my early childhood, when I was but a year or so older than, Mary."

Latimer took account of his nephew's appearance – a braided coat in a colour Latimer was not familiar with, ochre perhaps, and an embroidered waistcoat? The note he had retrieved and paid on his behalf was still current in his mind and could not be forgotten. Perhaps he was being harshly judgemental, the coat was likely old.

His occasional maid had brought in the breakfast dishes, placing them toward one end of the table. He took chocolate and allowed Vetch to serve him with some braised chicken and the larger part of a poached trout.

"I would have your company more often, Nephew." Latimer lifted his eyes from his plate and glanced at his nephew. Strength lay in decisiveness and he would not allow distraction to dislodge him from his path.

"I wish to discuss with you the matter of your trip north, Geoffrey." He tasted the chicken. "Trade, and most particularly the woollen trade, has been the bedrock of this city, Nephew, since the Exe ran freely and the cathedral was no more than a chalk sketch on the stonemason's slate. If we are to survive this lean time we must look to our known trade."

Latimer finished his chicken, picked at the fish and put down his fork. Geoffrey had not interrupted him. "There is a disconnect, Geoffrey, and I am anxious to reconnect with the farmers, weaving shops and cottagers I have done business with in the past. I wish you to begin trading again on my behalf." Henri took a seedcake from the stand and broke it in half. He caught his nephew in his direct gaze. "I have rarely employed an agent, Geoffrey, but I believe you quite able to fill that role."

"It is a plan, sir, and a worthy one, but I am doubtful that these weavers would see my appearance as any kind of substitute for yours. Let us sit together sometime in the close future and discuss the idea."

"I believe, Nephew, that the time for discussion and contemplation is passed. I wish for you to go tomorrow. We are still only a space into this day and there is plenty of time to make plans. I will arrange a sound mount for you and we will have time after this meal to look over a good map which I have already laid out upon my desk. It will be good practice to introduce yourself to the markets at Moreton and Crediton; they are the nucleus of life and trade there about, and will give you firm basis upon which to make your assessments. I will give you a full purse with which to buy fleece. You may decide not to make a purchase; I will leave this to you. The spinners and weaving families receive their wool direct; once it has been sourced, the farms have their own supply. I do not expect you to involve yourself in woven cloth as yet but this will be a beginning."

"Tomorrow, Uncle?"

"Even this prompt beginning will mean a gap of some weeks before any profit meets us. I will give you lists and descriptions of the farms I have done business with and the weavers I buy cloth from; a visit to any and perhaps all would be welcomed by them and helpful to me. There are upright men at Moreton who will advise and I will supply you with a letter of introduction."

"Will not the day following do, sir? I have a little business of my own to attend to."

"It will not, Nephew, we have sat in the doldrums long enough – lean times necessitate immediate action."

Breakfast had been over more quickly than Latimer had planned. Mary and Sophia, who had become bored with a wholly business-centred conversation and confused by their father's harshness of tone, asked to be excused. And Latimer and Geoffrey had removed themselves to the large sitting room where a crumpled map and several small well-thumbed books were laid out.

He knew the boy was shocked by this brusque mandate, and maybe the swagger had been replaced by a more 'tail between his legs' stance? Latimer had never been sure if anything much lay beneath the boy's peacock exterior, this errand might show him in a different light. They could depart together – although in opposite directions; tomorrow Henri intended to ride out to Lympstone and arrange for repairs to begin on *The Lady Rosamunde*.

Leaving his nephew to peruse the books and maps on his desk, Latimer retrieved his hat from the stand and went out. The Fore Street woollen markets had been doing business for several hours before he reached the main drag of the city. An easterly wind had brought clear skies and the streets were accordingly full. Latimer tapped his way through the crowds; he knew most of the traders here, green baize aprons marking out their profession, and he had shaken a hand or two, lifted his hat in greeting.

Predominantly a cloth market, long ells of serge and twilled kersey were laid out inside the Market House or displayed on trestles beneath the granite-pillared portico that ran along its front. But like a moth to a flame the cloth market drew other traders – Jannie-fortnights with trays strung about their necks selling liquorice sticks, sweat-meats and ribbons; bragging quacksalvers with bottles of physic and cure-alls for everything from impotence to the pox;

pie-men with hand-carts, women selling smoked eel unctuously displayed on whittled sticks, and cheap-jacks too numerous to count.

Historically narrow, the mediaeval streets ensured the crowds were tightly packed. With such lucrative passing trade many shops displayed their stock and wares on the cobblestoned pavements in front, goods and the paraphernalia of trade spilling out onto the streets. Towards the head of Fore Street where it was intersected by the turnpike road, the crush was a little easier and Latimer stopped to browse a table at the front of a book-binders. The innovative trader had expanded his field, selling velum, off-cuts of leather, endless laces and second-hand books. Planked trestles displayed all this in a jumble of interest that Latimer could not ignore.

As he began to examine oddly shaped pieces of leather, long laces that would surely find a use before the day was out, he saw his neighbour idly thumbing through a small book. It was unmistakably Rae – rarely did he see her out; altered circumstances made him less easy in her presence.

"It seems we are drawn to this same stall, Rae, and yet I could not tell you why if you asked it." Latimer lifted his hat and picked up a thick book he had no interest in.

"Mr Latimer, sir.' Rae had bobbed – any reference to their private intimacy avoided. "Is it not the possibility of finding something that others have missed which do draw us to have a second look?"

Henri rested his stick against the trestle and flipped open the book – she was wearing the short woollen coat he had seen her wear many times before, but with the addition of a dark ribbon, worn high on her neck and tied at the back.

"Or the need to make some order of it perhaps?" Latimer examined his book. She looked different today, just a small square of lace on her dark hair and no hat. He noticed the book she was holding contained painted prints – her other hand was occupied with the strings of a canvas package.

"I see that it is an errand that has brought you out, Rae," he said lightly.

"'Tis an errand that do release me, Mr Latimer." She looked up briefly. "I have been sent out to collect a package, come down this morning on the early coach from London and only a day since it left Cheapside." She swung the package in her fingers, keeping her eyes on the book.

"The country becomes a smaller place when goods may be transported at such speed." He placed his book back on the pile. "And what does your package contain?"

"Precious pigments I do believe, Mr Latimer, and other necessities that Alexander insists he may only find in our biggest city, although I cannot see what more any would want that could not be found here in our westward city." She turned a page of her book. "I do not believe I would like the crush of searching – in London, I do mean." He understood her meaning.

"I do not believe I would like it either, Rae. Now tell me, Rae…" Latimer picked up another book and read the spine, "how many hats does Trelawney have you wear this week?"

"One less than before, Mr Latimer – we have a cook."

"Then your release is explained. And does your new cook sit well with Mr Flood?"

"She do not, sir, but she has great knowledge of roasting and baking, and I am glad of it as I am more'n busy in the master's painting rooms."

"Trelawney is working then?"

"Oh yes, sir, he will work and work and has started two likenesses this week since, although Mr Luca is not so happy about it."

"Not so?"

"He is idle, Mr Latimer, and seems not to like it. Alexander has given him canvas and brush but he is restless still and has no interest for it."

"Ah," Latimer said remembering many other young bucks that had returned with Trelawney, outstayed their welcome – or become jaded and moved on.

"Your master must work like any other, I suppose, Rae, although I believe he has access to other monies and need not work as hard as some. The boy will have to be patient."

"But he will paint Mr Luca soon. Mr Trelawney says Mr Luca will make fine pose and this will make a glad change from the washed clean merchant's daughters he is used to. He has promised it and then they shall both be content." The bells of numerous churches and the chimes of city clocks had begun to mark the midday. "Lord deliver me, Mr Latimer, you have quite made me behind time and I must get this packet back to Alexander before he comes searching for me."

"Then I indeed apologize." He watched her indirectly as she carefully closed the small leather-bound book and placed it back upon the trestle.

"Will you not make a purchase then, Rae?"

"Oh no, I cannot, Mr Latimer. I intended only to look."

"And I also," he said candidly.

She was gone and Latimer watched her work her way through the crowds in the direction of Exebere Street, the canvas package held tightly to her chest.

Turning back to the trestles he searched the disordered books for the small volume she had been holding. He found it without difficulty, picked it up and thumbed through the prints – wild flowers perhaps, crudely printed in black Indian ink and then finished with watercolour. He flipped it shut, retrieved his stick and went into the book-binder's shop to make his only purchase of the day.

*

Standing later in his own wide entrance hall, he had felt the small purchase that he had placed in the lower pocket of his long waistcoat – touched it absently with his hand and then shouted for Vetch.

"The day is good, Thomas." He spoke without emotion, nor any particular kindness, which he had decided was a sentiment that had not paid well in previous dealings with his servant.

"Go to the top of the house, Thomas, and find my daughters; I will have them out of this house and into the world – if they are not already so?"

"I believe they are occupied within their rooms, sir." Vetch knew they would be there; Old Sarah always slept at this time of day and it was fortunate that the Misses Latimers were well used to managing without her.

"Do not disturb Mrs Sarah," Latimer had said with the same understanding. "We will be visiting St Mary's burial ground. Make haste, Thomas, the time runs on." He paused, felt the small rectangular book. "And when I return please find me, I have a little errand I wish you to perform."

Waiting for Vetch to return with his daughters, Latimer considered the future that he now felt he had. The house needed a stronger hand and now that he was well again he would offer it.

They had gone to the burial ground, companionably enough, although Mary was more sombre natured than he would have chosen, but this was eased by his younger daughter's enthusiasm. They had wanted to pray and he had encouraged it and listened to their childish chantings with a full heart. What heathen ways was he pushing upon these two innocents – he should at least join them, on occasion, in church.

There were primroses gathered in bright pockets around the burying place and he had encouraged them to pick some and lay them upon their mother's grave. He leant back against the boundary wall watching them, taking the weight from his leg. In many ways time had fled since his wife's death and the six years that had passed seemed no time at all – and yet the memory of her was so indistinct that it might have been a hundred years ago. Perhaps today was some kind of new beginning; tomorrow he would see Geoffrey off on his exploration of the moorland towns, settle himself on a good horse and go down to Lympstone. Bringing the *Rosamunde* back to life would be a new beginning in itself.

17

The smell of the fulling process was something that Geoffrey – cosseted, served and protected from the disagreeable necessities of earning a living – could never become accustomed to. Sitting in a comfortable, although thriftily furnished room in a building adjoining Blackaller Tucking Mill, he waited for William to gather his senses. There was an interesting view of the river – aged willows, small craft and ferryboats scuttling from one side to the other. The scene may have been pleasant, but there was nothing that could distract from the roar of the hammers nor disguise the smell of urine.

William Mudge lolled in a horsehair chair a distance from him. The drink from the previous evening was floating like a persistent mist around the innards of his body, giving him the look of a sick man. Geoffrey sensed this was an opportune time to call.

"You look like a man with the ague, William; was we so very drunk last eve? I cannot believe it?"

"We had an evening of it did we not? A cock-fight seems to drive a sober man into drink and a drunken one beyond redemption, and The Swan keeps as good a cellar as any, don't you think?"

There had been a slight dulling of their friendship of late and the reasons for this were closely connected to a swan-necked whore and a lodging house on the other side of the river. "I hear your good papa has travelled south?" Geoffrey had already indulged in an unequal and rather brief conversation with Josiah Mudge's fawning little clerk.

"So he has," William replied, blowing slowly through colourless lips in order to stave off nausea. "A relation of his, of mine I suppose, on her deathbed – gone off in the direction of Teignmouth well before I was from my bed. Praying, praying is the required physic and it is something I know him to be extraordinarily good at doing."

"When is he likely to return?" Geoffrey picked at his nails.

"Who can say, Latimer? How long is a weaver's yarn? A day or three I would hasten to guess."

There was a small table set between them and on it was a bottle of Bordeaux – revenue paid and not run-in, Geoffrey supposed. Geoffrey viewed the uncorked bottle with curiosity.

"A good bottle in a Quaker's counting house, sir?"

"We are quite amongst friends here, Geoffrey. You need not fear my papa's little clerk. He takes a drink as well as I and does not follow faith to the letter."

Geoffrey sat forwards, resting his arms on his legs – legs almost as long as his uncle's.

"I have come to you, William, because I am in dire need of your support. I find that I have been outfoxed. Despite my perpetual dragging of my reluctant feet I am to go north – and tomorrow and without forewarning!"

William looked at him with bloodshot eyes and poured a glass of Bordeaux for them both.

"And on a borrowed nag with only coin enough for the most meagre of hostelries, and confounding that," Geoffrey continued aggrieved, "I am to leave my whore to the enjoyment of others when I have most recently set her up in a quiet little garret across the river at considerable expense to my pocket."

"Outwitted, sir? By your uncle Latimer?" William restrained a smirk.

The monotonous hammering of machinery could be heard working away and was not a desired accompaniment to delicate conversation. "I am in need of that poxy little roll of parchment that is held so without need or use in your good papa's strongbox – the transfer document, William, the deed, the written agreement that confirms the ten per cent share and its encumbrances. We have talked of it much have we not?"

William was thrown back to previous encounter. A degenerative drunk he was, but his heart was sure and he loved his father – if not his father's faith. He did not have Geoffrey's determined requirement for possession and betterment.

"Must you have it now? I was hoping that you had changed heart. Cannot you talk man to man with your good uncle and have him offer you a better allowance – or lend you money to begin again in Dorset?"

"You do not know my slit-mouthed relation as I do, William, he will keep me poor and insist upon it. He lives like a semi-pauper and will not out his purse for any need." Although this was an unadulterated lie the statement did not prick Geoffrey's conscience.

"I wish only to borrow that dusty document. It has been sleeping in your papa's safe-box for a lifetime – I would wager some twenty years – and I must have it before the day is out so that I may make use of it while I am away."

"Fate do not always run straight nor expected, Geoffrey. There is every mischance that although this document has been idle for many years, it will be needed by some clerk or busybody tomorrow and then the thing will be missed. You must make allowance for that for it is I who will be a duck on the water."

"William, you make problem where problem need not be. If such unwarranted bad luck should be our fate then lay blame elsewhere and before your papa can argue upon it, I will have the document returned. I wish only to borrow against the share capital, an interest that my uncle will now, owing to his returned infirmity, never make use of again. It is sleeping, William. I need to wake it, use it and then return it to its rest. God forgive me for confirming it but my uncle is as sickly as a washer-woman's child in a breeding house and will never be sending serges to the fulling process again." He hoped the lie would not surface before he could accomplish what he must.

"I had not heard, sir, the talk has been that your uncle is well mended and pushing back to what he was."

"The grape vine of this city is ever false; the unexplained illness that laid him low has returned and I must make my own way in life for he will not be able to help me now."

"I do indeed see it is a plan, Geoffrey, but one that could see us both muddied in the mire if we are not so very careful."

William had lost all colour; having dishonesty thrust upon him when his preference would have been to return to his rooms and sleep until evening, did not improve his feeling of nausea.

"You need not worry, friend, I wish merely to offer it as security. Fate would not be so cruel as to send your dear papa or his clerk searching for the document when no interest has been shown it for nearly a decade. I will deal with it in haste, just a few days and then you can lay the thing back in that locked box where it may snooze on to eternity. We will not be discovered, William, and if we are you must put blame on that servile old man who creeps about these rooms with nothing better to do than keep watch on us." Conversation abated momentarily.

Thinking around his problems and looking for added security in his plan, Geoffrey drank his wine and continued on a different tack. "How goes your dealings in South Street, sir? That pleasant little doxy you had last sennight, do she still go well or has she moved on to better things?"

Geoffrey settled himself more comfortably in his chair, lifting his boots and resting them on the edge of the table. He observed the Quaker's only child, he hoped William would now ponder the consequences of falling out with a man who knew most if not all of his transgressions and might, if necessity existed, be willing to out them if his intentions were opposed.

William leant cautiously forwards, tentatively smelling the lavender on his handkerchief. "Then you must have it, sir, but do not keep it long away from its little chest, it will hardly make for a settled time knowing that I might have to explain the document's misappropriation."

"You will have no need to explain it, William, the thing will be done and dusted by the end of the week and we shall both be able to pay our taproom bills and choose the finest whores in Exeter."

Walking briskly down Exebere Street, the rolled document concealed under his coat, Geoffrey glanced instinctively at the milliner's shop. In previous times he would have easily been able to dismiss what he saw – the painted young women hanging about its door, the faceless gentlemen entering and leaving at all times of the day and night – but his new liaison made it all the harder. In his short life he had never felt commitment or loyalty to any woman – even his mother – lust and the need to take what he wanted had always been his driving force. He supposed his whore would be in the house somewhere and it bothered him, although he chose not to admit it. A mop-headed scarecrow of a girl was wiping the windows of the shop with a rag and a bucket of dirty water. There were three other painted harlots loitering around her; they were becoming brash. Upon his return he would forbid his doxy to return here – and then there would be no complications.

Uncle Latimer was not at home, Vetch had offered confirmation that he would not return for some time. Feeling the document, Geoffrey went quietly into the large low-beamed room at the front of the house and began surreptitiously to look over the maps laid out there, and fan through the numerous little books that shouted of frugal living and boredom. He felt the desk drawer, it was not locked; he drew it out and exposed the contents – a promising start. The paraphernalia of business long done was abandoned here. He began to carefully move sealing wax, sheets of neatly written figures and unused writing paper – the share certificate would not be here, Elcott held such things, but there were other useful papers. The document he had sourced from Mudge contained his own grandfather's seal and signature as well as Josiah Mudge's, but there was one more piece that needed to be fitted to the puzzle before he set out tomorrow.

Behind him he heard movement and the click of boots on the flagstones. Vetch was standing beneath the doorjamb watching him. Geoffrey looked up, his youthful face held in a kind of contortion of concern, this swept away by obvious relief when he saw who it was. Without comment, Vetch silently pulled the door closed and disappeared into the quiet house.

A small roll of heavy paper was tucked in a corner; he took it out unrolled it and secured it with a weight. The document was insignificant – he did not bother to read it, but his uncle's seal and signature were there, clearly, exactly as he had hoped. He re-rolled it, tied the lace and dropped it into his pocket beside the other. He closed the drawer carefully, his disturbance had been minimal. The prospect of his pending trip suddenly held an edge of excitement; he would not of course be fulfilling any of his uncle's instructions – but no matter, he would be leaving this city on a horse paid for by Uncle Latimer, and several days of unchallenged freedom awaited him.

18

Rae had watched Henri Latimer leave the house with his nephew as she had tied her apron, the pair well muffled against the sharp early spring winds in heavy-coats and scarves – the younger Latimer supporting a bound parcel. Her duties in the upper rooms had been quickly done and she had gone back to the kitchens, seated herself on the rickety cricket by the fire and picked up the goose she had begun to pluck earlier.

The new cook was standing against the table, making the kitchen feel smaller for her presence; coming at the beginning of Trelawney's return she was now well settled into the routine of the house – she was efficient, experienced and large. She was also a distant cousin of Elijah Flood's and between them lay an animosity which had roots in the distant past. The rotund woman was a Flood that had married a Coombely. She came at dawn and left – when Trelawney did not entertain – around dusk. Rae watched her large fleshy arms powerfully kneading the day's bread dough.

"The master do have fickle and whimsical tastes, Rae," she said without pausing. "Always requiring this and that, and when he is so offered his requirement he do complain that he has detested the same since he was a boy. If I am to raise pies and wrap puddings I would be better pleased knowing Mr Trelawney will eat them."

Flood had been at the top of the house dressing his master, avoiding doing the same for Luca, and laying the fires. Rae considered the lifeless lolling head and glassy-eyed stare of the fowl in her lap. Feigning her interest by nodding, she turned the bird over and began systematically plucking the white feathers from its breast with sharp purposeful movements. The cook began on another tack, one Rae had heard before – a dispute over quantities and cost book entries.

"That bible do make the man more high and mighty than he has a right to be. And I know as he can't read so how does he know how much sugar I must put in tomorrow's cider cake, or whether a brace o' pheasants be more'n a trio. 'Tis I who must cook it and I who must count the coin."

Before she had finished speaking Flood had appeared at the kitchen door – faded work-coat buttoned to meet his stock, grey hair pulled behind his head in a queue. He ignored the broad cook and spoke directly to Rae.

"You must run to the top of the house, Daughter. Your master has a mind to speak with you."

He was an upright man, well passed his mid-years and although his attempt to save Rae from wickedness often felt more akin to imprisonment, she felt no real animosity towards him and accepted his ways with resignation.

"Elijah, I have only just returned."

"Then you must go again."

Rae laid the half-plucked goose back in the basket amongst the feathers and slipped from the kitchen, leaving Elijah and his distant cousin to discuss thrift and prudency over generosity.

The light from the bright day and the fresh breeze pushing in from a part open window reminded Rae of all that lay beyond the city. She observed the disordered room, the incongruously placed scroll-backed bed now strewn with discarded clothing – shirts, stockings, a periwig and a half-dozen waistcoats Rae had never seen Trelawney wear. Alexander had met his promise and Luca was sat on the portrait chair, a silk coat buttoned over long waistcoat and a large quantity of lace showing at cuff and neck. Luca turned to greet her first.

"Rachael? What swift response you make when summoned. I cannot say I would be so quick to do this man's bidding."

"She does no bidding of mine," Trelawney shouted from behind his easel. "I have no charge of her. I know not where she is or what she does for most of her day." He kicked away a phial that had fallen to the floor and sought its brother on the cluttered table beside him. "Now you have quite disturbed the pose, Servant. Come you in before we lose all thread of what we do," and then to Luca, "Sit still, Luca, you have sat no more than a quarter of the hour and moved thrice already."

Rae did not speak whilst Alexander painted. She moved quietly into the room and sat upon a small dressing chair abandoned to one corner. There was blood from the fowl on her hands and she unobtrusively wiped it away on her skirts. Trelawney had painted on until Luca, who was a poor sitter, spoke again.

"Do you see, Alexander, you make her silent, demure, when she should be neither of these things. She is too young to be silent and too spirited to be demure."

"I have never had such a poor subject, Luca. You have no right observing what my servant does. How am I to concentrate on form when your eyes intentionally seek distraction? The little Egyptian has always been that way since I offered my guinea and brought her home." Trelawney stood back and assessed his work. "And now she must wait her turn, she has been at liberty far too long doing what she chooses." Satisfied he threw down his brush and looked disinterestedly at Rae. "In truth, Luca, if I have made her silent it is you who has made her blush."

Rae left her chair and began to gather up the numerous items of clothing thrown upon the bed, pulling her mouth into a small angry bow. Trelawney was wiping his hands on the remains of a shirt.

"Luca, why did we require my ward to attend us, the thought has quite gone from my head, you are a weary distraction – I do not know why she is here? If I must paint you then I must be allowed to do it undisturbed."

Luca was sitting with one leg hooked over the arm of the oak carver – he had already loosened the buttons at the knee of his breeches and removed his stock.

"Alexander, why do you offer this pretence that you misremember this and that when I know for sure that you remember all that is said and done in your presence?" Luca spun his legs round to look at Rae. "The dissenter, Alexander, the dissenter, sir."

"Ah, yes, yes. The dissenter." Alexander took off the long cotton coat he always wore to paint in and flung it onto the bed that was now clear from all additions – the quilt smoothed and folded. "Elijah Flood, a man of God. A man of his own God." He walked towards a tall chest containing half-a-dozen drawers and collected a small rectangular package wrapped in coarse paper, squinting at Rae in anticipation of the response he intentionally sought.

"It seems that this very morn a little packet was delivered to this house, my dear. Written upon it is but three bold letters." He pronounced the letters annoyingly slowly with unnecessary emphasis, feigning an inability to understand their meaning. "Flood had it tucked discretely in his coat pocket when he dressed us, did he not, Luca? And as duty says he must, naturally he handed the thing to me." To this there was a slight shaking of Luca's head but this seemed to be more in exasperation than agreement. "What say you to that, my Rachael?"

Rae's head had come up. "What packet do you have, Alexander? If it has my name upon it why did you not let Mr Flood deliver it where it was meant?"

"You are but seventeen, Rachael. We cannot allow such things to go unchecked, I must keep tally on your doings whilst you live under this roof, whilst I remain protector."

Such statements always rang with ambivalence – Rae could never decide whether Trelawney had been protector, master or gaoler during the time she had lived in this house.

"What things, Alexander? You do know that you care nothing for my youth and have never made any allowance for it in the past. If you have what is mine then give it along to me without interference."

"But interfere we must – must we not, Luca?"

"Alexander, do not require me to enter into your teasing for I do not approve of it."

"Dear boy, no, I see that you do not – but you must humour me."

The package had already been opened; the content was clearly visible. Rae scrutinised it with hungry eyes. It was rare that she felt fury or even irritation towards Trelawney, his ways were as they were and she had become accustomed to them over time, but at this present moment she did feel fury and if she could have done what spirit required she would have kicked him hard upon his silk-stockinged shins and grabbed that which was most privately and rightfully hers. He read the three bold letters on the front of the packet – written with some flourish.

"I perceive, my child, that these are not initials around which a name must be imagined, or some code to be picked over and deciphered." The half-open packet was in his palm and he held it unnecessarily close to his well seeing eyes. "But they are indeed a name and a name in its fullness. As God had no part in your naming, nor most probably in your conception and you have but one name – the one that I have given to you – I believe the anonymous little packet must be yours."

Luca watched her temper rise, folding his arms, assessing her, waiting for the sparks to set fire to the tinder – he hoped. The blush of her spirit rose upon her cheeks, the book was exposed; she knew where it had come from and she knew who had sent it but Trelawney played games, he would offer the book up when he was done – she must keep her temper until he did. Flipping the book open Trelawney read the fly, read what she knew he must have read when he had taken the packet from Flood.

"*To Rachael from Henri L,*" he read, "not much in the way of explanation – and no endearments." He closed the book as if disappointed. "A present, I propose, but nothing to link it to its giver other than a name." He held the small leather-bound volume out with exaggerated indifference but did not offer it to her. "I suppose it is yours, and if it is I suppose you must have it, but before

I hand it to you, you will tell me how it is that you receive such gifts from our sickly merchant."

She must be careful – if he detected spirit then he would tease her longer.

"I will not tell you, Alexander. I will not make a story just so you may be satisfied to have one. It was my packet and it is my book, so do not ask it."

"Do not squint at me with cat's eyes, my child, I have only your future well-being at heart. Here then, take it and hide it away in some pocket somewhere." She did not answer him but snatched it from him, searched her skirts and dropped the book into a deep pocket. "Will you not thank me then?" he enquired.

"I will not, Alexander." The floor about his painting table was littered with discarded brushes and phials; she bent and silently began to collect them in her apron.

"You have a black heart, Alexander." Luca was looking on with his arms folded. "Can you not see that she has an admirer? You have blundered in where you should not."

"I blunder nowhere, young man. I go where I wish. And how can you say my heart is black when I have made purchase of a sitter's gown. 'Tis a fine gown with a fine finish, the measurements come-by from whorehouse Jane – in the milliner's now and ready to fit." Satisfied with the disquiet he had caused, Trelawney softened his rhetoric, came forward to lift her chin. "Have I stepped beyond my mark, Rachael – teased you long enough? Come my black-eyed child, reply to what I have said and say you forgive me. You may have the gown whenever you wish it – and then I will paint you."

The gesture did not appease her; she would not be mollified. The suggestion that she sit for him was not welcome.

"Look upon that little Venetian watch in your fob-pocket, Luca, and tell what hour is approaching. My insides says 'tis late."

St Mary's clock was already chiming ten and Luca had no need to retrieve his watch.

"Do not work away in such a hoary huff, Rachael; you have the little thing securely hid now, let that be enough. We will take our breakfast on the half hour, you may return then to settle my pigments and brushes. Be gone with you now and send your temper back beneath that innocent's cap where 'tis normally hid." Trelawney waited for her to leave, amused by his servant's thunderous expression and pursed lips.

"You do not know when enough is enough, Alexander. I believe the girl acquiesces only because it suits her; you may not find her quite as tolerant of your whims as she grows."

The artist was sat in his own portrait chair, Luca opposite. The creative exuberance of the former had begun to settle; the boy was indeed quite beautiful, painting him involved an element of detachment from the person and the return to intimacy was welcome.

"We jest upon it, Luca, but what say you, do the hussy have an admirer in Latimer senior?"

"I know not of the man, Alexander, I could not say. I have seen him but in passing; he is a decrepit old widower and likely beyond caring. What is your tack here, Alexander? I know you to be a mischief maker and I doubt there is wisdom in it, either regarding the reclusive merchant or that fiery vixen – she sits upon her temper and you would do well to remember such."

"Mischief pleases me, Luca. It do stir the world to throw about a little mischief and serves it right."

The morning sun had risen higher and found its way into the house, illuminating the painting rooms. Trelawney put powerful hands on Luca's knees and felt the silk of his breeches and the taut muscles of youth.

"The pose has made me hungry, Luca." He cupped the boy's cock in his hand, assessing his want. "Silk breeches and a full belly must be paid for and I believe breakfast can wait until we are done."

19

His uncle Latimer's advice had been to go north on the Crediton road and then follow the pack-road on to Moretonhampstead. Never having had any intention of visiting either of the market towns nor any of the weavers between, it was more than fortunate that his uncle's suggestion sat comfortably with his own plans. The well-used turnpike would take him safely out of the city – if a little further north than he wished to be, but then once away he would skirt around the city drop down south and travel east eventually picking up the coaching road bound for Dorchester, perhaps towards the end of the day. He had waved his uncle goodbye with enthusiasm and fondness.

Having broken his fast in a busy roadside hostelry, Geoffrey had taken numerous minor tracks east, bridging the Exe and fording the Culm, and before mid-afternoon he was trotting along the turnpike towards Honiton. Behind him was strapped a woollen top coat, a leather satchel with all that he needed for business and a bound bundle containing a square of hard cheese, a loaf of freshly baked bread and a flagon of homebrew. He expected it to remain there. His small manor was at Marwood; he would go there, but possibly towards the end of the day when dusk fell, and when he could trot along hamlet lanes unnoticed. There were important business matters to attend to before he visited his mama at Marwood and it was towards the town of Axminster that he directed his horses head later that afternoon.

The wind was still blowing freshly from the east, the spring sunshine no match for it – he adjusted his collar, put his head down and cussed. The fields about him were becoming ever more undulating and the vistas less open. He pushed the horse on; it was familiar land now, although he felt no sense of homecoming. After half a mile of hard riding he slowed his mount from a canter to an idle trod, and patted the beast's withers with appreciation. He was relieved to be spared the tedium of picking his way along rocky tracks to any remote town or farmstead listed upon his uncle's itinerary – what mistaken sense of loyalty, downright hog-headedness made his uncle choose to set himself the task of making such an uncomfortable and arduous journey? Why had his uncle never paid men to do this work for him, other merchants had agents? Why had Uncle Latimer chosen to do all himself?

The road into Axmouth was an almost constant stream of mud-crusted coaches, farm wagons and unhurried walkers, at intervals the whole procession held back by wayward livestock being driven at snail's pace. Last year he had found need to visit an obliging notary living in the festering heart of the small town; if the man was still at liberty he would purchase his services again. Running his eye across the slate and thatched stone cottages climbing haphazardly up the hill towards the grey-faced Norman church, he tried to remember in which street the notary had lived. He would need to go there on foot and it would be wise to find livery for his horse. The London-bound coach he saw was waiting on the rough ground before The George, leather and swingletrees quivering between the restive team, the moneyed and the not so moneyed already seated. Considering his own future, he led his horse through to the busy yard and left instructions.

The notary's hovel had been easy to find, sitting almost level with the loom rooms. Geoffrey entered the single room, the notary was not alone: two heads looked up and the scrivener studied the young man who had just entered, assessing the cut of the stranger's coat and the quality of his boot leather. After a moment's hesitation and a space of time during which the notary tried to recall the young man's name, the ancient visitor had been hastily ushered from the room.

The notary stood, drew up a chair to the table and motioned for Geoffrey to sit.

"Have we met, sir? I have a sensation of familiarity."

"Briefly, yes. I do not expect that you will remember me. You made a simple duplication of a document for me."

The notary had remembered; peering at him more closely from under heavy brows he now clearly recalled the young man's history as well as his face, but did not make reference to it. "Indeed so. If I remember you travelled some distance to take up my services."

"Some distance," Geoffrey said without elaborating.

"Are you in need of assistance again, sir – you cannot be thinking of writing your will, at least not yet awhile?"

Glancing about him at the shabby furniture and the earth floor, Geoffrey felt in the pocket of his coat and took out the rolled paper. He laid it on the table.

"Ah," the notary said with understanding. He unrolled the paper and placed a pewter inkwell and a pair of circular brass weights along the document's outer edges, looking over it, taking in the seal and the signature and the first line of the document.

"Not a document of any particular age," he observed.

"No, not particularly." Geoffrey sat back and crossed his legs. "It is an agreement belonging to the family Mudge confirming acquisition of a property – my grandfather's property. The document also refers to the retention – by my grandfather, of a ten per cent share in that property."

"A tucking mill, I see," the notary said looking up. "There is some prosperity in these mills, is there not? I hear the woollen trade still continues well despite its antiquity and early beginnings – in contrast to our carpet weaving here, which is still in its infancy."

Geoffrey was not in the least interested in either the prosperity of the woollen trade or the Axminster looms. "Prosperity there may be, but the acquisition of my grandfather's mill was tantamount to theft. The ten per cent is paltry. However, I have not come to discuss such. The sister document belonging to my grandfather and the share certificate relating to the ten per cent – subsequently passed on to my uncle upon my grandfather's death – is lost. I require a replacement to be made, the share certificate in duplicate. You will have most of what you need on this document, seals and signatures – counter-signing." Geoffrey bit his lip and considered the ease with which he might defraud a bank or lending house into accepting a forged duplicate Deed and share certificate as surety.

"Exact copies, sir, in the ilk of the first?" the notary questioned.

"Exactly so, paper, ink and all." Geoffrey nodded. "I require also a Scrip of Entitlement benefitting me." He produced the small scroll he had liberated from his uncle's desk and dropped it onto the other. "My uncle's seal and signature is here, on the reverse I have recorded the name in which the shares are to be held."

The old notary ruminated for a while. "And confidentiality? I am always discrete but perhaps there is a delicacy beyond that?"

"Confidentiality, secrecy, call it what you will, it would be more than unwise to out any of our conversation nor the subject upon which we are talking. If you remember me a slight, I remember you well, and the work you produced for me – and the coin I paid to you. I do not forget such things."

The notary did not comment but looked critically at the documents set before him. "If I am to reproduce the seals and the signatures, as well as to replicate the look of the documents, it will take me some hours."

"I have a purse upon me – you will be paid well for your work." He uncrossed his legs and took out his purse.

The notary removed his wig and thoughtfully scratched a fleabite on his forehead. "When do you wish this delicate work done by? If I am to offer this service 'tis best I shut up shop for a while, declare illness or such like."

"I care not what you do or how you do it but I shall collect the documents complete in a three days' time upon my return journey." Geoffrey stood. "I expect to come into money in the not so distant future. I will need a notary of worth to continue to see to my affairs – let us hope that you can be that notary." Standing, he dropped a small coin on the table. "I will make payment in full when I collect these documents – good day to you, Notary." He ducked beneath the beam. The thing had been easier than he had expected – perhaps life would now turn a brighter corner.

By the time he had left the Bridport road and begun to work his way down the lesser tracks towards the hamlet of Marwood, dusk was already falling. The outbuildings and stables were just shadowy blocks as he approached, but even in the twilight they looked shabby; there should have been a light burning in the stable but there was not. He slid from his horse, led it round to have a better look. Once, in his boyhood, these stables had been full of well-groomed dancing creatures ready for the chase; when he had left they had contained just two fine hunters. The stable seemed unused, the doors standing open. Empty; why was he surprised? His mother had never felt any sentiment towards the things that he cherished.

The manor house was little more than an enlarged farmhouse with an outshoot at the back, low single-storey buildings straggling from both its wings. It would have been a fair inheritance if there had ever been enough money to run it as he wished – now there was none and it seemed his last two hunters had been sold or taken. He had yet to pay for them.

There was no servant to greet him and he had found his own way to his mother's sitting room. A fire was blazing in the inglenook – a short-lived flash of a fire made of kindling but with no substance. His mother was sat before it: she was well dressed and upright and stern, the image of her had been dislodged from his thoughts whilst he had been busy living his duplicitous life in Devon – now memory came back savagely. She greeted him without warmth as if he had only been gone for hours.

"There is dust upon your coat, Geoffrey," she said turning. He went forward but did not sit – the heat of the fire was repellent.

"I suppose it is too much to expect that you have afforded yourself a servant?" she said sourly.

"I have not, Mother, but I do not dress alone; there are servants within my uncle's house."

"Your uncle's house, Geoffrey – so there is no change in circumstance?"

Geoffrey did not answer; he took his mother's cold hand and kissed it lightly, then stepped back from the heat of the fire. The room was oppressive. He took off his coat, shook it and waited for comment. The candles had been lit, although there were fewer now than he remembered. A gilt mirror dominated one wall. His image was clear, unavoidable, and he saw his youth and the quality of his buttoned waistcoat; the image satisfied him but the room and the company of his mother did not. He felt her embitterment as strongly as the heat from the fire. She seemed old now, older than she was, older than he remembered – early widowhood had aged her.

"Your brother-in-law lives, Mama, but he has relapsed once, he may do so again. We must be patient."

"And while we wait what do you intend that I should live upon? I have just two servants and the butcher's boy swinging on the bell weekly for payment. The tenant farm pays a pittance. My father would always say the farm was not big enough to sustain a tenant, and now that it is shrunk to a meagre nothing it is no more than a dirt farm and the farmer a space above pauper."

Geoffrey straightened his lace in the mirror. Why exactly had he bothered to come here? He had nothing to report to his mother. Liquidity of capital, instead of being enhanced as he had hoped, was in fact diminished. It would have been better to stay away.

"I am aware, Mother, of the difficulties that surround this manor, but I had thought you would leave my stable alone, at least until I returned – I see there is nothing within but muck and straw."

"I will not live without servants, Geoffrey. The choice was simple – and as it is we have that horse trader on our backs, making demands and cussing that you had not paid fully for the beasts and had no right to sell them on."

"But I did not sell them on, Mother, you did."

"From necessity, Geoffrey, necessity, what else could I do? I brought a good dowry to my marriage expecting it only to be down payment, that there would be Latimer money in plenty to keep me. There is none, Geoffrey, and you return to me now and report that this situation is unchanged."

"These things are not of my doing, Mother, nor are they in my power to alter. I have done your bidding, reasserted my kinship, sat by my uncle's bed and professed to be interested in his business. But the man lives on, indeed he appears to be recovering despite all suggestion that he would not – we will not have his money yet."

"So what does bring you here, Geoffrey, if you have not brought conclusion?"

"The man does not allow idleness, Mama. He wishes me to continue business where he let go. I am sent to Moreton but I had a change of heart and thought I might spend time at Marwood instead. Life in the Latimer house is without luxury; the suggestion is that the household is poor, I had a need to come away for a while."

"And do you believe him?" his mother tutted, "that he is poor, or does he spin a lie and hide his wealth to put you off the scent? I have never heard of a cloth merchant yet that has not lined his pockets over time. Cloth is gold, Geoffrey, and flows continuously through that city."

"Believe him I do not, whether he spins a lie I cannot say. But I have seen his like about the city, they prefer to sit upon their wealth and wear dark coats rather than make a show of it. The house is sizeable and he runs a ketch across the channel to the continent and is not without assets."

"Then you must make a friend of him, Geoffrey, and wait. Perhaps patience will be rewarded." He viewed her from his detached position, sat in her usual high-backed chair, straight, unyielding and without emotion. The firelight had made grotesque shadows of her features making her look crone-like and inhuman. "What is it he wishes you to do? How are you sent here, Geoffrey?"

"I am not sent here, Mama. I am sent to Devonshire, to the hinterland of that county to do business."

"Are you to stay? There are no servants to air the linen and I doubt there is much on the slab."

"This night only, Mama. I have slipped free from Uncle Latimer's watchful eye but I must return as I am expected with either business done or a sound story to cover my tracks. I have a little business in Axminster and must be there tomorrow before the midday."

20

Some short distance into spring, with the sun worrying the coat from a working man's back one moment and sending matron's off to sit by bright fires the next, Latimer set out early to walk to the Waterbere Lane coffee house. His nephew had returned, his spirits were well, his second-best coat brushed and the pain and stiffness in his leg seemed to have become part of his existence and did not bother him overmuch. Tapping his stick with purpose he began his journey towards Cathedral Close intending to take a route he more often than not took, this route having the distinct advantage of avoiding Butchers Row. Spits of windblown sleet had begun to fall and he tipped his hat forwards over his face. All about him along Exebere Street people were doing much the same to headgear and coat collars. Rae was approaching him at a trot and he was directly in her path.

"Hell's Gate, Mr Latimer, 'tis change and change about; the sun and all it offers is barely beyond the river and now we are doused with snow."

In his haste to prevent a collision he had caught hold of her arms. He held them for a moment enjoying the sensation. She was noticeably smaller than he was and he considered how easy it would be to lift her off her feet – he did not let go.

"Indeed it is, Rae – change and change about." A flash of amusement ran across his face. "Haste and snowflakes, don't make such good companions, Rae, settle your feet awhile and tell me why you must run when walking will do."

"I cannot do else but run, Mr Latimer." Without comment she stooped and picked up his stick, handing it back to him and continuing. "But I thank you for your concern all the same."

"Why such alacrity, your errands must surely now be complete?"

"And they were." She swung another small package from her fingertips. "But I am sent out again to collect another parcel – it is malachite this time and was quite forgot before. Mr Trelawney must have it before the day has begun else he cannot work."

As quickly as it had begun the hard sleet flakes ceased to fall and the dark sky was replaced by pools of blue light and ribbons of yellow. As though the swirling sleet had hidden them from the world, the sun now seemed to show them in bright exposure. Latimer let her go.

"Good morning to you, Rae. Send my regards to your master." He tipped his hat.

"It is likely I will not," she said swinging away from him, the parcel dangling from her fingertips.

Sleeping late and enjoying the simple pleasure of fornication before they broke their fast, Luca was in Trelawney's bedchamber; the windows afforded an excellent view of the street and an excellent view of all that took place within it. Alexander, short and almost corpulent, was still in bed; Luca's nakedness put him in mind of some ancient marble sculptures he had seen. He leant across the crumpled bed, found his sketchbook, a piece of blunted charcoal, and began to run fluid, confident lines across the paper.

"Do tell what you see, Luca? And do not report that it is just the idle click-clack of the street below." Luca glanced over his shoulder, saw Trelawney was busy and remained as he was.

"I see a wild morning, Alexander, and the bootmaker arguing with his son."

"Your arse is like a ripe peach, Luca, I am absorbed. I see you are equally so and I doubt it is the bootmaker arguing with his fisherman son that holds your attention."

"It is your little vixen, Alexander, held in an embrace with the sombre merchant."

"An embrace – so she holds a secret from us. And do they seem to be enjoying this embrace?"

"I believe so, he has let her go now – she is coming towards the house with your package. Are you done, Alexander?"

"I am."

Luca turned to face the artist – drew on a pair of draws that he retrieved from the floor and began thoughtfully to pull in the strings.

"I suspect you will make worry for her, Alexander."

"I may, I have not decided yet, Luca. You need not burden yourself with her wellbeing, she has always been able to look to herself. She must bring my pigment and then we shall see how she is." Trelawney swung his short legs round and sat scratching his cropped red hair. "She deserves a worrying, don't you think? But I may not be so direct. There is interest to be had, sport, before I put a stop to it."

The coffee house off Goldsmith's was full to over-spilling. Latimer entered, ducked a little below the beam, searched above the heads of the animated gentlemen, who, for reasons not yet known to him, crowded into the low-ceilinged rooms. After much searching his eyes found Elcott and he pushed his way through the crush.

"What is the buzz, Edmund?" Latimer had to shout above the din.

"The buzz, sir!" Elcott shouted back from behind a small table, imprisoned by a dozen garrulous gentlemen with seemingly differing opinions. "The buzz is that Bute has resigned!" He beckoned to Latimer to come forward. "Make a way there, sirs – come forward, Henri, do, before your stick is clean knocked asunder." Henri did as he was bid and found himself a seat by the wall.

"Tell me in simple words, Edmund, I cannot make a head nor a tale of what is being said with all this gesticulating." He raised his voice to be heard.

"John Stuart – our Prime Minister, The Earl of Bute – has resigned. The Commons told but yesterday and the news just come down to us on the early coach."

"Then that is indeed news, Edmund, and a surprise to all no doubt."

"A shock, Henri, a shock to all, most especially his cronies and indeed his opponents within the house. He has barely settled into the post; it is less than one year since he came to the treasury and headed the government."

Elcott took the bench beside Latimer, almost grateful to be removed, at least partly, from the intensity and mood of the conversation. They continued their own in a more analytical manner.

"It seems hard to comprehend that it has been but two months since his successes, and the signing of the Treaty, and the country rejoicing in the war end and the beneficial results – if not the house." Elcott put a hand out to retrieve his hat, which was in danger of being trampled.

"Are there reasons beyond our knowing do you think, Edmund? It is a dramatic and finite end." As if to aid thought Henri felt his chin.

"My thinking is like, Henri. It is true he is unpopular and not just over the cider tax. But he is giving up great power – most would hang determinedly by their fingernails rather than lose all he had."

"Then we must continue to speculate, Edmund, as no doubt – if this noise is proof of sentiment – this house does now."

Despite the crush in the rooms and the probability that every man who had ever taken coffee here, however seldom, now filled the small spaces with informative gossip and knowledgeable oratory, one of the small boys who worked the house had managed to place pot and cups before them.

Edmund settled his empty cup back upon its saucer with respect. "I am afraid, sir, my own news – of some gravity – has been soundly beat in its priority."

"Gravity, my friend – you must out with it? I sense by your buoyancy your news will please us both."

"It pleases me, Henri, beyond measure and I suspect it will please you also." Henri waited, an ear cocked, his most attentive face offered in readiness. "I am to be married, sir, and before the autumn sits upon us."

If the news had come to Latimer a month before, surprise would have followed the statement, but his friend's trip to Bristol – the reasons for it, his prolonged absence and the loosening of his mother's apron strings – had suggested that Edmund may have had other business to see to whilst away. It was wholly good news and he was delighted.

"It is splendid news, friend." Latimer turned in the confines of their corner and took Elcott's hand. "I do not think I need to make second guess where you made acquaintance with your future wife. Offer me a name do."

"Emily, sir, her name is Emily. And make no second guess, your first will be correct. She is the young lady to whom the remaining funds from my client's will – her father – were dispersed. The money was of little consequence, and for that I am grateful; a level of complication that might have been there did not arise. She is quite without blemish and although she has sent me away to consider my proposal until I have spoken with my mother, I will not change my mind. As soon as I am able I will visit again and confirm our betrothal."

Having gratefully and successfully imparted news that he had held close for more than a week, Elcott sat back satisfied. Conversation was not as easy as it might have been; the noise and the fullness of the rooms made any kind of intimacy impossible, but Latimer listened as best he could whilst his friend made description of his time away.

Latimer's thoughts and matters relating to his heart were always kept some depth below surface but his own lack of social engagement sometimes troubled him. He did not mind it but he frequently asked himself questions about it. This prompted him to ask, quite without pre-emption, "Have I become more solitary since this injury, Edmund? Be truthful, I am quite happy to have your honesty."

"What makes you ask this, friend? Is it my news?"

"Perhaps it is, Edmund." It was not. "This last decade I have spent much time away from my home, social engagement has been limited. Yes, I know our meetings here have been sacrosanct but beyond this I do no socialize."

Elcott was amused. "I have never known you to worry over such before, Henri, why now? I believe you have been laid abed too long and now that you are up you over-question what is, or has been the norm. If you wish to go out and meet others socially, then do it. If this will give you no pleasure, then do not."

It would have been far too forward for Edmund Elcott to suggest that such a change in routine and attitude might lead to his friend finding himself a new wife to offer him succour in his widowhood – Mary Latimer had, after all, been dead more than six years.

Soon finding their small corner over-run and any meaningful conversation untenable, Latimer had thanked Edmund for his sound advice – although he could not retrieve any from it – and before the mid-morning had worked his way back through the jostling house to the Waterbere Lane door. So, he must do or don't do and please himself, which had always been his general view of life since responsibility was thrust upon him by his father's early death.

He left the gentlemen of the coffee house to debate Bute's unexpected resignation and walked south across the city towards his own house with the thought at least of seeking the company of his daughters.

The weather was still as fickle as Devonshire weather can be and he had expected another drenching. At the head of Billiter Lane he saw a familiar, although unexpected, figure approaching him – it was Trelawney. He had lived next door to the little man for many years but they had hardly ever spoken and very rarely had Latimer met him in the street.

"Latimer!" Enthusiasm resonated from his voice as brightly as his copper hair flashed in the intermittent sunlight. "I am out for some air and have a determination to do it whilst the sun lingers. I have heard that all has not been well with you."

Trelawney accepted Latimer's hand although Henri could not quite remember how he had offered it. He had no grievance against this man – he knew him and understood him for what he was. Painting and pleasure, whatever form that came in, balanced the scales evenly. From guarded and unguarded talk Henri knew the painter to be a self-absorbed, egotistical lover of life, itinerate and unpredictable – there was very little space in Trelawney's life for any other than Alexander Trelawney.

"It is in the past, Alexander, although I am a little encumbered still." He waved his stick in explanation. Henri offered no more – he did not wish it. "Has your stay in Florence been fruitful?" Henri knew that it had.

"Fruitful? Yes, most certainly so. But then I find it is change that brings about productivity – my return here has been equally as fruitful."

Henri felt an odd sensation of being hampered by too much knowledge and there was something in Trelawney's mood and lack of urgency to move on that told Henri he may still have more to say.

"I have heard that the cloth industry here is not quite as robust as it used? A living to be made still, I hope?"

"A living, yes, and the cloth trade, as you say, is perhaps not quite as lively as it once was. The industry of the northern towns sees them move forward more quickly than we; their mills are large scale and in part mechanised. But my living is well – if a little slowed by my injury."

"We should take a glass together, sir. I am not always at my easel and you surely not always visiting your markets. I had some good brandy run in the year before last, it awaits appreciation and another, like-minded, to taste it. What say we sup together soon?"

Bouncing around in Henri's head was the question he had so recently asked Edmund Elcott – was he reclusive, had he become reclusive of late or had he always been so? Henri had no desire to sup with Trelawney; he could not say that there was no connection, no common ground between them because of course now there was, but if choice had really been his he would have declined.

"Indeed we should, Alexander – we must find a space to do this."

"Let us find a space soon." Trelawney put his short but artistic hands behind his back and rocked a little in his buckled shoes. "Your little coastal boat, does she still run well or have you sold her on to fill a need?"

"*The Lady Rosamunde*, she undergoes repair, but all is well there and I have not had to part with her."

"Then I have a plan, sir. Come you to us the day after tomorrow. Sup and take a glass of good Italian wine. I have need to entertain a gentleman of my acquaintance and his good wife, I paint their daughter and there may be commission to paint the couple upon their estate. He is on the way up and may well have business he can send your way. What say you to that? Come, come and be victualled and hopefully find a little trade along the way."

Latimer looked over his neighbour's cropped head to the street beyond and the general scurrying of people going about their business. Pushed forward by a feeling of disappointment in his own lack of connection to the world at large, he felt suddenly moved to accept Trelawney's offer of hospitality – given a free choice he would not; ease and comfort came in drinking one's own brandy in one's own chair, but his brandy had near gone and his chair had become a lonely one.

"I expect to be dull company, Alexander, but I accept the gesture, yes, I would be glad to sup with you and your new patron. Thank you."

21

Swallows had already begun to appear in the city, firstly in ones and twos swooping down through coach house doors, searching brew-house attics, and then in clutches, fluttering specs floating high up on the warm soft air currents. Trelawney would have his sport and he chose to do this by inviting a mismatch of guests to his home to sup. The afternoon of that day was already upon him but there was no hint of discomfort or repentance on his flushed face as he worked industriously to finish some drapery on the portrait of his new patron's daughter.

As was expected of him, Luca was present in the painting rooms and he was already dressed in moiré coat and breeches. The waistcoat was heavily embroidered and the wide cuffs had been worked in the same way; he was the epitome of a young well-bred gentleman of some worth. Flood continued to refer to him as the young princock, but Rae forgave him his extravagances and enjoyed his comely presence – there was little else the artist's whore could sell to the world other than the sensual shell of his appearance.

"See, see this, Luca." Trelawney dropped his brush amongst the jumble of others on his painting table and wiped his hands. "Have I not told you? She has eyes like a cod fish! I cannot paint her. I must have one of the girls in, they have life in their eyes and their stare is saucy and full of affection."

"Alexander, you will have the girls here soon enough, do not paint more today, be done with it. If you do not wish to show the work to her mama and papa this eve, then do not show it and finish it when you are better placed – there is time yet to give it life."

"You are right, Luca. Whore House Jane and little Maggie. I always enjoy a session with Maggie – she makes such good pose."

Bored, restless for change, Luca stared from the window and picked at his nails. There would at least be entertainment tonight. Leaving his brush where he had thrown it, Trelawney sat on the edge of the scroll bed and watched Luca, understanding his mood but having no sympathy with it.

"You look like a man imprisoned, Luca. Is companionship such a tie? Perhaps I should find you activity that takes you away from that window and will dissolve that despondent look you hold upon your face. You are quite idle, my boy." He was smiling. "Do not find irritant, Luca." He put up his hand in a gesture of appeasement. "I accept that it is I who require idleness so that I may have your company."

"I do not argue with it, Alexander. Do not suggest that I do."

Trelawney scratched at his cropped hair as he considered Luca. "I would set a task for you this day – if you should be so good as to complete it for me?"

"It is not necessary to invent tasks, Alexander."

"I do not invent such – but I require a messenger, an advocate, a spy perhaps, and your good heart also."

"Then you have it." Luca turned from the window and looked at Trelawney through a curtain of pale hair.

"Go down, my boy, go down and see to my household. I care little for opinion, but I will have good victuals and a well-ordered table. See to it – report back to me and tell me how it goes. And find my disagreeable servant, our little Egyptian, and remind her that she is to wear the gown I have given her and that she is to join us when serving is done."

Offered a moment of solitude Trelawney threw off his painting coat and lay upon the bed, he was looking forward to the supper; people were so often unpredictable when set down in uncomfortable company, and he could not see any comfort in the company he had chosen to entertain tonight.

Henri Latimer stretched out his long legs and rested his head back against the faded velvet of his dressing chair. He had just come down from visiting his daughters' rooms and reflected on the promise he had made to his neighbour. A glass of his cook's fruit wine stood on the table beside him – he reached for it, twisted the glass absently in his hand and looked into the ruby depths, pondering the complications that accepting an invitation from Trelawney had brought him. Appeasing quickly come-up, socially aspirational landowners and begging for favours was not his way. But he would rise to it; it was time he made effort to socialize.

Vetch had shaved him earlier, laid out a little-used waistcoat and a good cambric shirt. There was some long time before he would have to leave his room and he was grateful for it. Geoffrey was home, sitting in the large room at the front of the house. The boy would have to sup alone tonight, but perhaps he might go down in a while and talk to him. His nephew's trip seemed to have gone well. The moorland towns and farms were visited and he had made contact again with some of the weavers. Once the fleece he had purchased had been carded and spun the chain would start to work again.

Below him, in the large sitting room, Geoffrey was dulling his rage, a rage that had come upon him during his last coupling with his whore. She was refusing to leave the bawdy house. Staying there meant sharing her, he had never got used to the practice of sharing anything and she had refused his company tonight, using some cobbled and cocked story about helping the bawd – he had not believed her. Taking her wrist in protest he had left marks, quite understandably. The strumpet had been pale of late and a concerning thought had sat in his head all week. Had he left his seed? Could that be why she was reluctant to leave the house? She would be wrong to think that he was prepared to share her with any bastard child.

Frustration swept over him. Plans were made and plans were continually broken or changed. The two or three weeks that he had expected to sit dutifully by his ailing uncle's bedside had now passed into months. The man was up and moving about freely, saints and martyrs, his uncle had even contrived a social engagement tonight; and he, a young man in his prime, with good breeding and his own manor, was reduced to drinking unpalatable English fruit wine alone in these dungeon-like rooms of this unfortunately placed merchant's house – it was untenable. The situation necessitated change – he would not allow fate to outwit him. With none of his uncle's appreciation but with equal thought, Geoffrey refilled his glass. There were things, plans, that sat waiting – audacity might be needed but did he not have that? The documents were secured in his room; in order to make them pay he would have to find an excuse to leave this mercantile city – and it would have to be soon.

Inside the head of the young woman who occupied his thoughts – whore and beauty – ran many concerns surrounding the young man she now termed as lover as well as client. Whilst her thoughts ran she was occupied in a room at the top of the Exebere bawdy house, winding Jane's henna-red hair into impossibly high mounds and fixing the gaudy periwig she wore above it. Despite her whoring life, which to all religious and pious men was the most-wicked, the most heinous, the most immoral of occupations, Mag had an honest heart. But left without option she had lied to Geoffrey Latimer – she could not tell him that she had agreed to sup with Alexander. Mag understood Alexander's black sense of mischief, they were to be part of it, and for that they would be paid well – and besides, the artist had promised to use their advantages in his next portrait.

Pale and fragile from a girl, Mag did not have a growing child in her belly; there was no alteration to the chemistry of her body and Geoffrey's worrying was quite misplaced. A last vicious beating from her husband had violently aborted her twelve-week foetus; she had been barely fifteen then and barren ever since.

Spending her day doing the bidding of others, Rae, however, saw no merit in the evening to come. Kept apart from the sisterhood of the bawdy house by Elijah Flood's resolve to save her soul, and with no determinate position in Alexander's household, she felt a sense of disconnection. If she had choice she would have chosen to remain in the kitchens – she had not been told that Henri Latimer was expected.

Towards the end of the afternoon, having done all that she had to do, she had gone unnoticed to her small room, squeezed between the bootmaker's shop and the kitchen store – a dark airless room with only one small high window to light it. To one corner a pewter jug and washing bowl was set upon a small table; there was little else in the dismal room apart from a low truckle bed, a chair and a half-dozen coarse nails banged into the beam where her clothes were hung. Rae filled the bowl and began to undress, unwinding the thin slither of voile she wore about her neck, releasing the laces on her bodice, dropping her petticoats to the floor. The undergarment she wore was of fine Holland cloth and had come to her from the bawdy house; she did not remove this but began to wash, first her face and then, scooping the water with cupped hands, beneath her arms and about her neck. She had tied up her hair earlier so that it stayed beneath her cap and it hung down about her neck in damp snakes. She took time to wash, drying herself with a square of muslin, patting the wet areas of her gossamer-thin shift – the small mound of her bush and the dark circles of her nipples showing through the cloth.

This room, her space, the place where she spent her private time, was isolated from the rest of the house: a heavy ledge and brace door separated it from the dank passage which served this remote part of Trelawney's tall house. The door was partly open and she glanced into the passageway; darkness engulfed the lower house early and there were no sconces here to light it. She went to the small table and lit the rush-light, placing it on the floor close to the open door, watching the flame throw light into the dark mouth of the passageway.

The sitter's gown was hung on a nail at the end of the small bed and she took the garments down – the hastily made petticoats and the stringed bodice. The colour was good, Alexander understood colour, but the sewing was coarse and the fabric cheap. She stepped into the skirts and fidgeted into the bodice. Perhaps Alexander was well meaning, she had given up any attempt to understand the man – affection for him stirred her conscience and she was suddenly sorry for thinking ill of him. She finished dressing, slipped bare feet into buckled shoes and picked up her apron, looking around the small space before she left it.

The rush-light was guttering mutton fat on the flags; she picked it up and pushed the heavy door wide. The single candle threw light into the late afternoon darkness of the unused passage, bringing it into relief – the dusty webs, the closed storeroom doors. She went forward with her cap and apron under her arm, the aura of light about her lighting her way. She heard a voice and drew back startled by the unexpected.

"You are so hid away down here in the pit of this old house I have had the devil of a search finding you."

Luca was leaning on the wall, one knee bent, his foot against the stone. Her grip was suddenly unsteady, mutton fat overflowed from the rush-light sticking to the back of her hand.

"Hell's Gate, Luca, what mischance and wrong reasoning has brought you here?"

She held up the candle and considered him – he was already dressed for the evening, dressed and dandified, fair hair caught at the nape looking the gentleman she knew he was not.

"No mischance, Rachael, and no reasoning, just a kindly errand." He pushed himself away from the wall and took the light from her holding it high, lighting the space from above.

"You may have found me just as easily in the kitchens, Luca. What errand do send you to seek me so thoroughly?"

"Alexander requires me find you, Rachael – I am to remind you that you must wear the sitter's dress and be biddable at his table this evening."

In return for a new suit, a full belly and a glimpse into a kinder world, Alexander had brought many a young man into this house to satisfy his needs, most had offered her no more than tolerance and indifference – Luca she was finding was a little different.

"Then 'tis a fool's errand, Luca, for he do know I will not go against him." She led the way to the closed kitchen door and he followed her holding the candle high above her head. "You must learn to know him better, Luca, for he is a man of games and whims."

The kitchen was filled with steam and clattering pans, the sound of cooks complaints and Elijah's low-voiced reasoning. He left her there and she put on her apron, pulled up her hair and covered it with her cap, thoughts of Luca gone – thoughts of a more practical kind filling her head.

22

Just before St Mary's clock bells chimed for the eighth hour Rae had gone up to light the wall sconces and tall pewter candle sticks that Flood had prepared in the large upper floor dining room. When she returned to the kitchens Elijah was waiting for her, ushering her up again to lay out the puddings. Now, dancing shadows ran across the darkly polished furniture and she placed damson tarts and gooseberry custard beside thin china serving bowls, and then returned to bring up a round of white cheese, dark bottles of cellar wine and decanted brandy.

A little after nine they had carried the warm dishes up and begun to serve the meats – and the trick, the game, the mischief had shown itself instantly. There were five seated at the table besides Trelawney: Luca, Alexander's patron, his wife and his daughter – and Henri, straight backed, self-control hiding discomfort, was seated between these two women. He acknowledged her with an awkward nod almost as though he had not thought to see her here anymore than she had expected to find him as a guest at Trelawney's supper table.

They had served pickled mackerel and flayed soul. Rae, following Flood's lead, had removed the plates and returned with bowls of finely minced chicken and hard eggs, veal sweet-breads in oyster sauce, a basted leg of mutton and a tureen of stewed peas in bacon broth. Then Flood had left and she had waited for direction; not one life but two – one role slipping seamlessly into another.

*

Trelawney was speaking, and not with any particular kindness. "Do not stand there loitering by the door, Rachael. Come, we will not devour you along with our sweet-breads, a place is set for you, take it." Rae had reluctantly removed her cap and apron. "There beside Luca and next to Mr Buckman." Trelawney nodded his red head between the two of them. "Then, my dear, you may converse with our merchant who is there opposing you from across the table."

Henri looked up and spoke levelly, concerned by her flushed face and agitated hands. "I hope that I will not, Alexander," he said. "I would not wish to oppose any of your dinner guests." He had been foolish to send the book – there would be a debt to pay. He was sorry that he had brought out into the open something that ought to have remained private.

Trelawney seemed in no mood to change course and continued. "But perhaps, Latimer, the title of merchant do not sit so well with you these days?"

"It is a broad description of a trading man, Alexander, covering many levels of business, although I have never found riches in it like many." He knew his reply was a little terse, to redeem himself he turned to Buckman's mouse-like wife. "I understand your husband has traded fruitfully for many years, Mrs Buckman."

Like many, Robert Buckman had begun his fortune by investing in Bristol slave ships; his wife seemed almost sucked dry by her husband's strength of character and success.

"Indeed he has, Mr Latimer, although I know not the whys and wherefores of his business. My husband proclaims that I am quite without understanding when it comes to the nuances of trade." She deferred to her husband.

"Trade is our bedrock, Latimer, there is great wealth to be had in the transportation of productivity. Even the most meagre of incomes ought to be invested in trade. Place a cargo under a reliable master – see it gone to the Africas, bartered with and exchanged" – there was a pause as Buckman altered the flow of his speech – "commodities purchased and then on again to the West Indies, cane sugar replacing commodities and then, God willing, home to England and a share in a tidy profit."

"God willing," Henri repeated examining the pudding fork laid on the damask cloth beside his plate. He wondered what Rae made of this man – her master's patron, someone she must offer a level of servility to. She had been held in a private conversation with the boy they called Luca – he had no idea what was being said, only snippets came to him. The young man was not quite in the mould of others who had come to this house over the years and Rae seemed to have a certain liking for him.

"I am told that you run a small ship yourself, Latimer," Buckman said, picking his teeth.

"The *Rosamunde*. She has been owned by my family for many years – aged now, but with a good sound hull and as quick as a dolphin. She is undergoing repairs and no longer has a crew. In time I hope she will sail and indeed trade again."

"Send me word, Latimer, when she is seaworthy, there is always cargo to be ferried from port to port and my barque is kept too busy elsewhere in the world to sail these coastal waters." Henri nodded, obliged.

Sitting back he took pleasure in the view that had been offered him. Perhaps there were certain merits to socializing even in such uncomfortable company.

"Do you paint, sir?" Buckman was asking Luca. Henri knew that he did not – Trelawney had intervened before the boy could answer.

"Indeed not, Robert. Luca has a penchant for the verse – do you not, Luca, for the rhyme, sir, and not the brush?" The boy's hair, Latimer noticed, was very fair, falling like a curtain over his face – a contrast he supposed to his own dull locks. Catherine Buckman, perhaps drawn to the classical unembellished good looks, ventured to offer her sweetest smile as her mother dared put a question to Trelawney's guest.

"Do you have command of the Italian language, Mr Luca – 'tis such a pretty language, especially if one uses it to write verse?"

"Sadly not, Mrs Buckman. I have only a simple knowledge of the tongue, I prefer to write in my own. Unfortunately, since I have been here I have had very little time for the verse." He threw a look of some malice towards Trelawney. "I am fully occupied watching Alexander paint – and he tells me he does so love to paint your pretty daughter, Madam."

Mrs Buckman almost blushed – Latimer was not so sure that this young man was all he seemed.

Rae was watching the mantle clock as she knew Trelawney would be – he had asked the whores to come late, make an entry, sit resplendent at the head of the table like two figure heads on the prow of a ship, well corseted, gaudily painted and saucy. If she could have saved Henri from this sham then she would have – but perhaps he did not wish to be saved, perhaps she had judged him wrongly?

Buckman's colourless daughter, Trelawney's prey, his latest object of ridicule, was speaking. "I wonder if I may ask, Sir, I have been considering it since we arrived and cannot find an answer to it – I see there are yet two more places laid at this lively table and wonder if 'tis a superstition? I have heard that some will not have seven seated nor seven guests and others are sent into vapours at the thought of thirteen on either count and will lay for a number that is satisfying to them."

"My dear, Miss Buckman, superstition must be viewed for what it is. I am far less complex, my dear – we are to entertain two more ladies, they will join us for the puddings and then we shall be a merry nine and I have never heard of a superstition surrounding that number."

Ever frugal with his observations, Henri waited for conversation to find him. The boy Luca had allowed Rae to be accosted by Buckman and now addressed him across the table. "I hear, Mr Latimer, that your injury was quite severe."

"Severe enough to keep me to my room for some weeks," Henri replied politely.

"I am told that it has left you only a space above cripple – I hope I do not give offence."

"I do not take offence if offence is not intended. It is true I am permanently with a stick but there is improvement daily and I must remain optimistic."

Presiding over the proceedings like a wigless judge, attuned to all that was said in his court, Trelawney interceded. "And what say you, Rachael, to Mr Latimer's returning health? Are you not glad that he no longer has his hand laid firmly upon death's door?"

"I am more than glad, Alexander, and I am sorry if he was ever at death's door. And I care not if he do carry a stick or no."

"My ward is glad for you, sir, is that not a comfort to you Latimer?"

"I believe your ward has a generous heart, Trelawney," Henri said turning respectfully towards the head of the table. Trelawney huffed, sensing perhaps the chase over.

"Luca, it is late – dear boy, look over the banister and see if you can spot the dissenter ushering in the ladies. I am in want of my pudding."

Luca had risen – a little too obviously compliant. Rae, sitting awkwardly on her stuffed chair, looked anxiously towards the door. A space behind Flood, the old servant's white hair and sombre coat in sharp contrast to their garish red skirts and fancy feathers, were two of the bawdy mother's finest daughters.

Henri's eyes went to seek Rae's and she returned his look with resignation. He supposed she would have been privy to this, but what she had obviously not been privy to was his inclusion on the guest list. He waited for the startled silence to evolve into something other – social preservation perhaps. Trelawney was eccentric, prone to extravagant ideas and these girls were his studio models and sat for him often.

"My dears, settle yourselves and I shall have Flood serve the puddings." Trelawney, delighted with the effect, begun to make introductions. "Jane, my dear, who here do you know? Indeed I should ask who do you not know – and Maggie such a pleasant addition to any table."

Warmed with drink and satisfaction Trelawney pushed the conversation on. "Latimer, I have heard tell that there are churches enough in this city to have opportunity to visit one each day of the month and still have some to occupy your time in the next, what say you to this suggestion?"

Now resigned to this pantomime Henri answered easily. "I would not argue with the idea, Alexander. I know there are many, and of every persuasion."

"Indeed there are – a church built in reverence to a score of saints, dissenters' halls in number, a brace of Jewish tabernacles and papist high house. In larger cities is it not the whorehouse, the brothel that wins out in number? I have pondered this, Latimer – do the appetites of men differ in this city, or is it perhaps that our houses are well hid?"

"I have never had the need to consider the possibility, Alexander, I visit neither with any regularity." He felt his comment bounce around the table.

Delighted Trelawney continued. "Perhaps we must conceive the possibility, dear sirs, that there may be a brothel of sorts in every street, even this one."

The candles, she noticed, were burning low and the pudding dishes had been piled on the sideboard without care. She wished to rise and help Flood but she had been forbidden. Henri was looking at her in her cheap blue dress with her hair untamed and her hands red with kitchen work.

Buckman coughed into his fist. "I hear you have two daughters, Latimer. Girls – still young. What think you to female teaching and boyish notions? I cannot say as I am in agreement with it. Do you tease their brains with book reading and pen writing? My wife would have it that Catherine should have her books, and here she is a girl of two and twenty with no sound suitor in her sights."

Sensing come kind of trap, Henri had answered honestly. "My daughters, as you rightly say, are young but they have great capacity for learning, especially the elder. I would not wish to hamper their understanding of things by disallowing such a necessary skill."

"My ward has a penchant for picture books, Latimer," Trelawney interrupted. "Even though she reads tolerably well for a girl of her birth – what is your opinion on such nonsense?"

"I can see wealth in all books; knowledge, inner-thoughts, scientific-findings, is it not a way towards wisdom as much as direct observation of the same – the picture book is surely both combined."

At the other end of the table Jane had her head back laughing, Buckman was filling her glass. Rae knew how it would be, every man a puppet if Jane pulled their strings – even Mag beside her seemed to have found some common ground with Buckman's wife. She watched them, the winners and the losers, the timid and the overconfident, and those under sufferance. She wanted to stand, clear, escape to the kitchens and wait until it was all over – go to the derelict balcony and watch the night.

Beside her Luca was attentively listening to Catherine Buckman.

"You may clear, Rachael. I believe we are done." She stood and silently began removing the pudding bowls – perhaps Trelawney had finished with her.

"Will you not light a pipe alongside us, Latimer?" Trelawney clicked his fingers in Flood's direction. "I do not send the ladies out."

Henri, the unchanging shell of who he was closed about him, nodded slightly in respect. "I'm afraid, Alexander, I cannot. I am little used to spending my nights away from my home and I have a little work to do before the morrow."

Rae saw he had stood and would not be persuaded to participate longer in Trelawney's mischief.

"Pity, business is a dull master sometimes."

"Don't forget my offer, Latimer," Buckman was saying.

"Indeed I shall not."

Moving away to the cluttered sideboard she waited for Henri to leave, waited until Alexander found other sport.

As she reached the ground floor Henri was still there being handed his hat by Trelawney's cook. She had never quite seen him like this, tall, erect – sombre.

"A delightful evening, Rachael, and an excellent meal," he said, the set of his jaw sliding into a smile.

Cook was gone bustling back to the kitchens and she stood with the pudding bowls clutched in her hands.

"Trelawney will be glad to know it," she said awkwardly.

"A discordant group," he said.

"A discordant evening, Henri."

"But not without merit."

She blushed. "How are you here, Henri?"

"I believe we must blame my enticement here upon a weakness of spirit, Rae, and a pocket of doubt."

She watched him go, drop his head as he found the door, looking back at her with a half-smile and an element of sympathy. "I hope it will not be too long before we meet again."

23

Sleeping well Henri rose early, dressed without the help of Vetch and made his way down to his breakfast room in time to meet his daughters going out.

"Sarah." He nodded to the old woman without smiling. "All is well?"

"Yaes, zir, well, thank 'ee zir." Obeying tradition she bobbed to him although he felt there was no need. Perching on the hall settle and laying his stick down beside him he spoke more gently to his daughters.

"It is a good day to be venturing out, the weather is quite fine. Come to me here and tell me where you go. Come, Mary, Sophia." They stood dutifully before him as was expected of them. "Let me see you. Turn around now. Let me see that you are ready to greet the world." They spun in their simple clothes, white lace caps sitting squarely on newly brushed hair. He held each child at arm's length and studied them, stern faced, intentionally holding back a smile. "Are your cheeks comely-pink and smiling?" He lightly pinched their cheeks in turn, replacing the serious-faced attention that they offered him with laughter. He let them go. "Now, where do you go, to the meadow or to shop – or someplace other?"

"We have not made the choice, Papa," Mary said, glancing for clarification at Old Sarah waiting for them like an overfull sack on a loading stool.

"Then I will make it for you." Henri sought an inner pocket, took out a handful of coin. "Go to Fore Street, or beyond if you wish it" – he opened his palm – "make impromptu purchase. That little doll you have under your arm, Sophia, do surely need a sister." He spread the coins about and pointed to a farthing. "This to buy a liquorice stick – if you so wish. And this…" he placed the tip of his finger on a larger coin "…to buy a penny wooden. You may choose, you may have both or you may have ribbons. Here, I will settle it evenly. A penny ha'penny each and be wise with your choices." He took hold of their small hands, placed the coins in each and rose. "Is Master Geoffrey down?"

Mary bobbed to her father. "No, Papa, not this day."

"Thank you. Be as good as you are."

Henri watched them go. It was a pleasant and welcome interlude, interrupting the more serious things he had set his mind to. He took his stick and made his way to the large room where breakfast was already laid out – and waited for Geoffrey.

He took oysters; Geoffrey had ordered them, he would have the same. By the time his nephew came down he was cutting a second slice of warm bread and nothing remained of the oysters save a pile of gnarled pearly shells.

"Nephew," he said brightly. The *Old Exeter Herald* was spread out beside him on the table. "Is it not a fine day to be alive?" Latimer pushed long fingers through untidy hair, the action sub-conscientiously prompted by his nephew's well-ordered appearance and tight queue.

Disguising the annoyance he felt in having his pleasant, solitary breakfast disturbed by this man, Geoffrey replied, "And so it is, Uncle." His uncle was looking altogether healthier than he ought to be, and he had eaten his oysters.

"Have no fear," Latimer said, reading his nephew's thoughts, "I am informed there are plenty more on the slab needing nothing more than a twist of the knife and a quarter of lemon." Geoffrey sat down opposite his uncle and rang the small bell kept on the table to summon staff. Latimer surreptitiously read the journal whilst his nephew ate. "Have you plans for the day?"

Geoffrey was certain sure his uncle had only contrived to be seated at this late breakfast time because he had a bundle of awkward and most probably unanswerable questions to ask him, ones that could not be countered without a lie. Discouraging himself from giving any reply until he had time to think he wiped his mouth on the cambric square sent along with the oysters for this purpose.

"Not of any certainty. Did your evening progress well, Uncle?" he asked without any interest in knowing.

"Tolerably well – a worthy table and an evening not without event." He would not say more and returned to his paper.

Geoffrey finished his porter and waited for his uncle to look up from his reading. "I wonder, sir, might I confide in you now that we talk of plans?"

Sometime soon he would need to take a trip into Dorset or possibly as far as Somerset, and seeing his uncle so improved and anticipating the questions that would soon be bubbling from his lips, that trip might have to be sooner rather than later. "My mama's health is less than good." It was an idea he thought he might use, an excuse to travel freely and without question – but he had not thought to spin the story quite yet. "I have received a letter this day." He took a folded paper from his pocket – the seal already broken. "She has some malady that brings her low and has asked for me." He laid the letter on the table beside his uncle's broadsheet.

The letter he had unearthed from his pocket had arrived some time ago and had lain there unread for several days. It would only be the usual bemoaning of life, more details of the families indebtedness – accusations on his slowness to alleviate his mother's suffering. Geoffrey knew Latimer would not read it.

"I would ask for a prolonged visit, several days perhaps, if you will permit it, sir? There will be no need to organize a livery horse for me, I will take the coach to Bridport – our manor is no more than a five-mile jaunt from the turnpike."

"I am sorry to hear your mother is unwell," Latimer said, assessing his nephew and this new idea. "Age brings complications."

"It do, sir. She is all of four and forty, and perhaps a little more besides."

Spinning around in his chair and stretching his leg Latimer said after a moment's thought, "Of course you must go, Geoffrey. I will pay for your ticket – let me have notice when you wish to leave and I will arrange as much."

It irked Geoffrey largely that Uncle Latimer always seemed to manage to outmanoeuvre him, and with no apparent effort. His intent was not, in point of fact, to take the coach to Bridport. He had no intention of repeating his last visit to his dour and complaining mother; his trip would be to Sherborne, or further if need be, taking him far enough away from this city and his uncle to achieve the secrecy that his plan necessitated.

"There is no need, Uncle, I have a little left of your allowance and my mama, when she is able, sends me what she can spare."

"I insist upon it, Geoffrey," Latimer said. "When will your trip be? Have you made any plans?"

"I thought the day after tomorrow, sir, or within the week."

"You must be quite anxious for her – I hope she is not worse than you have told."

"I am concerned, sir, she is quite alone."

"If the world were a right and fair place I would not keep you here, but if I am to pass the business on to you, then you must learn its quirks and turns. Most of what has come to me has gone in debt redemption and paying the mortgages laid upon the house – but there will be time ahead when profit will run freely again. I sense that it is capital that is required to re-build the prosperity of your manor farm."

"Indeed it is, Uncle." Geoffrey took a silent breath, cursed his uncle under it and then cursed himself for not having broken his fast at The Swan.

Latimer rose, stretched, his head coming close to the beams.

"I have a mind to trek over to Moreton this week, the wild air will do me good and the weather has changed for the better."

Geoffrey stood also, folded his arms across his expensive tailoring and looked out onto the street to hide his irritation.

"I'm afraid I will need a little clarity before I do." Latimer said. "The farms you chose to visit – marked upon my map? Pennymoor at Bridcombe, wasn't it? Good stock, wool of some quality and the whole family involved in carding and spinning. A well-considered choice, I have done good trade with them before and their cloth is sound, worked on a shuttle loom." Henri rasped his stubble and feigned poor memory even though his memory was never poor.

"And old man Yeo at Lower Venny, he works with his son and daughter-in-law, not quite the same productivity, they have but one loom, but I have done business there for many years." The heat was rising about Geoffrey's neck – unconsciously he ran his fingers between his gullet and his stock. "How many other farms did you visit? I have never run more than a dozen at any one time. The question remains, have they promised their cloth elsewhere or will they return to us?"

Latimer went to the window, looked out and then turned unexpectedly. "We cannot expect a weaver to wait indefinitely for our custom even if he has sold to us for some years."

Geoffrey considered his reply, his manicured fingers tapping the side of his breeches. "I am sure there will be no difficulty in them returning business to us, Uncle. I sensed there might be a slight disillusionment with the new clothiers, they are apparently quite irregular in their visits and poor payers."

Latimer considered this. He thought it unlikely that the Pennymoor family would have found the time to divulge such sensitive observations – educated to only the most basic level beyond their skills, they were hardly articulate.

"I believe, sir," Geoffrey continued, "it is you they would prefer to see and do business with. They do not know me from any other Adam."

"Then let us be heartened," Latimer said, looking through the window at the bright day. "I will visit while you are away." And, he added, reining in his optimism a slight, "I will take the pack road to Moreton and journey as far as this…" he tapped his stick against his leg "…allows me to do."

Geoffrey waited to be released. "The other thing," Henri said, looking squarely at his nephew and meeting his eyes, "the fleece you purchased at the Crediton sale – I see you have quite correctly entered it within the cash book but I cannot see to which weavers the load was sent?" Latimer fixed his nephew with cool blue eyes. Without searching, he took the small cash-book from a pocket and flipped it open but did not look at it. 'The Idely weavers, perhaps? Or possibly Yeo Cross? Let me have their names nephew and I will take pencil to paper now and make entry, and in a fortnight we will run up with some pack ponies and begin to collect our serges and then present them to the Quaker for fulling."

24

Preparing to step up into the Bridport Coach, Geoffrey shook his uncle's hand with all the sincerity of a perjurer. The unplanned meeting with his uncle had pushed things on, forced him to bring forward plans that perhaps had only ever been possibilities. And time was short; a visit to Blox had been necessary. By the time he returned Uncle Latimer would be back in the city and would know that Geoffrey had visited neither farm nor weaver; he could no longer dally between decisions. In order to quell any suspicion he must run a straight line. He could not alter the plans Uncle Latimer had set in place; he would either have to continue on to Dorchester – which was not his choice, as he had lost once too often at the gaming tables there and sense told him to stay away – or, alternatively, make the arduous and indirect trip from Bridport to Yeovil on a second coach.

The forged documents were secure in the inner pocket of his heavy coat, rolled and tied and ready to alleviate his insolvency. Refusing to join in any amiable introductions with his fellow passengers, he settled the brim of his tricorn over his brow, rested his head against the dusty seat cushion and affected sleep. There were two clear choices open to him: selling the documents – or the shares that they represented – and pocketing the money, or using them as surety and raising a loan.

The pale and flimsy little whore had given him her best before he had left. She had professed that she would miss him; he anticipated that she would. Compliant and receptive she had made no protest when his ardour had forced him to turn her arm. He might miss her – a little – and to keep her at the Seven Stars he had paid for both the room and her services in advance.

Rutted roads and a swaying coach, accompanied by inane conversation was the quickest way to send a man to sleep. Imagining a world where there were no complications, seeing the promissory notes, bags of coin and hearty handshaking that he felt must come to him when he presented the documents to an understanding bank, Geoffrey had passed into fitful slumber. He had already set other plans in motion and he doubted his uncle's trip would be as uneventful as he had anticipated.

Although common sense told him otherwise, Latimer had been determined to keep family together and believe his nephew honest. He did not mind particularly that he was wayward, preferring fine clothes and good living to work, and indeed had already found himself indebted. Latimer could see a certain unfairness in the way fate had dealt with his half-brother's posthumous child, but he himself would not have taken such a route; he was not like his father. He had aimed his helm in an opposite direction, solvency and constancy had been his reward, but now, almost fully recovered, common sense had begun to win out – he would make checks and assure himself that all had been done as Geoffrey had reported.

Returning from St Sidwell Street where he had settled his nephew on the Bridport coach, Latimer had passed through the South Gate and visited the livery on the Topsham turnpike. Although other merchants scoffed at his inefficiency in not keeping his own stable – and pack horse train – without suitable premises, and a desire to keep his trading to a level where he could oversee all its workings himself, he felt little impetus to do this. He stood in the yard at the rear, straight backed with only the slightest need for his stick. Since his return to health he had found sitting atop a good horse disguised all sign of infirmity.

The yard was busy – a half-dozen grooms worked in the small space, some holding fast to rearing mettlesome beasts others struggling under the weight of saddle leather and tack, muck-boys moving between it all with steaming buckets of dung. The head groom was a small man dominated by his boots; Latimer waited patiently while he finished tightening the girth-straps of a lively grey. Henri had always felt a sense of permanence here in this yard, solid and unchanging, but was not the world about him changing – the centuries old trade of turning fleece into good serge, buying from cottagers, many still with a single loom, hauling the woven cloth over the back of a pack horse and then bringing it back for fulling? Trading, bartering, shipping – the trade was honest and simple. In the north and middle lands of the country there seemed more of a hunger to expand, cottagers had moved into small factories and the shuttle loom had already made changes to productivity. Perhaps one day, after his time, the whole process might be mechanised.

He would not request a mount today, tomorrow would be soon enough to settle his suspicions and there were many pressing tasks to occupy his time for the rest of the day, including an intended appointment with his bedroom window to watch the evening light disappear over the city skyline.

"Such haste, Mr Latimer, in the leaving of us last eve and the puddings barely finished. Did your host not entertain you well?"

"My host entertained me well enough, the fair was substantial, the serving of it enjoyable and the company surprising – although not all to my liking – but the hostess, barring a few niceties to show etiquette, refused to talk to me."

Henri was leaning from his window, hands on the sill, stick against the wall.

"It is a falsehood, Henri – I did not refuse. I talked as much as I was able and all along with the risk of another teasing. And I am not hostess in that house."

"Well, I would view you as such – there was little competition for the role." There was some accuracy in his statement. "And did you receive a teasing once I had left?" Henri continued, watching her dark head, obscured by the few remaining slates on the gallery roof.

"I did not, Henri. Alexander, sat amongst his favourites, was far too occupied with himself and did not have thought for me."

"Then you are unhooked for a time."

"No, Henri, we are unhooked – for it was you who sent that little book and began his curiosity."

"It pleased me to buy it and to send it once I had."

He looked out towards the obscured horizon that was his view: the watery April sun had long since left the courtyard and the only evidence that it had ever been there was the reflected glow laying across the river as it set over the north-west edges of the city.

Rae did not answer him directly. "Words are so much easier to find when you are half-hid from another," she said. She had taken off her cap and idly spun it around in her hands.

"Your observation surprises me, Rae, and I am not sure it is necessarily a right one – did you not find pleasure in sharing a table with me?"

"And be made to sit starched back between Mr Luca and Mr Buckman, and have you look upon me wearing that foolish sitter's gown and all my hair a mess with kitchen work? I am not sure that I did, Henri Latimer." Henri pondered the need to keep his liaison with his neighbour's servant private, concluding that the spice of it was in the secrecy.

Rae leant on the gallery balustrade, arms folded, matching Latimer's.

"It is timely that I have found you here, Rae," Henri said after a moment. "This very day I have arranged for a mount and will be from my bed early tomorrow and on route to Moreton before the house has begun breakfast."

"Then it is timely, Henri," she said avoiding any note of disappointment. "And if you had not found me, how would I know that you were gone away?"

"Because you would reason me gone from my closed window, and you would know that if I were here it would always be opened to you."

"And if I am not here on this derelict walkway to greet you when you return, Henri, will you think me gone away?"

"No, Rae, I would think you hiding."

"And would you look for me, Henri?"

"Indeed I might."

"What takes you out of this city? Cannot your surly nephew go on your behalf? The man do look at me in such a way, Henri, and not a smile nor a good day coming from him."

"Then I shall have word with him. There is no requirement to be surly, his lot is far better than many and I ask little enough of him. But in truth, he avoids my company and although I have not heard rumour upon the subject, I would wager he may be keeping company."

Unable to tell an untruth, honesty always sought her out and she was torn between keeping a confidence and telling the truth. She hoped Henri would not ask her any deeply dug questions.

"I am glad you are able to make this trip away for it is only a short time passed that you could not think of it. I am glad, but I believe I will be better glad when you return."

"My good health is as surprising to me and I am grateful for it – but I shall keep this little stick for a while longer, and to answer your question, it is trade that takes me out of the city, that and a need to get atop of life again. I shall be away just a few days, and if you are not here waiting to talk to me on this decaying gallery when I return I shall seek you in your kitchen meeting house – and if you are not there I shall enter the lodging and confuse the bawdy mother into thinking I have changed my spots."

25

Buzzards were drifting far up in the almost colourless sky, shadowing the wooded valley of the Kenn. Latimer pulled in his mount and watched them: dark distinctive shapes, circling, changing places with one another and then floating effortlessly in the temperate air. He had already visited a weaver at Idely, his first call after leaving the city. The man, apologetic, confused and more than a little surprised, had neither spoken to nor had any dealings with any relative of Mr Latimer's. No, he would not have forgotten, and none of the fleeces brought to his tiny cottage to card and spin had come from any young man calling himself Latimer.

Self-consciously twisting a well-worn boot in the red earth surrounding his cottage, the weaver had admitted that he thought Henri dead. The continuous footfall of packhorses to and from the city across the Exe meant news was easy come by, and the reports were that the merchant was dead or near death and would have no requirement for good quality cloth in his next life.

In repetition of Geoffrey's journeying provisions, strapped onto the back of Latimer's saddle was a leather pouch containing bread and cheese and a stone flagon of cook's fruit wine – which had been ready corked and left out for him on the slab in the still room. Already feeling a level of discomfort from such a long ride, Henri leant back and reached for the jar. Unless sourced from one of the reliable springs in the city, water was of dubious quality – wine and ale were altogether safer. With lips made dry from the dusty pack road he drank gratefully from the cooling earthenware.

Looking out across the verdant land he considered the day so far and the concerns that it had already stirred. Much earlier this morning, waiting in the yard of the Holloway Street livery, Latimer had turned sharply to the sound of Edmund Elcott's voice. It shouldn't have been such a surprise to him, the young man often used the same livery.

They had greeted each other with a long-held handshake and Henri had wanted to know more about Elcott's progressing courtship. Sourced through the gossipy tittle-tattle that found him, and his daily business with the merchants and fullers, Elcott knew most of what was happening in the city and they had spoken for some time. Only some of this settled defiantly in Henri's head – enteric fever, mostly confined to the hovels about Rougemont, was proving to be endemic.

A third buzzard had joined the other two and the broad-winged raptors drifted off further up the valley. Another six or seven miles would have to be covered until he reached the Pennymoor's farm at Bridcombe, and he had not expected to feel quite so drained. Yes, it was true he had not travelled this far or anything like it for many months, but stamina seemed lacking; he would rest at Bridcombe, he liked the family and they were always hospitable. Henri never offered negativity before a thought but he knew that when he reached the farm the true character of his nephew would be out and he did not feel particularly positive.

Edging into the moor the road was isolated; he looked for the track to Bridcombe – he would need to drop down from the old pack-road and cross the Teign before he reached the farm. A disturbance of the dusty earth and the deep-voiced encouragement of the pack-train master forewarned him of a change in his solitude. He pulled sharply on the reins, turning the foaming mouth aside, feeling the strength of his mount, the horse's rebellious dance leading him backwards into the scrub. Leaning over the forelock, he stilled the beast, waited whilst the train passed him.

A dozen or more sturdy pack ponies, obediently in line with serges draped across their wooden pack-saddles, passed him in turn. As the last came level with him he drew himself up straight; the movement perhaps a little sudden, disturbing his equilibrium, sending his head swimming between his ears until determination restored his balance. He took this reaction as a warning – he should not expect so much from a body that not so long ago had lain upon a deathbed. Leaning forward again he ran a gentle hand down the chestnut flank of the powerful beast. He must take time, perhaps the Pennymoor's farm was as far as he would journey today – what point would there be in journeying further? If business had not been done here, then it would not have been done anywhere.

Even the dry spell could not see off the quagmire of mud and dung that dwelt about the farmyard. There were weeds and grasses growing from every receptive piece of earth, from the ancient thatch to the doorstep herbage. But it was not an unwelcoming sight, just the reverse: the sensation of timelessness, of souls having trod this way before his time, dispelled the sense of dark gloom that had begun to surround him.

The door to the cottage was open. He could hear the sound of a shuttle loom coming from the small cave-like room. He found a rusting chain and tethered the mare, pushed the door a slight wider, ducking his head under the beam. A fire was permanently lit in these low stone cottages, as much to dispel the damp as to heat the room and warm the pot. The two small rooms were divided by an oak screen and a ladder ran up to a loft. He could see the weaver working away in the second room, the stool beside a spinning wheel was empty. Losing lucidity again, Henri lifted an uncertain hand to the beam above him. He regretted not having his stick.

"Sir, is it Mr Latimer?" The voice came from behind him close to his elbow. "I assured myself that it were you when I saw you fording the dry stream, but then thought lay in doubt. Mother has gone off to Moreton market and 'tis easier to milk the cow where she grazes."

The young woman, swathed in white apron and cap, held a plump round-faced child upon her hip. Henri took off his hat in greeting.

"I intrude, forgive me. I expected the room full – it has been so previously."

"And so it normally is, sir, but a hedge is down in the lower field and Tom has sent the boys out along with Granfer to bring back the straying flock, and as I did say mother is away for the day." She observed Latimer's hand upon the beam. "There is a good old chair there, sir, if you would prefer to sit. Tom will not hear you. I'll tell 'ee and lay the babe down – fetch you a jug of ale all in the same moment, if you can settle a while."

"Thank you." Latimer sat heavily, gripping the arms of the well-worn oak carver and resting his head gratefully against the curved spindle back. When he opened his eyes again the clatter of the loom had ceased and young Tom Pennymoor was perched before him on a spinning stool.

"You are the last soul I expected to see sitting aside my hearth, Mr Latimer," he said, holding out a mug of ale. "No, sir, stay as you are. There is no need for any hurrying. Take a time to waken fully. 'Tis a long way out from the city and the sun is hotter than it should be."

Latimer had lost time. He could not say how much time had passed, but longer than the blinking of any eye and the settling of a coat tail. There were other people in the room, sitting or standing, crouching on the floor; the baby was asleep in his box, and old man Pennymoor was leaning on the door-jamb drawing on a pipe.

"I sincerely apologize," Latimer said, leaning forward and taking the beer.

"I had no intent to come upon you without warning and settle myself unbidden in your hearth-chair."

"We are glad to see you, Mr Latimer. Glad indeed, for we had not nor never expected to have your company again."

Reality dawned, the comment answered any questions Henri might put to them.

"I understand I am reported dead," he said lightly, the intent to question them upon his nephew's visit evaporating. They did not reply. "As you see the report is untrue." He put up a hand. "I am flesh and blood, although on this afternoon quite feebly so." He must run on a different tack. "Returned good health had duped me into thinking I might manage a trip out to Moreton, but I see now it is too far for one day. I hope to trade again in the close future and thought to visit the pack-road weavers – and old friends," he added. Latimer looked about him, his steel eyes unfocused and unusually quiet.

"Then rest, sir, there is no need to stir yourself from that chair until you are able. There be space enough for another body here for a while longer."

Henri ran a hand through his unkempt hair. He had an overwhelming need to put his head back and close his eyes – and he did not see how this tiny room could accommodate another in addition to the family that made it their home. "I thank you for your hospitality, a short rest perhaps." There was silence in the room whilst he supped his ale. It was this part of the woollen trade he best liked. Honest and simple, skilled men and women, without complexity, without greed. "I see your industry continues." Henri stood the empty mug on the slate hearth. "I hope we can do business again soon. Time runs through – I am unsure how many weeks it has been since I have taken cloth back to Blackaller."

"Five months, sir," the weaver interrupted respectfully.

"Five months," Henri repeated closing his eyes. "Then it must not be another five before I call again."

26

Glancing idly out across the empty courtyard with no direction to her thoughts save the absence of Henri Latimer, Rae slid a wide drawer from Trelawney's clothes chest and began to shake out a newly laundered cambric shirt. Henri had not opened his window last eve as expected; business, she concluded, had dips and turns and it was probable he had travelled a slight further than anticipated. She laid the shirt upon the open drawer and began to arrange sleeves and lace in neat folds before adding it to the clothing already piled on Alexander's dressing chair. His travelling chest was set open on his rarely used bed but she would not pack until she was certain sure everything he might need for his time away was prepared and in order.

A disjointed mix of likes and dislikes, favourable opinions and prejudices, Trelawney had decided he would paint at the Buckman's manor on the edges of the Haldon Forest, despite his refusal in past times to ever work anywhere other than his well-used rooms in Exebere Street. It was a change in habit, as was the endurance of his relationship with Luca – rarely did Trelawney's affairs last longer than a second moon. The table mirror was tilted at an absurd angle and she went to it and levelled it so that her own image came into view. It was not an image she knew well, mirrors were for middle-floor living; without vanity, she did not seek their reassurance.

For a moment she was caught by her own presence, was goaded into examining her own appearance. Womanhood and the changes it made to her body had come upon her unawares – she was far from child, had not been regarded so by the laws of the country for some five years. But unlike many of her age, she had not been taken by any man, either willingly or unwillingly – nor as wife – and if it had not been for the close proximity of Henri Latimer she might have felt the need to look outside these walls for a suitor.

She began to settle breeches, garters and stockings into the wooden trunk. The unreliable sun had been hiding for most of her working morning but now appeared from dark cloud to light up the courtyard. The brightness was an inducement to look out onto her city world and it pleased her to do so even though it was not a world that she had been born to.

She turned at the sound of a boot – Luca was idly leaning against the doorjamb.

"What view is this you pore over, Rachael? 'Tis dull surely looking out on such an empty and imprisoned little fish-yard. I can see nothing but the workings of household necessity and the bootmaker-son's enterprise." She did not look up. "Or do you find fondness with the view of fish buckets, laundry lines and whorehouse linen?"

He came into the room and stood behind her. Turning sharply, she found her face a hand's breadth away from his lace. She did not take his lead nor answer his goad but nimbly side-stepped, freeing herself without necessity to touch him or be touched by him.

"And what lack of better things has bought you here to stop me in my work and hamper my thoughts?"

"I cannot believe I hamper your thoughts, Rachael, merely push your day along. Company and talk do surely make a task seem more quickly done."

She began to fill the trunk with sharper movements than before. There was an adjustment in Luca's attitude towards her of late. In the early days of their acquaintance he had been willing to befriend her, to take her part against Trelawney; she did not understand the reason for the mood change.

"What confusion you are, sir. Are you not satisfied with the place you have and the thought that you are to stay at Haldon Manor and be treated in a lordly way?" Luca unfolded his arms and went slowly towards Trelawney's bed, laying himself easily upon it, indolently crossing his legs. "If you lie there watching me, Luca, you will muddle my work and the whole will take longer than need be." He was quietly dressed today, just a waistcoat over shirt and breeches. Avoiding taking obvious note of him, she moved to a cupboard to bring out wig powder and rouge.

"Then ignore me, Rachael, and work on – I will take your company as it comes."

She opened the lid of a small box and began settling the things inside. Her hair was loose and she pushed it away from her eyes.

"How long will you be gone away? How long will you stay at Haldon do you suppose, Luca? Alexander do not take himself off for such jaunts in usual times – his time in this county is most usually spent in this house."

"I cannot say, Rachael, I cannot say what interests him there – perhaps he has become more artist than money-maker and seeks the purity of his brush for a change? Or perhaps he needs distraction. He is to set the prosperous couple amongst their own belongings and fields."

Rae turned her back on him whilst she fetched small-linen from the top of the press.

"'Twill be at the least one week, I do suppose."

"I would say longer, although I am not privy to his thoughts."

"Then you must be glad of the change, Luca, and all that it offers – to live in a lordly way and dine at a fat table, will you not like it?"

"Perhaps I will, perhaps I must, there is little interest there for me unless there are others in our party – but perhaps I will make sport of Miss Buckman, she has me down for a poet and will not be dissuaded from it. Shall I learn some lines by rote, Rachael, and convince her that her perception is real."

"I believe you ought not, Luca, but I do not care much in any direction for it is you who must keep the lie running once you have begun it." She continued to search the drawers of the tall walnut chest on tiptoes. She heard him rise from the bed and drop his feet to the boards.

"Why do you choose this life, Rachael, when another freer one awaits you, so close you could smell it if you wished? Each time Alexander has a whim to be gone you wait obediently here for him to return, with expectation that when he does he will direct you through your life choices – between times you have no place in any life. It is a waste, Rachael."

She turned, linen draped over her arm. "Do not talk around in maizey circles, Luca. The only waste here is the time you do waste bothering me."

"You should welcome my bothering, Rachael – it seems to me that you have quite shut yourself away from life's options. Why spend your days in dun serge and workday linen when you could show the world a fancier view?"

"I do not wish to show a fancy view to the world, Luca. I am yet to know my path forward, and when I do I shall take it without guidance and most especially from you." She closed the lid of the chest shut with an abruptness that made the clasp rattle. "I am done here and I believe you are done here also, Luca."

There was movement in the passage – the sound of Alexander's small deliberately placed feet preceding his arrival. He looked into the room.

"This house is as quiet as a nunnery during vespers!" he said. "No sign of my black-eyed gypsy scurrying about my business and no slothful companion to offer me encouragement in my frustrated journey across that accursed canvas – and here you both are in one."

"Alexander." Luca had stiffened his back, pulled his waistcoat straight. "We are not far into the house, Alexander, and may be sought at any time." Luca moved about the room, looking for reasons for his presence perhaps. "Rachael finds quandary in packing your chest, Alexander. Do she fill the space with work clothes or do she fill the same with waistcoats and lace frills for gaiety and entertainment?"

"I care not, dear boy, what she fills it with – the lack of waistcoats and frills does not limit gaiety. I have far more interest in this day than the next and tedium is already stamped upon it."

He had studied Luca with the observant eyes of creativity. His lack of inclusion in this liaison fed his short temper and a need to have command of those he kept for amusement and facility had fuelled it further. He scratched his head through his cropped flame-red hair.

"You may choose how you spend your time when I have no need of you, Luca, but that need has not yet passed. I do not buy you chased buckles and brocade so that you may idle your time with my servant. I am parched dry with lack of affection and as stiff as a serge on tenterhooks."

Trelawney had turned on his nimble heels and Luca had followed. Left alone again Rae had not dwelt on what either man had said in her presence, she was thinking far more of the coach that would arrive with the freshness of the day and the quiet time that would follow her master's departure.

27

Returned now from attending his ailing mother, Geoffrey had agreed to meet up with Mudge. They had visited an unpromising whorehouse in a dingy little hovel off Bartholomew Street, then, finding the offerings not to his taste, Geoffrey had left. Hands in pockets he had crossed the city to The Swan where he had watched the last bloody moments of a cock fight, emptied his pockets on the next bout and feeling a sense of persecution had determined to cross the river to Alphington.

Picking his way along the cobbles of Bridge Street in the direction of the Seven Stars, cursing to himself on the state of the gutters and the obsession of slopping out from upper-floor windows, he assessed the events of the last few days. If the success of the thing could be measured in how much money he had left in the Honiton bank – or the weight of his cash box now firmly hid in a locked drawer in his rooms – then perhaps it had been a success; but if measured against expectation, it had not. He had been forced to visit both Sherborne and Dorchester in his quest to find a bank, and then latterly, a broker, who was willing to part with liquid cash in return for a solid holding in the Quaker's tucking mill.

The journey had started well enough; he had left the coach at Bridport, taken victuals and a lodging in the main coaching inn there, filled his evening with a game of chance, succeeded in cheated a deuce of old men out of their pocket change and left early the next morning on the coach to Sherborne. But luck had not been on his side. It was a dull town, full of dull men, repellent to any idea of doing business with an up and coming young man seeking to make a start in life. He had been forced to sell one of his documents to a dubious broker with premises along a back lane well off the busy central street. The price he had got had been a fraction of its worth. But he had not lost heart and having exhausted all legitimate establishments he had boarded the coach to Dorchester later that afternoon, spent a very uncomfortable night in a flea-ridden stopping house when the coach had cracked an axle, and arrived in the larger town looking more like a clodhopper come to market than the gentleman he was.

In Dorchester it was necessary to keep his head just a little tucked into his chest and avoid offering a greeting to any young lady, but he had got through without being recognised. But he had sold himself short. Drink and a night spent on a hard horsehair mattress had clouded his judgement – he had been coerced into borrowing against the duplicate document and now he was uncomfortably aware that he might live to regret the agreement he had signed.

Geoffrey bridged the Exe just as the spring rain had begun to find its way through his coat to the back of his neck. He went up, ignoring the pot boy who was loitering on the back stairs. Mag was not there – the emptiness of the room had displeased him and stirred more violently his possessive and controlling nature that lay a slight hidden beneath his smart clothes and well-honed manners. He had been watching for her when she arrived, seeing her first through the smutty but informative window which had clear view of Exe Bridge.

"Saints, Master Latimer – my life will be forfeit if you do insist upon jumping out so without warning. You have knocked the breath clear out o' me."

"I only await your return, Margaret, and must allow you know I am here when you do. I was resting in that joyless old chair and did not at first hear you enter." He sat at a small table and restlessly toyed with the empty mug and bowl that had borne her meagre meal of yesterday, viewing her with a jealousy bred from insecurity. She was flushed cheeked from her walk across the city and hollow eyed from a night working in the bawdy house. "I had expected you here, Margaret, I had things to tell but instead I have been made to wait and the thing has quite lost its urgency."

"Do not be bleak with me, Geoffrey, I am here now and your visit was not expected until later. I did not think you would come so early for fear your uncle would question you."

"He does not offer his presence just now. He went journeying across this inhospitable county with the sole need to catch me out and now, upon his return, has taken to his rooms and cannot come down. Vetch says he has the sleeping sickness and has bare stirred for days on end, so I am free of him for a while and may do as I please."

It was not news that Mag needed to be told; the gentlemen of this city may have their coffee houses but the whores and harlots of the houses had their sisterhood – besides, the man lived but a stone's throw from the mother's house and the talk had come to the whorehouse kitchen some days before.

"What news did you have to tell, Geoffrey?"

"I wished to tell you of my trip east, but now it has quite lost the moment. A little money has come to me."

"Then I am pleased for you, Geoffrey, for the lack of it do ever seem to trouble you."

"It would not trouble me, madam, if it were not always in such short supply and in such demand." He left the table and came to her, distractedly removing her tulle neck-cloth and drawing out the strings of her bodice. "Although I am loath to offer it, now that I am able I suppose I must pay that watch-eyed landlord." She placed a small hand over his and continued the task of undressing as he watched her. "And if I do and secure these lodgings a while longer, Margaret, there will be no requirement for you to go journeying to and from that house – it is far too close to my own and I do not relish the watching of you entering and leaving it." She dropped her skirts and he squeezed her small buttocks. "Leave that house, Margaret. I insist upon it."

"Master Latimer, I cannot leave the house yet awhile, I am obliged to the mother and I must oblige her; 'tis the way that life is and must be and it cannot be changed."

This was not a truth. If she had begun her life yesterday, if she had not been bartered for, sent off to marry her father's creditor bare a month after coming into her womanhood; if she had not been daily beaten by this man and if she had not learnt the ways of men earlier than she ought, then perhaps she might have taken Geoffrey Latimer at face, taken him as her lover and left the house. But knowing the world as she did, she must not trust him.

"Do not be angry still, Geoffrey, I am come to you now and have no need to return until later." She moved away to the bed and lay down, pulling the linen loosely over her small breasts as he liked her to. The colour in her face had gone and it pleased him to see frailty returned. He sat beside her and unbuttoned his fly.

"I may be angry as long as is warranted, Margaret. I do not believe my displeasure will be appeased until I am spent." He drew off his shirt, lay taut beside her, staring up at the ceiling. He felt her hand find his manhood and closed his eyes, keeping her dangling a little longer, refusing to succumb to passion until his sense of dejection had eased.

Since he had arranged for this inauspicious room in Alphington, come here most afternoons and lain with this whore, he had felt an urgency that he had rarely felt with any woman before. Need overcoming pride he drew himself up, aggressively pulling the linen sheet away from her breasts and harshly covering her mouth with his own. The urge to have her could no longer be deferred and he felt the smooth flesh of her thighs, rose up and entered her. The delicacy of her lips was unexpected, it was easy to imagine her virginal and unused.

"Say that you will not go back to the house, Margaret." He caught her hair in his closed fist.

"I promise, Geoffrey, I promise it."

28

Heavy rain was hammering on the sloping roof of the kitchen outshoot, great streaks of water running freely and without order down the glass of the casement. Rae was baking; the house was unnaturally quiet, always a quiet time the ending of the afternoon – a time when Trelawney, now decamped to Haldon Manor for this last week, often took to his rooms and slept.

She was making the hard-crust pastry Flood liked; with no time for his beliefs, feigning interest when she had none, Rachael often felt sadness for him and it pleased her to feed him well. Cook had gone the day after Trelawney – Elijah would not willingly have her in the house. The dough was too warm to handle and she let it rest away from the fire. Outside, leaking through every gap where a slate had fallen, water cascaded over the edges of the old gallery, collecting in the parapet and then over-spilling into the courtyard in erratic and spasmodic drenchings. She had opened the door and looked out; even the fisherman had given up his habitual gutting of river fish and withdrawn to the untidy shack that sufficed as storeroom.

For more than a week Rae had waited for Henri Latimer to open his window. Vetch, idling in the yard when he was able, often shared a pipe with Lisa. The news that the merchant's old sickness had returned quickly worked its way through the courtyards and kitchens of the Exebere Street houses; but knowing why he did not open his window was little succour to her anxieties. She was without resource to help him.

The sky hung heavy and dark above them, there would be more rain to come. Leaving the door open to alleviate the closeness of the late afternoon,

Rae went back to her table and began to mould paste into tin with dexterous, nimble hands. Somewhere over the moor the sky would be angrier still, she could hear a distant rumble. She pushed minced rabbit and hedgerow herbs into the mould, sealed and vented the lid and slid the meal into the brick oven already warmed with the ashes of the good fire. Elijah was at his meeting house and Trelawney and Luca, not such a passing passion this time it seemed, were gone to Haldon Forest and had not suggested a date for their return.

Rae felt no particular animosity towards Luca, he had not accountably done her wrong, but nevertheless, she hoped he would not return and that perhaps the cooling of Trelawney's heart or the opportunity of a better keeper might have already seen him move on to another city in the south-west – or perhaps to London. Upon this she did not concern herself overmuch, during the time that she had lived here Alexander had brought many a young man to this house. Luca was little different, except perhaps in his need to seek her out and fill her head with obtuse suggestion. In contrast, concern clouded her thoughts of Henri – if he did not come to his window soon then she would have to ignore scrutiny and seek him out.

Adding all manner of good deeds to his working day, Elijah Flood had not yet returned – he would be somewhere in the wide city, saying prayers for the sick or coaxing the unbeliever into Godliness. She cleared the table and collected the heavy bible from its resting place, opening the yellowing pages at the marker – finding more questions than answers in these ancient stories, she would not read it by choice. The heavy rain was splashing over the threshold, she closed the door and left the room with a mind to do what she had not been able to for some weeks. There is always a certain pleasure in a quiet house that has been full of bustle in the weeks preceding, and moving quietly from the kitchens she took the main staircase to the high-ceilinged and indisputably grand rooms that Trelawney used as his own. Leading off a small sitting room on the first floor was a study, and filling two walls of this were shelves of books – all manner of sizes, leather bound in every colour, dusty, unread and in many cases, misused. She had learnt to read here but she had not been in this room for some time.

A volume of work by Tobias Smollett was lying on the oak boards, its spine bent back, the pages curved with the impact of its fall. She picked it up, spun the pages shut, read an extract, following the words carefully with her fingers. The books were placed haphazardly upon the shelves, ordered in neither size nor content – it heightened her interest to find things by chance. Turning to seek out the standing stool she thought she heard an added sound in the house, detracting from the quiet – not quite a door closing and not a foot on an ancient board but something alien to the comforting silence of the house.

She listened, there was nothing more, and lifting her skirts she slid off her shoes and stood upon the stool.

Centuries of use and decay had given the house a life – a beating heart. Old houses were never completely silent, and distracted by what she had begun she put imagined sounds aside and continued with her intended task. The books were more disordered than usual and pulling out a volume here, where its head was upon its tail, and another there, where the pages had gone aslant and sat in bent confusion, she let time slip by without anxiety or the need to look at the mantle clock.

There was a dullness to the afternoon when she had finished and with an unread book by Defoe held tightly beneath her arm, she replaced the stool and moved from the small study through the sitting room adjoining towards the stairs that would set her down in the square hall where Trelawney's visitors waited. The house was well ordered and silent, not even a board was creaking now that the city was deluged with heavy rain and the associated dampness.

The kitchen door was closed but not clicked shut – she leant against it and heard the brass latch go into the mortise. Rain was still hammering on the outshoot roof, exaggerated by the still silence of the house. Fear of nature, wild and unpredictable weather systems, angry skies full of light and booming thunder did not bother Rae's thoughts; she had been born under a bender on the edges of a hamlet lost in the forested valley of the Erme – fear lay in confinement and in locked rooms, not in what nature offered up. An indistinct rumble of thunder could be heard heading up from the sea; she took a wooden paddle and slid the rabbit pie from its ash bed at the back of the oven, lifting it within the folds of a muslin cloth and placing it upon the scrubbed table. The distraction of book sorting had been only momentary and thoughts of Henri Latimer ran about her head sending up an assortment of worries and concerns and very few answers.

Prediction suggested that as Elijah had not returned for his supper the needs of his Meeting House had called him out into the city to do God's work. She would not wait for him and glancing quickly about her, seeing that all was ordered in the room, she picked up the square of pie she had wrapped in cloth, opened the squat door that lead to the passage behind the bootmaker's shop and made her way along the damp flags towards her tiny dark room. She lit her rush-light, hung up her work dress on the wall nail and washed. The candle was guttering in the airless confines of the small room and she lay on her bed and closed her eyes, considering the foolishness of the world and how etiquette, station and to a small extent the denial of her feelings for her neighbour kept her away from his beside. She allowed the thoughts to spin until thoughts became dreams and dreams could no longer be measured.

In the small hours of the morning, the spring storm had drawn itself up across the sea and unleashed harsh, jagged light and thunder over the mediaeval city. She pushed back her blanket and opened the latch, feeling her way along the dark passage to the kitchen. The rough curtain that divided Flood's sleeping place from the kitchen was not drawn and his bed was still empty. Being alone in the house did not trouble her and working her way back to her room she lay down – sleep returning without effort.

Awake but not fully awake, unable to ascertain if the feeling of breathlessness were dream or reality, she felt unexplained pressure on her chest – the warmth of another's body, tangible but still uncertain and unreal. There was no light in the room, no candle and only a small-paned window connecting to the dark world. Her instant protest came without question – instinct, the instinct of survival, made her try to shake the heaviness off, to call out. But before words left her lips a hand came swiftly over her mouth; the dark shape, surreal, without reason, without the essence of humanity, continued to crush her and each time she made to get up, to push it away, the hand became more forceful, the crushing sensation greater still, the weight more leaden.

The blanket gave little protection and she could feel the metallic hardness of brass buttons upon her skin, the roughness of a disordered coat moving against her until there was nothing between the dark shape and her body. Every time she tried to claw the hand away the hand crept further still across her face, into her eyes, distorting her nose, holding all effort back – the quick breaths of terror coming fast. As the hand engulfed her face the other seemed to bridge the heaviness and link to her exposed flesh so that there was no space between – until the dream became nightmare, until she had full understanding of what was to come.

In the end it was time that had beaten her; thoughts of pushing the weight off, of freeing herself, of getting away, had come too slowly to help her. And then the deed was done. The fighting, the struggle had been futile and over before it was hardly begun – the violent tearing of her chemise, the feeling of panic and the acceptance of the inevitable, the strange sensation of hard flesh and the pain and the force of entry, and then the abrupt removal of the heavy weight.

She lay waiting for the dawn, and it crept in slowly, more slowly than she ever remembered, first to her window and then through the open door. The house was the same, the view from her small truckle bed was the same, the dark passage, the sounds of the kitchen and the courtyard, all these things had not changed but she had changed – in the dark of the night a thief had come and in a brief moment of carnal lust had taken from her that which could never be returned.

Practical in every sense but numbed by the experience of the night, dry-eyed and expressionless, she drew up the bloodied bed linen into a bundle and mechanically began to dress.

29

In the quiet of the sick-room Latimer sat on his bed, the debilitating grippe-sweats had returned; enteric and other fevers were rife in the city running around the less affluent streets like wildfire, and to a man with a rational mind the existence of these notorious diseases was reason enough to explain away his newly returned infirmity. But his illness was different this time, not just a consequence of his poisonous leg. As well as fatigue he seemed to be laid low with a type of sleeping sickness; whole days were missing from his recollection, the distinction between this week and the last had been lost, and sitting now on the edge of his bed with his head resting in his hands he was uncertain if one week or two had passed since his visit to Bridcombe.

He knew the symptoms of some of the endemic diseases circling the city, although neither he nor his family had fallen prey to them before. Weakness allowed weakness to creep in, it was a proven fact. However, he did not feel his life was at risk, he was – between the periods of convulsive shakings and extraordinary fatigue – able to swing his legs round and get to his pot. With the spectre of contagion hovering about him he had allowed no one to visit barring his servant. Vetch had just left, leaving behind him a posset, which he would not drink, and a fresh jug of wine and water which he would but only when thirst necessitated.

In need of something stronger, he reached for his stick, crossed the room with the aid of the bedstead and located the half-used bottle of contraband he kept in a small cupboard above his press. Tucking it under his arm he made his way back to his writing chair. With some urgency to grasp this moment of lucidity he drank from the short neck, spilling a little and settling the bottle upright on his dressing chest.

His head had been level since he woke this morning and he hoped it would stay that way, at the least long enough for him to come back to his senses – perhaps the fever had run its course? With no time for physicians or apothecaries he had not engaged one; he would look for himself, and providing he did not pass any contagion to those about him then he would continue on as he was, without the intrusive meddling of any quack. More alert than he had been for days he lay down upon his bed in his nightshirt and ran over his time away – his meetings, the places he had recently visited to try to make a head and a tail of things – to understand why he had been struck again by this, or some other, sickness.

Time now ticked away clearly. The clock on the mantle gave a little after two – no more than a quarter of the hour had passed since he last opened his eyes. A light knocking had moved him to open them and now he realised the tapping was upon his own door. With no prompting the door swung open and the distinct click of Geoffrey's boots accompanied the young man into the sick room.

Henri closed his eyes again. He doubted this was his nephew's first visit – in all certainty one of many. Was the young man concerned for his health, was he anxious to know what Henri had learnt on his trip away or did he not expect him to recover enough to discuss it?

A chair was drawn across the floor. His nephew would be sitting beside him – Henri hoped it was concern that filled his head.

"Forgive me for not looking at you," Latimer said without opening his eyes. "I am afraid I will swim away to faintness."

Geoffrey had been about to get up and help himself to a glass of the excellent French brandy that his uncle kept secreted in his rooms – he was glad that the thought had not come to him an instant earlier.

"Uncle Latimer, sir. I am blessed with reassurance – I had not thought to find you awake."

"And nor would you have just a few moments ago, it is you coming tapping at my door that has woken me."

Aware that his uncle could not see him, Geoffrey moved, somewhat anxiously to the edge of the chair and looked him over. He was deathly pale and unshaven.

"Is there anything that you need, sir? Vetch tells me that you will not eat and will take little else but the wine and water."

Latimer felt there was an urgency to all that he said and did, he must be frugal in his responses – how long might he be lucid before he slipped away again into the dark place of nightmares and fevered sleep?

"Only your help with this lost time, Nephew. I sleep in the daylight and then wake in the dark. I have listened to the dawn and then found the next time I recount consciousness it is an hour or so preceding the following dawn. How long has it been since I returned from Moreton?"

"This is the third week, Uncle. But you have been fevered for the most part of it and could not possibly have recounted the days of the week."

"Then I must recount them now whilst I am able."

Latimer lifted his head a little, struggled upon one elbow and rested his head back against the oak board of the old bed. Although his thoughts had been jumbled since he had returned, since he had begun to drift between semi-consciousness and oblivion, in his head there was always a recurring thought – he must not let his nephew's dishonesty pass, whatever the state of his health he would expect explanation.

"I would prefer to wait until I can sit and converse with you in a manner better suited to business, but I fear I am not blessed with that luxury and must speak with you just the same." He closed his eyes again, holding on to lucidity. "You may tell me I am mistaken and you may give me reasons why I am mistaken – if you are able – but I have to report, Nephew, that my recent trip has thrown up irregularities which cannot pass without explanation." His eyes remained closed and even though he could not see him he sensed no change in his nephew's easy if not arrogant manner. "It seems that none of the pack-road weavers know you, have never had sight of you and to put this in a small parcel, Geoffrey, assume me dead."

Geoffrey's eyes went unconsciously to the jug on his uncle's table. This man did not have the better of him, would not have the better of him and was no longer in control of his own life. He would not feel done down.

"Give me explanation please, Nephew. There is money unaccounted for and I will have an account of it." Latimer now opened his eyes and fixed his nephew with an unblinking stare.

Geoffrey stood and moved into the shadows of the room. "In truth, I did not go to Moreton, neither to visit the weavers nor the farms. Nor did I visit the Crediton markets. You have been quite without flexibility in your dealings with me, Uncle. I have been used to doing business without interference, intervention or suggestion and I am quite able to continue to do the same here, but you will have me ride out to such widely flung places where I am neither conversant with the people or their business when all along the rewards for such are slight. I had a mind to do business in my own way – in the ways I am used. And I have. Your money is quite safe, if that is all that concerns you."

If he had not been laid so low already then Latimer may well have been winded by his nephew's response. He was a little lost for words. "God above,

Geoffrey, you must know that money is never all that concerns me. I would have honesty over it for a start. If you thought you were better placed, if you thought you had a better plan than I could offer, then you should have outed it. My business is the woollen trade and if you are to inherit it then it should be yours also – until I am gone."

Geoffrey sat again and looked upon his uncle's recumbent form with returned boldness. "Forgive me if I have displeased you, Uncle. I could not tell what I had in mind for fear you would not allow me to continue."

"And now? Are you saying that you may tell me now what you have done with the fleece money because the deception is complete and may not be upset? Why should it be easier to tell me now than before you misappropriated it?" Geoffrey rested back in his chair.

"I have bought a cargo, sir. Indeed that is not quite correct – I have invested your capital in a cargo of finished cloth, as a profiteer, as an investor." Geoffrey hesitated, spinning his yarn with the expertise of an accomplished liar. "The barque has already sailed from Axmouth and has returned with a variety of excellent Dutch tiles. Now sold, the buyers predetermined."

Henri raised himself a little from the bed. "How did you come by such business? I set you off on the turnpike to Crediton?"

"Indeed, and I had a mind to find an alternative business all along – but then the offer of trade came to me so I did not have to seek it out."

"Came to you? Where did it come to you, perched atop a hired nag on a dusty turnpike?"

"The inn along the way – just beyond our city walls, business thrives there, don't you know? In the rooms and the snugs that filter off the taproom."

"You mean The Carriers? I do not know – I have never experienced any business being conducted there barring the exchange of coin for run-in spirits."

"Then all has changed since you last had recourse to sup there."

Latimer pulled himself up onto his elbows so that he could view his nephew on a level. "I am bemused by your audacity, Nephew. In my present state of health I do not think my constitution will take more revelation – so do not explain more fully." He pulled himself square and dropped his feet slowly to the ground. "Pass me the gown. I do not believe I can confront this in my nightshirt." With effort Latimer worked his arms into the brocade dressing-coat and stood. The coat went to the floor and exaggerated his slimness and height. He faced his nephew a hand still gripping the bed. "I must retrench, Geoffrey. This explanation, this story you now tell – so at odds with your previous explanation – does not have the ring of truth to it either. You have lied and a lie so easily unearthed, in God's name – did you not think to adulterate your previous lie with some semblance of truth? Why not out with it at the start?"

"I see it was an error, sir, not telling you of my plans and then when it was done I might have been better placed to offer the truth – but then, some uncertainty surrounded my transaction."

"And now, with uncertainty passed?" On unsteady legs, Latimer went to his dressing chest, threw out the dregs of yesterday's half-drunk wine and water and refilled the glass with French brandy – he did not offer the bottle to Geoffrey. He drank. "In all my time trading I have not had such lucrative business come my way and most especially in a dusty way-side inn where the landlord is a drunkard and a thief." He turned stiffly to look at Geoffrey, searching his face for answers. The boy did not seem in the least perturbed by the implausible explanation he had just offered his uncle. "So be it," he said, already exhausted by the harsh words. "I cannot run around the bushes with it – I do not believe my head will allow it."

Latimer looked the younger man in the face, pale blue eyes as cold as ice. "If the trade has been done well, if my capital is returned, then I will ask no more. But see that the amount I sent you away with is returned to my bank in North Street in full. I expect it and shall know if it is not."

Geoffrey got to his feet, dropped his head in simulation of respect that he did not feel and closed the door as he left.

Latimer looked out of his window. How quickly fate changes the familiar simplicity of life. He lay down on his bed in his dressing coat and closed his eyes. He could not think upon what was, what had been and what he hoped might be again soon until he could face the world with more vigour.

30

Geoffrey had begun to frequent The Phoenix again. With the money he had made from the forged share documents he had paid his taproom account, and settled his argument with the Goldsmith Street moneylender who had fleeced him for almost double the amount he had borrowed. It irked him to be so cheated but he would not be caught again; and besides, The Swan had become less than comfortable – he had won a little too often at Jack High-Jack Low.

Now that his uncle was incapacitated again and kept to his rooms he might drink where and when he chose – no tricky explanations, no demands on his time and no requirement to seat himself in the dining room and offer up amicable conversation over a shared meal. The consequences of all this was that life had become a little solitary of late – and he had not seen Mudge for some weeks. The Quaker, determined to bring his only son back into the flock, had doggedly set about presenting William with a varied selection of dutiful Quaker daughters. William's social world had been enlarged and it was not to Geoffrey's liking.

He took a card from the pack, made a gentle arch of it in his hand then set it free like a nugget from a catapult, continuing in this vein until a dozen cards were spread across the table. A mood of despondency had engulfed him that could not be blamed on his solitude alone. He had spent the early hours of the morning lying with his whore; she was not with child and there would be no complications in that direction and no cessation of pleasure. Quite done with her he had come to The Phoenix and taken a late breakfast. Now he was reminded of his necessary and impending visit to Blox. The day that he need not visit the filthy herbalist could not come soon enough.

With only a day's grace before he had been forced to board the Bridport coach, and mindful of his uncle's trip to Moreton, he had been obliged to make a hasty visit to the hovel in Frog Lane. Blox had anticipated his requirements and had impertinently suggested an easier and more finite option. Geoffrey may have little conscience and an easy ability to lie, but this did not facilitate murder. There might, after all, be a judgement day, and although he was a gambling man he would not risk the possibility of any confrontation with the Devil. Assisting a man to his end was one thing, offering up poison was quite another.

Blox had offered him a tincture – flowers of Bittersweet Nightshade – and added a powerful opiate producing the symptoms of a naturally occurring illness and thus keeping suspicion at bay. The potion had done its job well and been easy to administer within the watered wine, but Blox did not have the power to overcome the unpredictability of Uncle Latimer, and Geoffrey might just be obliged to change tack again. Recounting his own, somewhat illogical and ungodly behaviour was not, however, the quandary that inspired his despondency – Blox needed payment and the more underhand, the more criminally inspired his requirements became, the greater the herbalist's demands. The tincture that was left in the jar would not last much longer, and if Geoffrey did not want his uncle up and bothering his business then he needed the old man to replenish it.

Perhaps it would not matter if he let the thing ride for a while. He could not face the hovel on this pleasant afternoon. Tomorrow would be soon enough. He collected up the randomly placed cards and returned them to the pack. Sometimes he did not know himself why he remained in this dull woollen city. He had never intended it to be so but there was a consequence to keeping a whore; she might not easily be relocated and although he cared not to admit it, he could not see a time when he would not want her.

His home in Dorset came into his mind – and his mother, a solid reason not to return just yet. Paying off debts had no draw for him, there were plenty of creditors waiting for him in the towns surrounding Marwood and there was a futility in paying debt with borrowed money. Time ticked on, the second week of May had already come and gone and he remembered grudgingly that there would be interest to pay on the money he had borrowed using the second share certificate. Although not quite as brutish and unaccommodating as the moneylenders he had done business with here, Geoffrey did not expect the man to wait much after payment day. There were consequences to leaving such a document in slippery hands – his whereabouts might be easily traced.

Returning the cards to a pocket and collecting up his loose coin, Geoffrey brushed despondency aside, and as he was not now intending to make a visit to Blox, he might seek out friendly company in that new tailoring establishment along Sidwell Street where he was little known. He placed his tricorn on his dark head and stepped out into the afternoon with nothing more in his thoughts than the warmth of the sun and the possibility of ordering a new waistcoat.

The kitchen door was closed against the dying day; Elijah Flood sat stiffly beside the cooking fire, his dark coat buttoned tightly to his stock, his hands held in closed unity. He might have been praying but he was not. He touched his closed fingertips against his lips.

"It would please me if you were to read a little longer, Daughter. I see that you are a slight tired this night, but the reading of God's word do so often bring a calmness that overcomes the need for rest."

Rachael had not the will to argue with him. She could read on for as long as he liked – it could not cleanse her of ungodly thoughts nor the feeling of self-hatred, of wretchedness or the belief that all that she had secretly aspired to had now been dismembered and thrown aside.

"Philemon has a verse or so more I believe, Daughter? 'If he hath wronged thee, or oweth thee ought.'" Rachael was reading from an ancient copy of *The King James Bible*; oversized and cumbersome, the fly torn and the leather cover hanging from its spine. The precious thing had sat beneath Trelawney's bed for months, if not years. Alexander often kept his chamber pot perched upon its sacred skin. Having viewed it with some distress for weeks on end, Flood had finally requested that he borrow it for his kitchen teachings. Trelawney had scoffed but the bible had been brought to the kitchens and had remained there since.

Rachael reluctantly ran her finger along the next line of the teachings of Paul, but did not begin – the pause was enough to prompt Elijah into changing course.

"Perhaps we have heard enough of The Epistle of Paul to Philemon. Try you Hebrews again – let us start from thirteen."

Turning delicate pages with the care that Elijah expected, Rachael began to read in her slow but deliberate manner. She would have preferred to read any other text than this, but lethargy had taken away her spirit and she would not argue for another.

"'Let brotherly love continue. Be not forgetful to entertain strangers: for thereby'… The text is quite marked and rusty, Elijah, shall I move on a space or try to continue?"

"Read where 'tis clear, the light is not as good as it ought – you must not struggle over it, Daughter, when slowed by tiredness."

"'Remember them that are in bonds, as bound with them; and them which suffer adversity, as being yourselves also in the body.'" The marked print was indistinct above her following finger. "Verse four, Elijah." She had read *Hebrews* before and knew it well enough.

"'Marriage is honourable in all, and the bed undefiled: but whore-mongers and adulterers God will judge.'" A great shudder of regret engulfed her body, uncontrollable and bitter. She stopped reading and dropped her forehead upon the page.

Self-pity, the analysis of things past – the need to return to a time gone by and make changes had never clouded her straightforward practical journey through life. Today she felt differently.

Opening eyes that had been closed in anticipation of hearing a much-remembered text, Elijah viewed the normally defiant and animated girl who was his fellow servant and his companion.

"Are you unwell? Does not the text please you, Daughter? We may easily choose another."

She did not reply – the first tears had begun, an unstoppable tide, falling onto the musty pages.

"Cannot you say, Rachael? It is not your way to show such emotion, especially over God's word." He observed her sobbing but did not come to her. Through tautness of manner and harshness of upbringing he could not comfort her. "Perhaps the text is a little worldly – might we not talk of its meaning?" He stood looking down on her, concerned for her but also a slight disappointed that his evening pleasure had been curtailed. "I do not remember a time when His word has distressed you so before."

With an impatient savage movement she drew her hand across her wet face. She did not answer him.

"Then do not read more," he said more gently. "God's word will wait until tomorrow."

He came to the table, placed a caring hand on the bible and carefully drew it away from her dripping tears. "It is enough, Rachael – we will say the first psalm and then you may go to your bed."

She watched him drop to one knee, as was his way, and start the familiar verse.

"'Blessed is the man that walketh not in the counsel of the ungodly, nor standeth in the way of sinners, nor sitteth in the seat of the scornful.'" On so many occasions she had followed his lead, unthinkingly repeating lines she had said since she was ten. She did not mouth the words now – her mouth was set in a hard emotionless slit. Eyes closed, Elijah continued. "'But his delight is in the law of the Lord; and in his law doth he meditate day and night. And he shall be like a tree planted by the rivers of water, that bringeth forth his fruit in his season; his leaf also shall not wither; and whatsoever he doeth shall prosper.'"

She could not say more, she would not have him finish. In her head the familiar psalm still echoed. "'The ungodly are not so: but are like the chaff which the wind driveth away…For the Lord knoweth the way of the righteous: but the way of the ungodly shall perish.'" She stood, knocking the chair with her skirts, producing a scraping sound on the flags that made Elijah open his eyes and struggle to his feet.

Although the afternoon had already gone through, a watery sun was still lighting the industrious Exe. This crisis of heart could not be borne in the confines of any house – the urge to have the sky above her head was stronger than she could bear. The wild world beyond the city walls would be her balm. Taking nothing with her save her pocket of coin, she ran from the kitchen, opening the wide door to the street and stepping out into the windy afternoon.

The Great Shilhay tentergrounds spread all the way down to the river, and lengths of serge were still strung out in the accommodating wind. She walked on along the edges of the leat towards the coal quay, untying her apron and pulling it impatiently from her waist – feet slowing as she reached the wharf. The industry of the woollen trade was about her everywhere, along the water's edge, on the ground surrounding the Custom House; a bustle of noise and busyness, of pack-ponies and carthorses, the sounds of hawsers being let go and crank-cranes and yard shovels – and the harsh, impatient voices of the stevedores. Despite the perpetual silting up of the river and canal, which allowed only shallow draught boats and barges to manoeuvre this far upstream, it was a place of endless activity.

Feet moving on unbidden, thoughts running unappeased through her head, she found her way to the river bank – although she did not know how. A decrepit ferry carried passengers regularly across to the shooting marshes; she viewed it with empty eyes, the ferryman standing on the boards, and the hunched shape of an ancient woman clutching a young baby to her chest already seated at the prow. The ferryman had called, broken her mood of indecision and despondency. She lifted her skirts, avoided taking the man's hand and seated herself close to the stern, searched for a coin, watching the tiller trailing the hindered Exe.

The child was sickly, she could tell the child was sickly – and the old woman seemed not to care for it, allowing its feeble head to loll to the side. She watched them, hardly present in this real world of survival and ultimate death – who were they, why were they here labouring across the Exe on this dilapidated ferry and so late in the day? Perhaps the old woman asked similar questions of her.

The boatman was unwashed and ragged, the remaining leather of his shoes barely holding sole to upper; he pulled hard on his oars, rowlocks taking the strain, powerful arms strong and taut. She watched the flowing tide and rippling wake and sat in silence as the boat worked through the central flow of the river. She did not wish to make conversation, she would rather not know the woman's life history, the reasons for her being there, and she had no banter to offer the ferryman. The opposite bank was coming closer and she waited for the boat to slow, for the raw unpainted wood of the bows to pierce the dense herbage and find the shallows.

The man stilled his oars, let the craft find its own way through the part-submerged sedge and flowering reeds. Spanning the mud-banks was a wooden pontoon, as broken and decrepit as the boat. Standing uncertainly, she let the old woman alight first, almost ready to grasp the baby if it fell, and it seemed to Rachael that it must. How many babies had fallen from desperate mother's arms in this isolated spot? The thought made her shudder and if she had seen reason in such beliefs she might have felt the fear that came with standing in places where souls are said to remain after death. But the shiver she felt did not arise from the thought of a haunted place, but the knowledge that it was often into these dense reeds and receptive mud-banks that the dead and the drowned were washed – this she knew was the resting place of many a bastard child.

Dusk had not yet come, the skies above the river and the reeds about her seemed full of the shrill cries of terns and gulls. The old woman had already begun to make her way slowly along the plank path and Rachael held back, she could not bear to look upon the sickly, needy child longer. With no more passengers on this bank the boatman dropped an oar down into the mud, freed the boat from the reeds and began to pull the craft out into the main stream.

Strong winds gusting up the Exe valley from the sea were pushing the fast-moving clouds northwards, rippling the surface of the water and running waves through the dense pliable reeds. There was no sound now, except the occasional shrill cry of a coot – life had changed and she must change and follow a different course. The wind drew up a strand of hair, teasing it and wrapping it about her face until the end found the corner of her mouth – she freed it, pushing the tendril back beneath her cap. In the north-west sky the dying sun was turning the clouds pink. She stood for a moment waiting for dusk to come and then turned in the direction of Alphington. Change had already taken her where it must and she would not look back.

*

Time and necessity pushing her forward, she had found it easy to slip unnoticed into the kitchens of the merchant's house; the Latimers' cook was not a young woman, most evenings the welcome comfort of her fireside chair sent her off into a slumber that she did not wake from until the early hours. Henri, his mouth drawn down at the corners, opium-induced nightmares still running unchecked through his head, was sleeping the sleep of the sick, deep and restive.

Rae had seated herself on the visitor's chair beside his bed and laid her cheek upon the soft comfort of the counterpane, her swollen eyes closed. His still hand was very close but she did not grasp it. She had come to say goodbye and it was better said when he slept – any kind word might unsettle her and then she might change her mind.

She opened her eyes and watched him for a while. His was not a peaceful sleep; it seemed that a conflict was going on within his soul and like any nightmare he could not speak it. Concerned for his wellbeing most certainly she was, but having lived alongside Henri through his recent infirmity something within her told her that he would survive this relapse – had he not survived sickness before? But despite her own reassurance a seed of worry still ran through her thoughts and it would have pleased her to stay here until he woke. That could not happen; fate had played a joker and the future no longer held choices. She rose, watched him a moment longer and then opened the door to the silent house. She had never been in this house before and understood that she never would again.

31

Although so often a requisite of a well-run climax, on this occasion Geoffrey had not felt the need for cruelty. No longer taut with want he relaxed the tension of his arms and lay spent upon his whore. Her frailty did not concern him; it was his right to have her how he chose – it was from his pocket that the coin came to keep her in these rooms. He rolled from her and lay upon his back. There was still an angry mark showing on her neck where he had abused her the previous day – today he had not added another.

Without inhibition or need to cover herself, Mag lay close to his side. He would not have her affection – he paid for her body and that was all, but he allowed her to come within the crook of his arm, tolerating her pale fine hair to rest upon his torso.

"Are you quite done, sir?" she said, turning a strand of long hair about a forefinger.

"I do not yet know, Margaret. I suppose you are anxious to be gone from here and return to that cheap place. There is little query over its comers."

"Master Latimer, that is not quite so, the bawd would not allow any Tom, Dick or other to come to us – she is quite particular."

It did not please Geoffrey to have her talk this way and yet the need to know where she went and who she had was too strong to disallow such conversations.

"I will stay for as long as you wish it, but if I am to go then 'twould be better sooner so that the mother can take stock of who is in the house and who is without it."

Geoffrey considered his options for the evening. Between administrations of the noxious tonic Blox sold to him – which was becoming ever more difficult to administer – his uncle would stir and recover enough to think himself well. It was like a game of trumps, he felt; just when Uncle Latimer began to have the upper hand, he would trump it and find a new way of keeping him to his rooms. Regretfully his deceitful activities did not come cheap; Blox was still owed payment and his continued cooperation in Geoffrey's quest to live his life unhindered was always in doubt.

There really were things that he needed to attend to at the Exebere house – tonight he would have to let the strumpet go back to the whorehouse.

"Then you may go sooner," he said abruptly, rising and pulling on his draws. "But see that you are purged before you return; I will not have you return to this bed when you are sullied by any foul-dick of a man cursed with the pox."

With sharp eyes that knew him better than he did himself, Mag watched him dress. "You are such the gentleman in that new waistcoat, Geoffrey, 'tis a fine one and would see you enter any grand place or assembly room – if you should so choose to."

Geoffrey pulled the well-fitted waistcoat down over his breeches and began to fix his stock. "You forget in your determined disobedience, Margaret, that I am master of both my uncle's house here as well as my manor in the next county. I do not need a new waistcoat to prove myself to be the gentleman that I am."

Mag was put in her place and she left the bed and stood naked before the grimy window.

"Business takes me this eve, but I expect you to be here before I return tomorrow." He pulled her nakedness against the harsh fabric of his waistcoat without tenderness. "Remember what I have said. I do not pay you to bring disease along to our bed."

Although they both knew well the dealings and activities of the three houses that ran side by side along Exebere Street, this was never spoken of, but prompted by what he had said, Mag could not help but mention the senior Latimer whom she had heard much tittle-tattle about but knew only in passing.

"Do your uncle still ail, sir, or is he up and about now and mending? I should not like for him to pass along to you whatever it is that sent him to his bed."

Geoffrey would rather not discuss his uncle – the question did not prick his conscience but it would always be necessary to make the wearisome effort of keeping it in a compartment of his mind where it would not.

"My uncle's health is of no concern of yours, Margaret – and be assured that the contagion he has will never come to me."

He put her aside and took his hat and coat from the back of the chair. When he reached the street, despite the brightness of the day, heavy rain had begun to fall. He cursed it and stepped out towards the Exe Bridge and the West Gate. An indistinct rainbow was forming, finding anchor in the wide river; he turned up his collar and walked on swiftly through the congested lower streets of the city. Blox had his hovel here and he intended to give the filthy ancient as wide a birth as he could – he had yet to pay him for the last draught.

He supposed he had no option but to return to Latimer house and sit for a while beside his uncle's bedside – he saw it as prudent. It would be expected of him by the mismatched servants of the house – the ageing cook and the revolting drunk who passed as nurse for his cousins, the occasional maid, and Vetch, a man who kept his aspirations quietly to himself.

Vetch met him in the hall and helped him off with his wet coat, shaking it out and removing it to a place where it might be dried. Geoffrey took the twisting stairs with long strides; the door at the head was just ajar. He looked through the gap at his uncle, his beard was near full grown now and his hair was tussled and wild. Even when encouraged into unconsciousness by opium Uncle Latimer slept annoyingly close to the surface – it could not be predicted when he might wake. Provoked into thinking it by Blox he had tried to persuade himself that death might be preferable to the half-life of a long illness, but he would not be pushed along – eventually he might reach that conclusion but not yet.

He sat beside the bed for awhile – Blox had become a thorn, he must pay the man but cash was a problem; it seemed to slip away at an alarming rate even though he felt he was rather frugal in his lifestyle. Uncle Latimer had never lived a lavish life himself; there was little in the way of worldly acquisitions lying about the house, even less up here in his private rooms. Geoffrey contemplated this whilst he watched his uncle turn for the tenth time – perhaps he might run through a type of inventory in his head. A good watch, a pair of stout leather boots – perhaps even a dead wife's earbobs might all be sold or bartered with, if he could find any. Bored with the pretence of concern he left the room.

There were five doors on this level of the tall house: one was his uncle's room, one a connecting dressing room, one his own and one a jumbled store cupboard; the fifth he knew was never entered – Mary Latimer had kept it as her own sitting room. He listened to the house, a floor above he could hear the childish chatter of his cousins but there were no other sounds.

There was no lock and one easy movement of the handle let him in, the neat furniture was covered with dustsheets and any remnants of female occupation had quite gone. He opened cupboards and drawers until his foray struck gold: a large chest was hid beneath a sheet. Squatting, he opened the lid, drew out samplers and thread, undemanding books, papers and quill, a pair of worn slippers, a cushion for lacemaking, but no spools. A small leather box took his notice. Disappointed at first, he tipped the contents onto the floor and ran a finger through the oddments. There were a few rings and indeed some earbobs. He put the rings on the ends of his fingers and the earbobs in his pocket; there was nothing particularly distinct about them and it was unlikely they would be remembered about the city after so many years.

As Geoffrey left the unused sitting room, Vetch was going into his uncle's room; several strands of greying string-like hair had come loose from his queue and hung down over his eyes. He turned to look at Geoffrey, peering at him through unwashed lank hair, the clarity of his vision hampered further by the near darkness that dusk had brought to the inner hallway. Geoffrey noted the small tray and the bottle and glass. It might be necessary to make a little more effort where Thomas Vetch was concerned. He anticipated his loyalties were sound – well he hoped they were – he moved about the house obsequiously enough, and yet Geoffrey could see how easy it might be for the man to find some duplicitous pleasure in playing uncle against nephew. Geoffrey nodded – Vetch dropped his head in acknowledgement.

Daylight had already been lost from the lower rooms of the tall house when he came down, and a sconce was lit in the entrance hall and a half-dozen more about the large sitting room. There was a distinctly unappetizing smell emanating from the kitchens, and the dullness and emptiness of the house – as well as the consideration of what might be being prepared for his supper – confirmed in his mind that the evening would be better spent elsewhere. Without the consideration that he might mention his leaving, he stepped out of Latimer house and walked in the direction of Goldsmith's and The Phoenix where he hoped he might find agreeable company and a little distraction that would fill his purse rather than lighten it.

His appetite had grown considerably since his late breakfast, and when he saw William Mudge settled in the snug chewing on the white flesh of a freshly roasted fowl – a plate of dough boys and giblet broth set before him – he was hopeful that all his aspirations for the evening might be met.

"Latimer, you are back amongst us I see." William looked up briefly and then returned to his meal. The relationship had naturally cooled and not just because of his father's determination to find him a suitable Quaker wife; William questioned what Geoffrey Latimer had drawn him into. Until recently he had managed to push the memory of his reluctant lending of the scrolled paper to the back of his mind, but last week his father had discussed with him the irregular correspondence he had received from a gentleman in Somerset, demanding share interest – this irregularity could not be explained.

"I have been back amongst you for some time, William, it is you who has been absent from these comfortable rooms." William was not sure that he concurred. "Chance seems to have set us down in the same place and at the same time, I am glad to find you here, William, I have an evening without plan and would welcome a companion. My uncle's cook has determinedly sent me away with the smell of charred offal lingering most unpleasantly in my nostrils and I have no intention of returning until supper is done."

"I hear your uncle is sickly again, Geoffrey. Luck do not seem to linger long with the man."

"Luck rarely intervenes in such things, William. The city is rife with seasonal fevers and grippe-like conditions. He is naturally sickly and will contract anything that comes his way." Geoffrey sat, lifted his coat skirts over his knees and watched William finish the fowl. "How goes your search for a suitably chaste and Godly wife, William? Is there likelihood that your old papa will succeed – have you stand before his God with a gold ring and a sombre wedding coat?"

"Do not bring the thought to mind, Geoffrey, I have been around the houses with these dull ducklings. I am constantly surrounded by them whilst they peck away about my feet. I cannot say if they are true or no and would ask the question would they be so eager if my papa did not own a tucking mill and the largest house in St Sidwell?"

"I did not have you as a cynic, William, and now my mind is changed."

William ignored the quip. "I will not have it, Geoffrey, I am one and twenty soon and will take who I choose to my bed, especially if she is to become wife and mayn't be removed from it until after death." William had finished his meal; this was in addition to the one he had eaten with his father earlier, a frugal and unappetizing mix of hard bread and cold meat. "The thing do have some merits though, Geoffrey." William contemplated the events of the last few weeks which had seen him enter a variety of houses, both wealthy and sparsely puritan. "Indeed some of the young women are jaunty enough, their company tolerable, and where there are sisters there are brothers also, and many a young buck who don't always quite see their life's future as their fathers do. They are like-minded, Geoffrey, surprisingly like-minded."

"How so, William?" Geoffrey had ordered the same plate as William and now sat looking at his meal, uncertain whether to begin with meat or dumpling.

"They like a wager as much as any and do not run the worry of being spied upon in any alehouse or backstreet cockpit."

"It seems you are quite well in – in this world beyond the meeting house."

"Indeed I am. There are rooms and places, in private houses and more public, where a man with a speculative eye might throw a dice or turn a card and it never be talked of."

"And have you seen inside these places, William, or is this just hearsaying in your ear?"

"Indeed I have, Latimer – and a merry night is had. A servant at the door and wine and spirits freely passed around despite their papa's and mama's leaning." William was hesitant for a moment – he could not quite make up his mind whether he might regret allowing Geoffrey to have these intimacies. He bumbled on. "I am due at such a house later this eve and I am quite certain sure that a prosperous young gentleman in a new coat, such as you are, would be welcome to come alongside me."

Geoffrey bit into a thighbone. "I am intrigued by the thought of it, friend, it mayn't be such poor policy to come along – I am tired of all there is to offer in these predictable places." He waved his hand in the air about him and then wiped his hands on an overworked square of muslin. "When will you start? Are we on foot or is there need to find a carriage?"

"We need not find a carriage, sir, for I have one already arranged. The house is a little way out of the city on the Longbrook road and will take an age to walk to, especially with the mud and the dung that has gathered up with the rains."

32

They had risen from the table sometime before ten. The coach William had arranged smelt of urine and mould but Mudge was right, it would not do to be trekking out towards Longbrook in this quagmire.

Perched within the coach he felt his coat for his purse: a brace of gold guineas and a quantity of silver coin. While he refused to feel any allegiance to this city, it did hold a certain interest for him. On the surface the monotony of its mercantile activities bored him, the predominance of churches over inns, the lack of real gentlemen of his standing and a social life he did not always feel lived up to expectation; but there were certain parts of his life here he would not wish let go of. One thing he did not miss from his life further east was the incessant bothering of his days by his mother, and he sometimes felt more in control of life here than he did in Dorset. Tonight he felt lucky, it would be enjoyable to sit and play – or make wager – in the company of gentlemen.

They crossed the Longbrook leat and headed out through darkened fields. The house stood alone surrounded by a wall; the coachman pulled up the lively pony and dropped them beyond the Gate, touching its rump with his whip and sending the beast off at a canter back towards the city. The candles in the windows, the lighted entrance – it had seemed a promising beginning.

Gaming was spread over three rooms, there was a familiar face here and there but none that he might call friend. A couple of rooms were set with tables; they were playing Quadrille and all the places were taken. He watched, leaning on the wall, a curious feeling finding him – a feeling of being misplaced, of being on the outside of things when he had expected to feel on the inside.

Snuff was offered and he took it although it was not a habit he knew well. William had introduced him as was necessary and then had moved away amongst the gamblers, hapless determination finding him a place at a table in the next room. Geoffrey had hung about assessing the mood and the wealth in the house – drinking all that was offered him.

Finally securing himself a place at a table in a smaller room leading off the others, Geoffrey had played just two games of Quadrille and then found the stakes too high and excused himself. These men, sons of the city, would not be cheated, could not be deceived into falling for his trickery – were not impressed by his gentility – and he would not embarrass himself by losing more than he had in his purse.

Coming up behind him now, some hour since their parting, Geoffrey knew Mudge had already reached that level of drunkenness when self-possession has been lost.

"Sir, is it not a lively place." William had placed a hand on his friend's shoulder to steady himself. "You will not find any old Jack in the pack here. 'Tis quite a select meeting and may be accessed only by a nod and wink and the asking." A bulge of air caused by strong spirit atop several jugs of good Phoenix brew came up from his gut and left his throat in a belch.

"I see that it is, William, and I also see that there is a tidy pile of money upon each table – bank notes and all." Geoffrey removed William's arm from his neck and propped him against the oak of the wall panels. Having a false sense that he had regained his balance without assistance William continued with renewed enthusiasm.

"And you are right, sir – some lucky brother will have the load in their pocket before the night is done."

"And how goes your purse, William? Do luck follow you, sir, or are you out?"

"I am out, Latimer. I suppose I should bless my dear papa for seeing me short each month. When my purse is empty it is empty, and as he is so well known on these streets there are none who will take my promise. It is a sure way to stay out of debt."

"It is logic of sorts, William, but sometimes when a man has gone so far down he must keep playing in order to come up again."

"I have no forte for the tables myself and barely wet my fingers, but never the mind, I am told there is a well-dusted pit behind these rooms and I'll wager there will be some lucky birds strutting their spurs about it. Birds is so much easier to make a prediction upon than cards don't you think?"

A corpulent servant with an ill-fitting coat and a short periwig had served them with punch. As they went through they could see the seats about the pit were taken, the noise floating above the bloodied sawdust intensifying as the spurs dug deeper into the birds' flesh – as the kill grew closer. Another cup of spirit inside him and the need to be part of this frenzy had seen Geoffrey plunge his hand into his pocket again and again, laying his money on the assured – so often the silver claw-end spurs of its opponent seeing it doomed.

33

The night and the dead hours of the morning had passed pleasurably enough – the beginning hopefully and full of promise, the ending frustratingly and none too clearly. Now, reality hit him along with the new day, and stepping uncertainly down from the coach as the grey dawn broke over the eastern hills Geoffrey was in desolate mood.

Inebriated to the point of imbalance, he stumbled on the uneven flags. Feeling for purchase on the ageing red wall of St Petrock's church and placing both palms against the stone, he put his head between his outstretched arms. After having won a little in the cockpit he had gone back into the house again and joined three others at a table. There was some recollection of promissory notes and of invitations to similar gatherings. He remembered searching in his pockets for the earbobs and the rings – he ran a hand into his inner pocket now, the earbobs were still there but only two rings remained. William was ever the fool – Geoffrey doubted the likelihood that any of the young men he had kept company with during the small hours were sons of Quakers. He had never gambled with such high stakes; these young bucks had not had to fight for their income as he had, they were sons of wealthy men and it showed in their recklessness.

Even this unhurried westward city did not sleep for long and there were already people about their business. A lamplighter was extinguishing a flame close to the turnpike crossroads, and an old man pulling a piss-cart was working his way cautiously downwards towards the river. The stench of the ammonia reached Geoffrey's senses; a sudden sweep of nausea filling his gullet, he put his head down and vomited, the contents of his stomach meeting his shoes. It was hard to tell if people were ending their night or starting their day. Geoffrey did not care either way.

It seemed easier to continue on down Fore Street, a less hazardous route – the activity of the butchery business would be well underway. After the rain of yesterday the strength of the May dawn had caught the wet city by surprise and mist was settling in the hollows of the valley, bringing a veil of dampness to the narrow and congested streets that bordered Exe Island. His journey was downwards and he drew back his shoulders to keep his balance and walked in the direction of the West Gate, which would take him, eventually, to his uncle's house.

Uncle Latimer came into his thoughts and with these thoughts returned the spectre of Blox. The tincture would not last indefinitely – he must pay him or go without. He walked on, focusing on the far distance, trying to ignore the stains on his new breeches. The river was in sight; the whole of this part of the city seemed to sit in a state of near permanent dampness. Blox must be confronted and soon; pushed on by a sense of persecution he determined to visit the old man now and be done with it.

The lane was empty, even the ragamuffins and beggars had kept to their pallets on this dank morning. No more than a few wormed planks, the door of the Frog Lane hovel was closed and held shut with twine. It was quiet about and quiet within. He pushed the door, stepped in and stood on the littered floor, regaining his balance, adjusting his eyes to the near darkness. There was no one here and he could not decide if this was beneficial to his cause or restrictive. His mind spun on in that illogical, irrational way that all drunks have when the impossible and the improbable seem easily within reach.

The shelves were a jumbled mix of phials, lidded containers and stone jars, corked and uncorked. There was something obnoxious soaking in a bucket beneath the apothecaries table, evidence of work having already begun. If the herbalist were not here – and there was no hiding place in this small room – then could he not find what he wanted and leave without confrontation? He did not wish to encounter the lash of Blox's aristocratic, venomous tongue any more than he wished to pay him for what he had already taken, and there was no coin in his purse even if he wished it.

Forcing his eyes into focus he began to look into containers and jars, removing corks, holding necks as closely to his nose as he could bear. Some were labelled, some not so, some in Latin; he made of it what he could. Senna, liquorice, peppermint, bark extracts, angelica and the well-stopped jugs of digitalis, aconitum and aloe. Deeper thought told him that he could never find the mix that Blox had previously prescribed for his uncle. He ignored this thought and continued to search for the familiar, clumsily knocking over jars, allowing the contents to spill out.

Added light came into the room and he heard a shuffle and turned.

"A thief in my house." Blox was standing behind him – he drew off the damp sacking draped about his shoulders and squinted through opaque eyes. "Ah, the man of stature and fine clothes but of no substance." He paused, speaking in a voice that did not fit with his filthy clothes and monk-like tonsure. "Would you rob me twice?"

Geoffrey turned, slipping the bottle he held in his hand into one of the large pockets in his coat.

"Your comment is malicious, sir, unfounded." He stepped back to allow Blox to enter the hovel.

"Then if you deny it you must explain it. I do not do business with any until the sun lights St Edmund's parapet. This is my time for gathering and if you had listened to any of our discussions in past times you would know it." Blox lifted the open basket he carried on his arm and placed it on the table. "You will have no more remedies from me, sir, until you have paid for the last and I wager by the level of your intoxication and the state of your dress, drink and gaming will have already emptied your pockets."

Blox began to sift through flower heads and herbage.

"You know nothing of me, Blox, not where I go nor what I do – nor even who I am."

Geoffrey's speech was still a little slurred. Blox did not answer but turned an eye away from his work to look at him.

"Then if you think it – it must be so. But hear me well, whoever you are, whatever your life, you will not have more until you have paid me for the last."

Geoffrey swallowed his nausea and steadied himself.

"It is hardly fairness that you should doubt me. Have I not paid you in the past and paid you well? You need not doubt me now."

"Doubt, sir, and inconsistency is written all across your egotistical face. Pay me or go, I have other business."

"I would have the tincture first, Blox – I have seen you mix a quantity of the stuff, do not think I will part with good coin before I have the thing in my hand."

The old man, still sharp-witted, had allowed his glance to flicker in the direction of an open wooden box. It was a glance of possession and satisfaction, but enough to set Geoffrey on the scent. Geoffrey covertly viewed the box through narrowed eyes – the jar, the size, the cork and the carefully tied Latin label were familiar.

"Then show your coin and I will mix you what you require."

"The mix is done, Blox, you know it, I remember from the last. It is here – this is the same as before. I can tell by the look of the thing."

"You cannot tell, you may only conjecture. Out with the coin and you shall have it."

Geoffrey had put his hand into his pocket in pretence of finding payment. His hand had found the earbobs and the remaining rings instead and he caught them up in his hand, held them out in his closed fist. "Here, take payment and let me have what I came for and we may part company the sooner." He picked up one of the bottles of tincture from the box and placed it beside the other in his pocket. "Here," he said opening his palm. "It will be more than enough to pay for the crushings of a few dried leaves and a thimble of brandy. Take it." With a flourish he threw the rings and the earbobs onto the earth floor amongst the debris of discarded herbage. "And see that you do not allow that venomous and free-running tongue to out any of our dealings. I will deny all – and who is more likely to be believed, a rancid herbalist with a spurious past, or a gentleman of the city?"

34

Rachael was kneeling before a long gilded mirror randomly propped against one wall. The striped cotton dress she wore was a discard of the bawdy house and had lain in the bottom of Jane's trunk for more than a year. Lack of appetite had seen the soft rounded shape of youth become noticeably taut and angular, and the waist of the dress was now neatly taken in to suit – a little lace had been added here and there in an attempt at modesty. All the vitality and vibrancy that had once shone from her face was now gone, replaced by lifeless powder and rouge, and an underlying sadness – the cause of which was known only to her. Jane was half sitting, half lying on the unmade bed, one plump leg crossed over the other. A buckled shoe moved up and down with frustration and a little impatience.

"If you must squat before that glass and make yourself look like something you are not, then I believe it might be better done in some other's rooms. I have no pleasure in looking upon you dressed up in that slatternly gown and painted up like a city harlot."

Rachael ignored the older girl and leant forwards to study her full lips. A small pot of carmine was balanced in her lap and she worked the paste with her finger, leaning closer to the mirror still and dabbing the mixture onto her lips to form a small unnatural bow where once her honest mouth had smiled out.

"I can have some sympathy in that you want to get beyond that pious old man's Godly preachings, but 'tis quite the wrong thing to go whoring no sooner than leave. I have pledged my heart that you would not and you have come so far along without – I cannot see as what has changed."

The preceding week Jane had found Rachael in the milliner's shop talking to the bawd. The old woman, shrunken with age and perhaps the harshness of a life lived by prostitution or the soliciting of others to prostitute, rarely left the dark corner at the back of the shop. Small of stature, it was her way to sit with her feet propped on a small footstool; the footrest was her money chest, and to dissuade any from attempting to remove it most times she sat with a long-tailed horse whip across her knees. Jane had gathered Rachael up and led her away, returning later with a concocted story to relate to the bawd.

Rachael turned to face Jane, almost unrecognizable now, her already dark winged eyebrows painted into unnatural arcs with the help of a burnt cork.

"Life must move on, Jane, and mine has, so it is hardly fair-minded for you to make comment upon my choices. The pot has little right to be calling the kettle black."

She turned back to the mirror and began to manoeuvre her bosom so that it sat more prominently above the lace of the gown. Jane picked at her long nails.

"I have told the bawdy-mother that you was chased away from your home but have no need of this house yet awhile. Rachael you are an enticement, she may run the house well and we are safer here than in most places, but she do not have a beating heart. Her life blood runs through that little box she keeps beneath her feet and she will have a man to you before you can say Jack."

Rachael looked into the glass without seeing herself and closed her eyes to cover her emotion, allowing Jane to continue.

"She makes a friend of me because I *am* her life blood and a favourite in the house and I may ask her favours, but she will send to you, Rachael, and then you will be lost and must take the consequences of what you do."

Mechanically putting the rouge tub and carmine back into the paper patch box – a level of beautification she did not need having escaped the disfigurement of smallpox – Rachael rose and spread out her skirts.

"Then if she wishes to send, she must send. I am no different from any other in this house, Jane. I am unwed and without family, I am seventeen and must make my way the same as others do."

Jane pulled herself up and slid off the bed, stood before the glass and examined her own image. She was near eight years older than the artist's servant but she had survived well, avoiding the pox and having to deal with only two pregnancies. The image before her threw back an uneasy comparison – Rachael was placing a hat on her starched chalk-powdered hair.

"You know it in your heart, Rae, that you are not the same as us here. You have the learning of letters and the reading of books. And you have Alexander – can you not wait for Trelawney to return? He would surely not see you here when he has had you as his pet for so long, keeping you safe. And Flood, I may not like his bible ways but the man would not send you to this."

The large brim of the hat obscured Rachael's expression, as did the processes she had so diligently gone through to turn herself into a willing harlot.

"Elijah do know where I am and will not have me back now that I have defied his thinking. He says I am no longer his daughter and does not know me. And Alexander is likely gone from the county. I am done with waiting on the man to decide where next he makes his living and who he makes it with. His money do not come from his brush alone and well you know this, Jane – and money may take him where he chooses."

Jane moved away from the glass and took up her own hat. She did not wear the lead and her box contained nothing more than chalk dust – it was rare for her to apply the carmine; berry-pap or vinegar worked as well and health and good looks continued to step along beside her.

"I am ready, Jane. We have run around this mulberry tree too many times and I am eager to be out of here."

"My thoughts upon the matter do not change, Rae, you may come along with me, but you are for the looking upon and not the mauling over and I will see to it."

They were ready to leave and Rachael stood in the older woman's wake. As if determined to fight her friend's defiance, Jane turned on her heel and faced Rae.

"Mayn't you look for a husband, Rae? A woman not yet bedded will always have hope of finding a solid man."

Rachael straightened her brim and closed her eyes as if impatient with the conversation. "I mayn't find a husband, Jane. You do not know all things about me."

Jane caught Rachael's arm, shook her gently, enough to make her open her eyes.

"Then tell me what it is I do not know. If I am wrong footed then tell me why."

"It is not your business, Jane, and if you was not so very urgent with your arm shaking I might keep my privacy, but now I see I am pushed along to tell what I would rather not."

She looked beyond Jane into the depths of the shabby untidy room unable to meet her eyes, took breath before she spoke. "I am already bedded, Jane – I am had, I am sullied and fit for nowhere but this house." Jane let go of her arm. "I have had no man, Jane, but a man has had me. So you see, I am whore already. Do not ask around it, Jane, I cannot have the thing aired over and over again and I must look to tomorrow and never back at yesterday."

Their destination was one of the lesser-known coffee houses just off Goldsmith's – at the door of the coffee rooms Rachael had turned.

"Forgive me, Jane, I did not wish to play haughty with you but do not ask me to explain – just help me along for a while until I know what path to take."

They stood aside to allow a group of gentlemen to exit the low door; if they had been from any other level of society, held any other occupation they would not have been accepted.

"Then I will not ask more, but I do not choose it, Rae – I would have the thing out where it may be looked over. And I cannot say as I am not saddened by what you say. I may have this life and survive it well but I would not have another take it without necessity. Come, we must go in, I have promised a young rogue to keep him in company and bid him safe passage before he is sent away to do business in the Americas."

She took Rachael's arm – the rooms were near empty, just a few gentlemen spaced here and there, sipping chocolate, broadsheets spread before them.

"I will agree not to ask you more, Rae, but you must promise me that you will wait awhile before taking any old man or young buck to your bed and moving down a path that you cannot turn back from."

35

June had begun to bring early light to Latimer's window, seeping between the drawn curtains, bringing slashes of sunlight to sit upon the dark boards of his floor. Unaware of anything other than his immediate surroundings for some weeks, Henri had no knowledge of events beyond his own four walls; but over the last few days his head had begun to clear – this time for longer periods. He had become accustomed to assessing time by the moving shadows on his wall, the lightness of the day or the blackness of the night; and although he did not wish to make prediction lest he be disappointed, it was clear that he was no longer falling into endless spells of stupor that saw him sleep through days and nights together.

Weakened by long spells of inactivity, he found he was stiff legged – without strength. He had called Vetch before the midday and had his servant take off, what was now, a full-grown beard.

"I thank you, Thomas, at least my chin has the look of normality." He viewed his dark gaunt features in the small mirror. Last week, he could not pinpoint when, Elcott had called. Vetch had chosen not to tell him directly and had taken it upon himself to fend him off.

"The notary, you said the notary had called."

"Yes, sir, the young gentleman has called on a few occasions – this last time I believe he had recently returned on the Bristol coach and wished to understand your continued absence from your usual meeting place. He has since sent word that he will call again."

"When?"

"Later today, sir, this afternoon."

Dwelling for so much of these last weeks in a surreal haze of incomprehension and restless sleep, the novelty of a simple conversation with his servant and the prospect of a more in-depth one with his good friend were lifting. He allowed Vetch to help him in into his dressing-coat. "Have him shown into the front sitting room when he comes – I will make sure I am there to greet him."

He allowed Vetch to go and looked about the room – a room that over the last weeks had lost its comfortable familiarity, fever turning furnishings into grotesque blocks, indeterminate and unreal. His window had been closed throughout his sickness and he moved cautiously towards it looking out into the yard. Rae, he had not seen Rae. How long had it been since he had spied her white cap and bowed head waiting for him to open his window?

A fire was lit in his sitting room sending mellow warmth about the oak panels and threadbare furniture. The weather had moved from unseasonal warmth to a dull coldness, better suited to a winter's day. He took a chair close to the hearth, pulling the long tails of his dressing-coat about his legs.

As his mind settled to the normality of life, remembrances of the preceding days before he took to his bed began to return. He understood now that his nephew could not be trusted, had spun a lie without hindrance of conscience, was deceitful by nature and most probably had aspirations way beyond anything Latimer could offer him. In a brief moment of lucidity Latimer had been offered explanation, but it would not wash. He heard the occasional maid hurriedly stepping across the flags towards his street door. It would be Elcott.

The young man stepped in from the street, there was a pause whilst he explained his visit and the maid took his cloak. Tentatively putting head and one shoulder through the part-opened doorway, Elcott greeted him. "Henri. Forgive me if this is inappropriate. My earlier visits here have left me with more concerns than answers."

"Edmund, come forwards and on no account carry concerns on my behalf."

Henri rose slowly, forcing himself to stand straight with the help of his stick.

"Please, do not stand, sir. The season has lost direction and I will be glad to air my coat-tails upon that little fire." Edmund stood facing Henri with his back to the fire. Quickly losing balance Henri sat abruptly.

"Have you time to stay for refreshment? I take only porter – there is plenty in the jug and a mug spare." Elcott watched him slowly fill another mug with dark ale. "Was there any pressing reason for your visit, or do you desire the company of a half-wretched invalid?"

Elcott, slightly embarrassed by the accuracy of the comment smiled briefly.

"There is nothing pressing, Henri. No more pressing than my knowledge that I have been remiss in offering you company, I would plead that my present circumstance mitigates. As you know, my heart is pulled in more than one direction – I have no wish to abandon my mother for long periods of time and yet my preference would be to spend the summer in Somerset." The heat of the fire had more than aired his coat-tails and he moved away to a cooler part of the room. "The consequences of my affections are that I have spent unaccountable hours sat aboard a dusty coach on the turnpike to Bristol and have had little time beyond to socialize."

"Ah, the heart," Henri said feeling his newly shaven chin. "We cannot predict nor control what it tells us, although I am little experienced in these things – but I believe it to be so. Perhaps there is no way through but to follow its direction. Have you set a date for your marriage?"

"September, it will be September, but I cannot say just when in the month. We must first decide where we base our new lives, and that, my friend, will include my mother. I would have Exeter but there are merits in centring a new business in Bristol."

"If you have the palate for the trade that dominates there then I believe your profession would be well supported."

"I am not sure that I do, Henri. My mama would prefer Devon, but there is always the possibility of settling near to Knowle Easton – a good life might be had there if sufficient custom could be found."

Latimer rested his head on the tapestry of his high-backed chair, although he was not particularly tired. "I am confident you will make a fair decision, Edmund – indeed I am sure of it."

Elcott took the top off his second mug of porter. "You say you are not much experienced in the matters of the heart, sir, but surely youth and marriage went hand in hand for you – indeed you have two pretty daughters to prove the point."

"They are a blessing and I would alter nothing," Henri said flatly. Intentionally or not he rarely brought to mind the difficult and sometimes querulous years he had spent with his wife. Perhaps it was wrong of him to push her memory to the back of all remembrance. "But I would not say the union was blessed – apart from progeny. Mary was dead before our fourth year of marriage. In truth I knew her little." He might have added that she knew him not at all, but instead he said, "Wedlock did not sit well with her and did not end well. Perhaps the fault was mine? We were not wed long enough to confirm it and I have never had any desire to repeat the commitment."

Elcott coughed and stood to look out at the changing day. "Many re-marry within a twelve month."

"Indeed they do, Edmund."

"What of your nephew, Henri? Does he continue along a straight path and give you hope that you may see him a solid merchant in full time?"

"Ah, nephew Geoffrey." Henri looked at his hands. He recalled his nephew's unrepentant telling of the well-articulated but seemingly false story of his independent business venture. "I have not shared his company for some time." He said no more – he would not black-mark a young man's reputation without proof. "To return to matters of the heart, Edmund, do not be despondent about my lack of female acquaintance – I am quite open to courtship should it come my way. Although I would not say experience guides me, I have knowledge enough to know that the heart is unpredictable but must be listened to never the less."

Looking at his time piece, Elcott rose and prepared to leave. "I must away, sir. It leaves me in good spirit to see you up and improving, but I have prepared indenture papers for a mother and her son out along Magdalen Street and must hurry there lest the mother imagines me forgetful. The boy is to be apprenticed to a sound wheelwright and will do well in the trade."

Latimer stood uncertainly, took the younger man's hand and was then left alone to ponder his own advice. After sickness, life seemed unexpectedly short and all things within it more pressing. He moved slowly to the writing table set close to the window, sat and took out paper from a drawer. Reaching for the inkwell he wrote briefly to Rachael.

Forgive me for my lack of attendance. If you find yourself lost, send me note by return so that I might seek you. I am bereft without our friendly intercourse and would restore this without interval.

He had read the simple lines twice, folded the paper crudely in four and placed it at the back of a drawer. Writing again with more energy he had omitted the last sentence, folded the paper, this time neatly, and sealed it. The house was quiet. He rose with the letter in his hand, moved to the door and standing in the hallway wrapped the panelling with his stick until he was heard.

Vetch had finally found him and taken the paper, reading the copperplate hand of his master and the name and respectful title of the young woman – a woman with considerably lower status than his own.

"I will have a reply, Thomas. The old man does not read and I will see this put into the hand of the addressee. Wait for reply whether verbal or written." Latimer turned away and began to re-enter his sitting room. "Find the occasional maid and have my daughters sent to me – I would prefer you do this before you leave."

Some two hours later, satisfaction replacing frustration, Latimer lay down on his bed knowing he had begun yet another journey back to health. He had enjoyed the softness of his daughters, their simple chatter and their liking for him which he felt must be heightened by his recent self-imposed exile, relieving their nurse of their care and having them join in the large downstairs room. Now he had no strength. The letter remained as yet undelivered but he would have reply soon enough, and then he could encourage life to return to the simplicity of how it once was.

36

Caring for her master's daughters was a task Old Sarah met with complacent familiarity, her daily responsibilities often eased by the intermittent sipping of cheap gin and pilfered spirits. She had been the firstborn of a family of eleven, had seen her mother birth half a dozen sickly babes and helped her parents bury most of these. Worn down and turned old before she was twenty, she had never married. Life in the Exebere house had suited her well. The master had not been a dutiful husband and had escaped to any place beyond his door, loitering along with a capable crew who did not need his intervention, sailing to and from the Lowlands, trotting out across the hinterlands of the county on a hired horse. And then when his wife had died he had stuck much closer to home, but the upper floors of the old house had always been hers – this was her home and she would die here.

A tray of hard eggs, curd cheese and dark bread had been brought up earlier and left for their meal. She had sat her master's daughters at their table and then gone away to her bed-corner to take a little refreshment herself. Rarely did duty allow her freedoms but this day had been exceptional; the master, newly from his sickbed, had requested that his daughters spend time with him away from the nursery, and instead of being obliged to wait until the dark hours to wander unnoticed through the house, she had been set free to enjoy this pastime in daylight.

She afforded gin from the few pence offered her as wages and supplemented her purse from monies given her for the needs of Mary and Sophia. The upper floors of the house lacked any kind of stewardship; hard drink could be found in all manner of places, left unattended or secreted away in unlocked cupboards. This post-noon, during her pleasurable time of freedom, she had wandered the upper house with the small receiving jug that she kept for the acquisition of extra spirits hidden in a voluminous pocket. This was now quite full and she decanted the liquid – a tincture perhaps, but brandy she was sure – into an empty earthenware bottle. She never took more than was noticeable from any bottle or decanter, returning the levels with her own mix of sugar water.

The pleasure was not for now, and when her charges had finished eating she would settle them with their pattern work and samplers and take a little nap.

Quietly entering the house after Vetch had gone to his bed, Geoffrey removed his boots and climbed the turning oak stairs to his rooms, passing the sick room without sound, lying down upon his own bed fully clothed. He had spent the early evening with his whore and then eaten at the Seven Stars; it had been a poor second to The Phoenix and he found the company on this side of the river altogether less amenable and the conversation quite base. The twin jars waiting side by side upon his dressing chest, intentionally lost amongst other applications and perfumes, taunted him. He had made no attempt to slip their contents into any bottle or glass, and he had not offered Vetch any spurious reason for the addition of this or that to his uncle's drink or victuals – although this would have been easy enough; Vetch asked no questions, sought no knowledge, and Geoffrey was certain sure he did not believe any of his well-prepared explanations.

In truth, he did not know what either of these bottles contained. The learning of Latin had been something to avoid and he remembered none. They both smelt of brandy – a tincture – but what else they contained he could not be sure. Geoffrey considered outcomes. What was it that he wanted? Apart from the very first weeks of his stay when he saw it his duty to ease his uncle from a life that he was unlikely to keep to the death he was certain to have, he had never felt the intent to finish him. Keeping Uncle Latimer confined to his rooms in a state of stupor where reason and thought would not find him suited Geoffrey's needs, but offering up the contents of either of these noxious looking bottles without surety of the outcome needed further thought. Would there be a judgement day? He could not say. A decision could not be made in haste.

He settled his head more comfortably on his pillow. If he thought only of surface things then life ran well enough. The fragile little whore he kept at Alphington still held his interest – his need was to master her, but although he felt he mastered her well in the confines of their room she would not sever her connections with the bawdy house. Whenever they came together it produced in him a brutishness that often made him despoil the wholesome pleasures of their lust. This thought made his gaze return again to the jars upon his chest. Money would always buy a harlot's time and perhaps a better place in which he might be served, but there was never enough in his purse and the thought continued to rankle, the question continuing to eat away at him – was his Uncle Latimer playing false with him, did he have concealed wealth? Only his death would out the truth.

Below the surface of light thought, his circumstance and predicament he knew were far darker. He was getting through the money he had raised more quickly than he had hoped. He deeply regretted repaying the fleece money his uncle had demanded be returned to his bank, and the interest on the borrowed sum, set at a very unfavourable rate, would be due in two weeks' time – he was unlikely to meet it. He sat up and moved the jars out of sight. Toying with these ideas with a clear head would never do. Changing his coat he left his room, passing his uncle's door again and noting that the sleeping sickness, induced by Blox's now depleted mix, had not yet passed, and made his way through the dark streets towards The Phoenix.

37

The endless hours of disturbed, fevered sleep, which over the last weeks had spanned not just the night but much of his day as well, had progressed into something quite different –this was progress as far as Latimer was concerned and for once he had felt rested when he awoke. He ran his hand through his overlong hair. He had asked Vetch to help him dress and his servant stood before him shaking out a linen shirt.

"The letter, Thomas – the sealed paper I put into your hand yesterday? Has the thing found its destination or do we still wait upon the Dissenter?"

Vetch offered up a clean stock from the press.

"We do not wait upon him, sir, I have been watching for the man. Unless he is called away elsewhere, he keeps good time."

"And so?" Latimer said, already impatient to have answer.

"The person to whom the paper was addressed was not at home, sir."

"Explain this please, Thomas – whatever knowledge you have upon the matter I would have it and as succinctly as you may give it."

"The young lady has moved on, sir."

Latimer may have assessed his dalliance with Rachael as secret but it was not completely so; Vetch had observed their meetings on many occasions. He disliked his master's turn-sided ideas and this flirtation with the whore's companion confirmed his belief that Henri Latimer would never be the gentleman that his father had been.

"Moved on, Thomas? Has she gone to join Trelawney? What does the man say? He must have explained her absence."

"He did not say, sir. He did not say further. I offered that he should put the paper into her hand but he said he could not."

"He does not know where she has gone, Thomas, or he will not say? A wealth of difference lies between." Henri absently tucked his shirt-tails into his breeches. He put his hand up impatiently before Vetch could begin again. "And do not give me any sit-upon-the-fence answer to this, offer me what you believe."

"Then if 'tis opinion you would have, sir, I would reason that the young woman has gone somewhere that fits poorly with the Dissenter's bible teachings, somewhere that she has often dallied when the old man is at his meetings."

Conclusion struck Henri like an errant packhorse even before Vetch had finished speaking. After a pause, he said, "You believe she has taken lodging in the house next to this – or do you perhaps know that this is so, Thomas?"

"Perhaps a combination of the two, sir."

"Then we can go no further with this." He moved cautiously across the room to stand before his glass. "Where is my note now, Thomas, did you leave the correspondence with Mr Flood?"

"No, sir, he would not take it in his hand. It is laid upon your writing desk."

Vetch held his coat ready.

"My nephew, I hardly expect that he remains in the house, but I would have this confirmed?"

The line of Henri's thoughts had not changed direction but he felt obliged to know what happened in his own house before he prepared to leave it for a while – and he would go out today.

"He is not within, sir – unless I am mistaken or he has returned unseen."

"I may not hurry it along, Thomas, but I intend to take some air once I have broken my fast. Will you see there is something light laid for me to eat when I come down?" His voice was harsher than it might have been.

Already moving towards the door, Vetch nodded his agreement. "Shall I put out a jug of porter, sir?"

"I would be obliged."

Left alone he considered what Vetch had said. He glanced into his glass, settling his coat – a sorry sight; recently shaved he might be, but the image that came back to him was of a pallid and ragged old man.

As soon as he had breakfasted, Henri had opened his street door and set out for St Mary's burial ground; having no affinity with any God, the quiet place seemed to clear his head rather than provoke complex thought. Early June may have seen in longer days, but the county was not always blessed with sun-warmed winds and humid nights; the North wind remained and the skies had still to clear. Perched on a low wall Henri looked blindly at the unkempt grasses of the old burying place – was it conceivable that Rae had taken lodging in the bawdy house? Elijah Flood's meeting house he knew was out towards the South Gate. He would find it if he took his time; he tapped his way slowly along the busy streets. Of course there was no certainty that Thomas Flood would be there, but the journey would occupy his mind and he must make some attempt at understanding why Rae had left the safety of the old man's kitchen.

Flood was there, still stiffly buttoned into his coat. He had recently finished cleaning the numerous pewter candlesticks that kept the small hall from appearing to be the dark slope-roofed hovel that it really was. Now he was kneeling on the stone floor, silver head bowed over closed hands. Henri might not follow the teachings of Elijah's religion, but he would respect a man in prayer. He waited until the Dissenter had completed his chantings and silent prayer before coming forward.

Having taken off his hat when entering the chapel, this was now caught awkwardly under his arm whilst he gripped the back of a coarse pew.

"Flood," he said in a low, reverent and almost whispered voice, a voice that surprised even him. He had not thought what title to offer Trelawney's servant, this man who had inadvertently become Rachael's protector, had done as much as any to keep Rae from vice – from harm.

"I would not wish to intrude upon your worship, but there is some urgency in my need for closure on an issue that concerns me." This clumsy indirect way of speaking would not do. Flood looked him over, blankness in his stare but no curiosity. The stick was a prompt and after a second glance, Flood understood who he was; they had passed at distance many times over many years and Elijah had served him at Alexander's evening. But standing there in the Dissenter's Hall, presented to him quite out of context; he had not recognised the merchant. Now that he did, Flood could not find a handle on why he might be there.

"The need must be urgent to seek me here, sir. But if it is not God's business you wish to speak upon then perhaps we should speak it without these walls and beyond this door."

Henri dropped his head in agreement and turned, replacing his tricorn as he moved back out into the cool rain-spotted day. Flood took a large key from his pocket and turned it in a lock that would have found pride on a cathedral door.

"The letter my servant passed to you, you would not take it."

"I would not," Flood replied, still as yet undecided why the reclusive merchant had sent such a correspondence in the first instance.

"But you know where she is."

"I do," he said shortly and then, catching the glint of Latimer's penetrating eyes and reading a little from them, added, "It seems that you may have second guessed her residing place also."

"Perhaps, there are few other options, but I must have this confirmed."

They began to move away from the meeting house, Flood surprised at the length of the merchant's stride despite his weakness.

"I cannot help her, Mr Latimer." Flood stopped, remembering his Christian teachings. Lies had no place in this world. "She has made her choice, she is stepping along a path that I have endeavoured to keep her from since consent found her, but she will not have my reasoning. She has chosen to live amongst the fallen, alongside base fornicators, to be amongst them and be as they are and to do as they do despite all that she has learnt from our good book. Whore she is and whore she will always be to me now. I will try no more to find her a place in Heaven."

Winded by this declaration Henri spoke. "Then it is confirmed," he said briefly, "and you can give me no reasoning."

"I cannot."

"Then when? When did she leave?"

"It is three weeks since now."

He considered this simple statement; three weeks, three weeks in which to grow into the house, three weeks in which to change from the innocent girl he knew to something he did not wish to imagine. He would not imagine it, he must accept what he had been told; but until he could stand before her and have her state clearly her reasons for this dramatic mind change, optimism must take him forward.

38

Two days of pacing his room, stick held tightly against his leg, body enfeebled by too many weeks lying in his bed, Latimer's temper had risen to a level where even Vetch had begun to turn a closed ear. It was not that the decision needed to be made – he had made it yesterday, before Flood had gone from sight – his reluctance came from the thought that the final outcome may not be what he hoped for.

Before the mid-afternoon Latimer entered the bawdy house. The squat bowed door and dirty lattice hid a dingy interior. He stood squarely in the small area that was set aside for the business of millinery. He was not alone: two gentlemen of trade in wigs and woollen coats had preceded him; one had a young woman caught upon his arm and the other was leaning on a high table which served as work space and coin counter. The place was close and airless as if it were permanently shut up away from the world. There was a point when he thought he might turn on his heels and run, and with every moment he spent in this oppressive place the less he was able to understand why Rachael had taken herself off here to live a life so much in inferiority to the one she had left, locked away behind closed doors and shuttered windows.

There were two girls working with thread and feathers towards the back of the shop and another, painted and sparsely dressed, idling her time near to the window. He saw this as illogical as the light at the back was so poor and then reprimanded himself for his naivety. The older gentleman and the girl had collected a purchase and left soon after his arrival, the other had been fetched and disappeared up the narrow flight of stairs which connected the shop to the house above.

During the two frustrating days of contemplation preceding, he had not thought beyond this point – now he was not sure of his course. He rarely visited the brothels of the city, but this one, almost on his own doorstep, was not a place he would ever go by choice. He noticed his hands were shaking, he suspicioned he would also be collected at some point, and then what?

A small woman with a hard face and a coarse wig came out from behind a screen. She faced him and he knew instantly who she was. He stood his ground, balanced his weight more evenly on his stick – the gossip surrounding this woman, almost entirely finding his ear through conversation with Rae, was almost legendary. He wondered how someone with such a small stature could hold such authority.

"Be not guided by the lid of the box, sir," she said looking up at him, pulling the leather tails of a small whip through her fingers. "There is much more within. If 'tis a fine straw bonnet you require then we can suit any taste – if 'tis the wearer of such a thing you have interest in, then we have stock and plenty."

"I do not need to see your stock, Mother. My choice is already made."

"Then we may suit you the sooner. Speak your choice and I will have a girl fetch her, if I am able. 'Tis busy times, the markets are in full flow and the streets lively."

"You have a young woman here, unsullied and unpainted, her hair is dark and she came to you quite recently."

The bawd looked him over. She did not know him, never leaving her cash box from one year's end to the next, but it only took one eye to see that he was different and that perhaps his needs may not be so easily met.

"I cannot recall such a one, sir." She lifted her chin in an attempt to raise her own stature to meet his. He noticed her chin was as hairy as a youth the day before his first scraping.

"You will know her, madam."

"I will know her? I know all who live here along with me. I know them because I am a good mother to them and keep watchful eye over them, but I cannot say such a woman lives in this house."

Latimer dropped his head, allowing his gaze to settle upon the bawd's face. She met his look evenly. There was no man of any class, of any disposition whom she had not had knowledge of during her long years of whoring; the merchant should not think she could conjure tricks.

"Our stock is of some quality, sir, will you not choose again? I can manage two and sometimes three if your coin is good and this be your preference."

"I do not wish to see your stock, not even if this can be supplied in tens. I wish to see the girl who came to you but three weeks ago, the girl who has settled many a day in your kitchens – if you did but know it – the girl who is deft with needle and thread and who you have paid good coin to for her work."

"Repeated askings and a hot head do not get you forward in this house. I cannot offer what I do not have."

The pasty, undernourished girls at the back of the shop had put down their needles and the harlot on display was now standing against the door. Latimer opened his coat, fumbled inexpertly for his purse, drew out a handful of coin and banged the money onto the counter.

"My coin is as good as any and I will pay you beyond what my requirements will be. If I do not find what I seek I will not ask for refund."

Gripping the pommel of his stick he turned on his heels, mounting the stairs and leaving the airless room behind him, rising up the narrow staircase more easily than he had anticipated. He stopped at the head. He had reached the landing above and now what – did he search, did he enquire, did he intrude? The house was a near replica of his own, but so unlike his own – this house was a brothel: dark, shuttered, without natural light, without life, airless and unalive.

His shoulders felt taut, he half expected to feel a hand upon them, dragging him away, a cudgel about his head perhaps, but the attack did not come – this was a wholly female house. Low voices and the murmurs of seduction reached him from darkened rooms. A boot on the base of a half-opened door revealed a buxom harlot semi-clothed and the naked rear end of her half satisfied client. What had he expected? What was he thinking? And then the thought came, hit him as hard as any cudgel. In the next room might it not be Rae in harlot's pose? What questions would he have to ask her then?

Finding stairs to the next landing he went up. There were about eight whores working in the house most days, he knew this already; many doors, many rooms – partitioned rooms smaller than in his own house. A harlot passed him in pursuit of her quarry, escaping, if only momentarily, to seek the communal piss-pot. White paint and lead-red lips, laces freed ready for work. He felt almost invisible; for years he had lived alongside this house, never queried it, had talked with Rachael of what happened here, knew some of the women who worked here. But he had not been thinking deeply. Between the toxic paint and the expected and accepted diseases, life expectancy would be short. But then set against the harshness of the world that would be theirs if they were not here, was not their life tolerable?

Temper falling, sense taking hold, he took more care in his hunt, unobtrusively searching rooms, opening doors closing doors behind him and now studying the painted faces that he found. He did not see quite how any young woman could change so very much in such a short space of time, becoming such a stranger to him that he might not know her – the thought was almost more alarming than the path she had chosen. In a small room at the back of the house with the window open to the evening air he found her.

The bed here was no more than a pallet with a thin straw mattress laid on top, and there was no man upon it. She had left the door open and he stopped, drew his thoughts together, unsure what he might say – he was not even sure why he had come and what he expected her response to be. He did recognize her, but she was different. He went forward to the open door and stood on the threshold; she was leaning on the wall beside the window looking out, she raised her head and he found he could not speak. How pertinent his omitted comment in his undelivered letter. He had found her, but whether she considered herself lost he did not know.

Her face was still chalk white and some remnants of carmine showed on her lips, but the surprise that he had anticipated was quite absent, which lead him to ask, "You anticipate me, Rae. Is this so?"

"I expected that you would eventually find me, sir – Hetty had forewarned me. Yes I knew of your searching."

All the easy conversation that he had become accustomed to had evaporated, and she had called him 'sir', not by his name. Although he had not honestly considered what he might find, this change he would not have expected.

"I am sorry you have had the chase. The bawd should have told you where I was." She did not meet his eyes. "It is not a secret notion to come here – I have made firm choice to do it and I do not hide from any."

"I knew of your choice, Rachael, but reasoning required more proof than hearsay could offer me." She glanced up now.

"Why would you think it such a turn-about? It is a path I should have taken since I was able."

Latimer did not want his anger returning. Most of all he did not wish to show this front to Rachael, whom he could never feel real anger towards. But her remarks frustrated in the extreme. He stepped further into the room.

"I must speak plain, Rae." The need to take her elbow, shake her until the dull shell of disinterest fell away was urgent, but he did not come close enough to touch her. "Why have you come here? Offer me motive, Rae. God in Heaven, Rachael, was not your lot an altogether settled one?" He paused and watched her eyes flicker, but the blank mask remained. "And you did not think to talk the thing through with me? You know if you had, I would have reasoned with you, stopped you, Rachael – might have stopped you."

He realised as soon as he had finished, the one thing she had not been able to do over the weeks preceding her self-imposed incarceration in this dead house was to talk to him. No, of course she could not and now he may as well have been conversing with the blackened lime-washed walls.

"'Tis quite a pleasure seeing you up and well, sir." She folded her arms, looking out over the courtyard, discarding his pleas like they were nothing. She continued, "With the will to get beyond the mother and the energy to rise two flights in quick time."

The breeze from the window was moving the ragged curtain, but her dressed stiffened hair, like a dead thing, did not stir. He drew his hand through his own hair in frustration.

"Will you not find me reason why you have come here – let go of your old life? I cannot think to leave you without knowing."

"For no reason, sir, excepting like all those who work here I have a need to support a life, my life. I could not remain living as I have, being neither one thing nor other, hoping for things that I may not have. And I do not wish to repent each day for sins I cannot find in my heart to admit to."

If she had taken herself off to any inward-looking convent and professed determination to take holy vows he could not have been more destroyed by her choice than he was now. "Life may be changed, Rae, but things can be gone back upon – there is no rule that says we cannot have a mind change. Come with me now and I will help you find another place, or you could go back to your home – it is your home, Rae. Flood does not have any right to keep you from the house and I do not believe Alexander would wish it."

The facade of her face remained as it was, even his rational pleading could not alter the cold dead look in her eyes. He pushed on – he would not leave her yet. "In full time, Rachael, this house will imprison you and take away your liberty, and you know the truth of it."

"If it is a prison, Mr Latimer, then the door is already closed and the key has long since turned." There was movement in the passage, Rachael glanced beyond him. A pair of harlots, less agreeable than any he had seen on the streets, supported the weight of a stocky man well into drink, his good suit despoiled by a mix of strong spirit and vomit. Latimer looked at her face, seeking reaction, revulsion perhaps but there was none.

"You cannot stay, Henri. You must go. This is a working house and not a place for idling and gossip." She pushed passed him and he watched her confidently remove the drunk's arm from the neck of one of the harlots and take hold of him, supporting the man, shouldering the burden. What misguided logic had she followed that had led her to this?

As much to himself than any other, and in some desperation, he said, "Do not feel you are lost, Rae. You are not lost. You cannot be lost when I know where to find you."

He watched her move away along the passage; he needed air, a basic need, unquenchable in this place. The heavy door of an entertaining room was closed against him and he turned, following the route along which he had come – his view of the world quite altered.

Now that the energy of the moment had gone, the flight of stairs to the shop below seemed arduous. This state of confusion and heartache, this desperate need for another, had left him alone until now; hard work preceding a marriage to a woman he did not much care for, and six years as a widower had not prepared him for the emotions that beset him now.

The milliner's shop was empty, the young women at the back continued with their needles and the whore had swopped places with another. The girl Hetty was there, twisting a rag about in her hands and leaning back on the counter talking to the harlot. He did not speak and tapping his way across the shop floor he reached blindly for the door and released himself into the busy street.

39

Boots resting on the sill of the low window, fingers impatiently drumming the arms of a dressing chair, Geoffrey idly viewed the Exe through the jutting casement of his Alphington rooms. Mag was laying on her front amongst the crumpled bedding, naked apart from a frayed neck ribbon. As she watched him, a small furrow had formed on her elfin features – there had never been a time before when he had not wanted her. The knowledge of men had come to her early; none had been of her choosing, except this one perhaps, and his lack of interest concerned her. There was no doubt in her mind that he was wrong-footed, intuition forewarned her; Jane baited her about him and reminded her, more frequently than she preferred to hear, of the life she had left, but she would have none speak against him.

"To share a problem will cut the thing in half, Geoffrey," she said lightly. The comment seemed only to increase the drumming and she sat up and reached for her shift.

"I did not say that you could dress," he said harshly, removing his feet and turning towards her. "My problems cannot be shared or halved. Your simplistic view of things does not buy you favours."

Wishing it were not so, but with no intention of sharing the complexities of his life with any whore, he stood and watched her, adopting that attitude of indifference that he employed to keep her in her servile place. The interest on the monies secured against the duplicate share certificate was overdue and he had heard through Mudge that there had been more rumblings over the other, the paltry sum raised dripping away like water in a holed bucket.

He sat on the bed beside her and began to ease his feet from his well-stitched leather boots. A little of the faith he had been raised with still guided him through some of life's more crucial judgments, and he blamed this ability of his mother's God to persuade him to follow at least some of the numerous commandments upon his predicament now. Right back at the beginning of the year clear choice had lain before him – he could have finished his uncle quite without difficulty, now it seemed altogether too late.

"Then if I cannot help them along, let me help them away." Mag knelt amongst the chaotic bed sheets, her small white breasts free, the blood-red marks from previous couplings now fading to pink. She helped him with his shirt. Geoffrey lay back as if spent already.

"You may not always have the luxury of a feather-filled mattress and a closing door, madam. It is a heavy expense from a not-bottomless pocket. Think on it and do not seek to anger me with your senseless remarks."

The experiences of her short life kept her from answering. The experience of her trade meant that words were not always a necessity.

"I need not go back to the house tonight if you do not wish it. Your uncle will be sleeping long and deep now that the passing of the gripe-fever allows him a more peaceful time of it? Surely you are free and need not think of returning?"

"Do not anticipate, Margaret, that my uncle will ever sleep in peace. He will not." The comment he realised was double-edged. "I have a mind he has quite the devil in him and would rise from his bed even if his head were severed and he carried it beneath his arm."

"This low mood will not help you forward, Master Latimer, you must take thoughts away from your uncle and offer them where they are better respected. You do know there is good salve to be had if only you will let me offer it."

Geoffrey lay across the bed, feet dangling from one side. He searched the ceiling above his head. Mould surrounded an irregular damp patch, the same leaking roof causing lathe and plaster to bow in an unsustainable bulge. The memory of the two jars of physic he had still to decide what to do with seemed to goad him, almost dancing before his eyes. Physic or poison, he could not say; but if he did not know, and this was the truth, then would not the giving of the latter be altogether accidental and the offering of the former only beneficial? Feeling his whore's pleasurable and now familiar touch he closed his eyes, banishing the sight of the bulging ceiling plaster – removing the spectre of Blox and his nameless potions to a pocket of his head where they could not bother him.

40

The bawd kept an orderly house and would have no brutish pimp taking profit where none was owed; no slatternly girl, pox-ridden or gin-soaked, kept company under her roof. Her girls were clean, still carrying the bloom of their early life – and no girl, no matter if the bloom of her young skin and the flash of her black eyes shone out beyond the fashionable determination to hide it, could live beneath her roof without working.

She watched Rae as she came into the shop, returning from a jaunt about the upper end of the city. There was no disgrace in soliciting company, working girls loitered on most prominent corners, and since the visit by the ailing merchant this girl seemed to have become more adept at the art of eye fluttering and lip pouting, for all the world like she meant to join them, but until now she had taken no man to her bed.

Deeper thought encouraged the bawd's habitual winding and unwinding of the leather whip-ends about her arthritic fingers; the irascible man had paid well for almost nothing and he had been determined that he would have his choice – might not others? Removing her feet from the chest, the mother stood and came forward, stepping into the path of her favourite girl and stopping the other from slipping away into the depths of the dark house. A good deal of easily won coin might be had from the younger girl; the time was right for her to lay her cards on the table. With little more than the stature and height of a child, the bawd lifted her chin to look at them.

"Home at last like homing birds fluffed up by trade winds." She tipped her head to the side squinting through small knowing eyes. "Jaunting here and

197

jaunting there, enjoying the fair weather like genteel ladies born for idleness."

"Your saying is always the same mother, and you do know we were neither born for idleness nor for to be gentry and have been working as hard as any. Work we must and work we do."

Jane had the gauge of the mother, knew her moods and held some fondness for her. If exploitation were the lot of all whores then she felt it less here than in any other house she had worked in.

Fighting poor eyesight and squinting even more narrowly, the bawd observed Rachael's neat person. "Well, madam" – she pursed her lips, a sterner face replacing the more benevolent offering – "you have been about house business and learning well. Now that you are rested and have seen your first customer might we not send another?"

Rachael wholeheartedly wished to correct her, but there was little point, the thought even preposterous – denying anything carnal had taken place between her and Henri Latimer. She drew the brim of her hat straight to cover her embarrassment.

"There will be times to come to send to, Rae." Jane had already anticipated this or similar interrogation. "Do not hurry her along and be not concerned that she is idle, Mother, she is not so – quality gentlemen need be encouraged and she is encouragement and plenty stepping out beside me."

"You have a mindset, Jane, and all to yourself, but you know as well as I that the artist's maidservant must choose her path and cannot dally on forever between one life and another."

Lethargy and disappointment and a feeling that she was living another's life in a nightmare that she could not wake from sat behind Rachael like a yawning mouth waiting to swallow her, and although she wished more than anything to be gone from here, a confused sense of determination to continue drove her forward.

"I do not sit between one life and another." Rachael spoke levelly and without emotion. "If you have men to send, then you must send. I will work my lodging the same as Jane, or any other." The voice she spoke with was not her own, the sentiment most certainly at odds with all that she was.

Showing a neat plump foot, Jane tapped a buckled shoe on the boards of the shop floor. "I will not have you pressure her, Mother. We agreed a fortnight or so and it has been little more."

"'Tis a loose account of time, Jane, better to have certainty. You know I cannot have a girl here whose only purpose is to lady about the place and read books."

Rae on the periphery of the conversation took an impatient and involuntary breath and toyed with the lace of her cuffs.

The mother looked kindly into Jane's rounded face, her pinched features forming into an unnatural smile. "So you have it, Jane, a mother must allow her chicks headway sometimes. We will leave it as 'tis until the end of the week, but I cannot see why the choice is so difficult to be had. This house is as worthy as those gentrified places I have heard tell of in Bristol and London, and I do know that a girl would not come to me if she had a better journey to make."

Jane was about to speak again, ambiguous reasoning determined to keep Rae from debasement even though she herself had carved an altogether satisfactory life from the profession of whore. Rachael spoke first.

"If you think I hover on the edge of things, I do not. And I have no need to be persuaded in either direction. I will have any man who has the need of me and can pay for his pleasure. If such a one do come to the shop mother you must send him."

A little further into the week Rachael was alone in the small room at the top of the house. Her forced seduction still remained her only experience of sexual intimacy. She leant closer to the mottled mirror and began the daily process of erasing all semblance of her old identity, applying a veneer of paint and powder that she hoped might convince not only others of her life change, but perhaps also her own ambivalent self. The action of leaning forwards, a sleepless night, a dawn rising and an empty belly had made her nauseous – she dropped the Carmen back into her box and stood to open the window.

Like the waning of the old moon and the waxing of the new, Rachael's losing week was predictable and constant. She had waited anxiously, but the predictable had not come, and although she tried not to dwell too keenly on the consequences of this, she knew in her honest heart that she had conceived. She stood, spread out the garish red cotton petticoats of her dress and went down into the kitchens to seek company – if not food. All along the dark shuttered passage of the upper floor the doors were closed. She walked quietly through the working house, remembering what she had told the bawd. Would she stand by what she had said – when the time came? She must, she must go forward and never look back.

The kitchen was empty, the cooking fire almost out. Hetty would be somewhere in the house. Only when she was chastised for her lazy indolent ways would the whorehouse drudge attempt to make account of her hours. Rae ladled water from the bucket, sipped it, but did not drink fully. She could not quench the thirst that she felt; all food and most liquid served her poorly now, brought forth a sense that her stomach was rising to her throat.

Hetty came into the room. Rae, sympathetic to this girl's unhappy, disagreeable nature which made most of those in the house take an instant dislike to her, spoke kindly.

"Just us this day, Hetty, all others asleep it do seem."

The girl heaved a bucket of slop towards the back door.

"I don't get much time for sleeping, 'tis up and down those stairs, doing the bidding of all and only one pair of hands." Arms folded and mouth pulled in tightly, Hetty leant back against the scrubbed table. There was an insolent look upon her face which usually preceded an insolent remark. She said nothing and instead dropped down onto a plank bench which ran along the length of the table.

The bubble of nausea that was sitting just below Rachael's windpipe abruptly moved up to her throat and made her retch. She went to the slop bucket and spat bile.

"You don't look too well, Rae. Perhaps you should have stayed abed with the rest of the house." Rachael did not reply but sipped a little more water from the ladle.

Hetty rested her chin in her large red hands and considered the new arrival, her stare more impertinent than concerned. "My mother was a one for the morning vomit. One month upon the next and then only a short space of time between, and on it would come again, seven years and five birthings, and half of them dead before they was grown."

"Each one of us is different, Hetty, sickness in the morning do not necessarily herald the coming of a child. There is all manner of reasons for the unpleasantness, so do not go telling things to the house that are not true." Rachael took a rag and began to clean the table. "I've a mind to take a bit of something before the house wakes – get yesterday's bread from the croc, Hetty, and sit awhile with me. It is surely only an empty belly that makes me retch." Rachael cut the bread and picked at a corner. If she had choice she would not choose the company of this girl over others. "The wool market and all that do go along with it will be turning business already, Hetty, could you not contrive a need and go along for a visit?"

"I could, if I had a mind, but what sense is there in that when the work that must be done here piles up behind me like dead leaves against a sluice gate."

For once Rachael lost patience. "Do as you will, it is your choice."

Hetty ran a critical eye over Rachael's painted face and evolving bosom.

"My mother always knew well before the eighth week. Some's bodies do change in an instant, whilst others may never know until they are too far gone to visit any abortionist quack."

"Hush you, Hetty, your mood do not sit well with me this morning and well you know this. A person may not always be well and hearty – it is the change in the air here and this idleness I do not choose. Fetch me the flour croc and the good yeast and I will bake today. I would rather you were gone from this kitchen if you have nothing more friendly to offer than foolishness and gossip."

Hetty weighed the prospect of a few hours of freedom and unhindered indolence against the possible confirmation of an idea she had formed in her head since the artist's model came here. If the thing were out, and Hetty had no doubt that the young woman, now stirring yeast into warm milk, was with child, others might be confused by the suddenness of her condition; she, however, would not be. People were such fools to think that they could hide away from all eyes by talking in a hush and dangling from backyard windows and decrepit overhangs.

The soft June morning won out. Insolence and disbelief splashed across her face, Hetty drew off her apron, adjusted her cap and stood by the part-open door. "I will slip out until the house is awake, for I am sure that the mother will know me gone even though she sees not a thing beyond her forearm and never leaves the shop."

Hetty was gone and Rachael worked the dough without the need to see it, looking out at the bright day and the sunlight that had begun to find its way into corners of the enclosed courtyard. The art of survival was not to think, not to consider the future, but to think only of the moment and the feel of the dough and the changing sunlight beyond the lattice.

Staying a while longer in the kitchens and then rising the two flights of stairs to the forgotten room at the top of the house, the rest of the day had offered nothing but idleness, passing frustratingly slowly as all the days before had. But nausea was an occupation in itself and although it had left her alone during the long afternoon, the feeling had returned unwelcome and persistent as the day came to a close. She lay drifting between sleep and wakefulness on the small pallet – Hetty's sudden appearance at the door brought her up from a shallow dream of solemn dark-coated men and half-drowned babes with weakened necks and hollow eyes. The mother had sent for her and she was to work the evening along with the rest of the house.

She had pinched her cheeks, rubbed carmine about her lips, moved slowly but deliberately through the working house to the milliner's shop below. She watched her own shoed feet descending the worn oak treads, uncertainty in every step, touched the hard matt of powdered hair with her hand and adjusted the front of her gown, reasserting her bosom.

Her gentleman was waiting in the milliner's shop below. She viewed him from the stairway – corpulent, broad faced and with a tight curled wig perched above his bloated face, he had the look of a parson about him. Clicking shut the lid of his worn snuff box, he looked up.

"Madam, be bold and do not leave me wanting."

A regular customer, he looked her over, assessing her. Rachael assessed him in return; he was the epitome of all she had observed during those days of reprieve when she had accepted the shelter of the house without the need to work it. Presenting herself to him she quickly dropped a knee and took hold of his fleshy damp hand as she had seen the other whores do. The odour of many days' sweat was on his clothes and the smell of strong spirit prominent on his breath.

"Sir, I would not leave you waiting nor wanting with intent, but this house is a cavernous old place and I must come from top to bottom to find you."

They went up, her customer following her light tread with heavy steps. Before they had reached the first floor he was already slowing, his breath laboured, his face red. She waited for him, trying not to see him even though she must look at him – everything about her feeling dull and without life.

"Give me your arm, madam, and help me along. You would not wish me done before I have been obliged."

Resolutely wiping away thoughts of his smell, the sensation of his corpulence against her side, his droning superfluous conversation, she took his arm and continued on up, refusing to slow, running headlong into what must be done.

He pushed the door of an entertaining room shut and came forward holding tight to the back of a chair, finding breath and then continuing on along his determined route of explanation that she had no wish to hear. The closed door was more than she could tolerate; she went to it, opened it a slight and returned to listen the monotony of his voice, to the description of a life in which she had no interest. He was a lay-preacher, preaching about the county, God had called him a decade ago and now he must do God's work.

Rachael hung about the foot of the bed, gripped the ragged ends of the dusty drapes for comfort, listening, viewing the part-opened door. Fear and revulsion had made her silent. He sat heavily upon a frayed armchair and she watched him scratch beneath his wig.

"If you are concerned upon the matter, I do not dally long about my task, upon the contrary. My needs are mostly urgent and may be met without difficulty."

Her lack of response to his continuous dialogue seemed not to bother him and she remembered all the imaginings she had ever held in her head about the working of this house – how it was, how the girls earned their living, the things she needed to do and to say – but she found her tongue had frozen in her mouth and her hands could not relinquish the drapes. His talk had moved from the past to his needs of the moment.

"I am celibate these two months gone and will see an end to it."

She watched the preacher remove his coat and throw off his wig. For the first time he seemed to have noticed her, the look of her youth offering him impetus. He began to unbutton his breeches flap, fighting against the flesh of his belly and the smallness of the unseen fastenings.

"Oblige me, young woman, and help me free from the restrictions of these infernal breeches. The buttons are quite impossible and will see me spent before I am released."

Perhaps if he was near done now the thing would be over in a moment and could be borne, could be got through and once done how easy it would be to offer herself again and again without thought? She let go of her support and dropped to the floor before him, unbuttoning his flap, involuntarily feeling the warmth of his flesh, breathing in the smell of his body.

"You may take time o'er it – a little handling will see me better ready and lay low these sweats."

He lay back in the chair and closed his eyes, anticipation of the pleasure to come bringing a flush of serenity to his urgent and overheated face. She drew her hands away and dropped them into her lap.

For the first time the reality of who she was, forged and formed by seven years of protected living and very little social intercourse, burned before her like limelight. She could not perform as they did; she could never work this house; and with this revelation came the thought of what might lie ahead for her if she could not.

"Madam, I have paid good money for an unworked whore and although I am not displeased with your comeliness and may accept a little naivety – may delight in it – I cannot sit a-waiting the whole eve without service."

Trapped by her own determination to take this life of harlot, with no path to follow that might take her away from it, Rachael considered the bleakness of her future. But could not time be bought by offering up some kind of coquetry, and as long as he did not lay hands on her she could act her part? Standing again, just a small distance from him she began to pull out the strings of her bodice, releasing the ribbons on her petticoats, for perhaps the thought of what she could offer alone would see him done and she might be done also and freed from this room.

He watched her undress – she could hear his heavy bronchial breathing.

"'Tis some subtlety you offer up, madam. Mute prudery and the black eyes of a heathen. When I have tasted what is on show you may have the servicing of me in future times."

She had taken off her stockings and began to untie the caned rounds of her pocket hoops with no plan beyond this point except perhaps the possibility of desertion.

"Then we are ready, madam." The preacher struggled from the chair, breeches migrating downwards towards his knees. He stood, gaining his balance, settling his paunch, his erect member showing clearly through his shirt-tails. "I will have the arse of you, young woman. It is a courtesy I offer my good wife. I will not fornicate face on face."

The deed that Rachael had thought might be easily done, seemed now to be surrounded by a sea of complication and doubt; the options open to her were diminishing moment by moment, but still she did not take flight. She offered him what he wanted, turned away, waiting for the thing to be over. His breath was on her back but his hands did not reach out for her, she could hear him mumbling behind her, at first questions came to her without answers – then she understood that he was praying.

Suddenly struck by the foolishness of the thing, the hypocrisy, she felt no guilt that she had led him forward, no desire to prove that she could live this life. Escape was a part-opened door and she took it, slipping silently from his reach, brushing the closed pious hands with her shift, moving beyond him, undoing in part what she had begun without consideration of what was to come.

It was dark when she reached the small room at the top of the house. The candles that burned in the greeting rooms were now behind closed doors, their light barely penetrating beyond. She found the stub of her rush-light, took tinder to it and lit it, the flickering light in the darkened room making ugly shadows on the walls. Kneeling above the flame and looking into the broken glass, Rachael saw her face as monstrous, unearthly like something from the pits of Hell so often talked about and read about along those years of bible readings and sermon.

She took a rag and some water from her jug, scrubbed hard at the red lips and white face. Her hair was a harsh matted web and she pulled at it, but the thing would not release and she took the sheers from her sewing box and cut at it until the mat lay on the floor beside her. Tonight she would be found out and tomorrow or sometime very soon she would have to leave. It mattered not – it was part of life, part of the consequences of life.

The child in her belly, the events that had overtaken her – this was the life she should have had, what her mother most probably had known. What foolishness to think that a pallet in Trelawney's cellar and her ability to understand the written page could lead her out of it.

In the semi-darkness she had filled her bowl and, still kneeling on the floor, put her head in the cool water, working the ends of her hair until they were free. She lay on the pallet as she was, in whore's clothing but not a whore. Not even a whore. Tomorrow she would change her clothes and then before she was cast out she would be gone.

41

Latimer had walked to the Waterbere Lane coffee house with conflicting thoughts, these thoughts roving about the pockets of his head with all the energy of a bull unleashed. Rae was lost; Geoffrey was a dissembler of the truth, a storyteller, a debtor or worse. His servant could not be trusted, was in collusion with his nephew. From the other side of his mind, the rational, level side came an alternative view. Rae was not lost, she had merely taken a different path – she was only lost to him. Geoffrey, his nephew, his kin, was no more profligate than many other young men about the city and judgement must not be made upon personal suspicion. Let proof be found first.

The broader talk in the house was of the sweeping changes taking place in burgeoning northern cities – the local chatter was of a fire in the northern quarter. A draper, praised for his efforts in putting out the fire, was then vilified for having chosen to rescue his pig in preference to his wife. On this morning, neither of these topics held his interest.

He took his coffee seated with Elcott. The young man's resolve to marry in September had not changed and his heart and his time were still thinly stretched between his home in Exeter and the small town of Knowle Easton. His business was well, his mother likewise and his prospects sound.

"You have quite confounded us all, Henri, by pulling back so quickly from ill health. These grippe-fevers can take a man out without warning – and have done so across this city." Elcott paused, looked at his cup for guidance. "Let us hope you are now free from these luckless humours – fate twists around us and seems impossible to predict."

Henri was not altogether sure that fate always controlled life, but it had in many senses controlled his own. "I must take what comes to me, Edmund. I have had many years when sickness did not touch me."

"And your nephew, sir?" Elcott said fiddling with the handle of his cup. "Are things between you improved or do they run along much as before?"

"No and yes, I suppose would be my honest answer to this, Edmund. Things have not improved and yes they run along in the same unsatisfactory way as before. We meet rarely, an occasional supper, breakfast if I have Vetch call me when he is down. He goes about his business, although I am never certain sure what that is. And of course I have been incapacitated and unable to take account of his activities for some weeks." Henri watched Elcott's restless hands as he twisted his cup in its saucer.

"Edmund, we have sat here on too many occasions for me not to know that the worrying of that little cup heralds disquiet." Latimer folded his arms and observed Elcott from beneath taut brows. "I suspicion that you may have things to tell me regarding my nephew, else you would not have brought his name into our conversation so soon. You may offer them up cleanly if this is so. I would rather have it from you than any other."

As if in surrender Elcott put up his hand. "I do have things to tell. You already know that the tittle-tattle of the town comes to me without my calling it, my quandary is always do I leave the tittle-tattle where it belongs or do I out it?"

"A fire will always produce smoke, Edmund, rumour or not I would be glad to hear what you have been told – it is likely there will be some accuracy in this gossip."

Edmund laid his hands on the table. "There have been enquiries, Henri, not directly to me, but they have come to me through an associate – he has premises close to mine, his business of the same nature but we compete little."

"A notary?"

"It is often the case in our business that a search must be made in order to locate our client's beneficiaries. This can in some cases be arduous and take many years. For these purposes we use an acquaintance of my associate – he has an ear for the running grapevine and is adept at finding missing persons."

Elcott rarely strayed from the point – Henri did not feel any level of impatience and waited for Edmund to recite the gossip.

"There have been enquires, Henri, regarding your family."

"The reasoning, Edmund?"

"A gentleman – and I use that reverent term loosely – has been seeking assistance in finding the whereabouts of the family of Latimer."

"Are there not others of that name within the city walls?"

"There are, but not who fit the hand-bill so snugly. The description was quite clear, Henri, Blackaller was mentioned."

"I am being sought? Indeed are we being sought?"

"You may jump ahead, sir, I believe you will understand that it will be Geoffrey Latimer who is being sought."

Henri rasped his chin and continued to observe Edmund from beneath his dark brows. "And what became of this enquiry, Edmund. Was there conclusion?"

Henri had already concluded that a blind man with nothing more to guide him than a bleached stick would be able to find the house of Latimer when connected with Blackaller Tucking Mill.

"Nothing more, sir, our acquaintance sought first clarification that the family Latimer was content to be found by this…" He paused searching for an accurate description. "Banker encompasses so much, but my friend's assumption is that this title would fit the enquiring gentleman loosely and it is likely that he is involved in the lending of money rather than facilitating the saving of the same."

Latimer huffed, folded his arms more tightly across his coat. "It is fool's errand to sit here and ponder the reasons for this search when we both know well enough the truth. I believe, in the light of my nephew's past misdemeanours, we must assume that debt continues to follow him like a hungry dog."

The mood of helplessness and despondency that had sat about Latimer since he discovered Rae had left her home and taken the life of a harlot was not enlarged by this new concern – on the contrary, it was replaced by a determination to take matters in hand, to offer up a fight and on both counts.

On this day, the Waterbere coffee house, rarely as busy as its rival in the western quarter, housed only a few settled gentlemen. The country was beginning to prosper in the wake of the successful Seven Years' War; the colonies ran as they always had, there was nothing of any great importance to mull over and the talk was inconsequential and mild.

Latimer noticed the whore known as Jane enter the house: a woman who rarely entered any room unnoticed, she was on the arm of an older gentlemen, and although a few heads bobbed up, the coffee house gentlemen soon returned to their business. The elegant woman had seen him, and before Elcott could begin again on the state of the packhorse roads, Jane was offering a good day.

"Madam." His respect for all women was sure and he made no distinction between this woman and any other neighbour offering him a greeting.

"It is of some fortune that I have found you here, sir, for I were not on the look-about."

Henri stood and then finding himself some distance above her head, perched on the edge of the table. He noticed her look was grave and he found himself caught in her mood.

"You have the need to find me, madam?"

"I do, sir."

He thought to offer her a seat – he saw the bemused and somewhat confused look of his friend and decided against it. "Then I am glad that you have found me."

"I believe we have a mutual friend, sir, and I do know that you have called upon her in the house."

Elcott moved his position so that he might hear all that was said.

"Yes we have and I have, but with no success – you may know more than me why this choice, this path has been taken."

"A little of it, sir, but I think not all of it, and you be right in thinking that it is upon this matter I was hoping to speak with you. I no more wish her this life than you, but she has a root of determination to have it."

Although she could not make mention of it, the murmur in the bawdy house was loud and if she believed the fullness of this murmur then Henri Latimer would need to make recompense.

"I cannot fathom this determination, this change of thought. If you have guidance there I would be grateful to hear it."

Jane did not offer it but continued with directness to a man who expected directness. "I have tried and tried again to keep her from it, and now worse has come for she has refused a man and the bawd will not have her in the house. You must call again, Mr Latimer, you must call and talk to her and waste no time between."

He studied her concern. What was she saying, what had changed? Rae had seemed so determined to continue to run along with the life she had so irrationally chosen. The whore Jane was being beckoned to, her time already belonging to another. He watched her go, considering what she had said, bringing in his brows more tightly. He suddenly felt that he was under water and the sea of voices about him had become inaudible and indistinct. He needed some solitude, he must think.

42

His resolve to visit the house was stronger this time, urgency born from what he had been told. He couldn't think beyond stopping this young woman from falling, falling below the level of the whorehouse – for many Godly men only a space above Hell. He would not have her disappear into the ether of low city life, to fall amongst the criminal, the destitute and the desperate. He would not have it, there would be solution.

Latimer laid his coin on the counter, ignored the bawd and went up; he knew where to find her – if she were still there. Jane had offered him the bones of the story, but she had not told him all.

The door was just ajar, he viewed it with optimism. By choice, Rae would not shut herself in any room. One knock and he entered; the room was dismal, unadorned, without memory of any who had lived here. She turned, all signs of the harlot he had seen before gone. Her hair had been shortened to just above her shoulder and hung in jagged clumps of dark curls. The questions he would like to have asked would not come and instead he began with simple explanation.

"I have come with some urgency – I was afraid you may be gone."

This time surprise was clearly etched on her face. She took her cap from the bed and began to push her shorn hair inside it.

"I am to go, sir, but I am at a loss to see the hows and whys of your knowledge of this, or the reasoning for your being here." The pretence, the mask remained.

A small parcel of her belongings was wrapped in a petticoat and lay on the bed.

"Jane, Rachael – it is Jane who bade me come and I am glad of it." All her wild dark hair had gone, the change in her had stunned him – he could not ignore her nervous and futile rearranging of her cap. "What has been done to your hair, Rae? Is there more that I should know?"

"It was an irritant, sir, and I have taken it off – see how much more easily it fits under my cap."

Before, he had stopped himself from taking her arm, but now he took it, held her so that she could not move away.

"Blessed Heaven, Rachael, at least call me by my name."

Unable to free herself, she saw him properly for the first time, searched his face and was sorry that he minded. It would be better not to have him mind, if she knew he cared it was more difficult to be free.

"Henri, I do not understand what you want of me – I will be fine and well about this city and neither you nor Jane should worry over my going. The whoring life do not suit me, I was mistaken in my choices, but there are other ways to live." He let her go. "Perhaps you do not believe me, but I know 'tis so."

"I am sorry, Rachael, but I do not. The lot of an unmarried woman alone, without money or family, is harsh. You know this, you understand this as well as I. Stay amongst friends, do not move out of sight to some unsettled place where none may find you."

"It is for me to decide where I live, Henri, our earlier friendship do not leave you with obligation. You must not mind my leaving nor concern yourself with where I go."

"I will concern myself, Rachael, and it is my wish to feel obliged – my heart requires it."

It had begun to rain and beyond him in the courtyard she saw the view that she had always had during those anxious weeks that she had waited on his health, anticipated his company. The remembrance was strong and fresh and a deep sadness swept over her.

"I am sorry for it, Henri. I am so sorry for it all. I did not mean to disturb your heart nor bother your mind."

"Rachael, I want you to disturb my heart, my mind and my life – if you would allow it to be so I would have this be permanent."

She looked at the pitiful bundle of belongings on the pallet bed – thought of the truth of things, the world that she understood much of despite the protected life she had lived. It would have been so easy to accept him, to lie, to let him believe she was still whole.

"A time ago I would have wanted nothing more than to have a permanent place in your life, Henri, although I never expected that I might. And now I cannot."

"Do not find reasons why you may not accept my help. I have talked with Jane – nothing has happened here, nothing more than your acceptance that you could not live this life."

There was suddenly terror written across her face. "She is right, Henri, in all truth nothing has happened – I could not do even that."

Knowing her honest, he believed her and did not understand her reluctance. He digested what she was saying before speaking again. "Then there is no argument," he said clearly watching her face. "Step out of this place, Rachael, and choose another life."

The terror on her face had intensified. "I cannot, Henri, I cannot – do not ask it."

So much of their unorthodox courtship had existed with physical distance between them, but now in this small room there were no restrictions and he took her limp hand from the folds of her skirts and held it.

"Then face me, Rachael, and tell me why you must refuse me. I will go nowhere until I have heard a convincing argument."

With a short impatient movement she freed her hand. Covering her face she dropped to the floor. Her words came quickly, jumbled and distorted, spoken through clasped hands.

"I cannot be wife to you, Henri, I can never be wife to you – I am not free to have you."

Henri perched on the low bed and spoke quietly to her bent head.

"I see no ties upon you, Rachael, you are owned by none, neither Trelawney nor this house. Why may you not? Tell me, I will know."

"I cannot be any man's wife now, Henri." She took her hands aside and looked mournfully into an empty corner of the room. He waited for her to continue. "I cannot have you, Henri. I cannot be your wife. I carry a bastard, Henri, another's child. I am used and sullied, a whore in name if not intention."

The honest admission stunned him, unsettled his balance. Frantically assimilating thoughts, searching for rational explanation he stood and slowly walked to the window. This hour, this moment was not the time for interrogation – for understanding what had happened to her, he should not try, but if not in the whorehouse then where had she conceived a child?

Did he want this woman? Would he take her unconditionally? What would be her life if he did not? He knew too well what became of destitute women who begat bastards. The thought chilled him. He did not turn.

"Then there is more reason for you to accept me," he said calmly, looking through the grimed window to the familiar court below. "It seems you have my heart, Rachael, and to keep it from harm you must also agree to have my name."

43

Ignoring the disapproval of his cook, the snub-nosed jealousy of his occasional maid and the downright distaste of Vetch, Henri had installed Rachael into the Latimer household the following day. The fear that she might slip away to a lower world without his knowing was real and concerned him more than any momentary discomfort he might be obliged to tolerate. Besides he had never cared much for others' opinion. He had not consulted Geoffrey.

Moreton market square had been full, he had observed but did not trade – his visit here was to be just a beginning. He had settled on a quantity of quality cloth purchased from weavers along the busy pack road, and now that the long June day was coming to a close, a night in this familiar coaching inn was a necessity. On tomorrow's dawn he would pick up the lesser-trodden tracks north, ford the upper reaches of the Teign and likely arrive in Crediton before the midday.

He had found a seat in the snug at the back of the White Hart, crowded now, men of business filling the low-ceilinged rooms with companionable talk of the day's successes – and misadventures. Supped and watered on half a hock of bacon and a tankard of dark ale, thoughts beyond his trade had begun to materialize and he had asked for a bottle of port wine to be left instead of more ale. Maudlin thoughts had begun to disturb him of late – despite his changed status from widower to husband.

Hardwick's law had made a swift and timely joining of hands far more difficult than he had anticipated. In mind of Rachael's delicate and changeful state of health, he had not wanted to wait three consecutive Sabbath's for the banns to be read. They were of the Parish, although his betroth's age and lack of parent or guardian had threatened to undo his plans, and following a little palm greasing they had been married by Common License at St Mary's Church on the twentieth of the month. Any who had stumbled upon the proceedings on this dull midsummer morning might have been surprised to find that apart from his nephew, his daughters and a close friend, the congregation was almost exactly divided between retainers and whores.

He stretched his leg, his stick was never far from his grasp, but he found he had less need for its support now. Informing his nephew of his plans and intentions had gone a slight better than he had anticipated. The boy seemed quite indifferent, almost as though he had already got wind of Latimer's sudden intention to marry. Elcott, surprised, had found delight in it. With health returning, Henri ought to have settled to his new situation; but he was far from settled and it was Rachael's state of mind that troubled him most.

Acceptance of her condition and what that might mean for their future together was a concern aside – his real unease was for her lack of buoyancy, of any flicker of contentment. She seemed reluctant to offer him any explanation of the getting of her child and he did not push her for detailed account. This lack of confidentiality wounded him and although they had consummated their marriage, her almost repugnant fear of his touch had added to his sense of hurt and confusion. He had taken her as his wife purely to keep her from the streets; it had been the proposition he offered up and he would not push her yet a while into repeating the experience – at least not until she had returned to her old self.

He refilled the pewter mug, drank more slowly this time. If he cared to admit it, his urgent desire to begin to trade again was fuelled by the need to leave distance between a woman he wanted but still it seemed could not have. But to complain of disappointment was folly; women, he understood, needed time to adjust – and then there was the complication of the child sickness.

The din in the rooms was becoming ever louder, he folded the rough doodlings of previous calculation and tucked them inside his account book, picked up his bag and rose. The bottle and mug were still on the table and contemplating the long evening to come; he took the fogged bottle by the neck and tucked it under his arm. Marriage was a paradox, he concluded; he should have remembered experience of it from the time spent with his first wife, but the memory of his daughter's mother was dulled to nothing and had rarely ever distracted him from business. Before his momentous decision to marry again, it had been his nephew who teased his thoughts; this night would be a good time to think his way forward on that account.

*

Sitting on the nursery floor, a wooden doll resting in her lap, small pieces of clipped cloth strewn about the oak boards, Rachael glanced a little slyly at Old Sarah. Asleep in her chair this last hour, mouth dropped open, chin vibrating a slight in accompaniment to her heavy drink-induced breathing, she was oblivious to all that went on around her. The look was traced and intercepted by both Mary and Sophia who responded with a giggle; neither Rachael nor her husband's daughters expected the old woman to wake until supper time. The nursemaid had not seemed to mind the newly wedded interloper spending time in this private kingdom, over which she had always ruled unchallenged; the old woman had welcomed Rachael's efforts to amuse Henri's daughters and was happy to literally take a seat at the back.

Rachael freed her folded legs from the restrictions of her new skirts. The bodice and petticoats were generously cut to allow for the future changes in her figure. Henri had taken her to a dressmaker in North Street the week before their marriage; the woman's business overlooked a well-known soliciting-ground – it had not been a good beginning to her new life as wife of a respected merchant.

With familiarity, Rachael felt the stirrings of late afternoon sickness, she rose to her knees, rested her palms on the floor, breathed until the nausea faded. Sophia looked up disinterestedly.

"Why did Papa have to go away?" She had been lying on the floor and drew herself up to a sitting position, and following Rachael's lead held a small square of cloth to the body of her doll. She was much engrossed in the task of dressmaking and continued, "And now he must miss supper and the jumping bugs will bite him all through the night so that he may not find any sleep."

Her question had been pertinent and Rachael could answer this fully – although her analysis may not have been correct on all fronts.

"He must begin to trade again and he mayn't do it unless he goes away, but he will return tomorrow and I do not think the bugs will keep him awake all the night."

Sophia was satisfied and all thoughts of her father's absence were temporarily eclipsed by the discovery of a bright square of velvet. Mary, neater and more ordered in her ways, was running large stitches across the remains of a cotton shift.

"One night is no time, Sister, you do not remember before he cracked his leg and was away for many nights each week. You are too young to remember."

"You are not so very much older than I, Mary, and I remember well enough."

"We will not argue upon what is remembered and what is forgot. We will greet your father well when he returns and miss him whilst he is gone."

The surge of sickness had made her efforts to concentrate on fine stitches impossible. Sitting back again and finding some comfort by folding her arms and holding tight to her body, she rocked herself back and forth, hoping that these two small girls would ask no question. Since she had conceived, her emotions had been unpredictable and muddled – she did not want this child, how could she want something that had come from violence? She did not want it and yet she could not help but feel it and know it and even care for it. Confusingly she wanted her husband, but could not love him as she wished.

Rachael stood, went to the window, breathed in a little air; it was a humid day and the skies were full of swallows, fluttering and falling, drifting high above the Exe. Distracted by the endlessness of the summer skies she did not hear nor note Geoffrey's arrival in the nursery; she turned to find him looking at her.

"Master Geoffrey." She stood before him, self-consciously smoothing down the bodice of her gown where she knew her child was growing, tucking up the ends of her shorn hair inside her cap. "Do you seek me?"

"Madam," he said dropping his head.

Sophia and Mary, less relaxed in his company than they had been since his perpetual absence from their daily routine and the removal of any minor affection he may have once shown them, continued as they were.

"I see a pretty scene of domesticity here – you are all so settled into it and so soon after joining us here in this tottering house." He took a chair, rearranging the skirts of his coat and smoothing down the knees of his breeches. "If I did not know other, I may believe you mother to these two girls. But then I do not believe biology would allow it."

Thirteen years younger than her husband, his observation was correct and she knew the comment was said without kindness.

"Sitting alone by some empty fireside do not please me, Master Geoffrey – I am better met offering a friendship and an afternoon's lesson in the art of thrift and needle sewing."

Seeing that he had nothing of interest to offer them and very little interest in them, Mary and Sophia continued to practise what they had just learnt with studious faces and an ear to the conversation.

"I can see that sitting alone would not suit, this silent old house must seem a world away from what you have known – lively days and livelier night times and the company of others." He sat back allowed his fingers to play out a tune on the arms of the chair. "So close to your old place, but so far removed from it in every other sense."

Well able to fend off his sarcasm but having neither the will nor the spark to do so whilst her insides were churning, Rachael seated herself close to him, making show of her new skirts.

"It do seem a world apart in some ways, but in others it is much the same. I must still climb three flights to come from bottom to top and make friends with Thomas Vetch to get my way with things, when before his place were taken by Mr Flood. The only difference in this house is that I may now tell the serving man to go to damnation where before I were threatened with the visiting of the place myself." She smiled having defused his meaning. "I had no mind of my old life, Master Geoffrey, so do not think it so, but in this one I am blessed with companionship and the security of marriage."

"Ah companionship, so you have it – apart from when my uncle chooses to trek the moorland wilderness alone in place of a cosy life at home with his new wife."

Rachael had taken up her sewing again, listening with mock interest whilst Geoffrey related – and also embellish – a loose story he had heard about the escape of a large hog from the slaughtering post.

Able to detach herself from the dialogue by dropping her head over her work, she allowed her thoughts to run on. Geoffrey was convincingly Henri's kin but there the similarity was ended.

"Before the blade could slit the beast's throat and bloody the sluices, the thing was up and away and trotting down the Stepcote hill with no more chance of being stopped than a bull at his work." Geoffrey's hands came down hard on the arms of his chair, watching Rachael's face, quizzing her reactions. He had no real interest in visiting the upper floor of the house, to spend time with his recently acquired relation and his cousins, excepting perhaps a certain curiosity and a black desire to bait his uncle's young wife. "I am told the beast was last seen swimming hard towards the west bank marshes – and a tidy sum of bacon lost and gone for all times."

The story was of some interest to Mary who asked, "Do hogs swim well, Cousin Latimer?"

"Indeed they do and speedily so, have you not observed their little cloven feet all ready to paddle their way to freedom?"

Her concentration seemed suddenly lost and she dropped her sewing into her lap and shrewdly considered the young man sitting next to her. Through Henri she had learned that Geoffrey Latimer held expectations above the status of his purse, that his father had died before he was born and that his mother had never forgiven the deceased man for his inadequacy.

"I am aware upon what business my uncle ventures out, but not when he will return. A matter of days or will he add plan upon plan?"

"Tomorrow, Geoffrey. It is but one night that he is away from us."

"And I congratulate him on it, madam. A union so freshly made should not be drawn apart so soon. You have barely been wed a week."

*

Old Sarah was stirring, Geoffrey pulled in his mouth with distaste. The revolting woman belonged in the kitchens – she left an unpleasant odour behind her and was a sorry addition to the upper household. The domestic scene had begun to bore him and he stood in his well-cut coat looking for retreat. Looking back at the scene, a worrying thought began to form – from this union might there not be progeny? Might there not be a male heir?

"I had thought to take supper elsewhere in the city, but I believe I will change my plans," he said turning back. "You are so newly come here, Aunt, I believe it would be a cruelty to leave you head and tail of that grand table with no other in between. I will have Vetch call me when you are down."

From arriving here to sit at the bedside of a dying relative and wait for the wealth that ought always to have been his to finally come his way, Geoffrey was now confronted by a complete turnabout of circumstances. His uncle was now married to a servant, a whore, and if all he had heard were correct a girl without the benefit of parentage. He felt surpassed, his position challenged, lowered by this unexpected change in the house. His uncle had courted this girl under his very nose and yet without his knowledge; he would be more watchful in the future.

44

Towards the end of the following afternoon, Henri was making his way down busy North Street towards the Holloway livery. The now dusty city was a contrast to the verdant forests and farmlands of the upper Exe. It was humid and close – he felt in need of a drink, his own bed and his wife. The thought amused him and troubled him all in the same moment – how would she be? He quickly moved away from the thought – if he expected little then he would not be disappointed; it was a way of thinking that he had grown used to over this last decade of his life.

The wide entrance hall of his house – near windowless, ancient slate flags creating a cave-like feel – was cool. He dropped his coat on to the settle and listened for the sound of voices. There were none. Expect nothing and live without disappointment. The door to the large low-beamed sitting-room was wide and he took a chair by an open window and rested his leg. There was little about to suggest that anything much had changed since Rae had come to live here, just small evidence of her being – a brace of books, the old writing box, once his mother's now hers, opened and ready for use, and a feather-filled cushion that had not been there before. Rousing himself from consuming thought, he called into the dark hall for Vetch and was heard by his occasional maid who had brought him a jug of ale. He spread his account books on his writing table and looked beyond them into space, considering the offered routes through life, the things that he could change and the things that he could not.

The sound of feet on the oak stairs made him look up, but the hoped-for reunion of his immediate family did not materialize – it was Geoffrey on his way out. He considered his nephew in juxtaposition to his wife, not so dissimilar in age, but where Rachael could no more tell a lie than she could close a door, his nephew seemed unable to distinguish between honesty and deceit. All morning Geoffrey's name had headed his mental list of things to be got through and there was no time like the present time to discuss what he must.

"I hope I do not keep you from business," Latimer began, easing himself back into his writing chair. He supposed he was on his way to Alphington, but he would not quiz him.

"Nothing draws me out that cannot be postponed, sir. You have made good time and we had not expected you until the evening."

"You will appreciate, Nephew, that there is a slight more necessity to return than before."

"Yes, sir, indeed so – a new wife would surely keep most men to their homes until the freshness were passed."

Henri did not answer this directly but followed it with his own observations, the piecing together of a puzzle that had long since kept him speculating.

"A woman will take a man's time and perhaps drain his pocket," he said lightly. "A good wife will have the worth of both of these." Geoffrey fiddled with his stock. "But perhaps marriage is not for you yet a while, Nephew."

"You would not deny me friendly company, Uncle, not when you are now enjoying the pleasures of such yourself."

"I would not, Nephew," Henri said leisurely. "It is provident that I am home before your departure, there are things we must discuss together. Before my marriage, before my attentions were taken to a different place, I had cause to talk with Edmund Elcott. As you are aware he is a man who sees and hears much of the commercial dealings of this city. And I can trust his reporting."

"This would be expected in such a profession as his, Uncle. A notary may deal with many men on many issues."

"And may hear through the chatter that runs about our trading streets, much of what lies below the surface of formal business." Latimer waved his hand impatiently. "Do take a chair, Geoffrey – my view of you will be eased by conversing upon a level."

They sat together – Henri looked at his hands, in no hurry to push the conversation on. "I am told, Nephew, that the name Latimer has been mentioned and indeed sought – my name and indeed yours, Geoffrey – about the underbelly of the city and I must ask myself why this might be."

Geoffrey moved to the edge of his chair, avoiding being caught in the hard gaze of his uncle's pale eyes.

"Indeed? Most probably some confusion, Uncle, there must be many families who share the name Latimer. I can think of no other reason."

"Just so, Geoffrey, and my first thoughts, but it is only this house that has a connection with Blackaller."

Geoffrey re-crossed his legs, the impatient jigging of his foot showing his agitation. "Then you must go on, Uncle, I sense that you have opinion on why we are being sought."

"I do not believe, Geoffrey – and on this I think we should be like-minded – that it is we who are being sought, but rather that it is you alone who is being sought."

Geoffrey rose from his chair. He had not paid the interest due on the money he had been loaned by the back street Dorchester bank – if bank it was – and although he had tried to push the thought to the back of his mind, he anticipated that at some point the hounds would be sent to find him, and now it seemed they had. Denial was his first option but perhaps a twisting of the story may be a better path.

"It is true that I was forced to borrow a little money from a bank in Dorchester, and I have fought these last weeks to keep interest payments to date."

Henri closed his long fingers together as if in prayer and continued to observe his nephew above their tips.

"This Dorchester bank, I imagine it is a counting house you and your family have done business with in the past, this indebtedness will not be recent?" Geoffrey waited until his uncle had made his point before he tried to counter it. "This leaves me confused, Nephew. Why send a debt-collector here and not to Marwood? And why Blackaller? The description that Edmund has been offered up directly connects the family Latimer with the Blackaller Tucking Mill."

"I have raised a little money for my needs, Uncle – since my coming here."

"I would rather it were to me you came for advice on the advancement of any monies – and Dorchester, Geoffrey, why there? There are banks aplenty in this city, I am known to more than one."

Geoffrey did not say, 'exactly so', but instead continued. "Familiarity, Uncle, it is a place I know well."

"Then Blackaller?"

"Did not this family once own the whole of the Blackaller Mill, in not so distant history? All loans demand security, Uncle, and our name and connection with the mill were security enough for the Dorchester counting house." He was straying too close to the truth of things and needed to side track. "And of course my own family, my mother's name and our holding in Dorset assisted the favourable outcome."

"And the favourable outcome being what, Geoffrey? I was not born the day before yesterday – the likelihood of any bank sending out a brutish collector without sound reason is remote. Were the terms of this loan favourable?"

In all honesty, Geoffrey had taken small notice of the agreement he had signed; this prickly interrogation he now found himself subject to was never in the plan of things. He would move away from the truth altogether and spin a lie. Uncle Henri was coming ever closer to picking up the scent.

"Quite favourable, Uncle, not a penny more than ten per cent run over the term of the loan."

"Which is?"

"Three years, sir."

"And may I ask the sum?"

"Fifty pounds, sir." He added, "Of which only twenty remains outstanding." The amount he had borrowed had been for one hundred and fifty, the unpaid interest had added to it.

Henri silently considered what he was being told. He must keep an open mind.

"Do not concern yourself over this, Uncle. I am sure there is some sound and reasonable explanation why we— I – am being sought. I have a six month interest to pay and will call at the bank when next I visit my mama."

"This interest, do you have the means to pay it?"

"I do, Uncle."

Latimer stood. He felt he was at the beginning of a new life, already strewn with difficulties, but nevertheless a chance to make changes to find some kind of happiness – he would not have this young man undo hope.

"Compound interest accrues at an alarming rate, Geoffrey – if not settled regularly. I have some responsibility for you whilst you live under my roof, if this loan may not be fully serviced I would rather you came to me before you are pursued by any debt collector. I would not wish to see you idling in the debtors' gate."

The moment of awkwardness passed more quickly than it ought given the seriousness of his comment. Although he had not sought to gain the upper hand, Henri felt that he might now push on with a plan he had made whilst idling his evening in Moreton.

"Whilst away, I have made purchase of a quantity of serges. These will need to be collected, Nephew." He watched the young man's reaction – although the boy's insolvency troubled him, rebuke was perhaps not the best path forward; occupation would do as well. "I have arranged for a half-dozen pack ponies and a good mount, the serge I have bought is already paid for and now requires collection. The task is yours, Nephew, and I hope you will take it with good heart."

The interview had been quite swiftly ended – his nephew, he could see, was eager to leave. The boy had not refused his direction, but he doubted he was happy with the idea. Never the mind – he would not have him idle.

He had heard Geoffrey close the street door, and in the time between he had sat peaceably watching the day beyond the window; but now there were different sounds filling the space, sounds of exuberance and childish chatter. He saw his daughters' light aprons and dark serge frocks through the part-opened door – Rachael was close behind them. The sight made him sit forward, his mood stirred into something akin to excitement.

He watched her, she stood on the threshold of the wide room almost as though afraid to enter it – or perhaps the fear was of him. Mary and Sophia did not have such reservations.

"Papa, we did not think you would be home yet, and you are come already."

"I am, Sophia, in haste, to see you both. They came to him and he held their soft heads to his waistcoat. He looked beyond them to Rachael. "In haste to see you all," he said, offering a hesitant smile.

"Have you been to the markets, Papa?" It was a question he expected from Sophia, but knew he would never hear from Mary.

"Ask and you shall not receive, make no demands and you most likely will. Mary, go to the hall settle and search my coat pocket, I have a certain recall of having purchased something for you there. See if I remember correctly."

Rachael, he saw, was studying him, her dark eyes unreadable. Their unconventional courtship had meant that each had rarely had an honest view of the other – was this reason for her reticence? He doubted it. He put out his hand and she came into the room and took it. He held it for a while, the small cool fingers, unsure but not necessarily unwilling.

"Are you well, Rachael?" He lightly kissed the back of her hand and let it go. "Better than before?"

"A slight, thank you, Henri." He could hardly believe that this was true, but could not say whether her lack of good health was due to the events of the last few weeks or the consequences of early pregnancy.

Sophia and Mary had found the brown paper roll that contained liquorice sticks and returned to the room. "I am certain sure that I heard your nurse call you a while ago, I believe you should climb up and see if this is so." Understanding very well his meaning, they did not make protest and he listened to their innocent voices as they climbed the stairs to the upper level of the house.

"We did not expect you yet awhile, Henri, I am sorry that you found your home empty and no friendly face to greet you."

"It matters not, Rachael, I had need to speak with my nephew – an empty house offered an opportunity to do just that."

Although he could not quite quantify the emotions he felt living with this woman he had come to care for long ago, he was not dissatisfied with the union. Rachael was safe and he must take succour from that, even though it seemed a veil had been drawn – a part of her left behind.

"Won't you sit awhile, Rachael." She sat in the low chair with the cushion. He sat opposite. "Will you have the story of my travels, Rachael? And then you may offer up yours and describe to me domesticity in detail." Seeing the veil remained he continued. "Or perhaps I should remove myself to beyond that wide casement and converse with you unseen."

"No, no, Henri, I do not wish that you remove yourself from my company, and I have no wish to remove myself from yours." She bit her lip and looked at him honestly.

"Are you content here, Rae? My daughters are not a burden to you?"

"They are not, Henri, and you know they are not."

"Then what is it that I must do to bring the brightness back to your cheeks? I offered marriage without condition and I have not changed my thinking."

"Then perhaps you should not have, Henri – perhaps you should not have offered it. I am quite unworthy and shall likely make you unhappy."

"My motives were entirely selfish, Rae, and you do not make me unhappy." The hand that had been limp in her lap now went to her mouth – he could not decide if this was to inhibit the sensation of sickness or whether her hand covered despair.

"I will try to make that so for always, and while I try you must wait for me, Henri – wait for me to catch you up, wait until I am right again."

45

Henri had not stayed long in his home and the following afternoon Rachael found herself without company. The child sickness would not leave her and she could not think of anything beyond it; picking up her needle, returning to her book was not distraction enough. Mary and Sophia were taking their midday meal and she had hastily exempted herself from their rooms.

Since their first awkward night together, her husband seemed to have decided that she was better left to herself – he had removed his night clothes to another room and then settled with some enthusiasm to the task of resurrecting trade. The consequences of this were that he had spent more of this last week away from his home than within it.

She walked about the room, hoping to alleviate the constant sensation of nausea. Emotions of conflict and contradiction had sat on her shoulders since first Henri had brought her to Latimer house. The pleasure that she ought to feel, now that she had been offered salvation and had taken a goodly name, were constantly opposed by the cuckoo in the nest – the child that was not his and the knowledge of its begetting.

After an unpromising start, the month was now settled and the bright day lifted her up from the gloom into which she often fell. Laying down the unread book on a chair she moved quietly passed the dining room and lifted the latch on the kitchen door. Henri's cook did not approve of her presence in the kitchen, indeed did not approve of her presence in the house, but respect for her master would never allow her to own it. Passing silently through the empty kitchens she let herself out into the warm courtyard, tipped her face to the sky and felt the sun. She had not spoken to Elijah Flood since the announcement of her intentions to enter the whorehouse; she did not wish this disconnection to continue and at least on this she could make amends.

She nervously entered Trelawney's kitchen. Flood was not there and she looked about, ran her hand over the heavy bible and remembered how it had been. Nothing much had changed here in the weeks that she had been away, and whether from habit or the need for simplicity and the normality of kitchen work, she lifted down the flour croc, slipping easily under the cloak of the girl she had once been.

"Rae?" It was a question. Flood had entered – was stopped in his boots by her unexpected appearance. Although he was not aware of all that had happened to her since the dark night of her undoing, he had heard of her marriage.

"Good day to you, Elijah, I hope I am not unwelcome. I have come to see how you fair – left alone without company and with nothing but bakehouse bread and a silent kitchen."

"'Tis not seemly for you to be standing before that old table white with flour – your place be in your husband's house."

At least his hostility towards her had dulled; he had as good as cursed her to Hell when last she had stood here in this kitchen explaining her choice.

"And nor is it, but the house beside this runs well enough without me, so may I not offer company to an old friend?"

Flood sat, she noticed his hands were discoloured by the red earth upon which the city was built, his nails thick with the dirt of manual toil. He looked tired and the top buttons of his waistcoat were unfastened.

"I am surprised that you would wish it."

"I do wish it, Elijah."

She would offer the hand of friendship, but she would not ask for God's forgiveness – she waited for him to suggest it. He did not, but instead ladled water from the bucket and drank.

"Have you had a burying?" she asked as she worked. Overtime, the meeting house had become his life; he would dig a grave or polish an altar stick as willingly as he would drop to his knees in prayer.

"I have, Mrs Latimer, the third this week." It was an oddity hearing him call her Latimer, a title she doubted she would ever become used to.

"And all from the meeting house?"

"Of the same family – fever is rife in the lower streets, but they are in God's kingdom now and will be better rested there."

She began to form the dough into mounds. The bible sat on a small table close to his bed, she wondered if he still turned the pages and then, because there was none to read to him, continued to imagine what was written in the text? He stood and went to the fire, reaching for the shuttle and placing a heap of brightly glowing embers into the oven in readiness for her baking.

"Trelawney writes us," he said returning to the table. "I thought to keep the paper until I could take it to the meeting house."

The folded letter was tucked beneath the bible and he collected it and showed her. Rachael wiped her hands, took it and sat looking at the writing. It was addressed to her. Along with remembrance of Alexander there was a painful stab of remembrance of another kind. She placed the letter back on the table, reluctant to resurrect what she wished to forget.

"Will you not read it? My master will not know what has happened here, and I believe he would wish to know – if you have the notion to do such, a reply would be proper."

"It will depend upon what is writ, Elijah, whether or no I make reply."

She put the dough aside to prove, took up the letter again and broke the seal. She would read it to herself first as she always had. There was a sketch of Haldon Manor and an irreverent profile of his host. The text began, *My worthy servant* – not so much in favour as she had been. There was obviously much to occupy him in the Haldon Forest, it continued: *We are gone away to Bristol and will likely move along to London when we have done with the scene there, be so kind as to convey my intentions to Flood and tell him he must settle the house at least for the next month.* There was a little more about the progress of his work and his access to biddable servants. She put down the letter and observed Flood's look of expectancy. She doubted he would find any satisfaction in it and in the stead of reading it she conceived her own.

"*My dear servants, the house here at Haldon is quite grand, a servant for each guest and more. I thank you both for waiting so patiently for my return, but now that my work here is complete – and successfully so – I am invited along to Bath with the family Buckman and will take opportunity to work there. I will return before the summer wains and hope you may find enough in the cash box for your needs between-time.*" She had omitted any suggestion that Alexander may still have a companion. "*Yours with sincerity, Alexander Trelawney.*" She returned the letter to its folds and placed it on a corner of the table.

The bread would not be ready for the oven for a while and the bible sat waiting, the heavy volume already open. "I have a little time, Elijah." She wiped her hands on a square of muslin, looking about the small room, considering what had been. "If you wish it I will read a verse."

Change had come rapidly, but life held no guarantees; reading as she always had would be a distraction and any distraction was welcome.

46

The heat of midsummer finally settled over the county, the sun as unwelcome as it had been missed. Geoffrey stood in the stirrups of his hired mount to alleviate his boredom; a line of pack ponies trailed out before him, the hooves of the train kicking up dust from the unmetalled track, a multitude of flies and insects dancing in the wake of the slow-moving line and their leavings. He jerked at the bit of his horse, allowing a little more distance to grow between his plodding bovine mount and the pack-team, watching the back of the carrier's boy as he rocked from side to side on his undersized pony. How savagely he missed his own stable and the thoroughbreds he had once kept there – for him change needed to come and could not come soon enough.

He slackened the reins and slid a hand inside his waistcoat, probed his shirt until he found his way through to the small irritating spot – one of many, the result of a night spent on a much-used straw mattress. Indecision did not normally hang about him, he rarely thought long enough to consider options and outcomes, but still the two bottles of physic sat unused on his dressing table. The degradation of riding this plodding nag, the uncomfortable night he had spent on the road and the deferral of his usual afternoon habits in Alphington had decided him: when opportunity arose he would experiment with a little of the tincture.

The serges hung limply over the wooden packsaddles – he had been completely superfluous in the collecting of the woven wool and was certain sure his uncle had only tasked him with this errand to unsettle his life. In an hour or so they would be entering the city by the North Gate; he had only to make his way to Blackaller where the Quaker's men would be waiting for him. Then he would be free, free to go about his own business.

Before St Mary's clock had chimed three he had left his hired mount at the Holloway livery and was making his way back towards Exebere Street. In past times his entry into the cavernous old hall had been met with the near silence of an underused house and the obsequious subservice of Vetch. Contrary to expectation today, Latimer House was a disordered mix of keening servants, whispered words and determined activity.

Rachael was standing central in the hall, her shaking hands grasped before her in an attempt to still them, her top teeth biting hard into her lower lip. Henri was looking down at her, concerned, but with the measured patience that he now reserved for all conversations with his young wife.

"I ask it only if you are able, Rachael, although I think it best policy. I would rather not have the burden of explanation until the house is settled."

Rachael watched her husband's daughters through the open door of the sitting room. They had been offered the privilege of using their father's desk and inkwell and were occupied in writing infantile script across a blank sheet of bleached paper – they had been set the task as a distraction, she did not expect this to be anything other than temporary.

"I am quite able, Henri, it seems the simplest thing to do and best for all." She let him take her hands in an attempt to stop them shaking. "It is just the thought that we were sat along with her for so long before considering the changes. I should have known it – I should have known the difference between a living soul with breath and one whose life has ebbed away."

"I might agree in all instances, but this one, do not run around things in your head, Rachael nor attempt to find blame. We should not be so surprised at her passing – I believe it is more expected than no." He let go of her hands and lightly touched his fingers to her pale cheek. "When things are calmer here I will explain to them what has happened."

Rachael picked up the flat straw-brimmed hat that she had laid on the hall settle and secured it above her cap – which she now wore daily. Henri may know what she had done to her hair but the rest of the household would not.

She had spent the early part of the afternoon as she often did, in the rooms at the top of the house where Mary and Sophia spent most of their time. It was an easy option, a valued distraction from irksome thoughts or the questioning eyes of house servants. She could not say how much time had passed between Sarah's last breath and the startling realization that the old woman was dead. Henri's daughters, she knew, had little expectation of anything other than silence and deep slumber throughout the post-noon hours, and the nurse may have already found her God before Rachael had even entered the room.

Henri had begun to give her instructions and she tried to listen to him, to focus her mind on the immediate rather than the past or the future.

"I think it would be wholly appropriate to go to St Mary's burial ground, the church will be open, go within if you choose it – my daughters find some comfort in prayer, it is a link they still feel they have with their mother."

She had glanced again at her husband before leaving him to do his bidding. She wished so much to have him comfort her, to restore that inconsequential benign dialogue they had enjoyed for so many weeks before her world had changed. The barrier she could not surmount had yet to stir in her belly, and she knew Henri had formed his own conclusion on why she could not lay with him – she doubted its accuracy.

Glancing up as his nephew had entered the house, Henri was aware of the boy's confusion. He did not have the time or the inclination to ask him how his trip had gone.

"Geoffrey, I would have your support if you will offer it." Henri's immediate reaction had been to send Vetch for a doctor, his servant had returned just before Geoffrey, unaccompanied.

"Thomas informs me that our Magdalen Street physician's preference is for the affluent living and will offer no help to the lowly dead. We must wait upon an apothecary."

Latimer viewed his servants with some irritation; he had expected some level of grief, of shock even, but not this desolate grizzling.

"Thomas, take the women back into the kitchen and find the cooking brandy. I doubt it is locked away, and if it is please liberate it and offer them enough to quieten their whining."

He stood alone facing his nephew and began his explanation. He saw no requirement to offer anything but fact.

"My wife found my daughters' nurse dead some two hours gone – the old woman cannot remain slumped in her chair as she is. I would have your help, Geoffrey, in settling her respectfully away from seeing eyes."

They took the stairs together, Latimer a little slower than his nephew, but quite unaided by any stick. The afternoon sun had found its way to the back of the house and the rooms were airless, stiflingly hot. He went to the sash, raised it and turned, looking at the woman's corpse. The lips were purple, eyes fortunately closed. He wondered if Geoffrey had ever had dealings with the dead before, but then perhaps he had been spared such base things. Reluctant to enter, his nephew leant against the doorjamb, observing the motionless body – unmoved.

"How long dead, Uncle? Not known you say?"

"Not known, Geoffrey – a physician would have put a time upon it, the apothecary will have seen many a corpse and will try."

Their brief conversation was curtailed by Vetch, the breathless apothecary close behind him.

"Thank you, Thomas, at least we may now confirm her passing and move her. A nursery-room chair is no place for a corpse. Do come forward, sir – if you would."

The apothecary, a man of some experience, removed his coat and dropped it on a chair – a serious man with the look of worry permanently hanging about his features.

"How old would you say the woman was, sir?"

"I cannot say with any accuracy – more than fifty perhaps. She was employed some six years ago to assist my daughters' wet nurse."

They watched while the sweating little man laid an ear to Sarah's chest – waiting for him to pronounce what they already knew. He lifted her hand then let it drop back to her lap. There was a bottle held in the other, the fingers still quite tight around it.

"Some stiffening has occurred. And of course this woman is quite dead. I would say has been so for something approaching three hours."

He released the stone bottle from her grip and placed it on the small table amongst her personal things – an empty plate and a half-dozen similar jars.

"Know you of these potions, sir? There seems to be quite an array here. I may not have the book learning of a physician, but might be able to help you with the reasons for her passing if clue may be found within them."

Latimer turned to Vetch. "What say you to these mixes? Quick-salves and physics do you suppose?" He sensed his servant's reluctance to speak openly. "The woman is dead, Thomas – do not be tongue-tied when offering up opinion."

Vetch stood stiffly some distance from the corpse, his unwashed hair loosened from the cord that formed his queue. "I believe she liked the spirit, sir."

"I think, Thomas, that even my daughters would have been able to furnish me with this fact."

Prompted, Vetch continued. "I do not own the truth of it, sir, but I would think it likely that brandy might be found in a one or two of these bottles. Although her pocket did only run to gin, I believe her preference was for something more refined and there is always leavings in a gentleman's house. I do not wish to speak sourly of the dead, sir, but I believe she had a nose for any spirit, no matter how presented and no matter where 'twas found."

All manner of mixes, decoctions, tinctures and physics being his bread and butter, the apothecary was already one step ahead, picking up a second jar from the table and smelling the contents.

"There is a distinct smell of good brandy here, sirs, but something beyond it also." He handed Henri the jar, Henri stretched out an arm and offered the same to Geoffrey. "The smell is quite dilute, but there is something other beyond brandy." The apothecary picked up another larger jar. "I would expect angelica to be found in most households, 'tis a singular remedy against all manner of corruptions and evils, although I cannot identify it here."

Geoffrey had taken the jar. Latimer observed him; the disinterest, even disrespect he had offered up earlier had been replaced with flush-cheeked agitation.

"My uncle has been unwell and to his bed on more than one occasion since the year turned." He went through the motions of sniffing the bottle and pretending to read the label. "I sought the advice of an apothecary in St Paul's at the onset. If the woman had a habit of seeking out spirits – in all their forms – she may well have chanced upon this mix."

Latimer handed the jar back to the herbalist.

"What remedy was offered, sir?" The apothecary spoke to Geoffrey.

"Peruvian bark as an infusion."

"A sound choice." He continued to smell the half-dozen or so jars and bottles displayed on the small chair side table. "I am quite familiar with it – but can find no evidence of its presence here, sir."

"Perhaps not, I had understood the mix was administered fully to my uncle and some time ago." He looked uncertainly at Latimer. "At my uncle's request, the attendance of neither herbalist nor physician were sought during his recent malaise. I believe I am correct, Uncle?"

"Quite correct, Nephew."

"Then is it not likely the old woman had other sources, found other mixes beyond this house?"

Latimer stroked his chin as he considered this. "Her habits, Nephew, we shall never now have full knowledge of." He turned to the apothecary. "Do you anticipate that her death is other than natural?"

"No, sir, no, I find nothing here to suggest it. It appears from these mixes the woman considered herself in poor health. Perhaps there may have been some contradiction with so many remedies being taken together. But her antiquity is not in doubt. It is not my field, but I would say, judging by the ruddiness of cheek, she may well have benefitted from a leach-letting and died through lack of it."

Latimer faced the open window, seeking respite in the soft incoming air. If any were to blame for the demise of this elderly woman, it was himself. In defence there had been many distractions, many issues taking priority over a top floor servant's addiction to strong drink. But he should have questioned things; he was well aware of Sarah's liking for gin, her habitual drink-induced slumbers. He understood the woman saw these mixes she had collected, all of which had either brandy or gin as their base, as physics – a helpmate in the inevitable journey towards old age – but he should have been more vigilant, more watchful. It was only by chance that it had been Rachael who discovered the woman dead; it could so easily have been his daughters. His wife most times kept a level head, but the finding of the old woman, without breath and slumped more firmly than usual in her chair, had unsettled her and she had come to him white-faced, stunned into near silence and told him what she suspected – by choice he would have had it otherwise.

There was little more to be gained here running over what may or may not have ultimately caused the old woman's death. Assessing the apothecary done, he turned and addressed him. "I thank you for your time and indeed expertise, sir. Let me know your fee and I will have my servant settle with you before you leave."

Henri had let the man go and they had removed the corpse to the small sitting room a floor below, a place unused for more than six years. Despite her propensity for hysteria, he would have his occasional maid go up and lay the woman out – he did not want the task to fall to Rachael.

47

Geoffrey closed the door of his room and sat heavily upon his bed. The Latimer household, a place of habit and dull living, constantly threw up the unexpected. He considered the scene he had just left; the old woman, who had no business surviving as long as she had, had been moved with some considerable difficulty to the room along the passage. He had been obliged to assist.

It seemed his cousins' nurse had been a thief, a pilferer, a wanderer of darkened corridors. He rose and went to the small square box-cupboard in his press; the brandy he kept there sat undisturbed between folded stocks and cotton stockings. He took it down, smelt the neck and filled a glass. He supposed it to be unadulterated, but what of the two bottles he had acquired from Blox? Before he had left he had placed them in a chest drawer he felt inside, found them, held each to the light of his window. He had never been certain sure what they contained, and now he could not even be sure that the mix was not a dilution of its original self. His mind was divided upon whether or not the concoction had played any part in the death of his uncle's servant. He put them away, drank the brandy in one and began pulling off his stock, removing his shirt. The afternoon's events had left him feeling tainted, soiled. He quickly washed changed his linen and unobtrusively left the house walking in the direction of Alphington.

The end of the working day brought many drinkers to The Seven Stars and the taproom was full. He worked his way through the bull-like watermen, undernourished apprentices and farm boys. Avoiding the landlord had become habitual, he owed the man more than four weeks' rent – buoyant trade meant he could rise to his rooms unnoticed. Mag had not yet arrived and he waited for her; sat in his usual chair, muddied boots on the sill, watching the river. Long days of summer made for short nights, and even though the clock had moved on darkness did not hamper his view. She was late, more than late – a niggle of anxiety allowed the thought that she may not be coming, which in turn fuelled his impatience, and irritability began in the close heat of his cousins' rooms.

Soon after the cathedral bells rang out across the city to mark the ninth hour he saw her appear from amongst the ramshackle buildings built across the bridge, walking without haste, without thought that he had been waiting for her for more than two hours.

"Margaret – what game do you play?" As she passed his chair he reached out and gripped her wrist, stopped her from going further. She looked tired, her pale hair still caught beneath the cheap wig she wore in the bawdy house.

"What time is it, Geoffrey? I have not the least notion. The eve has gone away at a sure pace."

Since adolescence, women had held little interest for him apart from what could be gained from their purse or the obvious pleasures of fornication. If he felt any differently about Mag, he did not accept it.

"If the evening has gone away at sure pace, madam, here in these rooms it has been held in stagnation and inactivity. I would have expected you some two hours since. Now as you see I have a grievance to offer up and do not think you can settle it with platitudes and fair smiles."

He stood still gripping her arm. The wig did not please him – without the obvious dressing of a whore his subconscious mind could be persuaded that this woman was pure, pure unto him, almost virginal with her soft uncoloured hair and her obvious frailty. He removed the wig, releasing her hair.

"There is good reason, master Geoffrey, for my lateness and if you will leave me go then I will speak it, but I cannot think upon anything other while your hand is so cruelly clamped upon my arm."

Without care he let her go and watched her move to the glass to brush out her hair. She sank into a low chair. "Make your story well told, Margaret, I would not wish to have had the waiting for you without sound reason."

"A sickness has come to the house, Geoffrey, and the bawd would not release me." She watched for reaction, deciding that honesty might not be well met, working with half-truths and limited detail, she continued. "We have a new girl come just this week gone – she has taken straightway to her bed with a malady. Tis nothing more than the gripe-sweats and will be gone from her soon enough, but there is another two so affected and I must see to customers and may not find liberty until I am done."

Admitting what she was did not normally unsettle his thoughts, searching out the detail beyond this was something he tried to avoid.

He stood behind her and caught his hands in her long tresses, preventing her moving her head. Mag put down the brush and waited for him to release her, for he would soon enough. It mattered not what she knew of this man – and of men and their ways in general – on this day with the house full of sickness and a girl laying close to death she could only wish him kind, needed more than harsh words and harsh handling. Her lower lids had filled with tears – he saw the image in the mottled mirror and he let her go.

"If you left the clutches of that whore mother you would not have such reliance on stolen liberty, and I should not be forced to lose time here by counting barges and crank-cranes."

The thought did, she knew, have some appeal, but the memory of her past life, the time she spent as a married woman, came to her to forewarn her. She ought never to put singular trust in anyone, never cut ties with the one place she might run to when danger required it.

"I shall think on it, Geoffrey, I will think on it more, but I cannot leave when the house is in need. Hetty do not deal well with these things and there is still fetching and carrying to be got through for all of us."

He removed her hair from her neck and lay his open mouth upon the white skin – in Geoffrey's eyes not a kiss, just a clear display of his need.

"I have a little head pain, sir, but will be well and good if I might lie for a while, and better still if you were beside me." She stood and helped him with his shirt.

He lay beside her and felt her smallness. He liked her lack of strength, her frail beauty, her desire to please him – life and all its irksome difficulties could be kept at arm's length when she joined him in this bed – lust was a worthy analgesic.

Although in practice they lived side by side in Exebere Street, in conversation this was rarely admitted to – even though there were friends and acquaintances and even relations now in common. In small part they each knew of the other's lives – Mag, he understood, would soon know of the Latimer servant's death, and he, in time, would understand that the fever come to Exebere was not of the passing kind.

48

A note had come from Blackaller during the breakfast hour. The child in whose hand the sealed paper had been placed had not waited for reply. Rachael was already seated at the table when Henri had come down – the broken remains of a saffron cake set before her.

Until recently, Henri had not regretted his lack of interaction with women or the absence of a sister, now he assuredly did. He was not dissatisfied with Rachael's permanent place in his home and he did not doubt that in time she would explain the still-blank details of her life between the eve of his journey to Moreton and her appearance in the bawdy house – and more pertinently the begetting of her child. Dissatisfied, he may not have been, but frustrated, both in his heart and in his sexuality, he was. Having a wife but not knowing her as wife had, in the first few days of their union seemed wholly acceptable; the thought of having saved her from the low world of destitution, abuse and even infanticide had been enough. He was not sure that it would remain so indefinitely.

His daughters had already broken their fast and returned to the hat of the house to settle over their books and script work. The occasional maid was no more effectual in watching over them than Old Sarah had been, but the arrangement suited his momentary need and Rachael seemed more than willing to spend her afternoons sat amongst nursery games and sewing thread.

He shifted his weight in the hard-backed chair the Quaker's clerk had provided for him – even the closed door did not deaden the sound of the pounding mill hammers. Although his health had returned in bounds, there was still necessity to keep his stick by him when he was out. He stretched his leg until the intermittent pain had passed and watched the timepiece on the mantle. Josiah Mudge, he understood, was a busy and conscientious man, philanthropic in all his dealings; but the Quaker rarely kept him waiting when an appointment had been made. The unexplained summons brought to his mind his nephew and the thought unsettled him. In all the time the boy had lived along with him in the Latimer house, Henri had always hoped for better things, a better understanding between them. He had been genuinely pleased, gratified, that his dead brother's child had wanted to interest himself in the family business. Lately he had come to the conclusion that it might be preferable for all if the young man returned to his mother. Sarah was to be buried in the morn of tomorrow; perhaps then the house could settle into the cleft of normality that he had once been used to – unless his interview with Mudge dictated other.

White-haired and ageing, Josiah Mudge entered the room, his clerk dutifully closing the door behind him. He settled himself behind the enduring desk where once two generations of Latimers had sat, the clerk busying himself in some far corner of the large room.

"I hope my summons did not unsettle you unduly, Henri, there is of course some urgency to this meeting – I would not have sent a boy so early in the day if there were not."

"If you have urgent need of my ear, Josiah, then I offer it without complaint."

Mudge moved some papers to the opposite side of his desk and then restored them to the place they had begun. "What I must tell you, what I have learnt most recently, concerns your nephew, sir, and indeed my own son." He paused, reflecting. "Although many in this city may think me an indulgent fool where William is concerned – believe me blinded by affection for the boy – I see his failings as well as any."

Latimer folded his arms and squinted at the Quaker from under taut brows.

"William is to be married. I am delighted with the proposed union and it seems he is not displeased with the prospect himself. Although I did not call you here to tell you of this news, you may have it just the same – I believe it is a starting point. I have asked to speak to you this day as I do not wish to have any insurmountable obstacle thrown in his path."

Josiah looked at his own broad hands and the papers beside them. "For some weeks past we have received communication from a Yeovil gentlemen, the writings in bold rustic hand and the meaning less than clear. At first, I handed these short notes, requesting details of our business here, indeed showing surprising enthusiasm for the fulling mill and the processes therein, directly to my clerk and then latterly to William." He looked up, considering the lean dark-headed man sat before him.

"Do not hold back on my account, Josiah. If this story involves my nephew I shall not be taken by surprise, and I presume by your hesitancy it does."

"Your presumption is correct, sir. It seems the Yeovil gentleman, a Mr Dundish, is in possession of papers which show him to own a holding in this mill. More recently, I dispatched my clerk to visit and although I have not seen these papers myself, my clerk assures me that they are genuine."

Latimer sat forward in his chair. "How so when apart from my minor holding Blackaller is entirely yours?"

"I'm afraid, Latimer, that they are your shares that are in doubt. They were sold in good faith to Mr Dundish via a Sherborne broker. My clerk tells me there is a Scrip of Entitlement benefitting your nephew, this document containing your seal and indeed your signature."

Latimer looked out over the working river and the canal beyond, considering what he had been told. "Then genuine they are not – until my nephew has learnt to live as his income dictates there is no likelihood that I would bequeath him anything, save advice and admonishment."

Mudge looked at his hands. "I would have chosen any other conclusion than the one I have reluctantly formed, Latimer, but I find I cannot shy away from it. It seems that there has been a lending of papers. I will not say that William was exactly coerced into offering these, but nonetheless, these papers – my copy of the long-made agreement between our families, the Deed that gives me ownership of Blackaller – was offered to your nephew. I believe this was used to forward the deceit – the documents held by Dundish counterfeit."

Henri ran a hand over his chin. "And you believe Geoffrey to be the initiator?"

"I have to affirm that I do – all knowledge points to it."

Latimer shook his head, allowed the breath of exasperation to escape from taut lips. "Then perhaps the boy is rotten. Although in the past I have tried to convince myself otherwise, I already know him to be profligate, lacking in honesty, and now it seems he may well be a forger and a perjurer to boot." Latimer ran his hand through his dark hair and mulled over the possible consequences of this new revelation. "If what you suspect is true, the consequences will be long running. The involvement of any constable will have him sent before the courts. A felony such as this could likely see him end his days at the end of a rope. I suspicion you will have considered conclusion – a path forward?"

"I have considered nothing else. I have only one son, Latimer, and there will most certainly be implications for William if this should find its way to any assize court."

"Then we must make resolve that it does not. Although a visit to the debtors' gate may be no more than my nephew deserves, and there would be a willingness on my part to allow him suffer it, this fraudulent reproduction of documents moves far beyond simple debt – I would not wish his transgressions to muddy the life of any other."

"I had hoped that we might be in agreement. My first suggestion is to buy back the shares, although Dundish may not be so compliant. He owns a small farm in Somerset and land in Devonshire and is likely seeking a foothold in the woollen trade at a broader level."

The Quaker hesitated, treading with care before venturing on. "The alternative is that you allow the shares to remain transferred, remain as they are, ownership unchallenged, and then seek compensation from your nephew. None but us will know that a criminal act has been committed."

Henri sat back in his chair and frowned at the working river beyond. To give up his holding in the tucking mill, a mill that his grandfather had fought so hard to build and to hold on to, did not sit well. And compensation, what compensation could he ever hope to ring from a young man already heavily indebted, with a moneylender sniffing at his heels and a pile of unsettled accounts left unattended in the next county? If it had not been for the respect he held for Josiah Mudge and further concern for his inept son, he may well have presented his nephew to the magistrate himself.

"Is the farmer persistent – does he have any wind of the truth of things do you think?"

"I think not, Henri, although I believe him persistent."

"More succinctly, Josiah, do I have time to consider a path?"

"Indeed you do, sir, at least until our hand is forced. Our aspirational farmer is quite intent on claiming his share of this business, his last communication intimated of a pending visit to this city and to Blackaller." Josiah looked up, the calm confidence of a man who knows his God disturbed by the conflict of heart versus faith. "It sits badly with me, Henri, but it seems I must break our Lord's commandment if I wish to save my son's neck."

49

Thought fixing his gaze to the wall beyond, Geoffrey released his member from his breeches and aimed at one of the overfull piss buckets set at intervals about the working yard of The Phoenix Inn. William Mudge was engaged in much the same activity; a greeting had been offered but was reciprocated with almost tacit correctness. The inn had been close, the yard even less agreeable. The sun, almost relentless now for near on a fortnight, had been about the east-facing cobbles since just after dawn, successfully promoting the stench of stale urine, kitchen slops and horse droppings into a miasma of odorous unpleasantness. Geoffrey waited before speaking again, buttoning his breeches, settling his waistcoat.

"Saints, William, you're like an apparition from a time forgot – I had not expected to find you offering up to any drink-house piss pot." William, he noticed, was darkly dressed, his usual flamboyance quite absent.

"I have been perched behind that counting desk since matins and even my father's impertinent little clerk bade me leave it for the hospitality of an eating house." William eyed his contemporary equably. "Besides, Geoffrey, if any is apparition it is you, sir – we have seen neither a hide nor a hair of you these three weeks gone."

Geoffrey shrugged, leant idly against a stone wall. "The city offers interest beyond this taproom and I am done with backhand dealers and eagle-eyed moneylenders. I suppose your teacup handling and plan making do offer up an interest of sorts."

"Of sorts."

"And marriage, I hear – a dull duckling, sir, or something other?"

"Something other, I hope, and a duckling may grow – she is of the faith and the union pleases my father; I will settle on it as I find I must."

"Must, William?"

"Must, Geoffrey, circumstance do sometimes dictate the treading of a careful path."

William considered the near dandy he had once drunk alongside and called friend. "Deuce, Latimer, these Quakerish ways do not sit comfortably with me and well you must know it – this suit, the need to spend the daylight hours looking along endless lines of counting and then the even hours sat in that dull meeting house seeking forgiveness – but I am backed into a corner and must do as I am bid to save my liberty."

"Liberty, William? Why so threatened – has your old papa hardened in his determination to have you serve his God?"

"Do not play fool about, Latimer, you must know the circumstance about which I speak."

"Riddles do fox me, William. Exactly of what circumstance do you speak?"

"Then you are yet spared the knife edge of your uncle's tongue, sir, for I have felt my papa's and shall feel it again if I am not compliant." William put his hands in his pockets and considered his contemporary's easy ways – his ability to shake off responsibility, his lack of moral reasoning. "The beast you have created has turned to bite and it is my hide that is at most at risk. The paper, sir – your uncle was called to Blackaller the day before last. The thing is out, Geoffrey."

"An innocent borrowing and an innocent lending, a loan secured and nothing more."

"Plenty more, sir – a deluge of block-hand notes, a declaration of interest in the mill and an examination of documents by my father's clerk. You may finish this story for me, Latimer, for you will know better than I."

"Perhaps I do, William, but I cannot see how this directly affects you. Deny all, sir, 'tis the best and only policy."

"I cannot agree. Unlike you, sir, I do not keep a whore that I may run to when times are difficult. I am set down amongst Godly men. I am without choice and must run with what God offers. What you have done is fraudulent, I am complicit. I am duped, Latimer."

Geoffrey pulled himself away from the wall and straightened; at last a small furrow of concern showed upon his indolent face. "How is this out, William?"

"Inevitability and poor reasoning, sir – and the latter is yours. I will do my father's bidding, marry his duckling and sit myself daily behind that counting desk and you, sir, must take the consequences of what you have done."

Geoffrey kicked at a loose cobble and watched Mudge's straight back and dark coat as he abruptly left the yard. So he had been unearthed, the shares perhaps sold on to another party – he had never before dug himself in quite so deeply, but there was no reason why any of this should hamper his life; the money had been useful and although now almost deplete, he did not regret its acquisition. And he had been his own master since he could look above his mother's head; he had no need to tolerate a grubbing from his surly uncle, he was well used to ducking when the arrows flew, well versed at avoiding creditors. Unavoidably this city still held interest and he would have to lie low for a while until this moment of difficulty had passed.

Weeks of heat with no more than the dew of morning to damp the dust had left the streets reeking of the river, and the debris of living, normally washed away by West Country torrents, sat in decaying heaps about the city. Picking his way carefully along South Street, avoiding the worst of the rubbish, he had formulated a plan, made a decision. He would remove himself permanently to Alphington and then do nothing.

50

Cautiously indifferent towards any God, Henri had never sought succour in any church building; but St Mary's burial ground, so often a place visited by his daughters – and their nurse – offered a form of sanctuary, the feeling born more from the tranquillity of the place rather than any reverence. They had buried Old Sarah the previous day; there had been only himself and Thomas Vetch present and they had laid her to rest without emotion. Perched on a low stone wall he leant forward resting elbows on long limbs and viewed the newly dug earth covering her grave, mounded now and bare. There had been no time until today to consider the revelations passed to him in confidence by Josiah Mudge.

He supposed he must confront his nephew soon, although the boy had made himself scarce of late – had not been home these last days. Before he did, he must first know his own mind; unusually for Latimer, at this moment he did not. Allowing the boy's own actions to catch him up remained a possibility, was more than a consideration – he no longer felt any need to offer a protective hand, his half-brother's child was obviously rotten to the core and no amount of instruction nor reproof would change things.

He considered his wife, a young woman he had shared spoken intimacy with before marriage but almost none since, and it was to Rachael he would have wished to turn, to discuss the future and not just in regard to his nephew. But he found he could not, he seemed unable to move beyond the first tentative enquiries regarding her health before a veil of sadness ended any attempts at closeness.

Earlier shade had been offered by an ancient yew, but now the pool of shadow was lost as the day moved on. He stood, picked up his coat and left the comparative calm of the burial ground for the bustle of West Gate Street. Although he had made no arrangement, he would visit the Goldsmith's coffee house in search of a friendly face and a receptive ear. Market day brought crowds to the city, but also drew them away from their usual haunts and the rooms were not overfull. When he had arrived, Elcott had been on his feet about to leave, but Latimer's narrowed brow and taut-lipped pique had made him change his mind. They had found a seat together in a quiet corner.

"Do you seek me, friend? You do not look like a man who has come to take refreshment and listen to the idle chatter of the city."

"I have not, Edmund, and I doubt I would have the patience for it if this were my intention." Latimer waved the serving boy away. "I find that I am between a rock and a hard place – the choices open to me poor and I would welcome opinion."

"Then I will offer it if I am able, this rock, this hard place, concerns an issue of a serious nature?"

"Indeed, I am damned whatever I do. To solve or at the least relieve this difficulty I must choose between purse and conscience. Neither will afford me satisfaction."

"I am in no hurry, sir, please continue."

"It seems, Edmund, that my nephew is not only a thief, but is also culpable in a scheme of fraud and deception. To take the story forward quickly he has contrived to duplicate and then sell on my holding in Blackaller."

"I have come to understand him a little through our conversations here, Henri, but this surely is a new and unexpected level of misdeed."

"Perhaps it is not unexpected, Edmund, but merely a continuance of his determination to have liberty removed. Mudge has the full knowledge of this misadventure, through deduction and in small part through the belated honesty of his son. We have discussed the way forward and I must make a choice. Weather I pay off the unsuspecting recipient of this forged share agreement or allow my holding to remain in these new hands, it is my purse that will make amends. If I do not take this route then I as good as send my nephew on his way to the assize court and quite likely the gallows."

Elcott tapped his closed fingers to his lips. "Is there no other solution? I see no promise in either suggestion."

"There is not. And this does not sit alone – he is already sought in two counties for debt and cannot evade his creditors indefinitely."

"Then perhaps you must allow the wolves find him."

"Perhaps I must."

"Do not take it as an impertinence, sir, but if you were to decide to help your nephew to untangle himself from the consequences of his actions, would your purse allow it?"

Latimer sat back and considered the question. "I believe that it could – I would not wish to lose my holding in Blackaller."

"Perhaps then, Henri, allow it run – let the fish pull on the line and see how far it swims. Have you confronted your nephew? Perhaps he will have explanation, perchance his own pocket might see him out of trouble – he has land."

"Indebted, I believe, but of some value."

"I am sorry I cannot offer clean solution. I have a little money of my own if you choose to take that route."

"I would never ask it and did not seek your company with any such offering in mind."

Henri felt the day's stubble on his chin and looked across the room towards the open door, his brow no less furrowed, his mind no less troubled. "I am resigned to a sleepless night, Edmund, for tomorrow I will confront him, and before tomorrow I will have made a decision. I would have sought you yesterday but, as perhaps you have heard along the ever roving vine of this city, yesterday we laid my daughters' elderly nurse to rest."

"Rumour spreads, Latimer, as you say – I had heard."

They had sat for a while with their own thoughts, good manners prompting Latimer to ask a little of his friend's continuing plans. Straightening his back, Elcott began tentatively.

"What think you of these new epidemics running about the city? There is a thinking about these rooms that this hampered river – in centuries past, the bringer of wealth and prosperity – now plays some part in the spreading of these diseases."

"I have heard a little, Edmund – are not such fevers and maladies always rife at this time of year?"

"Indeed they are, Henri, but this lack of rain seems to have propelled the contagion onwards, the moorland streams have almost dried to a trickle and no longer greet our river with any force."

"And the waterman's trade made even more arduous. I query what is found when the source is so depleted."

Elcott looked at the obligatory stick which was laid across the empty table. "I have had conversation with a gentleman – I deal occasionally with his papers, our long held association allows some intimacy in dialogue." He paused, already gauging his companion's reaction. "He complains that fever has spread as far as the southern quarter, has become a disagreeable interference in his life by having the gall to insinuate itself into a popular and regularly used whorehouse there."

No longer able to shrug off reports of fevers circling the city, Latimer faced his friend. "Enteric fever – I had not heard?"

"Perhaps your thoughts run elsewhere and I doubt the crone would wish it common knowledge, trade will be greatly hampered."

"I cannot decide if this new concern dulls the others or merely adds burden."

"Your house, I'm sure, will stay untouched – we cannot say with any surety why one household should be cursed when another is not. It seems that if you are free of it you will stay free. The elderly woman, what was the cause of her dying?"

"In simplicity, Edmund, gin and pilfered spirit – in addition, of course, to her ever-increasing state of feebleness."

"I have rarely wished that the city would be deluged with Godly rain, Henri, but I wish it now if only to belay this stench."

"Amen to that, Edmund. And now I must return and resign myself to an unsettled evening and hope the dawn will bring clarity."

It had not taken until the morning for Latimer to find clarity – although not upon the problem of his nephew's deceit. A brisk walk through bustling streets, baked dry by the heat of midsummer sun and now in dire want of a good washing, had focused his mind more keenly on the issue of seasonal fevers, and most pertinently upon the arrival of enteric fever in Exebere Street. The house was quiet when he arrived home, not even Vetch had bothered to meet him – it suited his purpose. He lay his coat and stick on the settle and made his way across the wide sitting room, his gait barely hampered by the injury that had caused him so much discomfort earlier in the year. His desk remained as he had left it. He moved some cost books to one side, pulled out a draw and found paper before seating himself. The inkwell was full and he fiddled with the quill before beginning.

His first wife, a pious woman with deep-rooted beliefs, had been dead for more than six years, and during that time, other than the occasional letter relating to his daughters' progress, he had never felt the need nor had the requirement to contact her family socially. He had no real liking for them – a sister and cousin-in-law centred near Tavistock, a mother now dead – but he knew them to be straight-living and honest, and a seed of an idea had formed as he had returned from his discussion with Edmund Elcott.

In his clear, uncomplicated mind he had set out the difficulties that surrounded his life. His nephew's possible arrest and incarceration, a sudden jolt to his finances and the need to draw in his belt, his continued lack of connection with Rae, but most troublingly the arrival of typhus in Exebere Street. With a steady hand he dipped the quill and began a letter to Mary Latimer's sister – his daughters, without a nurse would be better placed there during these unsettled and unsettling times; better in the care of their mother's family than here with debt and disease scratching at the door.

He wrote freely for a while, returning the quill to the well, reading what he had written and finishing the letter with the flourish of his signature. Satisfied, he dusted the distinctive loops and swirls of his handwriting, folded the paper and wrote instructions for delivery on the reverse as well as the name of the farmstead – some half-day's trek from the market town of Tavistock. It would be necessary to have Rachael accompany them. Since he had removed her from the whorehouse the distance between them had become ever greater, it might do her good to be away from him for a while. Although he supposed it to be some time in the future, once her child was born perhaps then they might restore the friendship and affection they had once had.

He stood, sealed the paper, collected his stick and coat from the settle and left the house walking briskly along Exebere Street in the direction of The Guildhall with the hope of entrusting the letter to a reliable clothier or even pack-leader. Having travelled the breadth of the county for many years, owning a plethora of acquaintances who made it their daily business to do likewise, Henri did not expect there would be any difficulty in finding a willing courier who might put his letter into the hands of his first wife's sister – and be persuaded to wait for a reply.

51

After enquiry, Henri had entrusted the letter to the keeping of a clothier's boy; the boy had been away from the city no more than two days and returned correspondence had been prompt – the reply, a slight curt, was nevertheless satisfactory. He held the letter in his hand now as he stood looking out through the open window. Rachael was away from the house and he had wandered distractedly to his rooms, rooms that were now occupied – at least during the sleeping hours – by his wife.

The problem of his nephew's dishonesty and insolvency had not gone away, but there seemed no likelihood now of confronting him upon either. Vetch had informed him yesterday that the boy had permanently left the house. Interrogation got Latimer no further forward – Vetch did not know where Master Geoffrey had gone or whether his absence would be permanent. Cynicism so often surrounding his relationship with his father's servant, Henri had not believed him. But if he should wish to confront the boy a short walk across the Exe Bridge would likely find him – for the present he would let the fish swim before thinking of pulling on the line.

The view from the window had always been a diversion and it was no less so now, although today it troubled him and on two counts: apart from the fishmonger salting a cask of river trout, the court was empty. He was aware of the reasons why – the thought reminding him that he had yet to tell Rachael about the sickness in the house. His other concern was of the sentimental kind: he missed what he had once enjoyed and enjoyed without complication.

He heard the street door close a flight below, the sound of Vetch's monotone voice as he mumbled a greeting, and then hurried steps on the stairs, light, lithe steps – Rachael's tread. He turned to greet her; she was a little breathless, her cheeks pink with the heat of the day and perhaps whatever it was that had prompted her to take the stairs in such haste.

"Henri, I had not expected to find you here."

"This view gazing is habitual and I was looking for you – indirectly."

He was aware that she had hardly heard him. She seemed agitated, flushed with something other than excitement. Standing before him she pulled at her hat, lifted it from her head, catching her cap along with it, removing the small circle of lace and discarding both on the bed. The tufts of her dark hair had grown slightly since her butchery, the ends beginning to turn under with the natural curl that came from her heritage.

"I have been walking, the heat do make me fretful cloistered up inside."

"Then I am glad of it, I would not have you cloistered for any reason sound or other." Henri stood with his back to the window, watching her. "Is there need for this haste, Rachael, do you have news to tell? I believe you would be better placed seated for a while than roving about this room."

"Roving do suit me just now, Henri, I cannot sit when my thoughts are troubled."

"And I cannot see you fall down." He reached out and caught her hand. "Take breath, Rachael, seat yourself until you are better able to explain to me why a simple airing has compounded your fretful mood."

"It is Jane, Henri – the house. I have chanced upon Hetty out and about on the Fore Street soliciting grounds."

He sat her in a chair and kept her there by pulling up another beside her. "Hetty?" It was a question.

"Hetty is working the grounds. Hetty is working in the house. There is fever there, Henri, and we did not know it. I should have known it, if I had not been so unthinking, thinking all the time about my own ailments when Jane is abed and most likely dying."

A surge of guilt ran through Henri, almost like a wince following an unexpected wound. "Is it so grave, Rachael, have you certain knowledge of this?"

"It is only Hetty's hearsaying, but it is enough to trouble me, Henri – it do seem the house is full of it for why else would Hetty be working if others were able to do it in her stead?"

Henri reached for her hand again, took it firmly, the need to offer some kind of solace was strong but he would not offer what was not welcome. "Do not take blame upon yourself, Rachael, it is likely the mother has kept things close – she would not wish the world to know that the house is so inflicted. You could not have known. You cannot accept blame for not having heard sooner."

"But I do, Henri, this fever runs freely about the house and I cannot sit here knowing what lies in wait for those beyond these walls and be neither helpmate nor friend to any."

She stood suddenly, relinquished his hand and went to the press in search of something, although she seemed unable to remember what. "I must go there, I must see Jane. She has been a friend to me since I was a child and I will not leave her in need."

Henri had risen also, his movement showing a new anxious energy that had not been there before. "You cannot go where there is fever, Rachael, a woman who carries a child must know how dangerous these things can be. Your own health will be doubly at risk. It is enteric fever, Rachael, contagion is real."

She turned, forgetting why she had gone to the press. "You know it. You know of it, Henri. Your knowledge is greater than my own. What know you of this fever, what have you heard?"

"Forgive me for not speaking of it sooner. But in truth I have heard little. The subject arose during a conversation with Edmund Elcott. If there had been opportunity to discuss such with you, Rachael, then I would have offered what I know." He paused, settling his weight, folding his arms. "But perhaps in hindsight, seeing your mood, I conclude that I was right in not telling you."

"Then you conclude wrongly, Henri. How can you think to keep this from me when you do know that I would be lost without Jane and all her sense and thinking – you cannot stop me attending, I will not be stopped from doing what I must."

He watched her again like he was looking afresh, his heart now removed to a place where it might not be injured. She had gone to the press again, sought and found a newly starched work apron.

"Rachael, you will not go to the house. I forbid it. I disallow it, and as my wife you will do my bidding. You will not bring trouble upon yourself nor will you bring disease to this house."

The soft kindly features of his face had gone taut, hardened towards her. He saw the look of fear in her eyes.

"It is my duty to go, Henri, an obligation owed."

"There is no duty wanting here, you have no allegiance to the whorehouse. You have led me to understand that you were never whore. You have neither obligation to offer help nor your husband's permission. I must forbid it."

The flush of agitation had gone from her face, replaced by the pallid complexion of troubled early pregnancy.

"I believe it would serve you better, Rachael, if you were to sit a while. I have much to discuss with you before this interview is ended."

She sat with the linen apron in her lap, subconsciously twisting her hands in the crisp folds. Henri condemned himself for his short temper, softened his approach but did not sit beside her, did not take her hand again.

"As you rightly say, I should have told you of all I have heard concerning our neighbouring house, but I have had thoughts beyond this, Rachael. I am head of this house, I accept responsibility for those who live within it, the typhus is a concern to us all, but further, circling around us there are certain financial issues that must be seen through. These issues may well have connotations to this family and for both these reasons I have decided that my family would be better placed away from this city."

The twisting had stopped – she looked up waiting for him to explain. The letter he had received lay discarded on a side table.

"I have this day received correspondence from family, a reply to my own letter requesting that my new wife and my daughters be received in their home this coming week. I have asked that they be made welcome there until such time as epidemic and business concerns allow me to collect them."

"I cannot do this, Henri. I cannot leave with the house full of fever, with no thought to the ending of it." Still defiant but now with a new concern she looked again at the crumpled linen in her lap. "Where are we to go, Henri, will there not be some chance to return in a short while so that I may at least have word of things, may seek Hetty once again?"

"There will be no returning yet awhile, Rachael. In truth, I cannot predict an outcome on either event and cannot give you an accurate offering of time. But you will do this, Rachael, because I ask it and I do not believe searching out a scullery maid who has less common sense than a wayward child will help any of us forward. The hamlet is a distance south of Tavistock, Mary and Sophia's aunt will welcome you – as I have arranged."

Sensing defeat, Rachael's protest was minimal, her concern of a deeper nature: she had witnessed a side to her husband's character that she had never seen before.

His stick had fallen to the floor and he picked it up and restored it to his side moving wordlessly towards the door. He turned. "The door will remain open, Rachael, I will not turn any key, but I expect to find you here when I return. I do not negate your desire to tend an old friend. I understand you believe this surface reasoning to be sound, but think more deeply and you will see that it is not. If you must have news of Jane then I shall seek it for you and this done I hope you will do what is asked of you – and willingly so."

52

Henri had been true to his word and in return she had packed their trunks without complaint. She could not say if it was solely Henri's concern for his daughters' – and her own wellbeing – that had led him to send her to a distant hamlet for a prolonged and open-ended time, or whether he had just lost heart. Her instinct was to restore the buoyancy of earlier times; she wished it but could not allow it. If she could have swept away the feeling of her own culpability in the seeding of this child, if she could have diminished guilt then she may have been able to disperse the mantle of self-loathing that hampered all intimacy with her husband.

Early mists had risen quickly, leaving the bright globe of the sun to heat the already dry and littered streets of the city. A short distance beyond the seventh hour of the day, the yard of the Mermaid Inn was a noisome mass of activity, a focal point for all manner of travelling business – pack ponies and carriers' wagons filling the wide central area, stamping, snorting beasts pulling against snaffle bits and bearing reins, and on the periphery a coach, newly drawn up, putting down a dozen passengers before yard boys set about changing the team.

Rachael accepted Sophia's small hand and held it in recognition of the child's understandable disquiet at the sight of so many powerful beasts gathered in such a confined place. Henri was a distance from them, she assumed negotiating their journey to Plymouth – he had said little to her during the three days that had come between his telling of his plans and their instigation. She took Mary's hand and drew her husband's daughters away from the central hubbub of the yard; the Plymouth coach was not yet come and she would have them settled in a quieter place whilst they waited its arrival from London. Through the moving beasts and general mayhem she could see Vetch tipping one of the yard boys to sit upon their chests – Vetch was to accompany them, she had not wished it but she had felt it prudent not to say so.

They entered the inn and found a seat away from the door; the place was almost as crowded as the yard. She waited, searching the smoke-filled room for Henri; he had noted them, briefly looked up, his face as sombre as his dress. Taller than the crowd, she watched him shouldering his way through the drinkers and travellers, dark brow held in a tight line of thought. He reached them without difficulty and spoke above the noise.

"Sound choice, Rachael, I would not have you remain in that furtive scrum when there is opportunity to avoid such." He found a stool and brought it beside them.

Keeping his distance for all of the next day following his refusal to let her enter the bawdy house, Henri had finally come to her and given account of what he had learnt about the sickness in the house next his own. She had no cause to disbelieve him – the typhus had affected five young women, Jane amongst them. Of these one was recovered already, Jane and three others were holding well to life and would most probably find health again, the fifth, apparently new to the trade, had died.

The heat of the day was already oppressive, seeping effortlessly into the airless rooms of the overfull inn. Although she had chosen to wear a thin dimity skirt and buckram bodice, a trickle of sweat had begun to form on the side of her brow. She wiped it away with her palm, taking stock of her husband – his face never an open book now closed to all scrutiny.

"How long are we to wait, Henri? Although I do not wish the time passed, the tightness of the room do make me wish to be gone from it."

"A little while, I believe – there can never be any great accuracy in the timing of these coaches, not when such a distance has been travelled already. There is a garden square beyond the yard if you would prefer to wait there."

"I would prefer it, if you will come along with us."

They stood, Henri forcing his way through the packed room, his stick a useful tool, and Rachael holding fast to the two small girls. "I will need to find Vetch," he said turning. "I would not have him wander off and leave your trunks to chance."

The garden square was an unkempt area of green, but seating had been built around a walnut tree, and apart from an elderly man being harangued by his plump wife, the garden was empty. Henri spoke to his daughters.

"Mary, Sophia, you must sit and dandle your legs awhile until such time as the coach may be boarded. Will you be happy to do this for your papa?"

"Why do you not come along with us, Papa – we would enjoy the coach all the more if you would come."

"Mary, I am afraid I am quite unable." Rachael watched him touch the child's cheek. "Besides, you have company enough and Thomas to keep a watch upon you."

Rachael had remained standing, nausea came and went – movement and unfettered air neutralised the feeling – a welcome respite from the monotony of continuous child sickness. Henri turned to her, this morning clean shaven; she imagined him seeing to himself while Vetch was away.

"Will you walk with me, Rachael? It seems we are at odds and I would not wish this to continue, in your company or without it."

She took his arm, felt the muscle tighten; it was the closest she had been to him for some time, since the first night of their marriage.

"Do not be concerned at the length of journey, even given that you must change coaches in Plymouth and then seek a cart boy to assist at Bickham Down – it is no more than a day's journeying to Venn Combe and shall be achieved within daylight hours."

"I am not concerned, Henri, and would not Thomas Vetch be better placed here with you? No sooner will he be come than he must turnabout and leave again."

"Allow him to assist you for my peace of mind, Rachael. I have asked that he sees you settled and reports to me upon both your safety and your comfort when he returns."

They walked to the end of the square and stood in the shade of a small oak sapling sprouting incongruously from a crevice in the crumbling wall.

"I confess that I am not well acquainted with my wife's family – Mary's family." He had corrected himself quickly. "But they are blood relations to Mary and Sophia, and I am sure will offer nothing but kindness. This situation need only be temporary, Rachael, and I will feel better settled if you are with them away from these seasonal fevers and the curse of my nephew's creditors."

"You will send me word, Henri, if things are worsened in the house?"

"I will send you word, I will write to you as often as I am able." He moved away from her to lean against the wall. "But I do not change my reasoning, administering physics and changing slop bowls in a whorehouse rife with enteric fever is not a pastime I would have my wife do whether or no she is with child."

She adjusted the brim of her hat to take some of the heat from her face.

"Perhaps now it is not the time for discussing the difficulties of marriage, but I hope that you will take what I say along with you upon your journey and think it through. There are too many things that have remained unsaid between us, Rachael, since we have lived as man and wife – and I would assure you know that this is not my wish. I cannot contemplate a life where we are ever distant. Although I do not ask it now, some honesty upon the parentage of your child might be a beginning."

She looked at her slippers letting the shade from her hat hide her face.

"If you do not ask it, Henri, then I cannot offer it. What good would it do for you to know things you ought not – the knowing would only be turned over and over and chewed upon, and then you would have the spitting out of it?" She raised her face, sorry for her impertinence. "I am grateful for your protection, Henri, but you must not feel bound to me. If you should have a mind change then you must own to it."

Henri pushed himself away from the wall. "Rachael, I will not have a mind change and I am bound to you. I have no wish to change this." He held her arms, the frustrations of three weeks beginning to erode the benign patience he had offered in earlier times. "You are bound to me and we will do what we must to make a life together. Go upon this journey, Rachael, and send me word of your progress – when you are able. I have been a little loose with my facts, suggesting that we were married early this spring. If you wish for your child to be born away from this city then so be it, I will take your lead on this, but come back to me as you once were." She felt his hands tighten about her arms. "I believe it is you who must chew things over and with this I am unable to help you, Rachael."

Vetch was coming towards them – grey string-like hair adhered to his head with sweat. Henri let her go and walked towards his servant. She watched him giving instruction. The thought of sharing Vetch's company throughout the day and for the days to come was not a prospect she looked forward to.

53

The coach from London arrived as it was expected, four broad-flanked paired horses ploughing up the dry earth with dancing hooves, the coach now dun coloured with mud and dust, bright lettering obscured. Within the half hour they had boarded, the fresh team turned, impatient heads nudging through the already opened coach doors. They had settled themselves inside opposite an elderly man with spectacles, his ruddy complexion heightened by a powdered horsehair wig – beside him the plump wife, but without her husband.

Rachael placed the small travelling trunk containing the things they might need for the day to come beside her feet. The smell of horse and leather was everywhere, mingling with the dust and mayhem of the Mermaid's yard. She had watched Henri speaking to Thomas Vetch, waited for her husband's servant to climb above. Henri had already said his farewells, kissing her forehead as he had his daughters' …as he had his daughter's. What was she in his eyes now – on a level with his daughters, not wife any longer, if he had ever seen her in that way? The coach lurched forward rearranging her hat – she removed it and watched the view from the open window as they had pushed on through the busy city towards Bridge Street and the Bon Hay tentergrounds.

Mary and Sophia were easy charges and before they had climbed the arduous gradients through the Haldon Forest, the girls were settled with picture books. As they had picked up pace on the downward run towards Trusham, Rachael watched the plump woman swaying with the movement of the carriage, several hours of travel stretched out before them – she supposed small conversation would be necessary.

"Madam." The woman spoke. "Will it be a long trip for you or will you vacate before the coach reaches Plymouth?"

"We do go all the way to Plymouth and then a distance beyond it." She saw the woman lift her head as though surprised by her uneducated soft local burr.

"And their father, I see you travel without the company of your husband – or perhaps he is your employer?"

A streak of perversity had almost goaded Rachael into answering with a lie, but she had not. "It is my husband who saw us upon the coach – whom we must leave behind. You have also left a husband behind, I believe?"

"In preference, young woman – quite in preference." The plump woman had pulled a bone pin from her hat and began to work it around the nape of her neck beneath her wig. "'Tis an uncommonly flea ridden coach, I fear, and we shall all be bit to pieces before we are released. What say you, sir, are we to have a peaceful time of it or no?"

Freed for a while from scrutiny, Rachael rested her chin in her hand and watched the passing landscape, the rising contours of the moor showing clearly now above farmland and thickets of dense woodland. How many times had Henri had this view from the back of a livery horse? How many times had he traversed the moor doing business with village weavers strung out across the core of the county? She could not say – in reality she did not know much of him beyond their stolen meetings and simplistic conversation.

Unwelcome, a wave of nausea hindered her thoughts and she brushed the folds of her skirts with the hand that bore her ring, any movement a distraction from the sickness that was rising again. The small leather-bound book was there in one of the wide pockets; she felt it reassuringly, took it out, but did not open it. Being banished to live with people she did not know was a consequence of all things that had transpired in the weeks before, not just the fever and Henri's concern over his nephew's dishonesty, but also their abortive relationship – a relationship that had never had chance to grow. Before this year she had had no expectations, she had not chased happiness – what was so very different now? She must take life as it was dealt her, succour her husband's daughters and make no complaint.

The plump woman was dozing and the bespectacled man had produced a broadsheet – she ventured to open her book. It was nothing more than pictures, some had been coloured by hand, but it pleased her nevertheless. A kindly meant gift given when life held few complications.

During the midmorning they had dropped down the hill into the narrow streets of Ashburton and changed horses for the second time at the Red Lion; the sun was still a bright sphere, but now, low cloud spilling off the moor had lessoned its potency. Victuals were offered at Ivybridge; she had taken none although the two small girls had seen off her portion of cold pork and coarse bread.

Tumbling free from the moor, fed by peat black streams and now shrunk with lack of rain, the Erme had stirred her subconscious – brought back memories that had lain so long undisturbed. She knew of this river but could find no familiarity in the small town that straddled its banks. As the sun turned to face them in the west, the broad skies and endless vistas they had watched all day began to run into monotony, the jerking motion of the coach becoming tiresome, and for a moment she had closed her eyes.

The last run from Plympton St Mary was mercifully short, the Plym now accompanying them to the edges of Plymouth where the narrow streets of this most easterly of the Three Towns seemed, at first sight, like the city she had left behind. They bustled with life and the detritus of life and yet this place was not the same, she could see no friendly face to it, no remembered building, no familiar landscape.

As they drew into the changing place, Sophia had gone excitedly to the open window. Sutton Pool was in clear view, but so unlike the quayside she knew with its barges and shallow draft ketches: here frigates and ocean-going barques with three and four masts filled the pool, or waited in the curve of the sound, shrouds unfurled, shrunk to toys in the distance.

"Madam." Vetch was behind her as she caught hold of the girls in the chaotic congestion of the yard. "I must pay a boy to get the trunks. There is a coach ready that will take us on towards Tavistock."

"Then do it, Thomas." She answered him flushed face. "You will need coin to pay him." She sought the small purse Henri had given her from the folds of her skirt pocket and gave Vetch what she deemed necessary. His resentment was poorly disguised – she understood this: why should a lesser servant, lately come from the whorehouse, be entrusted with his master's purse when he was not?

They stood waiting to board amongst the crowds, officers' blue serge mingling with the sailcloth uniform of the sea, working men in shirt sleeves and barefoot urchins busying themselves along the wharf – calling instructions, moving goods, heaving the great mooring hawser's over tethering posts. She raised her voice above the shouts and the general chaos of the port. "This place do seem a world away from our own, Thomas – do what you must do but do not leave us long."

He was soon gone into the crowds. She felt Sophia catch hold of her skirts, Mary her hand, it was a struggle to keep sight of Vetch and the Tavistock coach was not the only one pulled up here in this noisy bustling place. She

259

caught sight of the back of his coat, the boy with his cart just in front and the coach ready to leave, the coachman already standing above his team shouting obscenities at the boy as Vetch dragged their trunk onto the roof boards and strapped it in place.

Momentum began almost before they were seated. Two beasts only now, heavy footed, pulling hard up the hills towards the Mile House turnpike. Vetch had slammed the door shut, steadied himself and sat heavily on the dusty cloth. Cramped in a corner, she had taken Sophia upon her lap and then laid her head against the faded velvet lining waiting for the city to become countryside again, surreptitiously watching Vetch, in better spirits now that he was seated inside. Conversation between her and Thomas would be ever stilted, she understood this and she did not mind it. He would be gone soon, gone to return to Henri to report whatever lies or truths he chose to tell.

54

Waking early in the bed that he had not slept in since the first night of his marriage, Henri pulled himself to a sitting position and looked unseeing beyond his window towards the disorderly grouping of backhouse buildings and outshoots that made up his view. The house seemed lifeless, without energy, and if this were so then it was entirely his doing. The removal, the sending away of his wife and daughters, had been abrupt, barely pre-planned. Had his determination been fuelled exclusively by his concern for their security and wellbeing, or was there more flesh to his motives than he cared to admit? Enteric fever during these dry times was indeed rife within the city, it did not discriminate between rich and poor; it was unpredictable in the extreme and could carry a body off within days. And then there was his nephew's debt and the dishonest web of deceit that had been spun to fill his pockets.

Yesterday he had broken his fast alone; solitude held no pleasure now and he had removed himself to the Goldsmith's coffee house before the midmorning, but even an hour spent in agreeable company had not dispelled his low mood. Today he determined to move life forwards; if solitude could no longer be tolerated then he would see to business and leave the house to itself. He had visited the bawdy house soon after he had seen the coach off; keeping on the margin of things, he had enquired of Jane's health. She was holding to life – that was all, it was enough. He would write to Venn Combe later and reassure Rachael that all was well – at least for the moment.

Dawn had already found its way into his rooms and he rose, washed in the cold water left yesterday, found linen in the press, but did not shave. The stick was lying against the wall by the door; he grasped it, tucked it under his arm and sought his coat. His intention was to ride to Topsham; the *Rosamunde* had been re-rigged and now settled comfortably on the tide – he had only to pay for the repairs and the ketch could be moved.

A persistent knocking on the street door made him lift his head – visitors were rare, and this early in the day unheard of. The caller was determined and he doubted the hammering was made by fist alone. He allowed his cook to open the door and perhaps see off whoever was there. He waited impatiently at the head of the stairs for their dialogue to be completed, the white cap of his formidable cook just in his view, conversation inaudible. Logic and reasoning failing to quench his curiosity, he swung his stick to the fore and began to descend. As he reached the flagstone floor of the hall he heard the door close. His cook turned, presenting him with the flushed-faced innocence of a woman whose behaviour has been less than appropriate.

"Who in God's name was calling at this hour? Some lost soul in dalliance between hostelry and gin shop?"

"Indeed, sir, something along that way – the man were mistook, lost in a mist of misremembering and quite upon the wrong street."

"Then I am not required to attend upon any urgent matter."

"You are not, sir." The large woman, the flush of her cheeks even more pronounced now, subconsciously clutched her apron and began to wipe her hands. "Were you expecting to attend upon an urgent matter, Mr Latimer?"

Henri drew his brows together, considering his cook, not wholly satisfied with her explanation. "I was not." The day was already warm and leaving his doubt aside, asking no further questions he dropped his coat onto the settle. "I will have whatever you have ready. I intend to travel to Topsham – and if any other lost gentleman calls enquiring of me or no, you may tell him of my whereabouts and have him return towards evening."

The fleshy woman dropped a knee and took herself back to the kitchens where she could not be interrogated further – the shilling she had earned in directing the surly easy-tongued visitor to a hostelry in Alphington secured in the deep recess of her skirt pocket.

As he walked westwards through the city sometime before the middle of the day, Geoffrey was not in good humour. He put his hands in his breeches pockets and felt apathetically for their contents – felt the two half sovereigns he had been forced to accept in return for a finely cut coat and a rather pleasing snuff box. The lower streets abutting Exe Island were becoming ever more disagreeable, ever more foetid, ever more littered – home to low-life loiterers, tricksters and unchallenged urchins. He kicked savagely at a pile of loose masonry and sent a stone spinning off into the central gutter. Since it had come to his hearing that enteric fever was running through the southern quarter like a spark up a powdered fuse – this including the whorehouse – he had refused to accept Mag on her usual terms. If she returned to the bawdy house then she need not return to him. She had been acquiescent and now barring unforeseen eventualities, he expected her to be waiting for him when he returned to his lodgings.

The taproom held a dusting of souls, the landlord was resident behind his counter, spitting into the bottom of a pot and wiping out the scum with a cloth. Geoffrey had been forced to pay a portion of his back rent; for a while he need not dodge the insidious man's attentions. He did not meet the landlord's eye but continued on up the backstairs in the direction of his rooms. The door was locked, he rattled the knob, shook it.

"Mag, would you lock me out when I am in more need of sanctuary than a hare on open heath?" He waited for an answer. What was the harlot doing? He had been gone no more than the hour. He kicked the bottom of the door and fiddled with the knob again. "Margaret. Do not play fool-about, madam. You abuse my trust, next time I go out I shall turn that key and keep possession of it myself." He heard movement from within, waited impatiently whilst a key was placed in the mortise and turned. The door opened a slight, Mag's sorry face peering hesitantly between the gap. Temper rising he kicked violently at the uneven panels of the door sending it hard back on its hinges. Startled, Mag took a step back. She was partially dressed as he had left her, but she had draped her mantle loosely about her shoulders, a nervous hand grasping at the clasp.

"'Tis not any of my doing, Geoffrey, and I would not have wished it so. Things would have been better met if you had turned the key and locked me safely in."

He could see into the room but did not immediately enter. A squat, stocky man with all the characteristics of a villain and nothing to commend him sat perched on a hard-backed chair.

"You have a biddable strumpet, Master Latimer." The man searched Geoffrey's face with small pig-like eyes. "It has been quite a pleasure waiting here for your return, and the waiting made that much more interesting by being spun upon a coincidence."

Unsure who she was most afraid of Mag stepped backwards until she had the solid contours of a wide armchair between her and the two men.

"What business do you have, lolling in my rooms, and in my absence? I have offered no prior invitation."

"Business, Latimer? Business is exactly what I do have to discuss with thee." The man showed blackened teeth and rested back in the hard chair, adjusting the fronts of his coat so that the smooth pommel of a cudgel was revealed. "Come you in and take your ease. Bring a chair, Margaret."

Geoffrey stood in defiance, legs apart, arms folded. This man would want money, but the door remained open behind him, he might run if he wished it – Mag could make her own escape. He waited feet planted uncertainly on the boards, eyeing the man, considering him – he had met such men before.

"I'll take no ease with you, sir. I would have you state your business and then hastily remove your person and your malevolence from my rooms."

With the sly movement of an adder breaking cover, the uninvited visitor threw out an arm and caught hold of Mag's wrist, forcing her to sit reluctantly in his lap, the steel grip of his stocky arm keeping her there.

"Shut the door, Latimer, and offer up an ear while I tell you my story and then perhaps we may do business together."

"I have no wish to offer an ear to any monotonous tutorage, sir. I have neither the time nor the inclination."

The man stiffened, Geoffrey noted the thick fair hairs on the back of his broad coarse hands, the black nails – noticed his grip tightening about Mag's waist.

"You owe me money, Latimer. I have come to collect such."

"Just how do I owe you money, unless my mind plays tricks we have never met?"

"The money is owed to me through another party." Mag tried to release herself, the vice-like grip tightening.

"Saints, Geoffrey, do not tinker with this man while he has a hold of me."

The passivity that Mag normally displayed had changed to annoyance, not only with the man who held her tight but also with the young man who would not action her release.

"I am minded, from time to time, to purchase an unpaid debt – when all else has failed. 'Tis a worthy pastime that do bring me a steady income, I have the asking instead of others. And be sure, I am never refused."

"Then I refuse you, sir. It is an injurious lie, what proof do you have? You cannot insinuate yourself into my rooms, play rough and familiar with my whore and demand money without proof. How does this debt relate to me, I think you are quite mistook, sir?"

"The money is owed to a lending house far east of here, or should I say was – it is now owed to me and a twenty per cent annual yield on a hundred and sixty pound lending." He jerked at Mag's waist so that her face was against the stubble of his unshaven chin. "You sit pretty there, my frightened little harlot, and hold close to memory." Mag screwed up her eyes, refusing to be baited.

"I have indeed dealt with a bank in the next county, and it is true I am a little late with interest payments, I was due to travel that way later in the month. I had no concern that the lender would be anything but accommodating."

"And so he may, but as you see I am not."

Geoffrey ran his fingers between his stock and his neck but did not change his delivery.

"I keep no money here. Do you think me fool enough to keep any quantity of coin above this drinking house of sly-minded waterman's apprentices and itinerant footpads?"

"Whether I think thee a fool or no needs no answering. I shall have the money I am seeking and I shall have it before I leave – wherever it may be hid. Now what say we have a look about these snug rooms and give closure to the question?"

"I think not, sir."

"Then I must beg to disagree. 'Tis in my experience that a little searching do often haul up treasure." He stood, allowing Mag to escape his embrace, and with slow deliberate movements went towards the only chest in the room, lifted the lid, threw out a quantity of linen and rummaged with his heavy hands for any sign of a purse or cash box.

"You will find nothing. I have told you I keep no money here. Let us arrange for tomorrow after I have visited my bank, state what it is you are owed and I will see you are reimbursed."

"Let an eel escape the net when I have so nearly landed him?"

The money collector stood looking about him considering the room, its limited contents and singular door. Heavy shouldered, he began to cross the floor towards the wooden bed. He grabbed at a corner of the counterpane, dragging it to the floor. Finding nothing he picked up a pillow in turn, ripped at the innards, scattering the room with feathers.

This man had got the scent, his nose was obviously adept. Disregarding the morality of how he came by the money, Geoffrey felt an intense sense of persecution – this brute would not steal from him. He hesitated for a moment, then plunged forwards taking hold of the collector's coat, discontinuing the search. A muscular arm lashed out instantly, throwing Geoffrey back, sending him stumbling, colliding with the abandoned chair, striking his brow at force.

"Do not worry my temper, Latimer, if you wish me to spill blood then I will oblige thee o' that – but be damned, I will have what I came for."

Geoffrey got himself half up, still on his knees went for the man again – he caught his legs about the calf and pulled him to the ground, ham-handedly grappling with him on the floor. Temper rising in both men they rolled over, neither had the better of the other – the heavier grasping the younger about the throat, choking him, hampering breath, the younger reciprocating, releasing the fingers.

"For sense sake, Geoffrey, do not rile this man. Do not make challenge, he will leave you bleeding and take your money all in one." Frailty dissipated, refusing to stand by and watch while her lover was choked to death by a vicious bully whose knowledge of right and wrong was so blurred that only luck and good timing had kept him from the gallows, Mag dropped the mantle and leapt forward, tugging at the man's hair, finding the flesh of his head with her fingernails.

"Leave me be, you duplicitous little whore." He struck out at Mag with a fist, allowing Geoffrey the chance to right himself. "I will have what I have come for, Latimer, and I am not afeared to spill blood, be it yours or any others."

Disadvantaged and still prone, he fumbled in a pocket for his knife and drew it out. Mag watched wide-eyed, the remembrance of unparalleled fear making her pull back.

"Saints, Geoffrey, he has a knife – you must get up and run hard away from here. He will have no fear of cutting you whether it be for a sovereign or a penny cabbage."

Crawling backwards upon his elbows, rising quickly Geoffrey found youth was on his side. He could see the blade clearly now in the powerful hand – without thought he kicked out hard sending the knife spinning to the floor. Mag watched it spill free from the money collector's hand, spinning on the boards, spinning towards her feet.

Frozen for a moment she looked down on the knife considering options – revenge sat above the rest, but revenge would come with consequences. The collector was starting to get to his feet and before he could she snatched it up, closed her fingers about the handle, moved quickly to the open window and threw it out into the street below.

"If you think you can protect this weak-livered coxcomb by throwing that inconsequential cutting blade out of the window then you are mistook, I will have his purse just the same."

She watched his slow bovine movements. He was taking his time to rise. Crouched down and holding to the bed, the heavy leather pouch, secured to the bed boards with twine, was just visible. He got to his knees mechanically, snatched at the pouch breaking the twine and stood awkwardly feeling the weight of the purse in his hand.

"Today's business is done, Latimer," he spat. "I am not in the habit of leaving without finding what I have come for, this will see you free for a while longer. But expect my company again."

A small trickle of blood was running down Geoffrey's temple as he dropped, resigned, to the edge of the destroyed bed. He felt in his pocket again for the two half sovereigns. Mag was standing beside him, her naturally pale face now almost colourless. She took a corner of her shift and wiped the blood away from his temple and he felt her body through the thin Holland cloth, her small breasts touching his shoulder. She had been more than familiar with the brute – he would have her understand that he would not be usurped.

55

As July found its second week so the heat of midsummer was swept away by seasonal storms, grey flat clouds now hung over the western moor and it had rained heavily in the night leaving the summer grass sodden underfoot. Rachael picked up her skirts, lifting them high above the short sheep-grazed scrub; the small church with its stunted steeple and lime rendered stone was in view, the steep and arduous climb from the darkly wooded valley of Venn Combe behind her. It was the Sabbath of the first week of her stay, her husband's daughters were above her being helped on by Pamela, a slightly more approachable and kindly version of her cousin. She watched them for a while and then continued on to the top of the hill, the greyness of the day making her movements feel heavy, the climb leaving her breathless.

They had been met by a cart boy at Bickham Down and had walked the last three miles, all of it on uneven stony tracks running zigzag across the plummeting valley, descending until the oak canopy ran above their heads and all views of the world were lost. The sensation of being buried had done nothing to ease Rachael's anxiety at meeting with Mary Latimer's kin. Phyllis, born some years before her dead sister and now in her midlife, was stern mouthed and frugal with her words. Widowed for fifteen years, bitterness had fed her through those empty years until she had been joined by her husband's cousin, Pamela. Rachael had automatically dropped a knee and introduced them to Mary and Sophia, the girls now exhausted by their trip and made silent by the widow's black clothes and unsmiling face.

The decaying farmhouse that had greeted them sat lengthways against the steeply rising ground. Stark granite walls and a single chimney, dark slate and pagan finials rose up from the encroaching woodland – each tiny window as dark as night, the only sunlight dappled and without warmth. Pamela had bid them enter. A bright fire was burning in the inglenook, but even this and an open door to the summer's day could not warm the room.

Rachael stopped, looked back into the combe and listened to a lone buzzard calling from somewhere above the valley. She had yet to feel the quickening of her child. There were no outward signs of her pregnancy and the cousins had hardly acknowledged her condition. There was no particular path here, just a well-worn track; others were gathering now, Vetch and the gaunt woman who kept house for the cousins already within the churchyard. She placed her hands in the small of her back, relieving the dull ache that quite often settled there. Phyllis was waiting for her just outside the wall, lace bonnet tied tightly over a grizzled wig.

"The bells are rung already, we must hurry, Rachael."

"Forgive my slowness, Mrs Medland, this valley is altogether the steepest I have ever seen. I am sure I will become used to the climb in time."

"You will, as we all do, it is a necessity of life, and God's house can be reached no other way. I would have wished to have word with our preacher before the service, but now we are late I will have to defer until after prayer."

Rachael walked beside the elder Medland cousin, despondently listening to the assertive droning voice.

"Neither Mary nor Sophia have a prayer book of their own. I am not a wealthy woman, Rachael, and am not eager to purchase these – I am hopeful that our curate may offer a solution."

"I do not think their father deemed it necessary, we could bring only a pair of books each owing to the size and weight of the trunk."

"Then His good book should have been included amongst these. It is remiss of my brother-in-law not to have considered this."

They walked on, Rachael did not make reply – she had learnt her letters from Elijah Floods' ancient Bible. The teachings were ever familiar to her, but the books on Trelawney's shelves had always offered more interest and she saw no reason why her husband's daughters should give up their picture books to make way for any bible.

"You may take my arm if it will hurry you."

Reluctantly she put her hand through Phyllis Medland's crooked arm; she was taller than Rachael, heavy footed and intolerant of other's weaknesses. They walked incompatibly on, watching the girls up ahead.

"Although I would not normally speak of it without invitation, I am a little uncertain of your timings, Rachael, and as you are to live amongst us I believe it necessary to know when you are due. Surely your pregnancy must be quite soon begun. Thomas Vetch tells my housekeeper that your marriage is in its infancy, although I assumed by your husband's tone that it was other."

Rachael looked ahead of her, the heat of a flush climbing up her neck to her face. Henri had laid things out for her levelly and without complication and now Thomas Vetch had intervened. She doubted anything other than intent.

"Quite soon begun, Mrs Medland." Rachael was grateful that Phyllis Medland could not see her face. A lie was always hard to order.

"I have never had the curse of it myself. Five years married and fifteen years widowed and thankful I have no other mouths to feed."

They had reached the churchyard. Freed from the boredom and exertion of the climb, Mary and Sophia were dancing about the coarse grass picking valerian heads grown in the crevices of the church wall.

"Pamela, keep those girls from their toes and have them throw down that herbage."

Rachael relinquished the older woman's arm, in her heart unhappy with the harshness of tone, but acquiescing outwardly, avoiding offence.

"My dears, you have not the time to pick at wild flowers before the service – lay them down here and find them again when we return. I will help you add to them and perhaps Pamela will have a crock we may put them in." She looked up for support – Rachael had already learned that Pamela would do nothing without the approval of her cousin. Unmarried herself and without income, she was wholly dependent on her cousin-in-law's charity.

Rae lifted her head to the dull day, were they assessing her, she knew they would be assessing her – her youth perhaps, her inexperience, her unsuitability. She put a hand to her head and began self-consciously to tuck the ends of her shorn hair into her cap, adjusting the brim of her straw hat above it.

"Come, the bells are stopped. We must hurry and be seated before the sermon is begun."

She gathered the girls, leading them forwards between the ancient headstones to the open door. In just one week they had made this climb three times already, she expected to make it many times again before Henri felt it in his heart to come and collect them.

The tiny church with its sgraffito walls and ancient fortified oak door was never full: just a dozen souls, no more, proudly sat in family pews or huddled close to the back to avoid the wroth of the curate's drink-fuelled sermons. Thomas had stayed a full week, he had been given no particular instruction by his master and unusually he had found good company in Phyllis Medland's complaining housekeeper. They were sat on the far edge of the Medland family pew together. Rachael doubted Vetch had much liking for Sunday worship nor any other, but it was expected of him and he had climbed the steep path ahead of her and seated himself unobtrusively beside the Medlands' servant.

The tedious admonitions of the ageing curate were eventually over, releasing the congregation into the grey day. She stood in the graveyard looking down into the combe. The stones were unkempt, weather-worn, Phyllis was standing amongst them talking to the curate. Pamela had already taken the girls' hands, drawn them through the lychgate to wait in starched silence for her cousin to join them. There were restrictions enough here, Henri's daughters' would not be held in check constantly, on this bleak hillside of scrub there was no need.

"Miss Medland, I have a thought to walk a little before we return." She put out a hand to take charge of the small girls she had tasked herself to protect. "We will be just a step behind you and ready seated at table well before grace."

"As you wish it, Rachael." Overruled, she raised her chin and let them go. "I had thought you tired this morning and wanting rest."

"A little extra walking will not tire me more, Miss Medland."

"Will you wait for Phyllis? She will wish to know what path you take."

"I will not, she do seem to have a parcel of things to say to the curate, I shall not wait for her to finish her talking."

"Then go you must, but do not keep them out too long, Cousin Mary was always watchful of her colouring and she would wish the same for her daughters."

Taking charge, Rachael walked away from the church, evading disapproving eyes by dropping down the hillside out of sight. This was unconsecrated ground: abandoned, lonesome headstones protruded from the scrub, unblessed, unforgiven souls buried here without rite of passage. She knelt before one of the stones, watched Henri's daughters for a while, feeling the wind on her face, enjoying the freedom of the wild untamed landscape. The mossy lettering on the coarsely carved headstone was indistinct, the indentations weathered to nothing. She traced the simple wording with her finger – a name perhaps, an explanation? If death came she would not chose this place to be interred. What rest could be found here on this windswept hillside?

The congregation had moved away, even Phyllis Medland, and now the curate was returning to the sanctuary of his church. She supposed there would be other questions to answer now that Thomas had given her away. There was little she could do to undo Vetch's malevolence and must live along with its consequences, but she would write to Henri, enquire of Jane and tell him that she did not wish her child to be born at Venn Combe.

The eastern slopes were already in deep shade when they reached the bottom of the combe, the intermittent sun just touching the roof of the grey stone house. She could smell mutton fat and field herbs; she had no appetite and released the girls and stepped onto the uneven flags of the through passage. The kitchen door was pushed open and she could just see the back of her servant's dusty coat, his thin grey queue, and hear the muted voice of the Medlands' housekeeper. The conversation had stopped as she came level with the door. She did not care what was being said of her, but Vetch was her husband's servant and he would do her bidding.

"Thomas, if you please, I would speak with you."

"Madam?" She waited whilst he slowly stood – his stock was hanging loose and his waistcoat was unbuttoned.

"Did my husband give you any guidance upon the length of your visit here?"

"Guidance, madam, only to see Miss Sophia and Miss Mary settled."

"Then I believe that they are, Thomas. I wish to write to Mr Latimer and I require you to take my letter along with you when you return to Exebere Street. I hope you are quite ready to go for I would not want any delay in him receiving it."

"'Tis the Sabbath, madam."

"Tomorrow will be soon enough, Thomas. I shall ask for pen and paper and begin it after we have eaten." She could see the Medlands' housekeeper working at a floured table behind Vetch, face expressionless but listening to their conversation.

"As you wish Mrs Latimer."

She picked up her skirts and turned, crossing the passage to the Latimer cousins' sitting rooms. She did not know what Vetch had said but she would find out soon enough just how prickly his loose-tongued gossip had made her bed.

56

A day out of Rotterdam saw the eastern foot of the Kentish countryside break the horizon; the *Rosamunde* was handling well, meeting the dark waters of the channel with the enthusiasm of a newly released colt. The wind had been with them, a north-easterly had come up with the dawn, filled the sheets and sat behind them all the way, having Latimer's new and unfamiliar crew dance to its tune. The boy had been sick but the master and mate were skilled men with two decades of experience between them – the *Rosamunde* was in good hands.

He positioned himself close to the mizzen and rested against the gunwale, feet apart, finding his balance. As owner he was an unnecessary addition to the working decks, but taking passage to the Low Countries was a distraction he chose – and as it turned out a lucrative one.

"I believe the Romney sands will be showing themselves in an hour or so, Mr Latimer – the day is clear enough for it." The elder of the two men he had employed was aloft, trimming a slack sail. Latimer squinted in the bright noonday sun and shouted back.

"I will watch for them, John, the old lady will have us well on our way before nightfall."

Three days ago they had run out serges – some his own and some from Blackaller Tucking Mill. A dispute on the quayside between the master of a Plymouth ship and a dealer had allowed Henri to pick up a return cargo, bringing back several tons of gambis and bark for the tanning industry as well as a quantity of dressed pelts.

Making easy headway, scudding unhampered a mile or so distant from the underbelly of the southern coast gave him time to think. He changed his position, rested on the wooden rail and watched the green-grey outline of the distant starboard horizon. They expected to see the jutting head of Portland sometime before the midday tomorrow and make landfall before the end of the day. He stood, caught hold of a shroud and teetered along the moving deck towards the only cabin, dropping down and feeling his way towards the tiny galley and single cabin, squeezed between the bulkheads.

"Have you found your sea legs, Silas?"

"Yes, sir, thank 'ee, sir. I believe I have, sir."

"It is hardly the smoothest passage to begin a career on the sea – we are running at some pace."

The boy dropped his head to show his agreement; he had emptied his stomach within the last half hour and did not find discussing the state of his insides in the least beneficial. Confined to a cramped corner of the galley was a fixed cauldron set above a wood fire, the boy was pocking around the ashes with a singed stick.

"Will you need victualling, sir?"

"In no great hurry, Silas, what sits in your pot this day – the same as last?"

"Same as last, Mr Latimer, a brace o' rabbits and the last of the roots."

"Then the broth perhaps."

He watched the boy fan the damp wood to prevent it going out and then ladle thin liquid into a clome mug.

"Thank you, Silas. Has Able taken you aloft yet and had you follow his lead?"

"Later this day, sir, I believe."

"When you have quite done with emptying your breakfast over the side perhaps?"

"Yes sir." The boy had swallowed and set his mind to the tasks given him.

Henri bent his head, ducked beneath the low oak bracing and felt his way aft to a tiny cabin and raised bunk, a wry smile moving the corners of his lips. He sat with the broth and reached for his cost books. He had not yet had word from Rachael – he had expected a letter. On his return Thomas Vetch had been as tight lipped as ever, although in truth Henri had found little time to converse with the man since his stay at Venn Combe. As far as he was aware enteric fever still held tight to the house next to his, but the whore known as Jane was holding to life and although he was saddened by the absence of his family he had not altered his resolution.

Solitude, as it had in the past, focused his mind and he had already made a resolution. He would let the shares go – this last vestige of ownership in his grandfather's mill ought not to be held onto unconditionally. Time moved on and he would not cause unnecessary upset to the Mudge family, it was altogether simpler to let the shares go. He pondered this thought for a while. Fighting for so long for survival he had never considered accrued wealth – any monies made had always lain in his bank's vault's to pay for the next clutch of acquisitions, whether opportunist cargo or loom woven serge – he had never considered the money his own. It was time to change his mindset.

He did not open his cost books but lay back on the bunk listening to the familiar creaking of *the Rosamunde*'s ageing timbers. The mount he had ridden out from Exeter was a sober beast with powerful flanks and a biddable nature, he had ridden the mare before – it was time he had his own stable and he would see to a purchase on his return to the livery.

They had seen the nose of Portland before the middle of the following day and slipped into the mouth of the Exe with the sun still catching the west bank spit. Henri had left the three men, now in his pay, to see the goods off-loaded whilst he had finalised business. Now that the *Rosamunde* was seaworthy again she needed to be kept busy, and there would be deals to be done back in the city, and if not his own serges, there would be others – other commodities to ship along the coastal waters of the channel.

With the weather breaking but still warm, the house felt cloistered, shut up and unused, it was dark now and he did not bother to disturb Vetch from his bed. He went to the window, drew up the sash and sat looking out across the courtyard. He had a mental list in his head of the things he must do in the morning; the first was to enquire more fully of Thomas Vetch's visit to Venn Combe.

57

It had been a week since Rachael had written her letter, and a week since she had handed it to Vetch and watched him walk away up the steep track. Yesterday she had accompanied Phyllis Medland to a cottage deeper in the combe; Henri's daughters had kept close to her side, their usual curiosity now quelled, their need to do right, to avoid rebuke making them quieter than they ought. The day had been heavy with cloud, windless and stagnant. Phyllis, presiding over breakfast with her usual disagreeableness, had complained that her nieces' clothes did not fit the needs of their new life. Questions had risen in Rachael's head and she had asked, "New life, Mrs Medland?" Harsh-mouthed Phyllis had replied that she would not sit another Sunday in the family's church pew beside children dressed ready to visit some low-house theatre.

Rachael had questioned this again, seeing no requirement for change and most especially when their stay would be short. Phyllis had looked sourly down her long nose but had not changed her plans. They had sat in the small over-furnished room for some two hours whilst Phyllis bemoaned the girls' lack of self-restraint and tendency to fidget, selecting dark serges to be made into skirts and jackets. Alarm bells were ringing clearly in her head. This was not what Henri had intended, this was not what she wanted for herself or her husband's daughters.

Another Sabbath was approaching; the child sickness found her as soon as she lifted her head from the pillow, and she had stayed in her room. Knowing breakfast would be finished she took the dark stairs to the lower rooms – the quietness of the house worried her. Each morning since she had come here she had gone into the sitting room and sat with the cousins, attempting to settle to book or sewing, watching Mary and Sophia at their studies, listening to Phyllis Medland's spinning wheel turning monotonously in the quiet room; keeping to herself and waiting for prying questions which rarely came but were nevertheless expected.

"Do not lie upon the rug, Sophia, and in such a disorderly fashion. The chair has been with us for many centuries." Phyllis Medland spoke to the child without taking her eye from her spinning wheel; the necessary dexterity needed to both turn the wheel and feed the fibrous twisting yarn towards the spool did not allow her opportunity to look up. Sophia had learnt not to reply and instead slowly removed herself from a position she had adopted for most of her short life, picked up her chalk and slate, and sat herself at the table with her sister.

"Girls were never encouraged to throw themselves upon the floor when I was young and I see no reason to encourage this now."

Rachael attempted a smile, she had not the energy to challenge the older woman's philosophy – quite soon Henri's daughters would return to Exeter and pick up the life they had grown used to, and this time here would become just a dilution in the memory of their early lives.

The cluttered room was hot. Rachael put down her sewing and went to stand behind Sophia, overseeing her writing, observing the child as she formed bold repetitive lettering on her slate. Mary had been given a small bible by the cousins and was charged with not only reading the unfamiliar words but also of making some sense of them. There was silence in the room as there often was and Rachael returned to her sewing, her eyes lifting now and then to look at the world through the open window. She could not settle and had been disturbed throughout the lonely night by a nagging pain in her back. She laid her sewing carefully on a small table and went to the window; she looked out at the dense green of the oak wood in the distance, the drying shale of the yard and the carter's boy throwing scraps into the pig pen.

"The day has come on warm again, Mrs Medland. I'm minded to walk down to the river for a while."

Pamela raised her eyes from her own sewing.

"Will you, Rachael? The air there seems so low, corrupted by all manner of ills and menaces. The tide will be out and I am not sure what benefit may be found."

Rachael considered the spinster's small lace cap and tight unworldly features without emotion.

"I think that I shall, it is a broad river to look out on and the movement of the tide do always seem so full of promise, of change and new beginnings."

"This constant need for the outside is a contrary practice, Rachael. You have endured a city life before this, have you not? You will have had little offering of open spaces and unadulterated air in such a congested place."

"The Exe runs up to the City walls, Mrs Medland – as your Tavy runs to meet the Tamar – it is as free flowing as any river, and brings a certain life to the city. And our buildings are quite tall, we may look out upon the world – I have become accustomed to the way of things."

The dull ache had not gone away and she arched her back, watching Henri's daughters' – analyzing her emotions in regard to her husband, but finding no solace.

"Then be careful, my dear, the low-built cottages and hovels are near always beset by illness and disorders of the humours – our curate swears it is the nearness of so much mud and the stilled damp air."

"Many places are beset by such things, Miss Medland. Lack of food and harsh living do more likely bring about these disorders than making a life beside the river." She touched Sophia's head and the child looked up reassured.

"Do not forget, Rachael, we are charged with your care and wellbeing. It is to us you have been sent to keep you free from contagion and sickly city dwellers. You would be wise to stay clear of the hovels and cottagers."

"Then I shall walk until the river is in view, but not to its shore."

Phyllis Medland's broad industrious hand continued to turn the handle of her spinning wheel, her sharp ears taking in all that was said.

Waiting until her cousin had finished speaking Pamela continued. "Is it the house of your guardian that has taken the typhus, or another?"

"Another, Miss Medland, quite another. Mr Trelawney has been absent for some weeks and the house is empty save his servant. I am sure all is well and fine in the city now, we will hear soon enough when Henri writes us and then we may all return."

"Soon enough, I doubt such. These things are set to linger, become rife, endemic in no time. I am not sure that I would wish my sister's daughters to return to a city beset with typhus. My brother-in-law should have sent these girls to us before – I have always thought it nonsensical to have a man raise his daughters alone when he has the blood sister of his poor dead wife living and able to take on the task. I have suggested it in the past, but entertain it he would not."

How misguided they were to ever think that Henri would entrust his daughters to them for more than a few weeks; she was surprised that he had considered it at all.

"If I am to walk I shall do it now whilst Mary and Sophia are at their studies."

She turned quickly, the quality of her skirts reminding her of who she was. She slowed her pace and went to the stand for her hat. Her hair had grown a little and she had tied it tightly beneath her cap, pulling it back from her face as severely as the two matrons she was escaping from.

Ignoring the advice of the cousins, she had walked slowly down to the lowest part of the combe, passing the huddle of cottages and continuing on through the oak wood to where the Tavy met the broad Tamar. This river was altogether busier, full of small inland luggers, sail boats and broad barges running up and down the central stream all engaged in the industry that ran along the banks of this waterway – an artery running up to the valley's industrial heart. There was a small quay here and an old pontoon stretching out across the mud, the end just jutting into the tidal race. Without the cousins knowing, she had often been here before; it was a place she liked – a small crack in the wall, a view to a wider world.

She felt the sun on her face at last, watched the windblown reeds following the snaking course of the river as it wound its way south to the sound. The boards were warm and she sat down, rested her head on her knees. The child was there, she could just feel the presence of something that she imagined was a growing child. Reluctantly, she considered what was to come, how Henri would greet her when she presented him with another's child? The thought had no ending and she put it aside to watch the craft making their way towards the quay at Wellham.

At first the ache in her back had not been severe, but the same pain had begun to find its way to her sides, to where the child settled. She had no mother, had no experience of pregnancy or the birthing of children, but she could not have lived in such close proximity to the bawdy house without gaining some knowledge of herself – of understanding a little of what was happening to her. As she stood the intensity of the pain changed, gnawing into her sides, running about her back. She caught hold of the post, leant forward, warding off a spell of dizziness. She would have to return, beyond that she would not think.

The carter's boy was in the yard, a thin shoeless child of no more than twelve. He watched her as she went in; she tried to smile, but it seemed the blood had drained from her lips and the buzzing in her ears made her view of the world surreal, intangible. She caught the doorjamb, ran a hand along the wainscot of the through passage. The Medland cousins were still occupied with their work, but Mary looked up through the open door.

"Mrs Medland, Rachael is returned." Mary had stood, begun to come towards her.

The sound of the spinning wheel had stopped, but the buzzing in her ears remained, the pain now coming in waves, tightening about her middle like a girth strap.

"Could you help me, I have come on sick and need my bed." She groped with cold unfeeling fingers towards any hand, any arm that was offered, finding her feet enough to get to the top of the stairs, finding the door to her room.

There were voices around her, through the pain she was being undressed and then she was looking at the ceiling, waiting for the end, for whatever was to happen to her.

Sometime later reluctant hands had removed the bloodied sheet, what there was of her twelve-week child held in the arms of the Medlands' housekeeper. The early light of a new day had begun to find its way through the lattice again, the night had seemed endless, but now it was over. Tiredness held her in its grip, all sickness had gone, but with it energy and the ability to raise herself from her pillow. There were people in the room, a doctor she assumed, a filthy apron stretched across his girth – and beside her arm was a bowl, a bloodletting bowl, in it her own blood. The doctor had finished with her, took away the bowl and begun to place a bandage over the small knife wound he had made in her vein.

"I do not believe there will be any complication now, Mrs Latimer. A loss in the third month is always a risk to life, but you are through this now. Given your age and my administrations I anticipate a full recovery in good time."

Both Phyllis and Pamela were there talking to the doctor, Pamela ashen and agitated, Phyllis's stern mouth a hard slit.

And then at last the room was empty, sleep took her for a while sending her down into places where deep thoughts turned the mundane workings of the day on their head: the doctor and the boy whispering loudly but inaudibly, Phyllis Medland hovering over her like a grotesque black crow and Henri so far in the distance that no matter how she reached out she could not touch him.

Light remained, but the sun had already set over the deep combe when she woke again. Phyllis was standing close to the window, her back to her, hands grasped in the folds of her black gown. Rachael attempted to raise herself and speak, but something in the widow's demeanour made her shrink back into the pillow and remain silent.

Sensing movement Phyllis turned, there was a letter in her hand. Her face was unreadable, without compassion.

"You have a letter from your husband, Mrs Latimer." She held out the paper but did not bring it to the bed. Rachael got herself up onto her elbows.

"Thank you, Mrs Medland." The widow came forward and placed the letter on the chest beside the bed.

"Our doctor insists upon a fortnight's confinement and we must abide by his instruction. My housekeeper will attend to you."

Rachael heard herself speaking words of compliance, heard the movements of the stiff kersey skirts as Phyllis Medland left the room and closed the door. The letter was barely in reach and she groped for it, caught hold of its edge and dropped it onto the blanket. Henri's seal, the Latimer seal, her name. She pushed her slim fingers under the wax and opened the paper.

My dearest Rachael,

I hope your journey was less arduous than you anticipated and that my daughters enjoyed the novelty of the day. My pen touches this paper just the day after your leaving so I have little extra news to offer you. I have made it my business to visit our neighbouring house and must report that Jane is well enough at present and will likely recover.

 Once she has her cargo loaded it is my intention to see the Lady Rosamunde away from her birth and test the wind, this, my dear wife, will also take me away from Exebere Street for a while, but I will write again upon my return.

 I send my dearest love to you all.

Henri

She dropped the letter back onto the counterpane – so this letter, written some time ago, was not in response to her own; or perhaps this would be his response, just a spasmodic reporting, a smoothing over of the furrows that now existed in their relationship. Jane was holding to life – and she had survived the loss of the child and the doctor's meddling, but she could not stay here. She would write again, Henri must collect them and soon.

58

Henri searched the papers on his desk, uncharacteristically agitated; his impatient fingers rearranging thumbed leather-bound account books, discarded quills and aged paperweights. Vetch had apologised, although not in his opinion with adequate sincerity. It would have been so much easier to have offered the letter up directly into his hand instead of laying it down amongst the paraphernalia of his desk – now it was mislaid.

He caught his own mood, sat and made a more methodical search of the desk. Earlier this morning he had seen two young women – unfamiliar to him – perched on the bootmaker's leather crates in the court below his window. The bawdy house perhaps had shaken off the typhus, it was a good sign he felt, but he had been wrong: a simple questioning from his window had informed him of events that he did not wish to ever have to meet. Two more girls had died, and one of them was the whore known as Jane.

He found the letter at last; his name, Rachael's well-formed hand and unfamiliar seal. He took his knife and released the seal, sat back rubbing his chin, ice-blue eyes below furrowed brow searching the writing.

My dearest Henri,

We are here at Venn and well, although we are missing you much. Both Mrs Phyllis and Miss Pamela treat us with some pleasantness and we are comfortable in our rooms. The combe is quite deep, Henri, and not a little like our own situation, which makes us miss our home all the more.

I would be glad to have all your news and most especially news of our neighbours' house, if you can find it. Please take very much care of yourself and remember us.

Although I think it proper for us all to linger here until the heat is quite gone, I would ask you have us return to you, what is to come to me cannot be prevented but I would wish to return before my time, if you will allow it.

Mary and Sophia send much love and good wishes. I write in haste, Thomas is to leave with the dawn tomorrow and I have bid him take my writing along with him.

Your wife, and friend, Rachael

He had dropped the letter back onto his desk amongst the disassembled books and papers. Had he been a slight more farsighted he may have foreseen the consequences of his actions, but he had not. He must now write to his wife, and not only must he make a decision upon when he wished his family to return but also he must tell her that the very worst had happened to one of the few people who had been constant in her life – he must tell her that Jane was dead. The situation he now found himself in was of his own making; he had neither sought to help Jane nor had he allowed Rachael to offer succour – the consequences would be open-ended.

The paper and quill goaded him, but he had not the heart to write knowing what he must say. He left the room, gathered up his coat and hat, leaving his stick leaning against the wall, and went out into the humid day, his unrest showing in his dark pensive brow and his pale unseeing eyes.

Thin cloud hovered above the city, creating an even greater stink than was normal. There were a couple of girls loitering outside the whorehouse and a steady drip of gentlemen visitors – nothing unusual in this except for the past two or so weeks these normal activities had been curtailed. The fever may have passed, but it had taken with it three young women; he should have been gratified that his own wife was not amongst them, but gratification was not an emotion he felt as he walked south towards the river.

Pushing his way through the carts and pack ponies along West Gate Street, he analysed why he had come, why he had chosen to confront his nephew today – knowing the answer he pressed on towards the oldest part of the town and the Exe Bridge. The lower rooms of The Seven Stars were unexpectedly lively, he found his way to the counter and spoke with the landlord, placed a coin on the wood, but did not take a drink. The door he had been shown was at the top of a narrow staircase that led to no other – a private place he saw, a place to keep a whore undisturbed. He lay a fist on the door waited and the door was opened by the pale underfed harlot they called Mag.

"Mr Latimer?" His presence was met with surprise, his name a question.

He took off his hat, ran a hand through his dark hair. "My nephew, I have come hoping to find my nephew?"

"He is not here, sir, at least not just now, but I'll tell him you did call and have him come find you if you wish it." Mag dropped her eyes, Geoffrey did not offer honesty freely, but she had learned from the conversations they had during those passive times that followed fulfilment that he would likely find his uncle's company uncomfortable. Perhaps he owed him money and if he did she knew he could not repay it.

"I would prefer it if I could wait." Latimer walked past her into the room, looked briefly about him – he could not in all honesty understand why his nephew had chosen this life over the one he had been offered. Perchance he had not – had this life chosen him, a consequence of his lust for money and his disinclination to work?

The pale harlot whom he had shared a dinner table with and often seen going in and out of the whorehouse seated herself. He studied her, a little older than his wife, but with the experience of a woman twice her age. He noticed she was red faced, a little tearful. Fool that he was, she would know all that had happened in the mother's house even though she had taken her living away and thrown her lot in with his nephew.

"Unpredictable," he began tentatively. "The typhus is unpredictable, I had thought them safe."

"Yes, sir, I had thought that, I believed God had finished with them – would leave them be. And Jane she were so very full of life and never an ailment all of the time I lived alongside her."

"Death is a fickle master and knows no etiquette, does not always take the sickly first."

The young woman had begun to cry and freely so. It was a situation he was not used to and he felt clumsy and ineffectual. He viewed her woodenly and walked to the window to look out.

"When do you expect Master Geoffrey?"

"Oh, sir, I never expect him, I have learnt not to – he do come and go as he chooses, but of late he do seem to spend most of his time here."

Latimer stood silently, twisting his hat in his hands trying to find some solace to offer this young woman. The awkwardness of the situation was to pass more quickly than he anticipated; he could hear footsteps on the treads of the uneven stairs, he turned as Geoffrey came into the room. Not quite the coxcomb he had been: his coat was unbuttoned, there were mud splatters on his breeches and the line of his young chin was covered with the coarse hair of a week's growth.

"Uncle." There was a moment of hesitation, a crack in the brash confidence of a boy still to reach his twentieth birthday. "South of the river I see, and finding my little nest with ease."

"With ease, Nephew, but not by chance."

Geoffrey sat himself down heavily in a frayed horsehair chair and flung a leg over its arm. "Do you seek me alone or is it our biddable harlot who brings you here?"

"It is not, Nephew, it is you alone."

Latimer stood his ground, upright, arms folded before him, sharp eyes diminished to slits – holding his temper.

"Then I suspicion a matter of business has brought you here, Uncle?"

"A matter of business, no, what I have to discuss with you relates to decency, family loyalty – to honesty."

"Indeed, what a heavy burden you carry." Geoffrey withdrew his leg from the arm of the chair and stood a slight shorter than his uncle; the arrogance that youth and breeding promotes no less apparent than Henri remembered. "Have I not been loyal? Have I not lived quietly alongside you all these months on nothing more than the meagre allowance you offered me and the occasional patronage of my mother? Have I not done your bidding?"

"I see that I must be succinct, Nephew, and disagree with your observations. There is nothing meagre about the monies you have disingenuously contrived to pilfer from the family purse."

"What monies do you refer to, Uncle? The working capital I borrowed is now repaid – as you requested."

"You may treat me as a feeble dullard, Geoffrey, but I have a nose for the underhand. I have saved your duplicitous neck from the moneylender's henchmen once already. This new level of duplicity has gone beyond any unpaid tailor's bill or the misappropriating of fleece money – simply put, if the facts of what you have done runs before any court I think it likely you would find yourself bound foot and hand and loaded into the gallows cart." Geoffrey toyed with his stock, avoiding his uncle's penetrating eyes. "Be not in doubt, Nephew, I hold the trump card both of knowledge and of proof, and if I should so wish it could place that noose about your dishonest throat." Latimer waved a hand to prevent his nephew answering. "Do not worry my temper further, Geoffrey, by feigning ignorance. The forgery of documentation is a felony and would be tried in a jury court. If it had not been for the certainty that Mudge would be implicated along with you I would not have sat in silence and let you run on the line for so long. God's life, Geoffrey, did you not think you would be unearthed?"

"Unearthed, sir? How would I be unearthed? If you refer to my recent enterprise, a simple borrowing, a securing of a loan against the Blackaller holding, then perhaps I might agree that the dealing would run on the edge of things, but it amounted to nothing more than the necessary securing of a loan."

"I think not, Nephew, and I do not think you believe it either."

Latimer felt the pain in his leg return, remembered he was without his stick and changed his stance.

"I could linger here, Nephew, and continue to condemn you for the fool that you most certainly are, but I have not come for this and will not waste my breath. I have considered outcome, reasoning and solution, and I will tell you what my intentions are." He watched his nephew, sullen lipped, tapping his fingers against the skirts of his coat. Latimer doubted his indifference.

"Although it is within my power to see you gaoled, Nephew, I will not have your demise upon my conscience."

Mag was slowly making her way towards the door. Geoffrey put out a hand to stop her. "I have not said you could leave, Margaret."

"Let her go, Geoffrey, she is not party to this and need not hear more." Instructed, he let her go.

"This last holding in Blackaller was always symbolic, a sign that the Latimer family still held some status in this city and although I have fought for ten years to keep it, I feel no sentiment towards it now. I intend to let my holding go, Geoffrey. Unless I choose to make the truth known, your misdemeanour will not come to light. The fraudulent copy of my share certificate that you had forged by duping Mudge into lending you the deed is now in the hands of another, and to save your neck I intend to leave it where it rests. This, I would suspicion you already had wind of. Should you fall foul of the law in future times, Nephew, be sure I will not hand you from the mire of your own creation."

Latimer had left his nephew to ponder his future. A necessary interview and a distraction from the inevitable letter writing that he must do, but it was hardly close-ended – he doubted it would ever be in his nephew's capacity to run a straight path. When he got outside, spots of humid rain had begun to fall. He looked at the sky and replaced his hat; he intended to make an attempt at some kind of cohesion, and explaining his decision to Josiah Mudge would be a beginning.

Stepping out for Blackaller he felt the discomfort in his leg again. He crossed the lower leat and cut through the Bon Hay tentergrounds, limping and cursing the summer rain. Mudge was at his desk and Henri sat himself down before the Quaker, waiting for him to finish reading a heavy paper his clerk had laid out before him.

"Latimer, I had not anticipated a meeting today – have you something urgent to report to me?"

"I do – a decision and an interview, but nothing dire, it will wait until you have finished."

He sat back, now that he had made the decision to give up claim to his shares he was surprised at how little he cared about retaining a connection with Blackaller, the mill that his grandfather had owned and run before he was born. Mudge looked up and Latimer continued.

"I have recently left my nephew, I have told him that his criminality will not now lead him to the assizes, but as he had no thought that it would, I cannot say that he seems particularly grateful."

"Ah. Then I thank you for it. I had never doubted that you would not take this path, but I thank you all the same for saving William from a court case and a shameful admission. Would you take a beverage with me, Henri, it will be china tea if this suits."

"It suits well enough, Josiah."

Mudge nodded to his clerk who left the room to find a servant.

"This need not alter our relationship or our business arrangements, Latimer – you must run your serges through this mill as you always have done and without charge. It is none of your doing that these shares have been lost."

"Have you met with our Somerset farmer?"

"I have indeed."

"And the outcome?"

"He is satisfied that he has bought a lawful certificate and now owns a holding. Thankfully, I do not now need to correct him."

"Then we can lay it to rest."

A tray arrived, Mudge unlocked the small tea chest and they waited while the business of tea making was completed.

"I cannot help but feel a little responsibility for this situation, for the loss of your family's asset. But I sense no bitterness in you, Henri, no regret. Surely it must be galling to lose the holding when you have clung to it for so long."

"Logic says I should feel so, but I do not – surprisingly I feel neither bitterness nor regret. My life as you know has changed – I have a new wife, I conclude that some areas of my life needed to change and not just my domestic arrangements."

"Your wife, how is the young woman?"

"From this city, but well I believe. We have typhus in Exebere street – I thought it prudent to send her to relations." He paused considered what next to say. "She is with child."

"Then I congratulate you, sir, a child is always a blessing."

Latimer sat awkwardly on the edge of his high-backed chair sipping the beverage he had been offered; he had told no one thus far of Rachael's condition, he was not altogether sure that he had done the right thing in telling Mudge.

He returned his cup and saucer to a side table. He had always kept his relationship with the Quaker impersonal, business-like – although there was an undoubted friendship. To fend off further questioning he had hastily changed the subject.

"I sense the buzz of the city is altering, Josiah, perhaps you feel it also? There are still plenty of serges being sold across the county and beyond, but our markets are not what they once were."

"It is true that the woollen industry is in decline here, has been so for sometime, but I see no reasoning why it should not continue on prosperous for decades to come – at this decreased level. We have relied on its wealth for several hundred years, I cannot see dramatic change in the immediacy. Do you see a different future for us, Latimer?"

"I believe our trade will be affected by northern markets. Perhaps it would be wise to offer up flexibility when considering future investment."

"You are not alone in your observations, Henri, and decline here will mean prosperity elsewhere. Where others have made considerable wealth through broader trade, I have always been content to settle with the business of producing good cloth and needed nothing more. It is an honest profession and on this I know we both agree, if the cloth industry were to flounder what would take its place?"

"Trade, trade of other sorts perhaps, and at the base of things we are farmers, are we not?"

"And so we are, this red soil is ever fruitful although the commodity most suited to our terrain is of course sheep. We are not a seaport – our silted river connects us only indirectly to the oceans of the world. This fact will always hamper trade." Henri nodded his agreement.

"I hear that your brotherhood has been vocal in condemning the African trade."

"Indeed it has, there has long since been mooted discussion amongst our Quaker brethren upon the morality of trading human life. Speaking out is the very beginning in stopping this dark trade – but I fear we have many opponents. I do not expect a solution in my lifetime, if ever."

Latimer watched the rain falling on the river through the counting house window.

"To return to the issue upon which I came," he said almost absently, "I will accept your offer to run my cloth through your mill without charge, at least temporarily, and I thank you for the gesture." Latimer stood and took the Quaker's hand. "I do not believe I can intervene in my nephew's life further. I have told him that I will not pull him from the path of self-destruction again."

"Then let us hope that now you have cleared that path he does not find an alternative route to the courthouse."

59

Rachael's confinement had drawn on with monotony and with a sense of loneliness that she had never felt before, but ten days after the loss of her child the portly doctor had bled her for the last time thus allowing nature to take its course. Recovery had been swift. During this time of segregation and inactivity, Mary and Sophia had been forbidden her company and she had seen little of the cousins, Pamela visiting on occasion and then walking the room like a thief, toying nervously with her cuffs, refusing to sit, and Phyllis timing her visits to follow the doctor's when Rachael had little energy for conversation.

Being confined to her bed, the casement closed, had felt like imprisonment and she considered the outside world now, there would be a fresher feel to the days. When finally she had been allowed to drop her feet to the floor the Medlands' housekeeper, critical eyed and sullen, had helped her dress, assisting her into the still-unfamiliar hoops and undergarments that had been bought for her just prior to her marriage. She had stood before the glass noting her sallow cheeks, dark-ringed eyes and bloodless lips – she lay her hands on her empty belly. Although she had never wanted the child, had felt revulsion at its seeding, its beginning tied irreparably to the remembrance of her forced seduction, she now, inexplicably, felt its loss.

Joining the cousins in their sitting room after breakfast she had read to her husband's daughters until they had been shooed into the yard to play amongst the chickens in the sporadic August sunshine. She watched them now through the lattice; there had been subtle changes in the two small girls' behaviour since they had come to live in this deep combe. Although it had been less than a month since they had left their home, they had already begun to lose some of their easy self-confidence.

Phyllis Medland sat across the room at her spinning wheel, strong forthright hand turning the handle. Pamela was there in her usual chair beside her cousin, the book she had begun to read laying in her lap turned open on its pages.

"Do not stay long amongst us if you wish to return to your room, Rachael, the whole commotion of being midst young children must tire you. Do say if you wish to return."

"Thank you, Miss Medland, but I believe I do not, 'tis quite the longest time I have ever spent so without purpose. I much prefer company and occupation to idleness."

Rachael could see that Pamela was troubled by some close-guarded thought, a thought perhaps that might not be spoken of readily to her stern-faced cousin.

"It must be a great sadness to you that your child will not be going forward." Pamela dropped her eyes to her book. "And also for your husband, who must be told surely and soon?"

Rachael bit her lower lip and looked at her hands. She had not considered what Henri would say or what he would think, and she considered it now. He had married her to save her from the gutters, and now that there was no child perhaps he would feel his obligation discharged? She rose from her hard chair beside the window and moved about the room, restless, restless with this company, with this place.

"Phyllis dear perhaps you should write your brother-in-law – it will save the burden of explanation falling upon Rachael."

The wheel was temporarily halted and Phyllis Medland threw a look of impatience towards her cousin. "Save the burden, then the burden would be mine, would it not?"

"No, please do not, Mrs Medland. I must write myself, the letter must be mine. I will find heart in good time." She could not allow this line of thought to continue, she would not have Phyllis Medland write to Henri upon something so personal, something that the barren woman could have no understanding of.

"My cousin has fits of idealism which lead her to false conclusions. Men, in my experience, rarely have interest in these things – my brother-in-law has two healthy daughters, why would he care overmuch about another unborn?"

Forgetting her book, Pamela had stood, allowing it to fall to the floor. "Perhaps you are right cousin – perchance we should leave the telling to

Rachael. I anticipate that your husband will wish to have you sent back to your city life, Rachael, now there is less danger for you, less need for you to stay away?"

Rachael leant back on the wide sill of the window. She knew Phyllis Medland was watching her, assessing her with her emotionless eyes.

"On this I believe your husband will make his own decisions, Mrs Latimer. I will leave you to inform him of your changed condition, but I feel it appropriate that I should write him on other issues."

"Other issues, Mrs Medland?"

"Upon the issue of his daughters – Mary's children. This masculine upbringing offers them no favours, they are quite wild and without refinement – I would prefer them to spend more time with their blood kin and I have no wish to see them returned to some illiterate nurse maid who has no head for correction or for manners. My brother-in-law may wish his young wife to join him in his city life, but I see no urgency for Sophia and Mary to do likewise."

"Then you misjudge my husband, Mrs Medland. Henri has been constant in their lives since their mother died and would want them to return to Exeter as soon as they may – when the fever is gone, and that will quite likely be soon."

Phyllis drew in her small mouth in disagreement, the corners set in a downward curve. Pamela, uncomfortable between these two women more assured than she, excused herself, closing the door quietly behind her. When she had gone Phyllis spoke.

"My cousin does not enjoy contrary opinion, but now that we are alone there are things I wish to say to you, Mrs Latimer."

Rachael had sensed a greater disapproval since the doctor had given his opinions, she watched the other woman with black uncertain eyes.

"To say to me, Mrs Medland – upon the guidance of Mary and Sophia?" Rachael lifted her chin ready to hear what Mary Latimer's sister had to say.

The repetitive motion of the wheel, the twisting of yarn around the spool continued without interruption. "I do not hide my opinion, Rachael, so I shall speak plainly. God may generously bless a marriage union with a child, but children begat from fornication, through sinful intercourse, shall remain unblessed."

"I know well enough society's thinking, Mrs Medland, and have seen many a girl damned for it, but I cannot say as I follow the flow of your thinking."

"I believe that you do, Rachael. Your servant has a loose tongue and my housekeeper an eager ear – from them I know that you were newly wedded when you came here, it takes no more than simple reasoning and our good doctor's insistence to understand that your child was too well advanced to have been conceived within marriage."

Defiant Rachael lightened her voice; she would not allow Phyllis Medland to know how desolate her observations had made her feel.

"Thomas Vetch is an un-reading man, Mrs Medland, he do not always count straight."

Lifting her chin she took Pamela's chair, carefully arranging her skirts as she sat. The discarded book was at her feet and she picked it up. "As you say, Thomas do like a gossipy ear and your old housekeeper did certainly offer him one. And a quart and more of ale to loosen his tongue further." She flicked over the page, feigning indifference. "I am sensing that you may have more to say to me, Mrs Medland. I would rather have it said when I may have the listening direct than when I have turned away."

"More – indeed I do, although I am sure you will find a credible explanation for anything I have to say."

"It do depend upon what you have to tell."

"When your husband charged me with your care I had assumed he had taken a second wife from amongst the many good women of good family that make their living in this county. The Latimer family has been prominent in Devonshire for decades passed. Indeed my father was always in agreement with the union between my sister and Mr Latimer, and encouraged our family's connection." She paused. "But he did not look amongst the good families of this county, did he, Rachael?"

A blush had begun to run across Rachael's hot cheeks. "What is it that you have heard, Mrs Medland?"

The wheel stopped, Phyllis lifted her eyes, heavy with disapproval, her mouth in a slit. "What have I heard? What I have heard confirms my doubts, offers explanation for so many discrepancies. He did not seek a wife from amongst gentry, did he, Rachael, because you have no parent, and not only were you born without God's blessing, but you have been raised by a dissolute God hater, a man with a penchant for male company, and more than this you have posed unclothed for this man."

Rachael dropped her eyes to her book, she would not allow Phyllis Medland to see that her mettle was dented. "Do not take the bones of the story and turn them into something other Mrs Medland, if you are to condemn me for living under Alexander Trelawney's roof and offering a pose then you must condemn all those who have him paint their likeness – Lady, judge and rich men aplenty."

"But I do condemn it, Rachael, I condemn all that you are – I condemn your history, your occupation, your ability to hoodwink my brother-in-law into this dubious marriage. What example does your life history set for my nieces? When I write to Henri I will challenge his thinking. You may return to your husband, but my nieces will not."

Rachael looked at the print of the open book, her mouth pulled in tightly with annoyance. "Forgive me for sharp speaking, Mrs Medland, but I feel that sharp speaking must be offered for it will never be you who decides when Mary and Sophia may return to their father."

Phyllis pulled herself upright, adjusted the long grey ringlet that she fixed beneath her cap. "Youth encourages impertinence, you may catch your husband's gaze in your seducer's eyes and have him do your bidding, but I am not so moved. I challenge your supposition that Henri Latimer will want his daughters returned. You forget, although my sister lived as wife for little more than three years, I was well aware of the time she was left alone. You will not always keep your looks and then he will be about his business the same as any man, leaving you alone to feed your low thinking and immorality into my nieces' young heads."

"Henri will not allow his daughters to remain here without end and I have already written him to ask that we may return. Their future, Mrs Medland, is not for you to naysay."

"And have you yet a reply to your letter? I know that you have not, Rachael. I doubt he will bother himself overmuch. At the beginning of our conversation you encouraged me to say what I must, but I fear I have not yet come to the end of it. I accept that knowledge gained from hearsay is not always accurate and I had supposed a certain exaggeration, expecting my brother-in-law to have better sense, but I conclude that I may have been overgenerous."

"What is it that you have still to say, Mrs Medland?"

"This house that holds the typhus, the reason that your husband bid us keep you, is I hear more ungodly than the one you were raised in, and not only do the young women there shun all decency but accept you as their own, as whore, Mrs Latimer." Rachael ran a cool hand across her burning cheek. "A marriage band does not erase this. Can you think me willing to send my sister's daughters' back to a house so poorly situate and with a harlot as stepmother?"

"Whatever I plead, Mrs Medland, it will likely not change your opinion, but you will not keep Henri's daughters from him."

Rachael stood, looking down on Phyllis Medland's white starched cap. She had often felt the ghost of Mary Latimer in the city house, but here her presence was tangible.

"On the contrary, I have already spoken with our curate who supports my determination and will continue a dialogue with the reverend on his next visit – I will not have these girls sent back to a house encouraged into sin by influences so close to its door. Mary and Sophia will remain here, Mrs Latimer, but I see no reason to keep you under my roof longer. I believe you are quite recovered and in a week or so we will arrange for your trunk to be taken to the turnpike."

Phyllis Medland had begun to turn her spinning wheel again, dismissively watching the twisting yarn. Rachael closed the book, stood and placed it carefully upon the chair.

"Then I see there is to be no agreement between, Mrs Medland."

For the first time since the loss of her child she had felt the need to cry, not because of the acid tongue of Phyllis Medland nor even the emotion that follows the loss of a child, but for the frustration of her situation and the thought that she had done Henri a disservice by marrying him and creating complications that would run and run. She must think beyond this moment – away from this cold determined woman. Leaving the door open she went out into the late summer day to search for the sky amongst the cloying nearness of the dense oak wood.

60

His uncle was not at home, he knew this was fact having already extricated the information from Mag who had begun, although infrequently, to visit the whorehouse again. Vetch had let him in. As unreadable and as tight-lipped as usual, he had not queried Geoffrey's return to the Latimer house nor explained his master's absence. Uncle Henri was wandering the wastes of the county, Geoffrey supposed, or perhaps idling his time on that old tub he often accompanied across to the Low Countries – he did not care, he would collect what he had come for and be gone."

The house was like the grave; he felt a stab of annoyance at the futility of this grand house remaining in his uncle's ownership, a man who had not the will nor the inclination to use it as it ought to be used. If the day ever came when the house was his he would dispense with these threadbare furnishings and aged furniture and replace them with something more befitting a gentleman.

He took the spiralling staircase two treads at a time and entered his old room; it had been cleaned and the remains of his possessions carefully put back as he had left them, as if ready for his imminent return. There would be things here he could sell, although that had not been the real purpose of his visit. His chest was locked and he took the key from his purse and opened it. The bottles he had dishonestly liberated from Blox were there still and he retrieved them and put them in his pocket, threw a moiré coat he had felt no longer fashionable onto the bed and began to add other items of clothing and useful nicknacks to the pile. He bundled it up and walked along the dark passage, stopping outside his uncle's room. Level with the door he touched the handle, rested his hand there for a moment, recounted the times he had entered this room and the reasons why, spontaneously turned the handle and went in.

The cloth market had been doing business for some three hours when Elcott left his rooms to push his way along Fore Street in the direction of the river. A couple of days ago he had been visited by the constable; as a trusted notary well respected and known in the world of magistrats and keepers of the peace he had been called upon to assist in a minor investigation involving a landowner resident in St Sidwell. The man had accused his wife of attempting to poison him and sited a herbalist from Exe Island as accomplice. Elcott was needed to help the constable make a head and a tail of things – many of the bottles and jars in the herbalist hut were labelled in the Latin language. Small, nimble and upright he walked quickly with a light tread, threading his way through the market crowds, cutting down Bridge Street and finding the point of rendezvous without difficulty.

An open door invited him in and he ducked beneath the ragged curtain to find the bovine constable studying a labelled jar with a look of despondency and confusion written across his florid face.

"Sir, I am pleased to have your assistance – 'tis one thing mastering the reading of the English language, without being expected to master another with no thought to schooling. I'd offer that the language of the bible be quite unreadable to the common man."

"It is perhaps the intention, sir." Elcott greeted the constable and took the jar. "Aconitum – Wolfsbane." He picked up another. "What is it your felon is accused of?"

"'Tis a woman, sir, wife and mother – accused of poisoning, or at the least attempting to poison, her husband. The old herbalist were arrested three days since, although I, like the magistrate, has doubts upon the honesty of the story that has seen both she and he detained."

"Indeed, why so?" Elcott began to poke around the hovel, examining jars and bottles, crumbling dead and dying plants between his fingers.

"Why so? No particular reasoning excepting the woman herself, she is a God-fearing woman – why should such a one wish to do away with her husband when she has been wed to him for a decade and faithfully so?" He paused, lifted his tricorn and scratched at a scab on the top of his head. "If 'twas the reverse way I might have understanding, 'tis known the accuser has grown tired of his wife and gets his pleasure from a harlot in Magdalen Street."

"And the herbalist, how is he named, is there proof that he has assisted in the crime?"

"Hearsay, sir, hearsay and nothing more – the old man has a poorly reputation and is loathed by those who do not have need of his assistance, and those who come here for his medicines will never own to it."

"So there is no proven connection."

"No, sir, but the landowner has deep pockets and none will gainsay him."

"I fear my limited knowledge of the Latin language will be little help here, these bottles likely contain mixtures of substances – I could not predict the effects upon the body if they were administered."

They continued to handle jars and uncork bottles. "There are poisons here, without a doubt – digitalis, in simplicity foxglove, belladonna – but I understand these will only cause harm when administered in larger doses, as droplets in a tincture they will likely remain remedial."

"Plenty here that will hang the man."

"Indeed so, but this does not prove his complicity."

The floor was carpeted with spent herbage and the leavings of strained infusions; several jars had fallen from the table in the scuffle that had preceded the herbalist's arrest. Elcott crouched down, moved the dead plants aside and picked up a couple of jars.

"There is something other here, some gewgaws, I believe." He stood and held out his palm showing a ring and a grouping of glass beads. "An improbable find, I would not have expected gold and jewellery of this quality to be present in such a lowly place." He offered the earbob to the constable and held the ring between thumb and finger.

The constable examined it doubtfully. "Perhaps, but they say the old man were bread from gentry, it may be likely he had such things in his possession. But I cannot see as why he would discard such on a filthy dirt floor along with spent herbage."

Elcott examined the ring. "It is initialled, M E M – does this have any meaning?"

"No, sir, the man's name were Blox, none seem to know him by any other. I can see no connection."

He passed the ring to the constable. "I believe I am done here, there is plenty of evidence ag'in the man if that is what you seek, but then the hut seems an honest enough workplace and the herbalist proficient at his trade." Elcott stood and returned his hat to his head. "If you have reservation upon the honesty of the herbalist's accuser then perhaps, as these items were found amongst his possessions, you should assume them property, offer them up – he may be in need of representation."

The constable folded his hand over the coloured glass and gold band and dropped the items into his pocket. "'Tis a thought, sir, 'tis a thought, Mr

Elcott. I thank you for your time and knowledge. It may be necessary to call your name at the trial."

"Unfortunate, for I fear my findings will more likely put a noose about the old man's neck rather than save it." Elcott ducked back under the curtain and stood in the open doorway. "Perhaps we are both wrong-minded – perchance the lady had done with her philandering husband and sought his demise?"

"Then we must leave the law to make of it what they will."

61

The stones of the steep zigzagging track were warm underfoot. Her stride matching his, she followed the boy up the rising incline, each measured step bringing them higher above the combe, leaving the oak wood and the winding rivers behind them. Her trunk was tied onto the slow-moving cart and she watched the flicking ears of the mule as it trod the familiar path out of the valley towards the turnpike road. As the track had begun to climb more steeply the boy had snapped a hazel twig from a bough, occasionally and quite half-heartedly he laid it on the rump of the lethargic beast disturbing a dozen buzzing flies.

A week ago it had been made clear to her that she must leave, and a week ago she had made a determined choice about what she must do. Mary and Sophia had not wished her to go but she had hushed their tears by sitting with them and writing the letter she intended to send to their father on their behalf, reading it to them, folding it, keeping it clasped in her palm whilst she had said her final goodbye. Although she wished her marriage to continue she would not bring shame upon her husband at every turn – she would not fuel Phyllis Medland's claim on his daughters. He must have them returned and she would stand aside and allow this to happen without complication.

The turnpike road running north–south alongside the moor was flanked by scrub, barely any trees surviving the harsh winds that blew freely across the landscape both winter and summer. Rachael shielded her eyes and viewed the diminishing Plymouth coach, now shrunk to a vague blur in the distance. The boy had untied her trunk and was waiting beside it, idly tossing small stones into the ravine. She put a hand on the back of the mule feeling its warmth, holding the matted strands of its mane in her fingers.

"Are you sure the Tavistock coach will follow the Plymouth?"

"It has been so for as long as I've known 'en – always following, one passing the other a distance beyond Bickham Down. 'Twas so when my father stood here aside this road carrying up trunks for folks and will be the same again today." A head shorter than her but with the swagger of a grown man he screwed up his eyes and looked her over. "If that be the coach you intend, Mrs Latimer."

"I wish to visit Tavistock before I continue my journey, it is a simple thing and I may even take a route via Moreton, if I'm so minded."

He did not reply, but watched the Roman road for the first glimpses of the Tavistock-bound coach.

Kicking up dust, the coach had arrived, as many hanging to its outside as seated within, a collection of battered trunks, chicken crates and calico tied bundles strapped to its roof. They had found room for her trunk, although she had been obliged to give a coin to the rider to have him hand it up. With no more than ten miles between this meeting place and the beginnings of the market town, she had not minded the crush, avoiding any conversation, watching the green edges of the woodland and the short sheep-shorn grasses that bordered the turnpike.

A spell of dry weather had hardened the rutted road, but the harsh swaying of the coach was easy compensation for a quickly done journey. By mid-afternoon they had bridged the Tavy and slowed their pace, the team pushing on through the green-grey stone buildings and congested streets of the busy stannary town.

Although the old town, sitting upon the rock-strewn river, bore witness to a meeting of tracks and turnpike roads, it covered little more than two main streets. The coaching inn set in the heart of a labyrinth of smaller paths and trackways sprawled sideways from its base; its yard, kitchens and stables set behind it without thought to purpose or uniformity.

They were put down, the trunk lifted from the roof. She paid a boy to watch it and went into the inn to arrange passage – not for her but for her trunk. The trunk would be returned to Exeter via Moreton, but she would not accompany it. Passage confirmed, a slim man with a crooked mouth slapped a crudely printed label to its lid and tightened the strap. She found a coin from her purse put it into his hand and walked into the bustling streets, cutting from her mind any thought of regret or uncertainty.

The letter was inside the lid, when the trunk reached Exebere Street Henri would find it, ride out to Venn Combe and bring his daughters home. There would be no complication, no necessity to contest his suitability as a parent, no longer any connection with harlots and whores. She lifted up her skirts to keep them free from the littered cobbles. These were the clothes Henri had hastily had made for her, the clothes that portrayed her as the well-bred merchant's wife that she most certainly was not. She had hardly begun to enjoy the feeling of belonging, of protection – the bastard child she had carried had blackened all pleasure and now that short-lived moment in her life was over.

Most sellers and buyers seemed to be doing trade along the edges of the narrow streets, but here and there was a better quality shop catering for the new rich in this growing tin and copper town. It was for an establishment somewhere between these two levels that she searched, and towards a steeply rising hill where the track ran sharply back upon itself she had found a pawnbroker's and second-hand shop. Negotiation had been easy and for her willow hoops, buckled slippers and lace cap she had accepted faded breeches, a couple of calico shirts and a pair of well-made but much repaired shoes. Behind a ragged curtain towards the back of the shop, she had changed, winding what remained of her clothes into a manageable bundle, slipping her arms into the short woollen coat that had been hers when she had still viewed the world through the eyes of a maiden.

Now that her head was bare the fast growing dark curls that were a mark of her ancestry worried her face, framing olive skin and black eyes. There was a small glass standing in one corner of the shop and she caught her image, dissatisfied still, having not banished all that she was. She could see the shop owner assessing her, asking unspoken questions. It was almost as if he had read her mind and he reached across a pile of linen – no more than rags – and took down a felt hat turned up in three corners as was the norm.

"Tuppence," he had said handing it to her. She took it, offered him a penny and left the small dark room.

She had returned to the main street, bought apples and a hard crust pie and given a farthing for a jute bag and then stood opposite The Queens Head watching the coaches come in, drawn to this moorland nucleus by converging tracks and the benefit of a river crossing.

A mud-caked coach, already having travelled across one bleak moor in the preceding county drew up, allowing its occupants rest before beginning their journey again to Moreton and then Exeter. She waited, watching the yard boys unloading and loading possessions, watched her own trunk lifted up and secured to the roof; it was done and she would move on. The choice to remove all outward signs of femininity and travel as a boy was as logical as making sure she had eaten and drunk, and had leather upon her feet – easier for a boy travelling alone to avoid danger than a girl.

It mattered not which track she took, the Callington road would do as well as any. The day had run into late afternoon and cloud was rising from the west. The road was well used, a highway linking the important stannary town with the industrial heart of the valley. Mule trains and carts passed her, serving the hundred or so mines that prospered and failed here, plundering the rich seams of tin and copper, silver-lead and arsenic. She watched the western sky for the approach of evening and perhaps a pink flush seeping through the cloud, predicting a settled day to come. As she walked she was conscious that the cart she had heard approaching did not pass her, but idled alongside her slowing to her pace. She dropped her eyes to the ground and waited for it to pass.

"'Tis three miles to Lumber Bridge and another fifteen still to Callington." She put a hand on her hat and looked up; an old man, a tinker probably judging by the clanking paraphernalia hanging from the rear of his cart. "Take a ride or leave it, 'tis still fifteen miles to Callington."

She continued to walk, the cart matching her pace – she must find a level, remember that she was no longer who she had once been. The tinker wowed his pony and brought the slow-footed creature to a stop; she nodded acceptance, tipped the brim of her hat further over her eyes and put a foot on a muddied spoke, pulling herself up beside him, and waited for the cart to begin again. The halter had slipped from the tinker's grasp as the cart had come to a halt; she watched him groping for it, feeling the space where he expected it to be, opaque, cataract obscured eyes looking ahead to a scene that was obviously indistinct and without clarity. They moved off at walking pace and she removed the jute sack from her shoulders and pushed it under the seat.

"Was you buying or selling in that busy place?"

She answered honestly and watched the track. "Neither, sir."

"Returning home to family then?"

She wound the question around in her head before answering. The people she had lived amongst as a child were left behind in the wooded valleys that hugged the southern coast, and now she had let go of the family she might have had. "I have no family and I am not returning to anywhere," she said without emotion.

"No trade to be done and no family to return to? If not returning then might you be running?" The tinker chucked the pony on. "Was you indentured – running away from a master maybe?"

She supposed this was a test – if this man did not contest her gender, took her for boy, then perhaps she could travel without complication.

"I have no master, sir, and no one seeks me. I am not running and I was not indentured nor am I tied to any." His struggling eyes she saw were still fixed on the road ahead and she wondered what he saw, how he worked his trade.

"Left at liberty and no place forward? Ye must have a mind to tarry someplace?"

Did she? She had not thought – her single-minded determination to leave the combe, to set Henri free, had ended there; she had not considered a future beyond the leaving, now she must. Following the old man's hampered gaze she looked at the passing landscape. This county was laced with rivers, she had been born beside one and grown up on the banks of the Exe – a river was like a road and a river always led somewhere. These last few life-changing weeks she had often stood on the banks of the Tamar, a lifeline to the world beyond the cloying, imprisoning combe, and during that time she had often considered its destination – she supposed she must have a destination, a destiny also. "I am going to the river," she said, the thought newly formed.

"Ha, the river – 'tis vein and artery to this valley, the life blood o' trade in these regions. I've a mind to travel that way myself – no tinkering to be done in Callington, no money for it and the rich do hold to their coins more tightly than the poor."

She listened to the tinker's unsteady voice, felt the swaying of the cart and watched the verdant green of the dense woodland until without comment he wowed the pony. It was a prelude to a change in direction; they had reached Lumber Bridge and the old man jerked at the horse's bit, turning the cart, crossing the rutted surface and pulling off the main carting road to follow the pitted well-used track which ran south towards the river port.

Gradually the landscape in its true form became visible. Scared earth, scoured of all vegetation by man's thirst to have what lay beneath it, spoil heaps and poisonous russet pools contrasting violently against the dense woodland of ancient trees, and here and there set sentinel above it all, the granite chimneys of engine houses. She gave the tinker what remained of the food, listened to his stories and looked ahead as they picked their way between the litter of mining and the ever-moving trade of mining business that passed along this track daily on route to Tavistock.

The tinker wiped his hands down the front of his breeches, probing between his knees for an earthenware jug stored there, shouldered it and drank.

"Take some ale, boy, 'tis plenty here and 'twill see thee along another day."

Rachael took the heavy jug, shouldered it as she had seen the tinker do, and quenched her thirst as best she could. Flood had allowed only water and latterly the child sickness had prevented her from drinking anything other. She handed the jug back to the tinker, staying with her own thoughts, thinking of the broad contorted river that they now approached.

Dusk had found the valley before they reached the quay; the masts of sailing barges and the paraphernalia of the working quay were just visible in the half-light. The tinker pulled the old horse to a halt and climbed carefully down until he felt the familiar soft grass underfoot, handing himself along the side of the tired beast and taking the halter. Sensing his touch the horse flung its head up, jangling the bit, the tinker hushed it and led the beast on into a clearing at the side of the track. Rachael watched the old man as he searched the surrounding area for dried grasses, pulling up handfuls and returning to wipe the sweat from his beast. She reached for the jute bag and let herself down onto the densely grown late summer grasses. The tinker was still rubbing down the horse and in the half-light she saw how ragged he was, how thin, and felt a shudder pass across her back – the reality of an itinerate life.

He was talking as he worked, she hardly listened.

"Indentured." He drew the talk back to where he had left it, stopped for a moment, standing still, and then began again to rub the flanks of his horse with sure movements. "'Tis ownership, being indentured – I could offer you up a good learning without ownership. Teach you all the mending ways I knows – have you work alongside me and no need for such a paper to say so. I need fresh eyes, boy, the eyes of the young, such as thee. 'Twould give 'ee a free life with no chains and the road laid out before you whenever you should wish to tread it."

Rachael watched him but did not reply. Now she understood how he managed, how he afforded ale and enough food to keep flesh on his bones. The moon was rising, it would be dark soon and she would not be his eyes. She reached down to pick up the bag. She sensed him turn like a cat, he was quick for an old man, dark-skinned sinewy arms lashing out groping for her. He caught her arm, twisted it and she felt the burn on her skin – his grip was stronger than she expected, there would be requirement to pay for her free ride. She dropped the bag and stood level with him. Survival and the need to be free was a fundamental part of her being; she would not protest, she must force herself to make no complaint, let him think her feeble. She looked into his face saw his blackened tombstone teeth and smelt the urine on his clothes and waited for him to make his move.

"Smooth hands for a 'pprentice boy, I can feel 'em smooth and long-nailed. What kind o' work did you say you did?"

"I did not say."

He felt her arm now with his other hand and then the contours of her shirt beneath her coat and the femininity that she could not hide; she allowed it but not for long.

"You're no more boy than I am rich man. Why would a woman – a woman with a woman's shape, soft handed and unworked – want to be wandering the turnpikes o' this valley with nothing more on her person than a jute bag and a penn'orth o' victuals?"

Her arm was taut in his grip, her fist tightly closed, her nails now digging into her palm.

"A biddable 'pprentice boy might earn his keep tinkering, but a soft-handed woman has the means to fill a purse."

It had not taken him long to understand who she was, she would not be so easy with rides and favours again. Now she would free herself and leave. Facing him, feeling his need and desperation but knowing that she must not offer compassion, she kicked hard at the raggedly covered bony shins, twisted her arm and set herself free. The jute bag was lying on the grass and she stooped to pick it up. Tonight she must spend the darkness on this quay and tomorrow she would be gone, return to the places she remembered and begin again.

62

Releasing his foot Henri slid to the ground, dancing a little on his good leg to avoid putting too much weight on the other. A livery boy took the halter.

"Content, sir – with the purchase?"

"Indeed I am." Latimer patted the chestnut mare's powerful flank with appreciation. "As I am the pony, biddable both."

After years of rejecting the idea, he had made purchase of a solid chestnut mare and, in a fit of romanticism, a well-mannered sorrel pony to keep it company. He was pleased with both although the pony at present would have to remain unridden. The arrangement with the Holloway livery endured: the new beasts could be stabled there, but available to him only.

He walked the short distance to Latimer House in the heat of the midmorning. His visit to the pack-road weavers had been routine and without event; however, his thoughts had been far from routine. He was troubled by the happenings of this last month, regretful and now concerned that he had driven the wedge that unavoidably existed between his wife and himself deeper still.

The street was busy now, an assortment of people going about their business. He noticed the windows of the whorehouse were still shuttered – activity around these premises far more discreet than around the hovels in the back streets nearer the river. He turned sharply to his name; a small boy seemed to be pursuing him through the crowds.

"Mr Latimer, sir. Mr Henri Latimer."

He stopped, looked down on the child.

"Something urgent?"

The child handed him a folded letter and he rummaged in his pocket, he was anxious to have any news of his family. He studied the hand, but did not recognize it, a feeling of disappointment sending his brow together in a frown. Inexcusably, he had not yet found the heart or the words to write to Rachael.

Vetch was out and he was met by the occasional maid who bobbed and took his coat. "Perhaps that will explain the other, sir." She nodded to the letter in his hand – now that the house lacked a mistress the young woman found her tongue far too readily.

"Other, another letter?" He was hopeful.

"No, sir, a trunk. Mr Vetch has put it in the sitting room to await your intentions."

"A trunk, unaccompanied?"

"Yes, sir, come two days since, on a cart from The Mermaid, Thomas has paid the carter."

Latimer rubbed his chin. He could offer no explanation, perhaps investigation would enlighten him. The trunk was standing before the unlit fire; Rachael's trunk, the locked clasp intact, he remembered the letter he held in his hand – was this explanation? He took his paper knife and opened the seal, unfolding the heavy paper and reading the unfamiliar hand.

Venn Combe – August 16th 1763

Sir,

I find I must write frankly upon the subject of Mary and Sophia.

Since I have played host to your family I have learnt many things about their living that leaves me with concern. I have long since held the belief that a man may not and should not raise his daughters alone, their demeanour lacks formality and propriety and I see there has been no attempt to have them learn the teachings of our faith. I do not wish, brother-in-law, to offer only negativity but there is a home here, amongst their kin, a place where I believe they should have been installed on the death of their dear mother and I would have you allow them remain in it.

I urge you, sir, think beyond self and offer no objection to them remaining here at Venn where they may be free from the taint of city life and those who might encourage them away from Godliness into sin. This is most assuredly what their mother would have wished and I hope you will comply without objection.

We require only your compliance, brother-in-law, and your speedy reply is awaited.

Yours with sincerity,

Phyllis A Medland

He dropped the letter onto his desk, eyed the chest, more confused than concerned. The letter he had just read was sharply pointed. He ought to have anticipated Phyllis Medland's likely demands – he did not attach any seriousness to it and he would not comply. The key to the trunk, he assumed, was with its owner and he searched around for something to prize open the lock; he picked up the poker, forced it behind the clasp and wrenched it from its housing. He lifted the lid. This was the trunk he had sent his wife away with – Rachael's possessions, neatly packed inside it. Sat atop the folded clothing was another letter. There was no seal, impatiently he opened the folds, began to read.

My dearest Henri,

   I must write you again with haste and this time with much need.
   Please come Henri, come soon, have your daughters sit upon your knee and then bring them home.
   I know you will ask questions between these lines but I cannot answer them, it is time to return your life to the way it once was and have your daughters join you in Exeter.
   Remember me fondly.

Rachael

He stood for a moment with the paper in his hand, looking blankly at the open trunk. There was an inference in the letter that unsettled him – why would he wish to return his life to the way it was? He hated riddles and puzzles, and he did not consider a reply.

A bottle of brandy stood on a side table and he went to it, filled a mug and drank – then refilled the mug. He heard his servant come into the hall – Vetch had entered the house through the street door. Perching on a corner of his desk and continuing to assess the open trunk, Henri called.

"Please save yourself the effort of leaving and therefore the necessity of returning, Thomas. I wish to speak with you and urgently so." Caught before he could slink away to the kitchens, Vetch came forward carrying a bloodied sack from his visit to Smithern Street.

"I require both your assistance and your company, Thomas. I had not expected to travel again so soon, but I have changed my plans and this requires you to go to the Holloway Street livery and inform them of my intentions."

"Sir?" Vetch allowed the sack to rest on the flags.

"They must make ready both my mare and the pony for tomorrow." Henri looked at his servant, evaluating his reaction. "I intend to travel to Bickham Down and I would be grateful if you would accompany me."

"Would it not be simpler to take the coach, sir?"

"In this instance, no, it would not. I am aware of your preference for the coach and I apologize for the immediacy of my request, but it is imperative that I do not delay my visit."

Vetch had taken his sack to the kitchen. Latimer listened to the mumbled complaints and then waited for his servant to pass the open door again and leave the house on his way to the livery. He put the cork back in the bottle and took the stairs, limping slightly, having spent two days in the saddle already. Tomorrow he would visit the Medland cousins, solve the puzzle and put confusion to rest.

Henri assessed the position of the hazy sun, now directly above them but still not beyond its zenith. They had left the highway some time ago and were working their way slowly down the steeply descending track to the bottom of the combe. Since they had left the livery at dawn, Vetch had found little to say on their journey west – Henri had not minded, his thoughts were his own. *You will have questions between these lines*, his wife had said, and he did; impatience had often made him act on impulse, he hoped this trip, unplanned, would give him answers.

A boy, underfed and shoeless, was loitering in the unkempt area of cobblestones and shale that enveloped the Medlands' farmhouse. Henri tossed him a coin bidding him take hold of the pony. Vetch slid from the saddle, took the more powerful beast by the halter and waited for his master to follow.

"Another coin if I find them equable when I return."

Henri drew his stick from his bag and brushed some of the dust from his coat. The door was open, he took his stick rapped and then entered – the maid finding him as he waited on the flags.

He had not been here for more than eight years, and then it had been an introduction – an obligation he put upon himself to marry early and well, another building block in his determination to restore the Latimer name and find some solvency.

"Latimer, Henri Latimer," he had said removing his hat and tucking it under his arm.

The room was gloomy and he adjusted his eyes. He could see his daughters sat in the depths, a sudden stab of conscience met him; he had been wrong-footed in sending them away, he knew it, his decision more deeply rooted in frustration rather than any threat from the typhus. His daughters' heads were dropped over their learning and they had not seen him arrive. They turned, rose to greet him and then came to him, firstly hesitantly, then like a warm wind crossing a cornfield, full of life and purpose. He held them to him, felt their emotion, condemning himself for having allowed autonomy and dissatisfaction to persuade him to send them way.

"Good day to you, Mrs Medland, I apologize for not having forewarned you of my visit."

Phyllis Medland stood, tall for a woman, meeting his eyes. Another woman, lace bonnet tied tightly under her chin was seated close to the window – the cousin, he assumed; they had never met. He dropped his head in greeting and faced his dead wife's sister.

"I have come in reply to your letter and indeed Rachael's. I do not believe my sentiments can be accurately voiced with ink and paper."

"There was no need brother-in-law."

"Indeed I believe there is every need. Although I am grateful for your generosity towards my family I regret that I cannot comply with your request, selfish or no I have raised my daughters without disturbance or intrusion for the last six years and I shall continue the way I have begun. I thank you for your opinion, but I shall not defer."

Vetch was standing beside him, the door still open; he could see the maid idling within earshot. Sophia had taken his hand.

"Where is Rachael, Papa? Has she come along with you?"

"Indeed she has not, Sophia – my assumption has been that she is here with you." He tried to assimilate the consequences of this simple question. "My wife is, is she not here with you, Mrs Medland?" He looked at the starched-backed woman standing beside the spinning wheel. "It is not just the concerns of my daughters' predicted future that has brought me here, but indeed a trunk and a letter returned to Exebere Street unaccompanied."

"To answer you directly, Brother-in-law, she is not."

"Then where, between the two, here and her home – give me an opinion?"

"On this I cannot offer you accuracy, your wife left Venn Combe a week ago, with her trunk – the boy accompanied her to the turnpike."

"Then we must be concerned, Mrs Medland. She has not found her way home."

Vetch was fidgeting beside him. Henri spoke to him without turning.

"Thomas, have my daughters show you their room and help them make a bundle of their belongings." He waited for his daughters to leave and faced Phyllis Medland again – the younger cousin still had her head bowed over her sewing, although he noticed she was making no progress.

"You must tell me, Mrs Medland, for I am in ignorance. Why would Rachael leave you without first sending word to me and without my daughters? A journey across the county alone is hardly wise. What was her motive – did you not attempt to dissuade her?"

"I do not believe, Brother-in-law, your wife to be dissuadable from any course. She is self-minded and was determined to leave."

He shook his head; truth was often slow coming, any progress like crossing slurry in heavy boots. "Did she intend to return home?"

"I had thought it, but I am not privy to the young woman's thinking and I had no guidance upon her intentions. However, I am surprised that she did not return to you, I would have expected it. She seemed to possess a level of loyalty. You will most likely find her there when you return."

Premonition that he would not made him go over the simple words of Rachael's letter: she had asked him to come, to take his daughters home and then return to the life he had once had – she had not included herself in this.

Hospitality had not been offered him and if it had he would not have taken it, he leant more heavily upon his stick and rasped his chin. "Something has taken place here that has led my wife to leave prematurely, your letter talks of taint, perhaps dissatisfaction with the company my daughters' keep. Tell me, am I being led towards accuracy?"

"Accuracy, Brother-in-law, is something that you did not offer when negotiating your family's safekeeping."

"Then let me clear any inaccuracies now, what would you have me offer?"

"I do not believe it is a fitting subject for discussion in the company of a maiden."

"Then perhaps your cousin might permit us privacy."

Pamela Medland, head still down but listening intently, stood silently and went towards the door.

"Your new wife, Brother-in-law, is not the person you led us to believe."

"Did I lead you, Mrs Medland? I believe I merely requested you offer her sanctuary along with my daughters away from the endemics of city living."

"And so you did and I accepted my blood kin into this house and your new wife along with them. But since, Brother-in-law, I have learnt that your wife has a history that sits uncomfortably alongside her new-found status of merchant's wife."

"I did not think the searching of my wife's history would be a requirement in the offering of bed board and a watchful eye."

"Ordinarily perhaps not – I had thought your tastes more discerning, they most certainly were when you sought my sister's hand."

The inference was enough, he had already got a gauge of this woman's prejudices and snap judgement; he could not say what had happened here but perhaps enough to make Rachael's stay untenable. There was no need to further pick over the beginnings of her life. It need not go further – he would put a stop to it.

"Whatever you know, Mrs Medland, whatever you have heard may or may not be the truth. If it is then I know it already, if it is not I dismiss it, and if you cannot help me along then I must find answers relating to the whereabouts of my wife elsewhere."

"Indeed I cannot help you further. I could not prevent your wife from leaving, I anticipated she would reach you before the end of the day and I am surprised that she has not."

"Then we make no progress and as I have no wish to be travelling after dark I believe it beneficial to all that we begin our journey without delay."

"Your actions, Brother-in-law, quite contradict your politeness – you are far too forward with your assumption that I will allow such a hasty departure. I insist that you do not remove my nieces from this house without thought. Legally I may not be their guardian, but morally I believe I have some ownership of their upbringing. Raising girls in a masculine household has been misguided and has brought about a noticeable harshness to their demeanour that does them no favours."

"I must challenge you, Mrs Medland, my daughters are as I wish them to be and they will return with me today; you need no longer concern yourself over their upbringing."

There was chatter in the hall, Vetch had brought his daughters' bundles down and was waiting for instruction.

"Wait for me in the yard, Thomas, I am finished here."

The meeting, the stay would be abrupt and not what he had planned. He had attempted politeness – did he not owe these women that much? It had been his obstinacy that had pushed him to communicate with this distant kin whom, in truth, he had little intimate knowledge of – now his obstinacy must take him away abruptly and without rest.

"Again, I thank you for your hospitality." He returned his hat to his head and ducked below the beam.

Vetch was standing beside his daughters when he got outside. The boy was there – Henri felt in his pocket, tossed the emaciated child a sixpence, passed him his stick and began strapping the bound bundles to the pommel of his mare.

"I understand you took my wife to the turnpike to meet the coach?" He pulled the strap through the buckle with force.

"Yes, sir."

"And did you see her safely onto the Plymouth coach?"

"Not the Plymouth, sir, she were waiting upon the Tavistock."

"The Tavistock, why so?" He continued with his task, no more than a slight hesitancy showing his surprise.

"Preference, sir – she said she wished to make a visit there and then maybe take the coach to Moreton."

Henri settled Sophia before Vetch and Mary on his own saddle, took his stick from the shoeless child and tucked it into his bag.

"We would be wise to go north to Tavistock, Thomas, and find an inn. The Queen's Head will do as well as any." He led the mare towards the slate-stepped mounting block. The younger cousin was walking towards him – he took the halter again, patted the young horse's withers and waited for the dourly dressed woman to approach him.

"Do you wish to speak with me, madam?" He noticed the well-mended skirts and the small straw hat hastily fastened over greying hair.

"Yes, Mr Latimer, if you please, but I have not told my cousin of my intentions only that I wished to take some air. I would prefer it we are not observed."

Henri looked back at the house, its four dark-stoned walls pushed back into the hillside.

"Mount, sir, and ride a little and I will meet you in the lane."

He obliged, kicked the mare on a little way, slowly walking away from the house. The younger Medland cousin caught him up and walked beside him. He felt her unease; prompted, he spoke first.

"I am sorry for the abruptness of this visit – it had been far from my intention." He looked down on her covered head. "Do you wish to say farewell to my daughters?"

"Indeed I do, sir, but it is also to you that I wish to speak."

Her eyes were faded, unassuming – Latimer doubted she had much cause to smile.

"I have enjoyed your daughters' company, Mr Latimer, and I shall miss them, but see that they have done well in your care. I am sorry they are leaving, although I do not condemn you for it – but it is not about their wellbeing that I wish to speak but about your wife's."

"Rachael, I will have anything you have to offer on this and will bless you for it."

"You may not, sir, once you have heard the level of it." She paused avoiding the straying briars over spilling the hedge. "Although there was some disagreement between your wife and my cousin, I do not feel it warranted her leaving – I believe her stay here had become untenable for other reasons."

"Other?"

"Sir, I do not wish to leave you with sadness to accompany anxiety, but your wife is no longer with child – the child is lost."

His mare took this moment to side step and he settled her, holding to Mary, processing what he had heard.

"And her health?" He felt a lump in his throat, an emotion he was unused to. His expression was unchanged.

"Sound, Mr Latimer, although it did take a little time to return. I know my cousin to be a wise and resolute woman, but her judgement is sometimes clouded by misconception. She has formed an opinion that is at the core of your wife's discomfort."

"This opinion, would it have moved my wife to leave the safety of your home and travel unaccompanied?"

"It may, Mr Latimer, but it is not for me, an unmarried woman, to explain it. My cousin has great faith in our doctor's judgement and also in the efficacy of our housekeeper's gossip – she has concluded that Mrs Latimer has a past beyond your knowing."

Latimer rubbed his chin. "Then I can see my wife's dilemma. Let us hope she has returned to her home." His face was rigid – he looked ahead above Sophia's white cap and waited for the conversation to conclude.

"I am sure that will be the case, sir – given a little time to adjust to her loss. I felt there was a reluctance to write you and tell you she had lost your child."

"Then, now she has no need to." He spoke with a taut jaw. "I thank you for your concern, Miss Medland, and for your care during my daughters' stay."

He had tipped his hat, allowed the woman to bid his daughters well and then encouraged his mare on, rising up out of the wooded combe to meet the moorland scrub and the turnpike running north to Tavistock.

Familiar to him, although not a place he had often taken lodging, The Queen's Head had been receiving the last coaches of the day as they came level; dismounted they led the chestnut mare and the biddable sorrel pony to the livery at the rear. His daughters had been tired from the sudden change in their usual routine; he had taken a couple of rooms at the front of the inn and had the victualler send up a selection of meats and a loaf of dark bread. When he had seen his daughters to bed he had blown out the candle and lay in the darkness with his thoughts. Tomorrow he would put Mary and Sophia on the Moreton coach with Vetch. He would remain in this town a while longer, his hope was that Rachael would return to the Exebere house and explain her absence; but before he began his journey home he would know her path, make enquiries about a young woman, fitting his wife's description, travelling alone.

63

The streets of the woollen city had hardly begun their ascent from sleep, arrested in that quiet time that falls between the activity of the night and the early dawn. Mag had spent the night at the Alphington lodging – and without Geoffrey. Yesterday, after many months of profligacy and ill-judged borrowings, the non-payment of any bill considered too trivial to be bothered over, the constables had come heavy footed and with determination and taken Geoffrey to the debtors' gate.

The city was just waking, she passed a piss-cart trundling downwards towards the river and the tucking mills that ran along its banks, an urchin asleep in a doorway and a couple of gentlemen dishevelled from a night of over-indulgence. They noted her elfin features, her neatly drawn-in waist – she was in her finery, whore yes, but not of the lower kind. She took hold of her skirts and drew them obligingly in, touched the edges of her straw hat, tipping her head to acknowledge them.

Standing guard over the turnpike south and the tentergrounds beyond, the two towers of the South Gate, castellated walls and arrow-slit-thin windows, stood tall above the surrounding houses. She stepped into the pool of shadow they made, lengthened now by the onset of early autumn and looked up to the windows set square above the archway. She cupped her hands about her mouth and called.

"I am here, Geoffrey. I have come, my love, as I promised I would."
A voice, the voice of her keeper returned quickly.

"Have you got what I asked for?"

"I have, my love, I have it all." Standing so far below the high window, Mag could see no more than the shadowy shape of her lover – the outline of his dark hair, the contours of his chin, now unshaven.

A hand was extended from the narrow window, the end of several laces tied one to the other was thrown down. She caught hold of it, looking over her shoulder, grateful that the streets were still empty.

"I have been waiting since before the dawn, Margaret. God rot them, unless I can show a handful of silver I must live on gruel and fetid river water. 'Tis a cursed ambiguity – if I had a handful of silver to show, is it likely I would still be here in this stinking room perched above this gate?"

Mag put down the small basket she held over her arm, took out the neatly tied calico bundle that held a stale loaf and a square of cheese, and began to tie it to the end of the lace.

"Be quick, Margaret, I have no wish nor urge to share your offering with any other here. They will be on my back as soon as they have wind of my intentions."

"You must pull this up first, Geoffrey, and then I may send up the flagon."

The string was thrown out again and the earthenware vessel was pulled laboriously up disappearing through the window.

"Do you have the coat, Margaret?"

"Not the one you wished for, my love – you forget I had need of coin to pay the landlord. It is gone to the dealer, Geoffrey, but I have another – its warmth I do believe will be no less. Send out the cord and I will tie it to the end."

"If you have sold my coat and replaced it with an offering from the rag merchants I shall know it, Margaret, and shall see the misdeed repaid."

"I am pushed to do such things, Geoffrey, how else can I keep body together and bring you what I must if our purse is empty?"

Moving away from the wall, placing a hand on her hat and crooking her neck to look up, Mag waited for Geoffrey's head to appear at the window again; she watched as one arm and then a head came through the constraints of the arrow slit. The flagon was rested on the sill and whilst he chewed he drank.

"Have you yet visited my uncle?"

"I am loathe to go, Geoffrey, are you sure there is no other way?"

"Would I ask this of you if there were?"

"I doubt that you would, Geoffrey."

"Then you must go and today, I will not spend another night in this loathsome hole. Saints, Margaret, it is a trivial amount – these low-living workshop owners have more importance than they ought and will find devilish pleasure in seeing a man detained when they could just as well wait upon settlement."

"But the hosier has waited many weeks already, my love, and I believe he do feel the amount is not so very small."

"Would he be so easy with his writs and accusations if I had more standing in this city, if my uncle had backed me as he ought?"

"What backing did you wish for, my love – has not your uncle spared you from the debtors' gate before, and worse beyond it, Geoffrey?"

"Do not argue around the point, Margaret, I have told you to visit the man and you must do my bidding. He will not refuse you and if he does you must have him change his mind. I cannot believe he will allow me to rot here, I share his name and he has been ever precious about that name since he laid his hands upon my grandfather's money. It would help me better if you were to cease idling beneath this window and get yourself gone upon your errand."

"Then I suppose I must, but do not reprimand me, Geoffrey, if I am unable. Shall I come again tomorrow?"

"If my debt is not paid, Margaret, you will have need to come again tomorrow, and when you do bring me better news and something other than poor man's meat and yesterday's bread."

She stepped away out of the shadows, looked up, kissed her white fingers, sending the sentiment towards the fortified window.

"I will be quickness itself, my love, and pray for your freedom right up to the merchant's door."

"Then you will have to pray loudly, Margaret, for I suspicion you are a long way from Heaven's Gate."

Gone into the waking streets, Mag turned into Rack Lane, skirts lifted high above the cobbles. She had no fear of Henri Latimer – she would visit him. She did not wish to see the young man who kept her brought any lower than he was, but perhaps there was some requirement for retribution, another night on a straw-covered floor above the gate would do him no harm. Mag saw no sound reasoning why Henri Latimer should open his purse again, but she would ask it – although she would not beg.

Looking about his bed chamber with the eyes of a man who has begun to see the world through a mist of cynicism, Latimer finished knotting his neck cloth and impatiently thrust the cloth into his waistcoat. He could hardly believe he had come full circle, passing through interest to hope, union and anticipation of better times to come only to find himself back at the beginning – sleeping alone and without companionship.

He had not found Rachael. His wife, it seemed, had disappeared into the valley of the Tamar without trace. He could only guess at her reasoning – he did not accept it, but felt himself culpable in the abrupt ending of his relationship with the young woman he had so wanted and then saved from a life on the streets.

Earlier he had called Vetch, the man finally condescending to appear in his doorway looking surprised that he should have been asked to attend his master again so soon after having left him.

"Remove this home brew and have it replaced, surely there is something better in the cellar."

Vetch went to the sideboard and picked up the decanted wine. "I will look, sir, and report upon my findings."

"Do, and then have my breakfast laid out, I shall be gone for the day and have no wish to travel this city on an empty stomach."

Latimer had sat alone at the breakfast table, bleakly watching the clock and finding no lightening of his dark mood. He pushed back the chair, the abruptness of the action making it grate on the flags. Someone had pulled the chain on the street bell and he waited, looking over the empty table at the crumbs left from a broken oatcake and the half-drunk mug of wine. He would see no one today. He wished for no visitor whoever they were.

"There is a person at the street door wishing to speak with you, sir, will I send her away?"

A spark of hope upsetting his resolution, he looked at his servant with narrowed eyes. "A person, this is little help to me, Thomas. I cannot say whether or nay I wish to meet with them offered such a poor description – a name?"

"She did not give a name, sir."

"No name, then a description?"

Thomas had met the sharp rhetoric and impatience with his own obsequious disapproval. "A whore, sir, I believe – I do not know her name but I have seen her enter the whorehouse in times past."

Latimer squinted at his servant. "The bawdy house?"

"I believe the person is known to your nephew, sir."

Intrigue had got the better of him. "I will see her then. The sitting room – have her shown in and say I will attend shortly."

He had not seen his nephew's harlot since his visit to the Alphington lodgings and he had not expected to find her hanging on his door chain. She was standing in the large room at the front of the house waiting for him. There were tell-tale signs of her profession, but not obviously so, he had seen less well-dressed women on the arms of the city's most prosperous men.

"Madam." It suddenly struck him that she may have news of his wife, but this was soon dispelled.

"Forgive me, Mr Latimer, I had not wanted to come – I know how you do feel, sir, upon the issues of your nephew's misadventures – but I have most recently left him at the South Gate, the debtors' gate and I have promised that I would call upon you."

Latimer stood looking at her, arms folded, his mood as dark as his stubble. So Geoffrey had finally found his way to the gate? "The debtors' gate?" He repeated. "Incarceration after so long avoided – how long there?"

"Yesterday, Mr Latimer, the constables did come yesterday with a hammering and a pestering and a heavy foot and cudgels at their belts all."

"So much debt surrounds the boy I hardly know from which direction the summons would have come."

"A hosier, sir, and long forgot."

"Ah, silk stockings and lace perhaps – it is no real surprise to me, I have long since concluded that his internment is more likely than no. And the amount of his indebtedness?"

"I believe a sum above five guineas, sir."

"Can he not pay this?"

"He cannot, Mr Latimer."

So his nephew's pockets were now empty, the money would need to be sourced from his Dorset property, but then perhaps that was already indebted.

Henri wandered the room for a while, ran his hand through his hair, turned and looked her over. He could see why his nephew had been drawn to this young woman, harlot or not.

"And he has sent you to beg my pardon and ask that I recover this debt – as I have others – so that he may be released?"

"He has, sir. The gate do seem quite without comfort – but I shall not beg and I do not expect that you should help him again."

"You do not?"

"I do not, Mr Latimer. I know he has long tried your patience. But I shall not leave him to rot either. I will find another purse to settle this debt be it sooner or be it later."

"Then you offer more loyalty than a wife might." His own comment had touched a sore.

"I know of his failings, Mr Latimer, but I will not allow him to rot away in that place."

Expecting to offer no more than courtesy to his visitor and then have her ejected, Latimer had begun to see the merits in prolonging the visit of this young and honest woman. The meeting was a distraction; other than the strangers he had enquired of in the search for his wife, he had hardly spoken to anyone for some days. He had offered her refreshment – she had declined.

"Have you had news, sir, of Rachael?"

Uncertain if he wished to respond to her question, his dark brows came together in a frown. "I am afraid I have not," he said looking away.

"Rachael were a friend o' mine, Mr Latimer, but 'tis cruel to have left without a word and leave you searching for her in no place but all. My simple head do not link along with her reasoning."

"Nor mine," he had said before thinking and adding, "the issues are complex but I am as confounded as any regarding the reasons for her flight."

"I hear you have travelled up and down the river and across the moor and still no nearer learning the truth of her." She persisted.

"You hear much. It is true – I have drawn a blank and returned home hoping that she would reconsider her intentions, perhaps would already be here in the home that is hers."

"And have you now done enquiring, Mr Latimer?"

"For the time being, yes, I believe that I have."

"She will not dishonour you, sir, and may wish to be found more than she do know it. Perhaps you should seek the inns again and places where she might find honest work."

"I suspicion that you think me too quickly done, that I have given up too easily and should continue with my search?"

"I do, sir."

"This is a broad county, Margaret – she has covered her tracks well. I have no handle on her reasoning and no estimate of her thinking."

"If you were lost, sir, where would you go to?"

Latimer considered what she had said. "Here, I suppose, home. I believe I would look for some kind of familiarity – the security of the familiar."

"I believe I might also, sir – if I were lost."

Latimer nodded and shrugged. "You propose another search perhaps – I suppose it would at the least be preferential to this uncertainty." Walking the room again he looked at the street through the sash, without turning he addressed his visitor. "I have told my nephew that he must make his own life choices and take the consequences that come along with that, but I am contrary, Margaret, and as you have not begged I shall offer. I will pay this debt this time and it must be the last." He waited for a response – there was none.

"There is a codicil. You will not tell my nephew that it is from me that the money to discharge this debt has come – you must find your own reasoning." He rested his knuckles on the slate sill. "If you should wait outside my bank in Fore Street just after the midday I shall make certain that the monies you require to release him are passed to you."

He had dismissed her then, waited for her to work her way back to the

South Gate or wherever it was she intended to go. He picked up his coat and stick and walked across the city in the direction of Goldsmith's to meet with Edmund Elcott.

The streets were no less busy than was usual, but the end of summer always brought subtle changes to the city, not necessarily quantifiable but present nevertheless – the shadows in the streets, the almost indiscernible change in bird song, the variety of traffic using the highways that connected urban with rural. Latimer tapped the ferruled end of his stick along the littered cobbles and remembered the day of the hangings when he had first made this journey after his accident; he had changed and life had also changed, and even if he wished it the genie was now out and he could not go back to living as he once had – singularly and without company.

The young woman he had recently entertained had a point. He accepted that losing heart and patience had encouraged him to give up looking for his wife more quickly than he ought, but had he not tried to understand women's ways? His wife seemed no longer to be the girl he had innocently courted through the spring and early summer, and he had begun to feel he did not know her at all.

Distracted, September seemed to have found him without warning and Elcott's marriage day moved ever closer. His pre-arranged visit to the Waterbere Lane coffee house would be the last time he would meet with his friend before he left for Somerset, and he intended to wish him well.

Elcott was in his usual seat, Henri made his way to the table and greeted him.

"Edmund, my apologies, I am a little later than I anticipated."

Latimer took the notary's hand, sat heavily on the high-backed settle.

"Do not concern yourself, Henri, I never keep myself short of time when anticipating a long journey. I have a good while before I must meet the coach and my trunk is already packed."

"I would have wished to accompany you, Edmund, but I have been much away and feel a little burdened with other things – it does not make me good company."

"Then no news, sir?"

"None, although the interview I have had this morning, the very thing that kept me, has stirred my despondency."

"Then I am glad of it, Henri, I do not wish to approach my own happiness with yours crushed to pieces. What interview, sir, and with whom?"

"With the young woman who shares my nephew's bed – she came to report that Geoffrey has finally found his way to the place he has been heading since his mama allowed him his own purse."

"You allude to incarceration, Henri?"

"I do, to bride-well, arrested and taken to the debtors' gate."

Elcott allowed a flow of air to escape from his pursed lips.

"Foretold perhaps, but hardly anticipated. How large the debt?"

"Set against my nephew's history, comparatively small."

"And will you settle it?"

"As you know, I have refused to pay any more of his debts so I should not – although there is mitigation."

"Mitigation?"

"The young woman, although sent by him, did not beg for his clemency. Because of it I am minded to help."

Elcott nodded into his cup. "So you will free him?"

"I will free him." Elcott nodded, thoughts of his own mingled with his concerns for his friend. "The conversation then led on to other things – my wife is an acquaintance of the young woman. She predicts that I have not looked hard enough."

"And are you in agreement?"

"It seems that I must, Edmund, or how else am I to pass through this dark time if I do not have hope?" He rested his hands on his knees and looked at Elcott, attempting to lighten the mood. "How long will you remain at Knowle Easton – you must write me, Edmund, or better still return and bring your wife to dine?"

"A month, sir, I believe a month, as you know my mother is to make the journey with me this time and I doubt she will be rushed away."

"Then I wish you well, friend."

Before the boy had come to refill their cups Latimer had risen – they both had places to be, lives to be lived. He shook the younger man by the hand accompanying him to the door of the coffee house and left him to make his way to his rooms on North Street and collect his mother. Remembering his promise, Henri put his stick to the ground and set out for his bank in Fore Street. He would settle that which he had promised, but he would not visit the debtors' gate and he would not attempt appeasement.

When he returned home Vetch was out and he took the stairs to his daughters' rooms. It was regrettable, but he would have to leave them in the hands of his servants again – if his wife did not return to the house soon then he must find another maid.

Seeing they were settled with their occupations, he left them and made his way to the lower rooms; the large sitting room seemed unused, empty, changed. He filled a mug and took a drink. There would be no more purpose to his search this time than there had been before, but this time he would be searching with a level head. Although he felt more than a little concerned for his wife and he found it hard to comprehend her reasoning, he understood her self-sufficiency – in the short term he doubted she would come to harm. A surge of optimism met him; he went to his desk, took paper from the drawer and sat down, viewing the empty page, considering what he would say. It was possible that she might return whilst he was absent; if she did he would have many things to say to her. He dipped his quill. He would task Vetch with handing Rachael his thoughts – and this was one request that he expected his servant to carry out without deviation.

Pushing the signature ring he kept in his desk drawer into the soft wax, he sat back – there was some added activity beyond the window, a well-rigged carriage had drawn up, a brace of snorting beasts dancing to a stop just beyond his view. He stood and went to the window. Trelawney, Alexander Trelawney, had decided to bring his living back amongst them. Henri folded his arms and watched. This was Buckman's livery no doubt, although with Trelawney you could never be sure what allegiances the man might form.

He stood back and spoke to the empty room. "Ha. The world has changed, Trelawney, and I know not what you will make of it."

64

Startled by an unseen predator, a flock of grey geese rose up from the stubble field, grouping above the estuary and flying in unplanned uniformity towards the sea. She watched them go, scanning the panorama of worked fields and oak wood, pale sands moulded and shaped by the tide. The sand bar at the head of the estuary was beginning to show above the gently receding waters, the tide would turn soon and the path she had walked along would be lost.

Early autumn had brought a new freshness to the wind; the end of summer, a turning page, the ending of a chapter. Looking back over the last few weeks was like returning to peer again through a misted and distorted window. She picked up her shoes and settled the strings of the jute bag over her shoulder, replacing the tricorn, scooping up her skirts and tucking them over her arm. It was several miles to the turnpike road and she did not expect to seat herself on any coach going east before the end of the day. Tomorrow she would and tomorrow she would return to her home.

She climbed the wall that separated the enclosed courtyard from the cobbled lane behind, dropped down into the working yard, littered with the remnants of the businesses that shared it, but empty of any soul. Elijah was in the kitchen working a cloth over a stain on the sleeve of a brocaded coat; the room smelt of turpentine – a familiar smell and not unwelcome. He looked up and she dropped her bag on the flags.

"Daughter?" Old eyes questioned what he was seeing. "Rachael, home?"

She was not sure what he had heard of her recent life, of the abandonment of her new husband – he had already forgiven her for entering the whorehouse, perhaps he had forgiven her for this as well.

"I am, Elijah, and I have been travelling throughout this long day and felt the need to see remembered places."

"Then I will greet you, Rae, and be glad to do it."

She had need of physical contact, of affection; she stepped forward embraced him, waiting for some kind of response. Tentatively, he put an arm about her shoulders and then drew her away looking at her dress, her face, the changes in her appearance.

"He is home." For a moment she did not understand his meaning.

"Alexander, he is here?" She had not expected it; she had thought the house would be empty save Flood. "And does he travel alone?" She had to know.

"He does, Daughter, but solitude do not smooth his temper."

She allowed a shallow smile.

"Then nothing has changed."

"Will you go up and see him? I have told him of your marriage."

"And other things?"

"There is no need, Rachael."

There were the remnants of a boiled fowl on the table, Flood felt her hunger. "Eat before you do, we are without a cook and I must do the best I can, although Mr Trelawney rarely dines at home."

She had eaten, ladled some water from the bucket and gone up, moving through the familiar house as though she had never left it, acutely aware that the person she had once been was lost.

The room was as chaotic as she remembered it; Trelawney, squat, russet–headed, was working at his easel.

"Alexander." Automatically she bobbed. Throwing a rag to the floor, he turned, looked at her briefly and then returned to his work, whim prompting him to show indifference rather than surprise.

"I understood from that little doxy that you were gone from the city."

"I was, but now I am come back."

He assessed his work, a bold wild landscape, and put down his brushes amongst the mayhem of his table. "Then come to me, Rachael, have I not missed you and called each day for you to be fetched up and brought along to join our party?" These comments had never held any substance or truth and she let him continue. "But I hear you have been far too busy to entertain such a thing."

"I have had a life to live, Alexander."

"Married, my little Egyptian, married and to our sober merchant."

"Are you well, Alexander? You have no company?"

"I have not, nor do I need it." He was watching her as he always did, with

327

the searching eyes of a painter. "What garb is this you present yourself in, my Rachael – I had expected finery, or is your husband too mean spirited to open his purse?"

"He is not, Alexander, I have been travelling."

"And from the other side of the county, I hear."

"Who talks to you of such things, Alexander? You know much of my life without me having the telling of it."

"The doxy, Rae, that frail, slim-limbed little thing."

"Mag?"

"Yes, Maggie, offering me feigned vulnerability and harlot's blushes – will you dine with me, Rachael?"

"I cannot, Alexander, the coach arrived but a short time ago and I am yet to enter the Latimer house."

"I hear your husband has gone away again and so soon after having returned."

Next to the landscape was the portrait of an older woman, just begun, a few assured lines depicting her hair and mantle; she made a pretence of studying them. He had heard too much, more than she wished him to know.

"Is this the news Mag brought to you?"

"In part, you must not be annoyed that I have heard things about your merchant – perhaps before you – I asked it of her. I have been away for many weeks and have heard nothing of the city and this street, so I must have all the chatter that surrounds it."

"You do know then of the typhus."

"Indeed I do, and Jane – I am laid low with sadness, of all the whores in the crone's house, I had not expected Jane to be taken, no other caught my eye as Jane did."

"Jane?"

"Jane, my dear – although our little Maggie had not come to impart any such news – her lover, her keeper is confined in the gate. I have offered to have her sit for me."

"Geoffrey Latimer, imprisoned?"

"Your relation now, is he not? My, my, what happenings and all in the space of this summer – will you not take refreshment with me, Rachael? You have quite lost your bloom and look in need a glass of canary."

"No. No, Alexander, I cannot. I must find Thomas Vetch and tell him I am home."

He had already turned back to his work before she had left. She closed the door, rested her palms on the half table that stood in the long dark passage and closed her eyes against the dim light. Jane was dead, dear God, Jane was dead and she did not know it. Why had Henri not written her – why had Henri not told her? The reunion she had hoped for would not now happen, Henri had gone and Jane was dead.

She let herself out, the street was busy – she stood looking up at the whorehouse watching the gentlemen coming and going, business as usual, assessing Latimer House, unchanged by time, incongruous now amongst its neighbours. Vetch had answered the bell and she walked past him, stood on the flags, dropped her hat onto the settle.

"Mrs Latimer." He was obviously stunned by her arrival, but she would not explain to Henri's servant where she had been nor why.

"Where is my husband, Thomas, is he home?" She knew the answer but she would have him tell her, let him say where Henri was.

"I am afraid he is not, madam, Mr Latimer left some days ago."

"Where did he go, Thomas, what were his plans?"

Vetch picked up the misshapen felt hat, turning it disapprovingly in his hands. "I believe he has gone to look for you, Mrs Latimer."

There was satisfaction in his tone, even ridicule. She went to leave him, to mount the stairs, to seek out the room she had slept in before she left, but then stopped.

"And Sophia and Mary?"

"In their rooms, madam."

"I will have my coat and hat brushed, Thomas, and a jug of water and a kettle sent up." She turned to go into the broad low-beamed room she had shared but only briefly with her husband.

"There is a letter, madam."

"A letter, Thomas?"

"Upon Mr Latimer's desk."

She took off her coat and handed it to Vetch. The sun had left the street now and a sconce was already lit. The letter was propped against the inkwell; she took hold of it, sat in a fireside chair and broke the seal.

My dear wife,

There are always penalties for loving and I pay mine daily. Your need to leave me has left me desolate, I cannot know your reasoning. But do not think me wholly hard-hearted, it was my determination that sent you away and mine that forbade you from visiting a needy friend, for this I ask forgiveness.

With heavy heart I must tell you that the typhus has taken Jane, cowardice has kept me from telling you earlier, if it will help your sadness I doubt any could have helped her.

I am away from this house because I cannot live with conundrum and I will search for you until I have knowledge of your whereabouts. If you have the reading of this then you are home and I beg you wait here for me until I return so that I may know at last your mind.

I will make my starting point Whimple Street close to the Sutton Pool – Thomas Vetch will have knowledge of my intentions.

Your supporter and friend,

Henri L.

65

Arrow straight rays, piercing the dense clouds, returned light to the marshy wastes between the three towns. It had been another fruitless day; he had done as the whore Margaret had suggested and yet he knew he was no nearer finding his wife than he had been the previous day. The pool was busy, scores of vessels rising on the incoming tide. He slowed his mare, let her settle into a gentler pace – the streets here, some cobbled, were wet, the gradient making it easy for a horse to stumble. Now that the navy no longer had use for them there were destitute sailors and vagrants on every corner, some openly begging and some too far gone in drink to consider a future. There had been displaced soldiers and returned sailors on the streets of Exeter, but not in such numbers.

Lost in his own thoughts he came level with the Hospital of the Poor's Portion, a group of beggars were sheltering against the forbidding stone of the walls; he took note of them but did not see them for more than they were. Working his way through the crowds he sensed some added disturbance behind him; he turned to see a man with an ear missing and a livid scar running down one side of his face close on the hindquarters of his mount – gesticulating, alluding to some grievance Henri could only guess at. The man had grabbed at the flank of his horse sending the mare's legs clattering on the wet cobbles, sidestepping until she found her balance. Instinctively, Henri had reached for his stick but a level of empathy had collided with his temper making him think again. Settling his horse, he took a coin from his pocket and threw it to the sailor.

Whimple Street ran perpendicular to the pool. He had chosen the inn here because he had used it some years ago, but the place had obviously undergone rapid change and he was not sure it had been a good choice. Relieved to be through the streets, he kicked his horse on under the coach gates into the small livery yard at the side of the inn, let the stable boy take the bridle, dismounted stiffly and stood gathering his thoughts. He supposed there would be a time when he would have to give up his search, but that would not be yet.

The inn was full. He crossed the taproom to the stairs, found his room and threw the panniers he carried onto a chair. He was tired, his leg, although profoundly improved since the beginning of the year, did not respond well to long spells in the saddle. The coarse mattress was inviting and he lay on his back, contemplating tomorrow. Sleep had soon taken him down into that unpredictable place of dreams and when he had opened his eyes again his belly reminded him that he had missed a meal.

He re-tied his stock, looked about the small room and picked up his stick, felt for his purse in the deep pocket of his coat and went down into the large room that ran across the front of the inn. There was a table empty in a corner; he caught the eye of the pot boy and had him bring ale and something to eat – a rancid mutton stew and a slice of stale bread. Thirst quenched and adequately fed, he assessed his surroundings: a different mix of men here from the inns and taverns of his home. The proximity of the sea, the Dock to the west and its improving popularity with the navy had swelled these streets during the wars, changed the face of them he supposed. This change was evident even here, the blue serge of an officer, most likely on half pay, and the red of a group of marines just visible through the bustle of the room.

The pot boy filled his mug again and he resigned himself to an evening of inactivity.

"'Tis full to the gunnels and not a space for a body anywhere." An unfamiliar voice broke through into his inner thoughts.

Latimer looked up, forcing himself back to the moment, the taproom and his failure to find Rae. A broad man with a weathered face and a periwig which was sat aslant over his wide-featured face was standing beside his table looking down at him.

"I see you have an empty chair here, sir." The man held the neck of a bottle in the sturdy fingers of one hand and a pewter mug in the other. "May I take your company whilst I finish this good wine – and perhaps share it if you have a liking for the stuff?"

Henri looked him over, saw no acceptable reason to decline and waved a hand, suggesting he sit. He would have preferred separateness, if separateness could be had in such a place.

"Will you help me along with this bottle – it would be a service and then I will have cause to request another?"

Distracted for a while from his own mood Latimer finished his ale, pushed the mug towards the stranger.

"Capital, sir, if a man is to lose himself in drink, 'tis better to do it in company than alone, do ye not agree?"

"Your thinking is reasoned, sir." Henri responded dully, cynicism clouding his every thought. "But the need to lose oneself in drink is often born from honest contemplation, which I have found so often holds hands with solitude."

"I see that you have perhaps had such times most recently."

Latimer did not reply and let the man part-fill his mug again. The bottle was gone and another called for – the ruddy-faced man had become suddenly contemplative, absorbed in the reasons for his drinking spree perhaps?

The level of taproom chatter had risen since Henri had sat himself down in this corner, the content of numerous conversations being had around him lost in the expected babble of the busy rooms. The naval men were still grouped about the counter, their easy talk spilling across the heads of the drinkers, confident, intrusive now.

Prompted perhaps by the snippets of dialogue that reached them above the rest, Henri's drinking partner began on another tack.

"What man would be a sailor, eh? What man would be a sailor who has choice of any other occupation? Are you a man of the sea, sir, or linked with the trades that run alongside it?"

"I am not, at least not directly so," Latimer answered with honesty. "Neither sailor, rope walker or cooper nor any other trade relating – I run a small ketch out of Topsham to the Low Countries, my trade is cloth."

"Ah, it would have been my guess, sir – and not from these parts, from the woollen city perhaps?"

"From my birth, yes." The man seemed satisfied, Latimer watched him refill his mug.

"Do you have sons, sir?"

"Daughters and still young."

"Then you are blessed, hold them to you and keep them safe and if they should marry, sir, never allow their husbands to wander alone in this city – 'tis beset with evil and brought low by those who have menace in their hearts. Young men and honest robbed of their liberty for straying too close to this vipers' nest."

Latimer frowned at the vehemence of the statement. "I am a long way from this thought, sir, and doubt I will have the concern of it."

The man seemed not to have heard him and continued to elaborate. "Sons – a comfort and a necessity. I had two such once, young men and hearty. Born to stand upon the sod, plough a field and thatch a rick."

"You farm, sir?" Henri had not wished to hear the stranger's life story, but manners and the lack of alternative seating prevented him from avoiding it.

"Once I did, but 'tis gone now, farm and family all, gone this last year past. I am quite on my own now, sir, my wife dead from a broken heart, buried alone and those she bore sewn into a sailcloth shroud and dropped into the sea."

The man's thoughts were more maudlin than his own – and it seemed for good reason. "They chose the sea over the land?"

"Chose, sir? What choice they? The press-gangs do not offer choices. A cudgel about the head and a blade to the throat is persuasion enough and will see a man's liberty taken with no questions asked on whether 'tis of their choosing or no."

Henri moved his mug to one side; he would leave soon, stand and find his way through the congested room to the stairs.

"Another, sir, the bottle is not yet empty."

Henri put his hand over the mug. "I thank you, no. I must take myself off and find my bed."

"Ah yes, the evening moves on."

The farmer was restive now, something foreboding sat about him, something that Henri could not at that instant fathom, his agitation tangible, hands groping into the open fronts of his coat, plunging repeatedly into deep pockets, eyes wandering the room without reason.

"Do you believe in justice, sir?" He had refilled and then emptied his own mug.

"I believe there is too little of it." Henri, now more than uncomfortable in the farmer's company, had moved to the end of the settle.

"Then our minds are like. Is there a reckoning do you suppose?"

"Before God – perhaps?"

"Before God and upon this earth?"

"I believe there is, what runs around will often come around and catch the perpetrator unawares."

"Too slowly done, sir, I have not the time to wait for life to find its way. Ought not justice to be demanded, sought, and in this lifetime and on this earth?"

"Perhaps, but justice in the eyes of one man may be injustice in the eyes of another."

Following the man's line of thought, watching his well-ordered, deliberate movements, Henri cursed himself for his slow wittedness. This man sought retribution? He was sure of it; lost in his own frustration he had not thought deeply enough about other's predicament. This man had nothing to lose and retribution, here in this room of red coats and his Majesty's officers, might be easily found. A prickle of fear ran down his neck.

"If your intent is to find your own justice – unless you wish the Devil to take you – I wholeheartedly recommend that you do not find it here."

Henri's voice was exigent, authoritative. He noticed that the hand had gone into the coat front again; whatever this man intended, Henri realised he was too close to his coat sleeve to avoid the consequences of it.

"The Devil may take me, sir, and willingly. It should not be a concern of yours."

"But indeed it is, sir, indeed it must be. I have no desire to see the run of your story darkened still further – and most especially when I am sat at your elbow."

Knife, pistol, Latimer had not been certain which. Now he saw the muzzle of a pistol. "Point that across this room and in this company and you are a dead man," he said cleanly, with a level of urgency but without fear.

His immediate reaction was to bring the farmer's arm down, prevent him from firing. He grabbed at the coat sleeve, caught the cuff, the arm like steel – his grip quickly thrown off.

'You must leave me do what is requisite, my need for your company is done, sir. I have long contemplated my end and I will see justice done and find some peace before I stand before any God."

Before freeing himself from the confines of the table Latimer knew he should try again – surely it was not too late. But self-preservation was a stronger emotion; since his youth he had stayed clear of drinking-house brawls, the consequences of this one could mean the end of his liberty. He could see the pistol pulled free from the belt now, held in a shaking hand, the muzzle pointed into the room.

The crack of the shot was audible, unmistakable even above the din, instantly bringing the room to attention. The ball had gone wide of its mark, missing the officer, taking the pot from the hand of one of the marines, shards of earthenware and ale showering the sleeve of the naval man.

Rapid activity had followed a stunned silence. Latimer was standing inching his way along the settle to get beyond the shared table, to get away. He heard the shrill sound of a whistle from somewhere in the room. A table was upturned, a scuffle now, the sound of chairs scraping the flags, bottles breaking. He would get out before the brawl engulfed him, took him down and made him part of it. Grievance between the press and the men of this city was ancient; he knew it, understood it but wanted no part of it. Calculating his chances of escape he began to push his way to the stairs, two marines were moving towards him, burly, fortified with drink, cudgels and hangers visible.

A man with menace in his eyes grabbed at his coat and Latimer pushed him hard on the chest.

Forcing his way, avoiding confrontation, he got himself to the back of the inn; a short staircase led to the upper rooms. He could see the farmer, reactionless, his failed attempt at retribution had brought him to the point of hopelessness – beyond despair. A marine had pinioned the man's arms behind his back, another let his cudgel find the back of his head. The attempted shooting of an officer in His Majesty's Service, witnessed by the whole room, was unequivocally a hanging offence – there would be no escaping the hangman's noose and Latimer knew he could not be seen as accomplice.

Shaking off a hand, pushing his way through, he got to the stairway. He saw there was a youth barring his way, gripping hold of the heavy banister. A man was sent stumbling backwards and the youth lost his hat, the short hair came free – the dark eyes were unmistakable. Stunned by the unexpected he did not waste time seeking explanation – he stooped, picked up the hat and returned it to his wife.

"God above, Rachael, what foolish notion is this?" He took her hand, began to climb the stairs, pulling her on, leading her into the dark passage, towards the door to his room. There was danger here and that danger was now doubled. He slammed the door shut, dropped the iron in the latch. A conflict of emotion ran about his head, this was Rachael, his wife whom he had not laid eyes upon for weeks. She was here, she was real and if found with him her freedom might be forfeit along with his.

He pulled her against him, protective, possessive and grateful, and then held her away, studying what he saw. She looked at him, unabashed, in no way ashamed of how she looked nor what tenacity and disobedience had led her to do.

"I have been looking for you," she said. Her face was flushed with colour, the mop of dark unruly hair putting him in mind of an urchin.

"I see that you have."

"I have read your letter, Henri – I have been back to Exeter."

"And did I not ask you to wait?"

"Did you expect that I would?"

The corners of his mouth had softened.

"I do not believe I can answer that question without thought, and this I do not have time for at present. A pistol has been fired, an officer's life threatened and a man will hang for it. We cannot stay here. I was persuaded to share a bottle with this man; when rational returns false conclusion may be made."

"I have the sorrel pony," she said.

"And a convincing disguise I see."

There were boots moving about on the boards outside the door, Latimer waited for them to recede and then peered out. Perhaps going back into the taproom was not a good idea. "Did you ever climb a tree as a child?"

"Many."

"Then this casement offers us salvation."

The casement, tiny squares of lead and glass, opened easily. He collected the panniers from the chair, looked down onto the sloping roof just below the window and threw out his hat. Keen to be away from the inn, Latimer offered his hand, she took it and sat herself on the ledge, hesitating and then dropping down onto the roof below. Turning, she looked back to the window, he put his finger to his lips and let himself down beside her.

"Where is your pony?" She pointed and he nodded, crouched down, let his legs dangle over the edge of the roof and dropped to the yard. The unlikely spectacle of a portly ageing farmer firing a pistol into a gaggle of officers had drawn onlookers into the hostelry and the cobbled yard was unusually empty.

"Take care, Rachael, the slates are broken."

She dropped to the ground, a couple of loose slates following her and smashing on the hard ground about her feet. Latimer caught her; a new experience, feeling her warmth, the sensation of her touch, his wife – even though she presented herself as a boy.

The pony was still saddled, the jute bag tied to it. He watched her confidently remove the tether, lead the pony out and climb up. His own mare was in a different part of the stable, but now the yard was no longer empty, a street hawker and a child were peering in at the window of the inn.

"Go quietly, Rachael, as if idleness were your friend. I have yet to marry saddle with horse and then I will join you. The Citadel is close company and this unrest will likely see marines on these streets. Take the pony to the pool and wait for me near the quay."

The reluctance he felt in sending her off was soon overwhelmed by the urgency of finding his own horse. Two seamen were leaving the inn from the side door – Latimer ducked back into the dark stable and watched them. Their steps were uncertain, they stumbled as they walked. He watched them disappear under the coach gates and took breath. He thought of the farmer and his fate; he hoped punishment would be mercifully swift.

The chestnut mare was tethered at the back of the stable, snorting impatiently into the dim light, the saddle was thrown over the buttress and he lifted it down, got it onto the mare without disturbing her and buckled the girth strap. He led the mare forward, looking out through the broken stable door into the yard. The shrill whistle he had heard before came again, then the sound of boots on cobbles. Although his view was obscured he could just make out the archway connecting the livery with the street: the red uniforms of marines, reinforcements perhaps, brought here by a report of deeper unrest – whatever had brought them from their barracks they were here now in the yard preventing his exit.

Some of the half-dozen or so soldiers had immediately entered the inn, two were left as sentries – he would have to hope that they were kept busy whilst he found another route, and if he could not the consequences would be dire. In his single-minded quest to refill the family's coffers he had travelled much; one inn, one livery was much the same as another. There would be another way out of this walled and enclosed yard, he need only find it.

He tied his mare to a nail inside the stable, a few more men were in the yard now, all made querulous by a nights drinking – it was the distraction he needed. The brewhouse and kitchens were housed in an off-shoot from the main building; the kitchen would be busy with servants but the brewhouse may not. He backed along the wall and found the door half-hanging from rusty hinges; he pushed the base with his boot and stepped inside. There was a door on the other side; he hoped it might lead to the street behind. He went to it, found it was bolted, but not locked. Glancing over his shoulder he reached up, slid back the long bolt and looked out, an alleyway and then beyond it another street. If his mare did not give him away – if he was not seen – this door spelt liberation.

He went back for his mare, repeating his cautious, well-considered steps. Most of the marines were still inside the inn, the two at the gate were kept busy preventing any leaving. He took the bridle, encouraging the beast forwards, getting into the relative safety of the brewhouse. Before he went to collect his horse he had closed and bolted the door; he reached up now and pulled back the bolt again silently, led his mare out into the dark narrow lane and closed the door behind him. Hopping on one leg he got a foot in the stirrup, pulled himself up, bid the mare on and moved unseen into the crowds.

The approach of early evening had not lessened the activity about the pool; the flood tide had lifted the hulls of ocean-going ships and fishing smacks alike, intensifying the industry which ran about them. Avoiding Whimple Street, he picked his way towards the quay along lesser streets, negotiating the shacks and wharfs that ran alongside, searching through the crowds – working men and those in drink, gin-filled prostitutes and half-starved urchins. He saw the well-worn tricorn and familiar coat. She was waiting as he had bid her, the sorrel pony now agitated in hostile surroundings.

The crowds were thicker than he would have liked and the mix of red and blue serge amongst them bothered him; peace brought men home and soldiers back to their barracks. The chestnut flank of his mare was noticeable next to the working ponies and heavy-footed drays and he did not wish to curry attention; he watched her for a moment considering his options. Although his heart had suddenly felt whole again he would not draw Rachael into this predicament that a chance meeting and shared bottle had brought him to – absurdly he wished she had not found him.

He reined in the mare, allowing her to kick the cobbles whilst the crowds milled about him. The sorrel pony was almost as noticeable as his own mount – but the boy who sat her was not; he was grateful for it. Without taking his eye away from the dusty hat and faded red of her jacket he worked his way between slop vats, filled caskets and tethered barrels, keeping his head down, watching for changes in the mood of the crowd.

She saw him approach her. Close to her, a boy was running barrels down a plank from the back of a cart, each one like a runaway iron wheel on a granite path. The pony was becoming skittish and she touched its withers and calmed it, looking for a way forward.

Glancing about her she saw the red of a uniform – two – there were others but these were closer. Her subconscious urged her husband not to approach; she would be fine and well, Henri should not approach, but he was and she could not prevent it. Another barrel, she moved the pony back, the red-coated soldiers were nearer and she felt the pony's fear, side-stepping, snorting. The pony seemed as desperate as she to leave this place, but the barrels continued to roll and the pony danced backwards, the soldiers now beside her, colliding with its rump – a torrent of abuse, a hand on her leg, gripping her breeches. For a moment she had lost sight of Henri and then she saw him, still mounted coming towards her through the bustle of the quayside.

He could wait no longer. He doubted the two uniformed men had any connection to the melee he had left behind, just two more soldiers in drink – if they did it made no difference. The pony was bucking; he went forward and caught the rein at the bit.

"We must leave," he said.

"Are you sought, Henri?"

"I hope that I am not." His face was sombre, unreadable, his head calculating the seriousness of the situation – now that she had become his accomplice.

"I am hopeful their reasoning will be lost in the scrum. The farmer is arrested, that will most likely be enough. Keep close but ride behind me, it is my intention to set water between us and this pool before light fails, only then will I know us safe."

66

Eventually they had begun to pull away from the compact port, working their way around the pool into narrower, less busy streets, skirting to the rear of shipwright's yards, fish cellars and the holding houses that fronted the water. He clicked his horse on, rode in silence until the shacks and tumbledown buildings clinging to the outskirts of the town began to thin and the cobbles became earth. Away from immediate danger they may have been, but he would not trust his emotions – this was not the time for questioning or for trying to understand where this young woman, his property, dressed now as boy, had been.

"We must find a track through the scrub," he said looking across the open watery land edged with the evidence of quarrying. He turned his head so that she could hear him. "There is a fly-bridge of sorts across the Cat Water – it should see us safely away from town."

He felt unaccountably awkward in her company; he could not say why, but nothing could have prophesied this ending to the day and now he seemed not to be prepared. Conversation, dialogue, was imperative but where to make a start.

They found a track and he set his horse's head towards the river. "The track is a little narrow but the scrub low-growing," he said, looking behind him tentatively, liking what he saw. She met his glance and quickened the pony to keep pace. When he turned again she was still watching him.

"You look well upon your new purchase, Henri," she said lightly – an irrelevant comment, but one he did not mind. "What brought you to change your thinking?"

Discussing his decision to change the mindset of a lifetime may not be pertinent, but perhaps it was a way back to the easy, uncomplicated conversations they had once enjoyed. Deeper discourse could wait – be satisfied with what you have, do not stand on the boards and rock the boat over. He answered her honestly.

"Whim, Rachael – I cannot explain it any other way. The sorrel pony was always intended for you, although I am surprised that you prized it from the protection of the Holloway livery presenting yourself in boy's breeches."

"I have more than one disguise, Henri, and the boy there do know me well enough. It was at his suggestion that I take the pony in the stead of any other."

"Then have I not been foresighted, Rachael?" He caught her smile, satisfied that a kind of innocence had returned to their dialogue.

They crossed the Cat Water on the Fly Bridge as he had suggested, entering a landscape altogether different from the one they had left behind: harvested stubble fields and hamlets with a single light – the cart track going east far less used than the higher turnpike.

"I am minded to keep going until the light leaves us," he said, taking stock of their location. "There is a place we can stay, it should be easily found before we are forced to have the half-moon show us the way." He looked ahead for a while negotiating the track. Turning his head he said, "This landscape will hold some familiarity to you, will it not?"

"A little, Henri, although the world do seem quite a different place now."

"Memories seeded in childhood perhaps should never be revisited for fear of disappointment."

"Perhaps, Henri," she said thoughtfully.

A silence fell between them, companionable but restrained by the unfamiliarity of their new intimacy. Dusk was coming to the September evening flushing the sky pink, darker cloud spilling in from the sea. Pomphlet Farm lay some distance behind them now and Henri adjusted his seat, searching for a track running south – finding it he kicked the mare on, dropping down into a ravine already in deep shadow.

"Can you forgive me, Henri?" she said to his back. "Can you forgive me for what I have done?"

Involuntarily he drew in his breath. So far any real intimacy with his wife had evaded him but now the mask seemed gone – would the change he had hoped for now come, a new beginning perhaps?

"If you ask forgiveness for things that have happened before our union, then I must. I must forgive, it will lead us nowhere if I do not, and besides I hardly know what it is I am required to forgive. If you ask me to forgive you for not returning with your trunk, then you must first explain your reasoning."

She did not reply until they had negotiated the steep rock-strewn track.

"I thought you better without me," she said quietly.

"Then your opinion was misguided, Rachael." His mare stumbled on a loose stone and he waited until the ground was firmer. "And your change of heart? Where did you go that made you alter your intentions?"

"I had a need to go back to the beginning, Henri, to the beginning to remember who I am and how it was."

"Here?"

"No, not this valley, but not such a distance from it and not so dissimilar."

The dark ribbon of a small brook was just visible through the yellowing autumnal grass, the bank trampled and muddied by field cows. An unexpected need to unburden his thoughts made him push forward with things he knew he must say.

"I feel I must also ask for your forgiveness Rachael. It was inexcusable of me not to have written you at Venn and told you of Jane's passing, and conscience stabs at me twofold. I have been misguided – misguided in sending you away and misguided in my choice of destination. Common sense should have told me that it would not suit. I have been to Venn, Rachael, as you required me to do and I know that your morality and character have been challenged."

The path had widened and she came level with him. The evening was still, the half-light wrapping them in shadows. Without looking at her he continued.

"And your child, Rachael – if Pamela Medland had not cleared her own conscience then I would not have known of your loss. It disturbs me to think that your life may have been forfeit, and there in that place without welcome – the place I had sent you, perhaps to appease my own frustration."

The clouds had thickened and the first spits of evening rain began to fall. Through the thicket he watched for the open blackness of the water where the brook abruptly ran into a creek.

"I had not anticipated this drenching, Rachael," he said apologetically. "A poor greeting, but less than a mile, I believe, then we may shake off these wet things and begin again tomorrow."

The thin, almost subterranean brook had disappeared and the creek became one with a wide jagged inlet, dark trees obscuring the flat water, weedy rocks and silt just visible above the receding tide. She followed him as he urged his horse along an overgrown track, keeping her own pony in check, avoiding strewn angular rocks until the rarely used path became a broader track. She wondered what he thought, what his intentions were, why he had left the highway to search amongst the thickets and harvested pastureland instead of seeking an inn. It occurred to her that she did not know him. Her fear of the flesh – of the act of love-making – had opened a gulf between them as wide as this salty tidal waterway that had begun to show itself in the half-light. She wished to make amends – if she was able – only then might she begin to know him.

A fork in the track revealed a house, empty, silent, unlit windows showing like dark sockets in a fleshless skull. He handed her down.

"Who would leave such a place empty and without heart, Henri?" she said standing on the wet grey shale, the mizzle and the dense encroaching woodland forming a circle of uncertainty and otherworldliness about her.

"Oh, do not think it is without heart, Rachael. Come let us put a light in the window. I am certain there will be no objection to us seeing out the darkness here."

A ramshackle outbuilding built of the same grey stone as the house stood separate from it, the courtyard about it enclosed by low walls. She watched him take her pony and lead it into the open-fronted barn with his own mare and she waited whilst he made the best of what he could find there, the fine rain wetting her face, cool on her lips, her eyes almost blinded now by the density of the darkness.

67

He thought she looked small and unsure in the struggling moonlight and he quickly found the key beneath a heavy stone, turned it in the box lock and pushed open the door.

The lofty entrance gave access to a labyrinth of rooms; to one side the connecting room was empty, stone mullioned windows, church-like, arched and without lead or glass faced onto the dark courtyard. To the other, the granite arch revealed a roofless hall.

Suddenly uncertain of himself, he questioned his decision to come here instead of finding an inn; but to him this house was familiar, almost comfortable. How it appeared to his wife he could not say, bleak perhaps – a lifeless ruin. He caught her hand and guided her through the windowless room to another, sparsely furnished but habitable. Leaving her standing in the near darkness, he found the tinderbox, struck the flint and lit a candle.

"Take off your coat and leave it dry, Rachael." He shrugged off his own and threw it over a chair. She was quiet, wide-eyed; he watched her take off her hat and coat, lay the jute bag on the table, following her eyes as she looked about.

"Who owns this house, Henri?"

The fire was laid and he crouched, touched the lighted candle to the kindling and watched the flames flicker and rise. He stood and looked at her squarely. "I do," he said, watching her response.

"You do, Henri?"

Unconsciously, he rubbed his leg. "The house came to my father through his marriage to my mother – although he never came here. I knew nothing of its existence until his death."

"But you have never talked of it, Henri – not to me."

"Not to any, Rae. If we own to it, Rachael, each of us knows little of the other." He put a hand up and touched her cheek. "And perhaps we do not need to know all there is –perhaps some things are better left untold."

She was looking into the next room and he lit another candle, offering the flame up to the wall sconces, bringing life to the two habitable rooms. He spoke as he went. "Near ruin it may be, but it does not tax my purse or my time, although I feel a nagging sadness when I come here. There is a hamlet barely half mile from here, small payment to a family there keeps what is left of the house habitable – at least for my limited needs."

He returned to her, touched his lips on her forehead and then moved away to feed the fire, settling the log with his boot, watching the sparks shoot into the dark recess of the chimney. Women were unpredictable, even the most level-headed, and he would not predict her mood.

"The day has been long for us both, Rachael – take your sack and find your bed, there will likely be water already drawn and in the jug."

There was no dispute in her mind that she had wronged her husband, in the early weeks of their marriage understanding this had not been enough – action had not followed her determination to make amends. But now she had sought him and found him and was returning home with him – life must not return to the way it was.

She held the candle high, lighting up the sparsely furnished room with the oversized bed and dark drapes. There was water in the jug as Henri had said and she dropped the bag on the bed and shook out the contents, tired as he had suggested. The water was cold and she washed as she always did – slowly, mind on the day, things to come, collecting thoughts and resolutions. She dropped the shift over her head and looked at her image in the dressing mirror, a stranger looked back. Henri had not yet joined her and she waited, seated on the edge of the bed, looking at the image. When he did not come she blew out the candle, lifted the cold linen and lay taut and still until sleep found her.

When she woke the sconce light was dripping tallow and the darkness outside the window was as dense as when she had laid down. Henri was not there and she stretched out her arm as if searching for him, but knowing already the bed would be empty. She pulled back the heavy cover, dropped her feet to the boards – the door was still part open and she could see the dying fire and the flickering candles.

The profile of her husband was clear. He was sitting in a wide chair close to the fire, his neck cloth hung over its back and his boots and stockings drying in the hearth. Crossing the room without speaking, she knelt down and put her forehead on his knee. Although his eyes had been closed he was not asleep. He put his cool hands on her sleep-tangled hair.

"Rachael, are you not tired enough for sleep?"

"I have been dreaming, Henri."

"What do you dream of that will not allow you to sleep?"

"I have been dreaming about you, Henri."

"Pleasant or no?"

"Vexing."

"And?"

"My dream is simple, Henri, and comes to me often. I am standing looking across water and although I cannot see your face I know it is you standing on the other bank. And the river seems so shallow and I know I must cross it, but as I begin the water becomes heavier until it holds me fast like river mud."

"And you do not reach me?"

"I do not."

"And this has disturbed you?" He sat forward and she raised her head. "Sit with me, Rachael." Standing, she then sat tentatively in his lap. She could feel the warmth of the fire on her bare feet and the comfort of his shoulder beneath her head. "Dreams are always about what has gone before and never about what will come, they should not disturb you."

There had been almost no intimacy since the beginning of their relationship; the touch of another, the pleasure of companionship was novel and welcome. "Why do you not come to bed Henri?" she said. His eyes were paler than she remembered, contrasting against the dark jagged brow line.

"Habit, my love – diffidence, perhaps." She had allowed him to kiss her, at first his touch was so light his lips had felt like gossamer. She put a hand to his face and touched the hard stubble of growth, the action changing his mood to one of urgency. "Do you wish that I should?"

Apart from the initial and unsatisfactory consummation of their marriage, her only experience of what happened between a man and a woman were the harsh fumblings of force – contemptuous and unwelcome – but she would not allow her husband to slip further away from her, not allow him to sense her fear.

"I do, Henri, I do wish it."

The contours of her body were obvious through the fine cotton, she felt his touch and sensed his need. He moved in his seat, running his hand over her shift and then beneath it, feeling her nakedness, putting his face in her hair and kissing her neck. He let her down, rising and taking her hand.

"Do you fear me, Rachael?"

"I do not fear you, Henri, only that I may lose you again."

68

Dawn, coming later in the river valleys of the west, now brought a pale light to the room, showing up the ancient drapes and well-worn furniture. He watched her sleeping, he would let her sleep longer; he had a mind to see the late summer sun rise over the land that was his. He collected his breeches and shirt from the floor, looking back, remembering the unexpected, her change of heart and his subsequent change of mood.

He dressed and let himself out into the watery early-morning sun; the ground was wet, every blade of grass, every leaf saturated. Two tall and misaligned granite pillars marked the boundary of the immediate house and courtyards and he walked slowly towards them, put his hands in his coat pockets and stood for a while looking out over the neglected woodland. Weakened by thin cloud the sun was rising indistinctly over the creek bringing mist to the hollows. For a while he stood looking about him, the sight pleased him, even in its neglected state the land was good. Satisfied, he turned back, glancing up at the empty windows and roofless walls of the once fine house – this morning it did not bother him, his mood was sanguine, expectant. He had come to a point in his life when he had begun to realize that the pit of debt and uncertainty that had chased him during his adult life had most assuredly been filled, solvency – ground level – now he might build a life and take some pleasure from it.

In a while he would wake Rachael. He had wanted her for so long, had often considered if having her would be a disappointment; it was not. Looking down the weedy path to the house he could see a young woman standing central beneath the door arch; she was wearing simple blue skirts and her dark curls were gathered up with a comb, the woman was his wife. He took pleasure in the scene, slowed his pace, taking his hands from his pockets and self-consciously running his hand through his hair. At some point they would return to Exeter and the life they had yet to build – but perhaps not yet.

69

Sitting before her dressing mirror but taking no heed of her own image, Mag turned her face to the window and watched the gentleman she had most recently entertained walk away from the Alphington inn. He was soon lost in the crowds and she returned her eyes to study the image in the glass. From this position she could see the room behind her; it had until recently been meagrely furnished and masculine, now gewgaws and linen lay about – the bed was tumbled and her working dress was on the floor. Time would be running on and she had an appointment – there was much to do before she could make her way across the city. Disinterestedly, she removed the coarse powdered wig that she wore for business and began to scrub the heavy paint from her normally virginal face. Standing, she lifted the buckram bodice and well-made but simple skirts from the peg and began to dress; plaiting her pale hair into a rope, she looked again at her image, picked up the small basket standing by the door and let herself out.

It was later than she had planned and the streets were already busy with market traders and merchants' boys. The walk to the South Gate was not so far, but the biweekly cloth market had brought many extra people to the city's already thriving streets. Standing beneath the window of the makeshift prison she found she was not alone. Their rendezvous had been specific, both in time and place, and she stood below the agreed window and seeing no face behind it, picked up a handful of loose shale and threw it up against the wall.

"Geoffrey, my love – I am here, I have come as I said I would."

The face of the young man who was inadvertently paying her rent appeared just behind the opening.

"I see that you are. Did we not agree cock-crow? Your time-keeping is slovenly."

"Oh, please forgive me, Geoffrey, for I have been working – working for you my love."

"If I must pimp my way to freedom, Margaret, then let it be swift and quickly done, but not at the expense of our meetings – do you not know that I am bitten to death, sickened by filth and laid low by the company I must keep?"

"I have what you asked for, Geoffrey, send down the string and at least take the victuals I have brought for you."

Running through what had now become a well-practised routine, Geoffrey took the calico bundle and threw out the string for her to attach the extra clothing he had asked for.

"I am a way forward, Geoffrey, each day I do add a little more to our purse – it will not be long, my love, before you may buy your freedom."

Just visible through the slit window, Geoffrey ripped at the poultry leg with his teeth, his full and untidy beard soaking up congealed fat and jelly.

"Curse the man, Margaret." He bit the cork from the bottle and drank more than half of it before he spoke again. "Curse my miserly uncle – I would have expected him to open his purse. Am I not kin? It would hardly have made indentation into that pile of coin he keeps so snugly locked away to have offered the little I owe and set me free."

Margaret was crouching down, industriously tying a shirt sleeve to the string. It was not his own – she had long since pawned his gentlemanly things; she had found the most threadbare on offer but at least it was free of lice eggs and fleas.

"But perhaps he do not have the wealth you suppose, Geoffrey."

"Do not be fooled by the man, he has been merchant for these ten years past – what merchant here about, most especially one living as pauper, does not own wealth? He wishes to teach me a lesson, rectitude, recompense – I have not played to his tune. I have always known he despises my gentility. The man is perverse and unreadable."

Having completed the tasks demanded by her lover, Margaret leant back against the stone of the crumbling wall and looked at her new slippers.

"Should I perhaps ask him again? Although he could not help you I believe him genuinely sorry for your misfortune. The merchant do have a family of his own to look to, my love."

"Saints and martyrs, Margaret, do not – the man is a cold unfeeling fish. You must make my freedom your priority – be minded of it, be minded at all times."

"And I am, my love, each day I rise alone in Alphington and have no other thought in my head but your freedom." Margaret scuffed the loose mortar at her feet, admiring the buckles on the front of her slippers. "Should I perhaps ask the bawdy mother to help us? She will make you loan of the monies you owe. You may owe the debt to her and return it when you can – she do like to add to that little chest and the interest would help her along."

"Be indebted to a whore mother, Margaret – surely you can see this as intolerable?"

"Then you must wait, my love, you must wait until I have earnt enough to release you. It will not be so long and then we can be together again and I can offer you all that you have missed."

"Cursed Heaven, Margaret, do not manipulate my ardour and put me in mind of what I am missing."

"Forgive me, Geoffrey." She had picked up the basket and was standing some distance away from the window. "I must go soon, but I will come again tomorrow. It will not be long, my love, not so very long until we may settle your debt. Then we may lie together as we once did and be never more hampered by magistrate nor constable."

"Saints, Margaret – saints and cussed martyrs!"

Lightning Source UK Ltd.
Milton Keynes UK
UKHW011941270120
357693UK00002B/82